In the Steps of the Shadow Warrior

It was too late now for caution. More sinister creatures, naked in their demonic hideousness, were now pouring through the entrance into the temple. Now they were surging after him, their angry cries like the hissing of vipers. He did not have the strength to run. Step by wearying step, the young warrior drove himself forward.

Nothing could discourage him now; no power in this dimension or any other could daunt him, no force drive him back. Too much was at stake: the great city of Ar, the very survival of his race, his beloved Srana. Clutching the Demon Sword, his jaws clenched determinedly with the strain, Branwe continued his way into the innermost recesses of the temple.

Ask your bookseller for the
Bantam Spectra Books you have missed:

THE DARKSWORD TRILOGY by Margaret Weis and Tracy Hickman
Forging the Darksword
Doom of the Darksword
Triumph of the Darksword

Darksword Adventures by Margaret Weis and Tracy Hickman

PHILIP JOSE FARMER'S THE DUNGEON
Book 1: *The Black Tower* by Richard Lupoff
Book 2: *The Road to Purgatory* by Bruce Coville
Book 3: *The Valley of Thunder* by Charles de Lint
Book 4: *The Lake of Fire* by Robin Bailey
Book 5: *The Hidden City* by Charles de Lint

THE RIFTWAR SAGA by Raymond E. Feist
Magician: Apprentice
Magician: Master
Silverthorn
A Darkness at Sethanon

Daughter of the Empire by Raymond E. Feist and Janny Wurts

ROSE OF THE PROPHET by Margaret Weis and Tracy Hickman
The Will of the Wanderer
Paladin of the Night
The Prophet of Akhran

THE UNBALANCED EARTH TRILOGY by Jonathan Wylie
Dreams of Stone
The Lightless Kingdom
The Age of Chaos

GUARDIANS OF THE THREE, VOLUME 4

DEFENDERS OF AR

Jack Lovejoy

SPECTRA

BANTAM BOOKS
NEW YORK • TORONTO • LONDON • SYDNEY • AUCKLAND

DEFENDERS OF AR
A Bantam Spectra Book / April 1990

ISBN 0-553-28453-3

Published simultaneously in the United States and Canada

Bantam Books are published by Bantam Books, a division of Bantam Doubleday Dell Publishing Group, Inc. Its trademark, consist-
ing of the words "Bantam Books" and the portrayal of a rooster, is
Registered in U.S. Patent and Trademark Office and in other
countries. Marca Registrada. Bantam Books, 666 Fifth Avenue,
New York, New York 10103.

PRINTED IN THE UNITED STATES OF AMERICA

RAD   0 9 8 7 6 5 4 3 2 1

DEFENDERS
OF AR

Chapter 1
The Blue Dragon

▲——▲

A potboy at the Blue Dragon, the most popular inn in all Kazerclawm, saw many strange folk come and go, and this year's festival had attracted the strangest young Branwe had ever seen. Outlandish in fur and feature, with accents so gutteral that he could hardly understand them, some appeared to him downright sinister. It would be a relief to get away from their probing questions for a while, and he hung up his apron and hurried from the kitchen.

The sprawling three-floored structure was comfortable rather than elegant. It stood just inside the Watersmeet Gate, and never closed its doors. Certainly the dragon sign over its front entrance looked more inviting than the species ever did in the wild. The walled courtyard behind was disposed among a congeries of stables, cisterns, curing sheds, and kitchen gardens. Normally the old inn lodged a transient clientele of merchants and travelers, itinerant craftsmrem, artists, wandering scholars, and some shy and guarded people of no evident means or profession, suspected of being magicians. It was now packed to the very storerooms with festival tourists, although the rankers from the local garrison—who sauntered in nightly to drink and dance and, sometimes, brawl—always seemed to find room for themselves.

There was plenty of room at the moment. Early afternoon was usually a slack period, even at festival time, and a pair of raddled old scullery wenches, once dancers at this very inn, toiled with dust rags, brooms, mops, brushes, and pails; chairs were stacked on tables, and all but one of the waiters idle. Out on the dance floor a lone soldier was practicing for a

1

forthcoming duel, under the critical eyes of his seconds.

Branwe watched for a moment, then shrugged. His own martial dance was already superior both in technique and execution.

The walls were a fantastic array of scenes, painted over the years in various styles with varying degrees of skill, by itinerant artists unable to settle their tabs by any other means. A full generation had passed since one such artist had framed the mirror behind the bar with ornamental gemstones. Common crystal, really, but so artfully cut and set, in a glittering rainbow of colors, that it was still the pride of the Blue Dragon. Nobody dared polish it but old Mamre herself, the innkeeper's wife.

Branwe found her polishing it now, with the silken cloth she used for no other purpose.

"If you don't need me for anything special," he said, "I'll be off to school. It's the last afternoon class before festival recess, and Master Hoobel wants me there as early as possible."

"Oh, that Hoobel." Mamre shook her head, half amused, half exasperated. "Nobody has more schooling, or knows less about schoolkits. No doubt he wants help with his class today," she added drily.

"The young scamps learn more tricks than lessons, from all I hear," commented her husband Grujekh, a sleek little mrem with shifty eyes, polishing a set of wine goblets down the bar. "Everybody needs all the help he can get at festival time."

This last he muttered as if talking to himself. That a common potboy should learn to read and write had always seemed to him a waste of good time. But so long as the arrangement did not also waste his good money, he did not press the argument. His wife could show her claws, when she chose.

"Run along, lad," she said. "You worked hard this morning, and we're sure to have another big crowd here when you get back. I just hope they're a handsomer lot than the gang we had in here last night. Never saw such mean-looking folk."

"They all paid their tabs," said her husband, continuing to polish the goblets, "so I don't know what you're complaining about. The way some of 'em looked at your mirror, I thought they wanted to buy it." He chuckled.

"You know it's not for sale, at any price," she bridled. "Nobody who knows the Blue Dragon would insult me with such an offer. Although it's natural they should admire it, I suppose. Probably never saw anything so fine, in whatever outlandish corner of the world they're from. I could hardly understand them, the way they talked."

"You had no trouble understanding their money though, did you?" Grujekh winked cynically.

Mamre glared at him and started to reply, but then just let the matter drop. It was years too late for her to expect her husband to change his stingy, grasping ways.

"Get all the schooling you can while you have the chance, lad," she said, returning to Branwe. "It will be important to you someday."

"Just don't dwadle on the way back," Grujekh warned him. "That's important to you right now."

The snow-capped peak of the Kazerclaw glistened like opal, or at least like one of the crystals in the frame of Mamre's prize mirror, in the afternoon sun. It dominated the barrier mountains, just as the walled city of Kazerclawm at its foot dominated the passage from the eastern deserts. Its one scalable slope was restricted to citizens, and the Sacred Gate always well guarded. Not in all his years as a potboy at the Blue Dragon—all his life, in fact, for he knew no other—had Branwe been able to penetrate the mystery he knew overhung the towering peak. Mamre had merely shrugged when he asked about it, while her husband returned the same answer he had for all such questions: "Don't meddle where it's none of your business." Only a creature with wings could reach the heights from any other direction.

Not that Branwe had any passionate interest in mountains. It was just that he was beginning to question things he had always taken for granted, for every day the familiar seemed to him stranger and more mysterious. He was certain the Kazerclaw was more than mere rock and snow, just as he knew there was surely more to life than kitchen drudgery and mopping up after sick revelers. The female dancers at the Blue Dragon, this last year or so, rarely missed the chance to rub themselves against him whenever he passed. They had schooled him in subjects never taught by Master Hoobel—although his first excitement was soon tempered by the realization that they were just as wanton with any presentable male. Especially the rankers from the garrison on payday.

Until accepting the post as monitor in Master Hoobel's classroom, in exchange for lessons, the odd scraps he had picked up from these old soldiers—sometimes teasing him, sometimes in drunken earnest—had been his only schooling. He had also picked up a cracked sword from the armory trash barrel, and practiced sword drills and military dances whenever he had spare time. Grujekh saw to it that he had precious little of this, and he knew that his martial skills thus far were barely those of a raw garrison recruit, much less a true warrior. But even a humble potboy can dream . . . .

Never had the streets seemed so colorful. He had heard rankers grumble over their cups that the whole city was being turned into a carnival, instead of the first bastion of the eastern marchlands, and that revenues badly needed to repair walls and siege engines were being diverted by the frivolous young governor—a recent appointment of the even more frivolous young King of Ar—to ornament his own palace.

Kazerclawm was certainly a carnival today, and he paused to watch a village troupe in traditional costumes, rehearsing a traditional dance for the festival competition. Only the grandest villages or city-states could afford to reserve a public dance pavilion for their rehearsals; nor were their glittery costumes so obviously homemade. But this small troupe was wonderfully enthusiastic, and he admired their agile leaps and whirls for a few minutes, before at last squeezing through the crowd gathered around them.

A stone dragon, its left ear battered by neighborhood urchins, marked the next crossing. Significantly, it was usually to the left that he turned, toward one of the most battered quarters in the city. Mamre had never told him how she first became acquainted with the old wizard who lived there, but she always saw to it that Branwe had enough time to run errands for him. Lately, he had also helped with household chores.

The old mrem was now gravely ill, perhaps dying. Why he was known only as the Sentinel was a mystery—he had dwelt in Kazerclawm longer than Branwe himself had been alive—but there was nothing mysterious about his choice of backstreet lodgings. Prudence more than poverty dictated that he live as obscurely as possible, although he was certainly poor. Magicians were always distrusted, sometimes feared, even hated. Twice in his lifetime Branwe had seen magicians stoned by hostile mobs. He had to be cautious himself at times.

Branwe's peculiar gray-blue coloring was rarely seen in this part of the land, and never in such unblemished purity. Few wondered about a mere potboy at an inn. Who knew his father? Or even his mother? Who really cared? Travelers came and went; the dancing girls at the Blue Dragon were notoriously promiscuous. That might explain any color of fur. Mamre had told him only that he had been found in a closet one morning. He was not the first kit so abandoned at the Blue Dragon; but in his case she had decided to raise him, being childless herself.

Not until Srana came to tend her ailing grandfather had he ever been sensitive about his lowly station. She was his own age, but seemed so far above him in every way that he was always shy in her presence—a feeling he experienced with no other female. In fact, those he courted at the Blue Dragon—or who courted him—were both charmed and amused by his very boldness with them. With Srana it was different. Her beauty and education, her poise and sensibility, were beyond anything he had ever known before; but she also brought with her the mystique of the White Dancers, whose moral authority was preeminent throughout the land.

It was mostly because of her that he had accepted the post of classroom monitor with Master Hoobel. The oddments of learning he thus gained might be a shallow reflection of true education, but he felt somehow less like a common menial now, when he ran errands for her grandfather, or helped with some heavy chore. He knew that servant's wages would be a burden for them and accepted only the loan of books as recompense, although he said publicly that he was well paid for his labors—or he wouldn't have done them. This claim allayed suspicions about why he visited the house of a magician so often.

Unconsciously, the old wizard's journeyman, Nizzam, also allayed neighborhood suspicions about the household. A tyro who had pompously convinced himself that he was a great wizard, his self-centered posturing and conceit made him such a figure of fun among the neighbors—a fact of which he was blithely unaware—that he thereby averted the usual fear and distrust of magicians, and perhaps some rough handling.

Branwe was sometimes tempted to handle him roughly himself. Nizzam considered all manual labor beneath his lofty status, and treated those who performed it with a sniffy condescension. His advances toward Srana generally took the form of reassuring her that she was worthy of him, despite her lack of fortune. It was at such times that Branwe found it the most trying to avoid dealing him a few reassurances of his own. He might have to one of these days, in spite of his intentions not to cause Srana additional care. For Nizzam's pretensions swelled in proportion as the health of the old wizard declined.

Turning right at the stone dragon, Branwe soon found Master Hoobel himself enduring some rough handling by his own neighbors.

". . . I had to count my ice pans three times to be sure." Branwe could hear the angry complaints halfway down the block. The stocky, aproned shopkeeper had hooked Master Hoobel's gown with a stubby claw, so he couldn't walk away. Neighbors for blocks around complained about the racket from the one-room school, but not a sound now came through its shutters or open door—a very suspicious circumstance.

"I thought my memory was slipping," continued the outraged shopkeeper. "All my berry niblets gone! Not your common grade either, but my finest dewberries! They thought I wouldn't notice, because they hooked the ice pan too, and rearranged the display case while my back was turned. Do you know where I found the empty pan? In fact, I never did find it myself. It was old Wincwyd." He waved his hand in the general direction of the spiced-fish shop down the street. "Found it by accident in his trash barrel. Don't interrupt! It was your brats all right. Who else would have done such a thing? It's not the first time either, but it had better be the last." He shouted this last through the open door of the classroom. "I'll be watching. Just let me get my claws on 'em, and see if they ever play tricks on anybody again! My very finest dewberries yet!" He stalked angrily back toward his shop, grumbling threats every step of the way.

Shopkeepers and their customers shook their heads in disgust up and down the street, while neighbors glowered down from windows. Despite his vast learning, Master Hoobel was still mystified that so few kits and she-kits could wreak so many pranks on an entire neighborhood. Had they devoted half their ingenuity to lessons, they would all be geniuses.

"Branwe? Is it really you?" The old schoolmaster squinted at him. His fur was ungroomed, his long purple gown was disheveled, and he had a harried look in his myopic round eyes. "I'm so glad you could come today. So very, very glad." He led the way through the open door.

Branwe could not remember the class ever being so quiet and well-behaved. But he noticed that several of the furry little faces had bluish-green stains around the mouth, suspiciously like the color of dewberries, and he caught sly exchanges of winks and the twitching of whiskers among them as he crossed the room to his stool.

The classroom had once been a cooper's workshop, and a system of ropeless pulleys still hung from its high ceiling. The firebrick walls were decorated with pictograph cards, maps, and popular drawings of the governor of Kazerclawm and the boy king of Ar. A brown chalkboard ran the width of the room behind the schoolmaster's desk. There were exactly twenty pupils—twelve kits and eight she-kits—seated at four long tables, whose tops were battle-scarred with initials, names, and caricatures, scratched by furtive little claws.

Branwe displayed his own claws as he sat down in the corner, where he could attend to both the schoolmaster and his class. The gesture was not missed by the latter, and they had long since learned that he would back it up; also that he was not only tougher than they were, but quicker and more agile. Whatever knowledge they gained here was learned during the afternoon session. Their mornings, when Branwe was not present, were often a riotous shambles.

This morning must have been just that, and the old schoolmaster looked warily up and down the benches, as if suspicious that the present nice behavior was only a prelude to renewed mischief. But although dreamy and naive in worldly matters, he was experienced enough to realize that the last session before a festival recess was not the time for new lessons, even with young Branwe present.

"Gerna." He beckoned to the she-kit at the end of the front table. "Bring me the *Dragon Book*, please."

The kit behind her tried to hook her kilt as she rose, but she agilely dodged him, and tweaked his whiskers so that he sneezed. There was a giddy burst of laughter, and several kits leapt up onto their benches, ready for mischief.

But Branwe, anticipating them, was already on his feet—arms akimbo, eyes narrowed with warning—and they at once resumed their seats and angelic behavior. He too reseated himself, but never took his eyes off them for an instant.

"Thank you, Gerna." The schoolmaster took the big book from her, and she smiled innocently at him. No doubt she made an entirely different face as she turned away, because a titter rippled through the room.

Again Branwe was on his feet; again the twenty kits looked angelic. But this time he did not reseat himself. Only on special occasions did Master Hoobel read from the collection of old tales and adventures known as the *Dragon Book*. It was always a favorite diversion with his unruly charges; but the book was so big, and his old eyes so myopic, that his head was always buried from sight while he read. So open an invitation to mischief was seldom long resisted.

When Branwe was not present, that is. He too was fascinated by the tales of magical animals, dragons, sorcerers, and the reptile-demons of the Old Race, which had ruled the planet eons ago, before the rise of the mrem; but he listened with an admonitory eye on the class, which remained quiet and attentive throughout the reading, although the old schoolmaster could no longer see them from behind the big book.

One tale especially fascinated them, a tale even Branwe had never heard before, about how the All-Mother punished the old reptilian race for its evil magic by sinking their homeland beneath the sea. He was so moved in fact that he could feel his fur rise with excitement, as if he were actually the warrior he had long dreamed of becoming, in the midst of a great adventure. He would one day have cause to recall this story, but at the moment the class drew only the most obvious interpretation from his rising fur, and looked very angelic indeed.

Master Hoobel was gratified at so attentive an audience. It was popularly believed that he read from the big book the way he did because he was thus shielded from missiles. In any case, he did read, and read, and read. What Branwe had expected to be mere classroom drudgery turned out to be a day he never forgot. Nor did the old schoolmaster ever forget it was the day before a festival, and he was shrewd enough not to press his luck. He dismissed the class early.

Branwe kept them in good order as far as the door; but then even he could do no more, and they fairly exploded into the afternoon sunlight with wild whoops, shouts, and squeaks of joy and high spirits. Windows were flung open, neighbors grumbled complaints, and shopkeepers up and down the street took up defensive positions.

Branwe, still excited by the tales of magic and adventure, could not help but be affected by such exuberance; but he remained behind, and helped the old schoolmaster straighten the benches and tables, and clean the room. He carried the *Dragon Book* back to its shelf with the reverence felt only by those to whom books are precious things. The sole book at the Blue Dragon was the innkeeper's ledger, and nobody else was allowed to read it. Except his wife, of course.

"It's hard for you, isn't it, young Branwe?" said the kindly old mrem. "Well, well, we all must follow whatever destiny the All-Mother has decided for us. Now do you remember any of the history taught in class this last week?"

He listened patiently while Branwe recited the major dates and events since the foundation of Ar, down to the death of the great Talwe. He had two of the early half-legendary kings confused, and won a battle for Ar that in fact had been lost, but otherwise recited with credit.

"Very good, my boy. And don't worry about not getting the names and dates of the early kings down pat. A lot of that history has no more substance than the tales in the *Dragon Book*. Although even those tales have at least some substance. After all, there are dragons, and some herd animals do wield magical powers."

"What about the All-Mother sinking the ancient homeland of the Old Race beneath the sea? Did that really happen too?"

"Who can say?" The old schoolmaster smiled whimsically at him. "We know so little about the rest of the planet, that I suppose even such wonders as that are possible. But now you'd better run along. I know what your master thinks about schooling, and I don't want to get you in trouble. I also know, alas, how much work there is for you at festival time. So run along, my boy. Run along. Don't forget, classes resume the second day after the festival ends."

Branwe did hurry away down the street, but not in the direction of the Blue Dragon. The early dismissal today was an unexpected boon. So long as he returned to work on time, Grujekh would have nothing to complain about—except as a matter of principle. Turning the corner, he wove his way through the festival crowds toward the armory.

The crowd here was already ten deep around the courtyard-like drill field. The soldiers did not like drilling under civilian eyes; their captains were still angry about it. But the new governor had thrown open the drill fields to the public at festival time, as a donative in the name of his patron, Tristwyn the boy king of Ar. Military discipline had relaxed since his accession to the throne. Branwe had overheard rankers at the Blue Dragon whisper that morale would have plain collapsed, but for old Severakh.

It was as much to see that legendary old warrior as to watch the drill itself that Branwe had come here today. He saw Severakh standing in full battle armor at the far side of the field, which was nearly a half city-block in dimension, surrounded on all four sides by two-story barracks, an infirmary, an administrative office, and a multidoored refectory. He recognized the martial dance now being performed—also in full battle armor, despite the official relaxation of this old tradition—as a maneuver popularly called the "grope." The complex sweeping, weaving movements were not merely ornamental; at least, not under Severakh's stern eye. In real combat, a horde of bandits or desert marauders would have found itself quickly outflanked and their defenses shattered. It was fascinating to watch the grace and agility of such powerful, heavy-armed mrem. All eyes were upon them.

Then all at once he was fascinated by a movement closer by. Hookpurses sometimes lodged at the Blue Dragon, and he had been taught their techniques, so he could alert Grujekh or Mamre of any attempt to rob a guest. This particular hookpurse had the look of an old professional: well dressed, but not too well; well groomed, but not conspicuously so; everything about him nondescript. He too seemed to keep his eyes on the martial dance. But slowly, smoothly, almost imperceptibly, he extended a single digit of his right hand; then just as slowly, smoothly, and imperceptibly he extended its retractable claw.

Hooking the purse of what looked like a prosperous village merchant, he locked his arm, and rose stealthily on his tiptoes, so no rotary movement of his hand would betray him. The purse vanished up his sleeve, and he began to insinuate himself backwards through the crowd.

"Well, well," said a brawny young mrem, as he seized one of the hookpurse's elbows, while his assistant seized the other. "If it ain't our old pal, Fefo. We just dropped by to tell you that we've reserved your usual lodgings for you. They're underground, and some folks say they're a trifle damp, but you can get used to anything in time. And you'll have plenty of that, Fefo."

The assistant, who was even brawnier, chuckled at the crude sarcasm. He was joined by a few people in the crowd nearby, who understood what was happening.

"Keep a grip on him," ordered the brawny young policemrem. "I'll round up our witness. All right, lad. Come along."

Branwe was surprised to see the policemrem looking right at him. He started to protest, but was brusquely silenced.

"You saw it all," said the guardsmrem. "We were watching you. Don't worry, you're not in any trouble. We just need your testimony down at the lockup, then you can go home and we won't bother you any more."

Branwe sighed and followed obediently. There was no point in arguing. He was more worried about how he would explain his presence here at the armory when he reported late for work.

▲

Chapter 2
The Sentinel

▲ ——————————————————————————————— ▲

There was no pattern to the labyrinthine dungeons. The first settlers in Kazerclawm had stored their water supply in underground cisterns. As the city expanded, so did its need for water, and the new cisterns were delved in conformity to the underlying rock structure, rather than to any ongoing plan. Then, with the completion of an aqueduct under the auspices of the late King of Ar, the cisterns were abandoned. Those directly below the fortress were now used as the city's lockup.

"Hello, Fefo," said the turnkey, a pawky little mrem with a humorous round face and neat whiskers, whose principal object in life seemed to be taking good care of himself. "Been sticking your claws where you shouldn't again? You know what we said the last time you were our guest." He picked up a metal beaker from his desk and shook it, grinning waggishly at the tinkle of hundreds of extracted claws. In the settled regions of the land, declawing was reserved for murderers; but Kazerclawm was a frontier city, the resort of rogues and vagabonds, and its criminal penalties accordingly more severe. "Amazing how fast my collection grows at festival time."

This section of the old cistern had been partitioned off into tiers of small cells. Several of the prisoners had bandaged hands. They glowered evilly through the bars at the waggish turnkey.

"The registrar's on his way," he continued in the same bantering tone. The insignia on his uniform indicated that he was a career soldier, in his fourth hitch of service. That he was still a mere turnkey, literally as well as figuratively the lowest rank in the army, bespoke his military repute. The only light came from an oil lamp on his desk, and he had to peer into the shadows to see who was standing behind the two brawny policemrem and their prisoner.

"What? Is that you, Branwe?" he exclaimed. "I'm astonished to see a good lad like you brought here."

"Hello, Cajhet." Branwe stepped forward. "I haven't done anything wrong. I'm just a witness."

"Well, that's a relief," said the turnkey. "The Blue Dragon wouldn't be the same without you."

Branwe smiled to himself. He had saved the pawky little mrem more than one sound thrashing at the claws of his fellow rankers. An inveterate gambler, Cajhet was at times not only reduced to mooching drinks but even to pocketing loose change from the bar and tables, when he thought nobody was looking. His reputation for skulking timidity seemed well known to the two brawny guardsmrem.

"Right under old Severakh's nose." The chief shook his head at the sullen hookpurse. "Remember how strict his orders were? Gnashing his teeth and pounding the table, he was."

The assistant took up his cue: "Never saw the old mrem so mad. Think we should bring Fefo here to him in person?"

"Say, you may be right. The trouble is we can't do it ourselves. We're already overdue back at our posts. We have the legal right to impress any public official into police service, of course. But who could we get?"

"Why not Cajhet here?" asked the assistant.

"The very one! I should have thought of that myself. As soon as the registrar takes our evidence and that of young—what's his name, Branwe—here, Cajhet can take the prisoner straight to old Severakh in person. Not only will he be doing his duty, but it'll be a grand opportunity for him to really get acquainted with his commanding officer. What about it, Cajhet? Want to talk to Severakh? Should we send him word to expect you?"

The turnkey looked so mournful at this prospect that the two brawny guardsmrem could no longer restrain their laughter. Even Branwe had to smile. Cajhet was often teased by his fellow rankers over his mortal dread of ever meeting the fierce Severakh face to face. He grinned weakly as he realized it was all a joke.

There was nothing funny about it to the prisoner, however. A bandit or sneak thief could still make a living after being declawed, but a hookpurse was out of business if he no longer had anything to hook purses with. He remained sullen and motionless while the registrar completed the legal documents, only raising his eyes once, with a look of vindictive malice, as Branwe ended his testimony. The evidence of guardsmrem could be discredited in court, but not when corroborated by an independent witness, even a common potboy.

Branwe caught the malicious look. If he himself remembered every detail of the crime, there was no doubt this Fefo would remember every last detail about him. What if he got word to confederates on the outside? Branwe was not afraid of danger. It might even be a blessing. What better excuse for carrying a sword in the streets, or drilling until he was master swordsmrem? Perhaps he would mention the incident later to Mamre.

Right now, he needed an excuse for his tardiness in returning to work. The Blue Dragon would be thronged by now with soldiers, tourists, merchants, and festival revelers, drinking, dancing, laughing, gambling—and angrily pounding their tables when there was no potboy to refill their goblets quickly enough. No excuse was valid with Grujekh, if it cost him money . . . .

The snowcap of the Kazerclaw glowed red-violet in the setting sun. More celebrants than ever thronged the streets. Branwe skirted a crowd straggling around a troupe of acrobats. The towers of the Watersmeet Gate were silhouetted against the twilight at the end of the street. If the garrison now seemed merely ornamental to some, and patrols beyond the city walls—against the protests of old Severakh—had been curtailed by the new governor as an unjustified expense, the gates were still shut punctually at sunset. There had been more and more reports lately about attacks by liskash upon travelers benighted outside the walls, and the last stragglers were even now pouring in from the countryside.

The sounds of revelry from the Blue Dragon meant that he would not get to bed until hours after midnight, but they were also a consolation. He might be so busy that Grujekh would not find a chance to berate him for his tardiness—

"Branwe," a voice called softly to him out of the crowd

across the street, and he at once forgot all about being late, or the long hours of drudgery before him. "I came looking for you, but Mamre said you had not yet returned from school."

Slender and delicate, with all the enchanting grace of a White Dancer, Srana had never seemed more beautiful than she did now. She was a flawless cream white, and wore a simple white gown and chaplet; her white scarf framed her lovely young face like a halo.

Shy and self-conscious as always in her presence, he stammered out the incident of the hookpurse. He did not want her to think him slack or undutiful.

"My grandfather sent me." She lowered her eyes sadly. "Can you help him tomorrow or the next day? He needs someone to bring down a case of books from the loft and, well, Nizzam isn't very strong."

Except in conceit, thought Branwe, but he only said: "There's usually a slack period in the early afternoon. I'm sure Mamre will give me a couple of hours off, when she knows it's to help your grandfather. How is he today?"

Again her eyes looked sad and distant. "He sleeps poorly, and hardly eats anything at all. He doesn't complain, but I know his dreams trouble him. His mind is being probed, and he's worried that he will soon no longer have the strength to resist."

Branwe had heard many rumors explaining the presence of so mighty a wizard in so remote a frontier city: that he had been banished here by the great order of wizards known as The Three, that he was their agent on some cryptic mission, even that he was treacherously in the service of the Eastern Lords. Nor did anybody really know why he was called the Sentinel. Whatever the reason, he had first settled here early in the reign of the late King of Ar, and was now an old mrem, sick and dying. But for the nursing of his granddaughter Srana he would probably not be alive at all.

As Branwe tried awkwardly to comfort her, he was alerted not by an unusual noise, but an unusual quiet. Having grown up at the Blue Dragon, he knew instinctively its every mood. Nothing could be more ominous than sudden silence on a festival night. He knew what he was supposed to do, but could not leave Srana just standing alone in the street.

"You must do your duty, Branwe," she said. "I understand.

Go now, but be careful. Evil has entered the Blue Dragon. I sensed it there. Farewell, until tomorrow."

He was not sure what she meant, but did not take her warning lightly, as he dodged and jostled through the crowded street toward the rear of the old sprawling caravansary. He had witnessed her powers of healing, and suspected that her danger sense was no less magical.

The brawl erupted just as he reached the kitchen door. He was nearly bowled over by two scullery wenches, then had to jump out of the way of several timid patrons also seeking cover. Shouts, curses, cries of pain and anger, daggers and claws bared; it was the most vicious brawl he had witnessed in years. He dived into its midst with the recklessness and agility of youth.

Not to fight, but to salvage as much inn property as he could. This was not much, as it turned out. The old rankers from the garrison remained aloof, taking up defensive positions at one corner of the dance floor. Nor did the female dancers—other than with shrill curses and swipes of their claws at any male so imprudent as to accost them—really get involved. The heavy fighting, surprisingly, was concentrated around the bar. He heard a cry from Mamre, and raced in that direction.

She was trying frantically to claw her way past the brawlers, so angry about something that tears stood in her eyes. Then one of the strange outlanders, who seemed to have instigated the fight, blindsided her with a cowardly punch, knocking her against the wall. Branwe snatched up a stool, leapt like an acrobat onto the bar, and brought it crashing down on the skull of the nearest outlander, unfortunately not the wretch who had punched Mamre.

Then he in turn was knocked sprawling. Bruised, his left arm cut by a shattered wine jar, he picked himself up ready for more. But the fight was over. The strangers had carried the man he had stunned out the front door, and were gone. He heard Mamre weeping, and was afraid she had been injured, but discovered it was only her prize mirror. It lay shattered on the floor behind the bar, its gem-encrusted frame hacked and broken.

She knelt beside it as if it were a stricken child. One by one she picked up the loose gemstones, carefully dusted them off, and laid them in her apron. Then in an agony of loss she began searching all over the floor.

"The wretches!" she cried. "They've stolen the big violet stone. Why did they have to go and do that? It's just cut crystal. It doesn't mean anything to anybody but me. It was my favorite." She dabbed at her eyes with the corner of her handkerchief.

Then Branwe realized that Grujekh was lowering at him, as if none of this would have happened if he had returned to work on time.

▲

Reeking alleyways; secondhand clothing shops; stalls peddling rags, broken crockery, and rancid-smelling meats and fish; beggars and thieves (often indistinguishable); cheap lodgings to let; gambling dens; and abandoned fire-scorched buildings. The taverns here were the lowest in Kazerclawm, their dancing girls the most lascivious. The sun had barely set and there had already been two murders in the quarter. Of the several robbery attempts, all but one was successful, and in that one the thief had been taken red-handed and stoned to death with paving blocks by a street mob.

And yet Srana walked these grim streets unmolested. The meanest bowed to her; the most vicious stepped aside to let her pass. Her mystique as a Dancer elevated her above the plane of everyday squalor. That her powers of healing served even the most downtrodden without payment lent her a kind of awe.

She kept her eyes on the wretched pavement before her as she crossed the street to her grandfather's humble dwelling. A high garden wall screened it from the neighborhood; stepping through the gate was like entering another world.

"I was beginning to worry about you," Nizzam greeted her in the vestibule. His sleekness and fine grooming left no doubt that he was inordinately pleased with his own person. He considered exercise a waste of effort, and high round-shouldered paunchiness made him look years older than his true age, an image his pompous manner tended to confirm. "It's already after sunset."

"I was detained." She removed her white scarf, and smoothed her gown. "The two Sanandazh kits were more seriously ill than I had expected. Did my grandfather rest comfortably while I was away?"

He shrugged resignedly, both at her grandfather's chances of recovery, and her frittering away precious healing powers on slum urchins. He also seemed to have resigned himself to spending the festival night at home. His nondescript, almost shabby attire was in contrast to the priestlike robes he generally affected in the streets.

He said, "I missed you while you were gone, Srana. You know that I consider you worthy of my affection, and that when your grandfather at last passes on—not soon, let us hope—and I assume my proper station, for which I have long, perhaps too long been qualified—"

But Srana was already on the way down the corridor to her grandfather's sickroom, leaving Nizzam to shrug resignedly again, and follow after her in a manner consonant with his dignity.

The old wizard lay propped up with pillows, his bed strewn with old books, charts, and parchment manuscripts. His feverish eyes seemed too large for so gaunt a face, and there was a tremor in his bony old hands as he moved them restlessly from book to chart to manuscript, as if uncertain which he wanted to consult next.

Srana sat on the bed and began to groom him. Then she checked his pulse and examined his eyes. "You haven't rested as you promised, Grandfather," she admonished him gently, "and you haven't taken the elixir I brewed for you this morning."

"I didn't want to sleep, today of all days." His voice was weak and hoarse, and it was obviously an effort for him to speak. "I'm most vulnerable then . . ." He fell silent as he noticed Nizzam standing in the doorway.

"You know I'm ready to help you in any way I can, master," he said. "Those who assail your dreams would find me no mean obstacle to their magic."

"Thank you, Nizzam," the old man said wearily. "You have always been a diligent scholar. But now that my granddaughter has returned, I see no need to detain you any longer."

"Then I have your leave to, uh, inspect the festival preparations?" cried Nizzam. "I won't be long, I promise." He hurried from the room.

"He's up to something, of course," said the old mrem. "Probably some conceit he's persuaded himself is important, for no other reason than that he's involved in it. Poor Nizzam! Not all his grinding away at his books has taught him yet how little he really knows."

"Please rest, Grandfather." Srana continued to groom him. "You mustn't overtire yourself."

"It's too late to worry about that, dear. There's no cure for old age. But whatever Nizzam is up to tonight, I'm glad he's out of the house. If he hadn't so deviously wanted to go himself, I would have had to devise some pretext to get rid of him. As you guessed, I didn't take your elixir. The intrusive wills trying to probe my mind have now become relentless. They sense that I may soon be unable to resist them. Will young Branwe be able to help us?"

"Yes, Grandfather. You know that dear Branwe can always be depended on to help us. I don't know what we would have done without him," she added softly. "He'll come tomorrow afternoon—unless the trouble at the Blue Dragon detains him."

"Another brawl? Yes, I suppose that's to be expected at festival time." He looked curiously at her. "Or is it more than that? Your danger sense is keener than mine."

"There was something evil there. Exactly what, I don't know."

"Like your feelings when you first came to Kazerclawm to nurse me?"

She nodded. "It's strange, Grandfather, but I've never lost that feeling."

"Let's hope you never do, for there is indeed danger here. The evil beneath the mountain never sleeps. Nor dare we relax our vigilance until the Third Eye is discovered." He wearily closed his eyes for a few moments, while his grand-daughter watched him with concern. At last he recovered: "I have been going over my books and papers, as you see. The work must be completed soon, because I know I have only a few weeks to live, perhaps only a few days. No, no, my dear, this is no time to beguile a dying mrem, no matter how well meant. It's a time for rendering accounts. That's why I want all my remaining books and manuscripts hauled down from the loft." He had to rest once more before continuing. "It's also the time for you to learn why I was appointed Sentinel here in Kazerclawm."

"Does Nizzam know the reason?"

He nodded. "As the nephew of a great wizard, he was thought to be the ideal apprentice, who would one day supersede me here. Alas, he has inherited his uncle's dignity, without his uncle's genius. I have tried to raise him in the best traditions of The Three, but he seems interested only in the trappings of wizardry, not its substance. He does indeed know about the evil beneath the mountain, but like too many young wizards these days he does not realize that it is eternal."

"Rest for a moment, Grandfather." She continued to groom his tufty gray fur with the soothing hands of a healer. "If you become too excited, or overtire yourself, you will be unable to tell me all I know you want to say."

He started to protest, but realized the wisdom of her advice. There was indeed no cure for old age, but without her ministrations he was certain he would have died months ago. Had she, rather than Nizzam, been appointed his successor, he could have died in peace. It had seemed a pity to him at first that one so naturally gifted in magic should become merely a Dancer. But he had been assured by her friend and teacher, no less than the legendary Sruss herself, that her natural gifts there were no less extraordinary.

"You're right as always, my dear," he said. "You've been patient with the whims of an old mrem, and I appreciate the sacrifices you've made to nurse me. Be patient with me a while longer, for there are things you must know before it is too late." He studied her young face, awed by its beauty. "I've taught you as much magic as I could in so short a time. I regret only that I didn't begin sooner. Now learn, as you have never learned before. Though I violate the stern mandate of The Three in divulging this information, the peril justifies me. The evil brooding beneath the mountain has not waned as we hoped, but grown ever stronger and more menacing. Nor dare we act to destroy it, until we ourselves are stronger. Exactly how much our united powers would be remultiplied by the Third Eye . . . Yes, yes, my dear, I know I'm becoming excited again." Once more he rested until he was calm.

Hours passed, and Srana never left his side. With rests and pauses to nurse his waning vitality, even a brief nap, he managed at last to relate a tale more dreadful than even the worst foreboding of her acute danger sense.

Exactly how or when the Eastern Lords first took Khal into their service was unknown. Nor was it known where the reptilian sorcerer learned to wield an evil magic surpassing the powers of The Three. Such was his cunning that he devised a means by which the entire order of wizards might be overthrown. The Eastern Lords supported him, for they well understood that The Three were a resolute obstacle to all their schemes of conquest—even if the mrem themselves did not. The primordial homeland of the Old Race had perished in a natural cataclysm, eons before the beginning of mrem history, but not the source of its evil magic.

The Khavala was a stone of flawless beauty, and yet it was not a gem like any other known in this world; for it did not in fact belong to this world. It was imperishable, for it did not really exist—at least not in this dimension. The very elements from which it crystalized were alien; yet they induced powerful reactions among the familiar elements whenever the catalyst of magic was present. Where there was no magic, there was no reaction. But a mere sliver of the Khavala could have turned the shabbiest bush wizard into a mighty sorcerer.

No ship of the Eastern Lords could have passed safely through the mrem fleets that plied the Southern Sea, or its pirate islands; certainly not with a reptilian sorcerer aboard. But Khal's agents discovered a mrem noble—bitter, impoverished, and spoiling for revenge—whose lands and titles had been wrongfully confiscated by a rapacious warlord. He was commissioned to lead a crew of bandits, declawed criminals, and highland renegades to the Shadow Islands, the remnants of the lost continent. A magic sword was forged for him to combat its demon guardians.

Only for a single night, when a rare conjunction of the three moons focused over a single point in the Shadow Islands, did the evil dimension conjoin this world. Then alone was the Khavala accessible. But greed, mutiny, and faulty navigation—it seems that Khal himself knew of the Shadow Islands only through vague legends—so delayed the expedition that it nearly arrived too late. Reptile demons assailed the crewmrem, and many were dragged into the evil dimension for torment.

The Shadow Warrior, as the mrem noble came to be known, was sorely beset. In desperation, in the midst of frenzied combat with the guardians of the Khavala, he tried to hack the stone from its setting. There was magic in his sword, though not enough to withstand the forces of the evil dimension, and it shattered in his hand. But so did a whole corner of the Khavala, and he managed to escape with the fragments; only one of which was of considerable size—the fragment that has come to be known as the Third Eye.

Returning to the port of Namakhazar, far to the south, the Shadow Warrior had premonitions of treachery, and sent the largest fragment alone to the waiting Khal. The premonitions turned out to be true. Once Khal had what he thought was the Khavala, he rewarded the surviving crewmrem by having them executed. The Shadow Warrior escaped, appalled at the evil he had unwittingly loosed upon his own kind.

"We were still more appalled," concluded the old wizard, "for we better understood the nature of that evil. The Shadow Warrior atoned for his misjudgment by coming directly to The Three with all the remaining fragments of the Khavala. There were seven in all, though not even combined were these powerful enough to overmaster Khal."

"But I don't understand, Grandfather. I've always heard that The Three were invincible, that such were their powers that the mightiest were immortal."

The old wizard smiled indulgently. "A fable, my dear. An old, old fable. Long ago, a small, select group of magicians covered their operations by creating a myth that there were three all-powerful wizards in the city of Ar who never died. They pretended that this gave them secret and invincible powers. One look at me should dispel any notions about immortality," he sighed.

"Yet The Three are an obstacle to the Eastern Lords," she encouraged him. "You've said so yourself. And there's more than just a small, select group now, and not just at Ar."

"Yes, we've recruited over the years, hoping that quantity might somehow overcome a decline in quality. Many today call themselves members of The Three, who in past generations would hardly have been more than bush wizards—and the recruiting still continues all over the land. Not that mere numbers did us much good against Khal, even with all our magic remultiplied by the seven fragments of the Khavala in our possession. His magic was too powerful, his fragment so large he could actually afford to waste some of it, having it cut and polished into a jewel he called the Third Eye."

"Because of some flaw in the stone that gleamed like an eye?" Srana guessed. She realized now that her grandfather was determined to finish his narration tonight. All she could do was nurse his strength, and try to keep him from exhausting himself dangerously.

"The Khavala is flawless, and like no other stone in existence. It is of a ruby color, but with a weird phosphorescence, like the fury of malice. Like Khal's own eyes. He wore it in a uraeus on his forehead, and it remultiplied his powers a hundredfold. He was invincible."

"And yet you overcame him?"

"He overcame himself, before he could turn all his evil magic against us." He looked up at her with feverish eyes. "Never forget that Khal is alien to us in every respect. His intelligence may reach ours in magnitude, but is utterly different in kind. It is really just bestial cunning evolved to a high degree of effectiveness. Instead of concentrating his new powers to achieve his ends, or those of the Eastern Lords, he indulged himself like a spoiled child in orgies of vengeance. Only thus were we able to take him unawares."

"But not the Third Eye?"

He studied her lovely young face with a look of profound regret. "Oh, why couldn't you have been named to succeed me here as the Sentinel?" he groaned. "Then truly might I have died at peace."

"What became of the Shadow Warrior?" She tried to calm him by changing the subject.

"Dead, along with his entire family. Whether Khal had agents abroad, or the Eastern Lords, we knew no more than we knew the location of the Third Eye. He hid it just before being subdued, and in such a way that the hiding place could never be forced from him, because he himself did not know it. His agents acted for him, just as they wreaked his vengeance upon the Shadow Warrior."

"Then that was what the two wizards who visited you last

summer meant," she said thoughtfully. "I overheard them both mention a search, and both seemed to despair of ever succeeding. Are they still searching for the Third Eye?"

"For over a generation now. The two you mention are only those who have visited me while you were here. All of The Three have at one time or another wandered the land in search of the Third Eye. The great Mithmid has devoted himself to it like a religious quest. In a way, I suppose, it's just that. For until the Third Eye is found, the very existence of our race is in jeopardy. Nor can we expect help from the people. If they did not believe in their original peril, how could we expect them to believe that the peril still hangs over them? And you know their attitude toward magicians. The fools! They think reptile demons are only the stuff of bad dreams."

Speaking softly, grooming him with the hands of a healer, it took Srana several minutes to calm his growing excitement.

"Reptile demons," he continued at last. "We know that Khal was learning to summon them forth from the evil dimension, by remultiplying his powers through the Third Eye, perhaps even learning to pass into that very dimension, and become more powerful still for working harm against us. Striking when he least expected us to, while he indulged himself in the most bestial forms of vengeance, we were just strong enough to overcome him, but not to annihilate him utterly. Only if we ourselves had gained possession of the Third Eye could we have done that, but he was too cunning for us."

"Then what became of him?"

"He lies entombed beneath the Kazerclaw, no doubt brooding on new orgies of vengeance. All the power of The Three, remultiplied by all our fragments of the Khavala, were needed just to enclose him in a vault of enchantment. The Kazerclaw was chosen because its only scalable approach is through this garrison city. The Sacred Gate is still well guarded, but who can say for how much longer. Tristwyn seems to outdo himself in folly with each passing month. Had it not been for the old king and, well, those who advised him, the Sacred Gate might never have been guarded at all. No stranger has passed through it in my time here, I can assure you."

After several moments, he added in a whisper: "But my time is almost over now."

"Can't Sruss help you? It was she who advised the old king, her son, in the first place, wasn't it? We still communicate with each other, so I could tell her—"

"No, no, my dear. A great Council of The Three has already been summoned, although I'm afraid it will be Nizzam who attends in my place. Besides, Sruss has enemies at court, who seek any opportunity to destroy her."

"Do you mean Rhenowla, the queen mother? I can't imagine anyone else who could be Sruss's enemy. You loved Sruss once, didn't you, Grandfather?"

His eyes misted over, as if gazing back upon a world that was gone. "A hopeless and distant love—I was never such a young fool as to think it could ever be anything more. Many in my generation felt that way. And you say she is still beautiful?"

Srana nodded, but noticed that tears were beginning to well up in the old mrem's eyes, and changed the subject.

"Will Nizzam take your fragment of the Khavala to the Council of Wizards, assuming you can't attend yourself, or will you keep it?"

"He must have it when I'm gone, I suppose," the old wizard said reluctantly. "Whether he will be allowed to keep it, to become one of the Seven, a full council must decide. But I must not give it up yet a while, for I could no longer survive without it. The lingering illness which has sapped my vitality has also diminished my powers of magic. The intrusive wills that now probe my mind relentlessly would be irresistible had I nothing with which to multiply such powers as remain to me. You've never seen my fragment of the Khavala, have you, dear?"

She shook her head, more and more concerned about the feverish exhaustion in his eyes. Somehow she must get him to rest. But she rose from the sickbed in order to fetch the mysterious fragment for him, at his direction.

"No, no, I have it with me always. I suspect Nizzam has poked and rummaged into every corner of the house, looking for it. But it's been right here all the time." He drew his familiar lavaliere from beneath his bed gown. Its pendant was a gold seal engraved with a circle of runes; there was a secret catch, and he opened it.

Srana again sat beside him, and peered curiously down at what looked like no more than a sliver of broken glass—except that it shone with a ruby phosphorescence. It was astounding that so tiny an object could confer such vast power. Still more astounding, even terrifying, was the thought of how much more power resided in the Third Eye—or in the Khavala itself.

"Did the Shadow Warrior ever reveal its exact size?" she asked. "Or shape?"

"He described it as being like the living head of some creature from a monstrous race. Given the circumstances under which he saw it, though, even that vague description is suspect. After all, he was fighting for his life, assailed on all sides by the guardians of an evil dimension. I'm sure that not even Khal himself really knows its exact nature."

"Only that it granted immense power," she added thoughtfully. "The power to work great evil."

"To Khal, yes. But only because he was already a sorcerer of great power. The stone multiplies force; it does not create it. If one is not powerful in magic to begin with, there is nothing to multiply. Nothing but a shiny sliver of rock."

They gazed down in silence at the tiny fragment of the Khavala, glowing mysteriously with a strange otherworldly light.

▲

Chapter 3
The Evil Beneath the Mountain

▲————————————————————————————————————▲

Two other pairs of eyes were gazing down at another ruby fragment at that very moment. The mug-house stood less than two streets from the Blue Dragon, but a whole world separated it in character. So unsavory were his surroundings that for once even Nizzam's pompousness was deflated. He had never suspected there were so many villainous types living here in Kazerclawm. Or were they all outlanders?

"Of course I recognize what's on your ring." He tried to conceal his growing nervousness with a display of omniscience. "My master has an identical fragment. He keeps it, uh, always within reach."

"Then you've discovered the secret of the lavaliere he wears around his neck?" The young mrem seated at the corner table with him spoke in a gutteral accent. "Very clever. I was sure The Three could count on you." He glanced over his shoulder to reassure himself that no stranger was within earshot, and lowered his voice. "The events of the next few days could determine our very survival. Your master was not suspicious about your coming here tonight?"

Nizzam shrugged, as if to say that his master's opinion was of no consequence to him, although he had in fact been taken by surprise. The lavaliere! Of course! He could hardly suppress the twitching of his whisker pads, at the thought of having missed so obvious a hiding place himself. Once more he glanced nervously around the low mug-house. The five villainous companions of the young fellow seated with him had ranged themselves along the bar, isolating their table from possible eavesdropping. One of them had his head bandaged.

"I hate this sneaking about after dark as much as you do," the young mrem continued. "But I'm sure you know yourself why it's necessary. We of the younger generation must redeem the mistakes of the elder. They would hold us back if they could. Yes, I can see that you too have suffered from the lack of recognition by a jealous master. A master who would still hoard all the glory for himself, if he could. What a shame! That such learning should be denied its just reward out of senile envy."

Nizzam frowned down at the table. He had felt for years now that his merits were slighted, that The Three were being disinformed about his progress. Why else had he not already been qualified as a master wizard?

The young mrem studied him for a moment with cunning satisfaction, then lowered his voice to an insinuating whisper: "Hold out your hand." He slipped the ring, whose bezel mounted the sliver of ruby phosphorescence, onto Nizzam's finger. "If your master hinders your advancement, be assured that The Three know you for what you really are. But have you the courage? That is now the question of questions."

"I believe I can be counted on to do my duty," Nizzam replied pompously. "Though some may not think so."

"We do," said the stranger. "Oh yes, we have long waited for just such a mrem as yourself." There was a hint of mockery in his voice, but Nizzam was still too rapt in his own grievances to notice it. "If your master has withheld due respect from you, I hope he has at least not withheld a full account of what lies entombed beneath the Kazerclaw."

"He has tried to," said Nizzam. "But I am not without mine own sources of information."

"Then we needn't mention any names? Good." He glanced suspiciously over his shoulder, then leaned forward and whispered: "A flaw has been discovered in the vault of enchantment. Not even your master, the very Sentinel himself, for all his imposing reputation as a wizard" —Nizzam snorted— "was alert enough to detect it. Let us be charitable, and say he has merely outlived his reputation. Once upon a time he may have had the prowess, even the courage, to attempt such an ordeal as I am now proposing. The Three fear that he might still attempt it, though no longer capable, rather than see another rival his glory. Or do we misjudge him?"

"You do not. He would rise from his very deathbed, before allowing anyone else a chance to earn recognition."

"So we feared. It has also been suggested that he might turn others against you in his own household."

Nizzam looked quickly at him, then lowered his eyes. Could that explain Srana's coldness toward him? It must. He had made it clear to her that, no matter what she lacked in fortune or noble ancestry, he considered her a worthy consort for the eminent position he would someday assume. Yet her response had lacked the warmth to be expected from a she-mrem in her position. Could her grandfather indeed be poisoning her mind against him?

The young mrem again studied him with cunning satisfaction. A sneer crossed his face, but he quickly suppressed it.

"All the power of The Three has been concentrated into forging this telesma." The golden pyx he now set on the table was engraved with occult runes, prominent among which Nizzam recognized the name Khal. "I needn't ask if you can read the incantation? Good. Then we can proceed at once to the actual ceremony . . . ."

Nizzam listened intently to the details of the task before him. He was barely able to spell out the incantation engraved on the pyx, but pretended to know its full meaning, although in fact several of the key runes were utterly unknown to him. Nor was he displeased to learn that there were things unknown to his all-knowing master. Once he demonstrated his prowess, The Three would no longer be swayed against him by disparagement, and the beautiful Srana would grant him all he desired of her. But first he must accomplish the task. There were official obstacles to reaching the mountain at all, and only a wizard bearing a fragment of the Khavala could enter it. Now it seemed there were defenses surrounding the very vault of enchantment.

"I must first return to my home neighborhood," he began.

"Not to beg your master for leave, I hope?" the stranger chided. "No, no, of course not. Pardon me for even suggesting that you can't come and go as you please. Of course you don't have to tell anyone about this undertaking. The terrible danger threatening us all has made me nervous. Fortunately for us," he added with another hint of mockery, "you're the strong and independent person you are."

"I hope so," Nizzam said complacently. "No, I must return to my home neighborhood merely to obtain an official pass. Two citizens must vouch for me, and register with the garrison duty officer. Then at the mountain itself . . . Well, there may be other, shall we say, formalities."

"Pronouncing the name Kazerclawm,"—the stranger's own pronunciation was almost unintelligible—"as well as other words that would betray a foreign accent? My own master warned me of just that problem, else I would probably have had to carry the telesma into the mountain myself. Thank you for your sensitivity. I don't envy you your ordeal."

Nizzam shrugged, as if he were an old hand at derring-do. The stranger watched him with the same insidious cunning he had used earlier to provoke a brawl at the Blue Dragon. He kept his right hand under the table, for it was still swollen from the cowardly punch he had thrown at the innkeeper's wife.

▲

"It was my mother's honor I was defending," said Cajhet. "I was a lad about your age, Branwe. But nobody was going to insult my mother, and me not do anything about it. Yes, I fought many duels, in my time."

He did not bother to add that he had invariably been thrashed, nor that he had enlisted in the army as a consequence. He stared morosely down into the dregs of his third brimming goblet of iced wine. It had turned out to be a sultry night, and he was still thirsty. He had lost a wager over a knife-throwing match, and now had no more money; though that might have been finessed—there were opportunities galore for free drinks at festival time—he came on duty again just before dawn. To be reported drunk or asleep on watch could mean facing old Severakh in person—an ordeal he had successfully dodged for years. He pushed his goblet away and rose stiffly to his feet.

"Time to toddle, lad. I'm a soldier, and take my duties seriously, though others may not. You've had some trouble in here tonight, I hear. Brawlers, eh?" He tightened his belt, and threw out his chest. "Lucky for them I wasn't around, or they'd have got some brawling they might not have liked. I take no nonsense on the job, or off. 'Night, lad."

Branwe watched him slink timidly through the revelers still crowding the Blue Dragon. Female dancers performed a lascivious highland romp, accompanied by the throbbing beat of drums, pipes, and scrapers. The musicians were drunk, as were most of the waiters and kitchen help, taking advantage of Mamre's absence. She had retired in dudgeon after her prize mirror was damaged in the brawl. Branwe alone had not celebrated right along with the festival celebrants.

The throb and beat and skirl of the music ceased, and a wild and ribald hullabaloo rang through the inn. One of the dancers rubbed enticingly against him as she passed. The rankers in the crowd were hardly in a condition to perform with credit in the military exhibition tomorrow. He wondered if they even cared any more. Morale had deteriorated even faster than preparedness, since the accession of the elegant new governor.

Returning from an hour of kitchen duty, he discovered that meanwhile Mamre had also returned, and had had her prize mirror remounted on the wall behind the bar. Three jagged cracks flowered upwards from the lower right-hand corner of the glass, whose replacement would cost little trouble or expense. Repairing the gem-encrusted frame was a more delicate matter, and she stood on a wine chest, trying to refit the loosened gemstones into their proper sockets.

Branwe made his way toward her. He needed time off tomorrow to help Srana's grandfather haul some books down from his loft, but as he approached the bar he had second thoughts. This was obviously not the opportune moment for his request.

"I'll haul the wretches in front of Severakh myself, if I have to," Mamre complained bitterly. There was still some swelling on the side of her face where she had been punched. "By the scruff of the neck, if I must. They'll pay damages. Oh yes, they will! And just let them try and peddle the beautiful gemstone they stole. Violet as the morning sky! I've passed the word already. Every dealer in town will be on the lookout for it."

"They'll never recognize it then, if that's the way you

described it to 'em," volunteered a scrawny elderly patron seated at the bar nearby. "That the socket it was stuck in? Well then, the stone is probably just plain red, like a ruby. See how that one socket there is dark blue, while all the others are backed by tiny little mirrors? I bet that's why the stones glowed the way they did." He withered under Mamre's angry glare, and hastily added: "Don't really know anything about it, of course. Mighty pretty, though. About the prettiest thing I've ever seen, I expect." Which was the last observation he volunteered on any subject that night.

Branwe helped Mamre down from the wine chest. She had had no success in refitting the loose stones, and he climbed up and examined the sockets himself. There were no prongs or flanges; the stones had evidently been held in place by some invisible adhesive. Only an expert craftsman could refit them.

Mamre sighed and shook her head. There was nothing more she could do about it tonight, with a thirsty crowd rapping the tables for food, drink, and entertainment. She sent Branwe back to work, and stalked off toward the kitchen. Those scullery wenches and musicians who had taken advantage of her absence would know better the next time . . . .

▲

There were four sentries posted at the Sacred Gate, only one of whom was still awake, and even he himself barely glanced at the pass in Nizzam's hand.

The air was still and sultry. The Kazerclaw loomed into the cloudless night sky, glistening with the supernatural radiance of two of the planet's three moons. The hubbub of thousands of revelers reverberated from the city below, while beyond the gate all was as still as death.

"Kazerclawm." Nizzam pronounced the name as only a native could, and the sentry waved him on, too sleepy for any deeper investigation, too bored to care why anybody wanted to climb the mountain at this hour of night.

It had been months, in fact not since the old wizard became too ill to leave his sickbed, since anyone had climbed the grim mountain path at any hour, day or night. Nizzam himself had never been there before. An ancient wall, built by unknown hands, indicated that the impregnability of the great mountain had been recognized eons before the garrison city arose at its foot. Landslides and gravitational creep had wrenched gaps in the wall; a narrow path wound through one of these, and when it emerged on the other side Nizzam found himself out of sight and hearing of all living things.

He patted the side pouch of his robe; whether it was to assure himself that the telesma was still there, or hoping that it was not so he could honorably turn back, was unclear even to himself. Tongues of black volcanic rock seemed to pant like overheated animals. The echoes of his footfalls whispered behind him as if he were being followed. He reminded himself that his powers of magic, redoubled by the mystic stone glimmering on his ring finger, were more than equal to any danger he might encounter.

In fact, what dangers could he encounter? Sheer precipices on all other sides of the Kazerclaw left this the only scalable face; there were sentries posted at the gate below; most important of all, The Three had prepared some nasty surprises for any alien sorcerer who teleported himself there—an improbable feat of magic in any case. Reassuming his pompous airs, he ascended the winding path, silvered with moonlight, at the fastest pace consonant with his dignity.

The cave entrance was not a natural formation, at least, not entirely. The adit of some prehistoric mine shaft? Typically, the old wizard had never deigned to instruct him in the topography surrounding the vault of enchantment. The strange outlander who had brought him this commission, a journeyman wizard like himself, may also have suffered wrongs from a jealous master. But nobody had ever been so belittled or held back as he had himself. That would all be changed after tonight. Then would his merits at last be recognized. Then nobody would hold him back, ever again.

In spite of diligent study, he had never succeeded in stretching his range as a fire-starter beyond a few inches—so close, in fact, that he was in danger of singeing his own whiskers whenever he attempted the feat. Unhitching the lantern from his belt, he had to concentrate for several minutes before a feeble glow at last ignited its wick.

The stout wooden door was studded with nails, but there was no lock, nor any need for one. No ax or battering ram

could have burst it open; no ordinary flame so much as
scorched it. Nizzam opened it at a touch.

One glance inside confirmed his suspicion that this was
indeed a prehistoric mine. The shaft had been delved out of
the living rock by the crudest of tools; its floor dipped un-
evenly and bent to the right. He had heard about the debate
which had followed the entombment: whether or not the
passages to the vault of enchantment should be sealed. It had
been decided to leave them open, for no mere rock could
keep a powerful sorcerer from teleporting himself, once he
possessed the power. Besides, it was better that Khal remain
accessible, in case the Third Eye was discovered. Only then
would The Three be strong enough to annihilate him. But the
ancient tunnel, its props fallen or rotted through, seemed
ready to seal itself at any moment. Nizzam glanced nervously
at the ceiling again and again as he tiptoed ever deeper into
the mountain.

The little golden table had three legs, and was engraved
with runes; it stood in the entrance of what seemed to be a
large room, or perhaps a natural cavern, and Nizzam raised
his lantern and peered inside. He could see nothing except
that the mine room or cavern opened into an even larger
cavity beyond. He did not enter. He probably could not have
had he tried, for this was the vault of enchantment, and the
little golden table concentrated all the united powers of The
Three.

He smiled as he thought of the way he would tell his
master how he himself, Nizzam, had succeeded where The
Three had failed. Of course Srana would be present. Nothing
her grandfather might say against him afterwards could then
poison her mind. She need not even apologize for failing to
appreciate his merits. It was hardly to be expected that a
she-mrem of her youth and inexperience should possess a
mature judgment.

He held the lantern up so he could read the engraved
characters on the telesma, recited them as if he actually knew
what they meant, then placed the golden pyx at the very
center of the little golden table, just as the emissary of The
Three had instructed him to—and that was that. He congrat-
ulated himself on so easily redeeming his master's oversight,
but as he turned away, to retrace his steps back up the

prehistoric mine shaft, he was startled by the sound of foot-steps, footsteps so alien that his fur stood on end, and the lantern light trembled eerily on the cavern walls around him.

The creature walked on two legs, with a curious stalking gait, as if creeping up on its prey. But this was no mere cave reptile. Green-white flesh, a wide mouth, eyes that glittered like twin rubies, and a sloping forehead; it was almost chin-less, with no external ears. Its iridescent robe shone weirdly in the trembling light, its barbarous array of jewelry glinted electrically. Its hands were partially webbed, and its many rings worn oddly close to its fingertips. It ignored Nizzam as it stalked toward the little golden table.

At last he realized that this could be none other than Khal himself. He had always envisioned the liskash sorcerer en-tombed in some kind of sarcophagus, but evidently he was allowed to roam at large within the vault of enchantment. Nizzam reassured himself that its confines were impregnable, and compensated for his initial fright with a ridiculous swagger.

"If you think to exploit any flaws in your vault, Khal—oh, yes, I know who you are—it's too late. My name is Nizzam. Unknown to you now, perhaps, but a name that you and your kind will soon have to reckon with. That's right, look down at what I've brought, and despair. The telesma seals your fate. In this case, literally so."

The reptilian sorcerer glanced at him for a moment; there was neither anger nor resentment in his glittering ruby eyes, but only a kind of sardonic anticipation, like a child at last permitted to indulge itself in some long-denied pleasure. Then he bent and picked up the telesma.

Nizzam gaped. But if he was astonished that no shock or concussion drove the sorcerer back, he was astounded to see him calmly open the engraved casket—something he himself had been unable to do, applying all the knowledge and power at his command—and withdraw a great phosphorescent jewel. Nizzam reeled giddily and almost fell. There was no escaping the horror of what he now saw before him, a horror so overwhelming that at first his mind refused to accept it. Even more excruciating was the knowledge that he had been duped. The lantern again began to tremble in his hand.

He had never seen the phosphorescent jewel before; no one had for over a generation now, though great wizards had

searched everywhere for it, high and low, in every corner of
the land and beyond. It was the Third Eye.

"So it was all just a shabby trick," he heard himself saying
in a hollow, quavering voice.

Khal ignored him as if he were some mere clamoring infant
or house pet. He made an occult pass, and the mystic stone
seemed magically to become indeed a third eye, glimmering
between his real eyes from a golden uraeus.

"Yes, I have heard that the bauble grants power," Nizzam
continued to rant hollowly, as if more terrified of silence than
of Khal himself. "But you will soon learn that I too wield a
powerful magic, that I too—" He gaped at his ring finger.
The fragment of the Khavala was gone.

Dark laughter echoed through the caverns, as if he were
being mocked out of the shadows all around him by a thousand tormentors. The ring was now on Khal's finger. A triad
of ruby eyes leered sardonically at him.

"Have no fear, Nizzam." Khal's voice was raspy and gutteral,
like the hissing of vipers. "You have done me a valuable
service. In no other way could the Third Eye have been
returned to me. For many years now I have pondered a means
of communicating with my servants. Only lately have I discovered that means. Be assured that you are precious to me."
His whisper seemed more sensual than cruel. "Too precious
to squander in haste or greed. Besides, as you say, you are a
powerful magician. So I'll have to take care not to offend you.
But first I must assure my servants that you have indeed
performed your service, and that they are now free to perform theirs. I shan't be long. Meanwhile you may go wherever you like, for I shall always know where to find you."

Dark laughter again echoed mockingly through the caverns, and then Nizzam found himself alone. Dazed, mortified
by what he had done, his mind reeling with terror, he stum-
bled up the long shaft toward the surface. He shut the
entrance door behind him, and was foolishly relieved when
he was unable to open it again. He literally staggered into the
open.

Then he flinched, as the whole world erupted below him.
Green fireballs arched over the city of Kazerclawm, and from
the dark countryside surrounding its walls rose the battle
cries of thousands of barbaric voices: rude, violent, and greedy

for plunder, seeming to rise out of the very ground. The response from the ill-guarded walls was tardy and confused. The *thud-thud-thud* of battering rams against the gates echoed through the streets before a lone bugle timidly summoned the garrison.

Nizzam was again relieved, as he thought about his own escape. He would surely have been summoned up with the supernumeraries; even if he didn't do any of the real fighting, he would have had to work until he was exhausted, hauling supplies and ammunition to the troops. And what if the attackers—whoever they were—sacked the city? What would have happened to him then? Yes, he was well out of the way up here.

It only remained for him to stay out of the way until the danger passed. He wished now that he had brought food with him. He didn't like missing meals. Oh, well, whatever happened to Kazerclawm, he himself would be safe. It could be only a *razzìa* of desert marauders, perhaps reinforced by bandits and highland renegades. They would at worst sack the city, then retreat with their booty before the King of Ar had a chance to dispatch a relieving force. It shouldn't cause him more than a day or two of personal inconvenience, and he began probing along the ancient wall for some snug gap where he could bed down for the night. Leaves and dried grass were everywhere, and there were berry bushes on the lower slopes.

Then he noticed that the fireballs had ceased, and peeked warily out from behind a heap of wall rubble. He spotted Khal on a height strategically overlooking the city, among a group of mysterious hooded figures, tall hooded figures, one monstrously tall. Who they were, or what they were doing there, he did not care; and still more warily he drew his head back. In times like these it behooved one to mind one's own business, and he stealthily resumed making himself comfortable for the night.

And it was well that he did, for a closer look at the hooded figures would surely have robbed him of a night's sleep—if it did not cause him to think he was already sleeping, in the midst of the most terrifying nightmare he had ever experienced.

Khal himself was unusually circumspect: "A battle is not a war," he said in a low rasp. "Be sure your masters—that is, our masters—realize that tonight's victory is but a first step to conquest. Powerful forces are still ranged against us, forces which I alone command the sorcery to overcome."

Huge round eyes glared suspiciously out at him from beneath drawn hoods; lizard claws extended beyond full sleeves. Every figure in the semicircle confronting him ranged over six feet tall, one over eight feet. If they represented the Eastern Lords, they also represented the various races of liskash; never trustful of each other's motives, even in a war of extermination against hereditary enemies.

"The Eastern Lords have done much for you, Khal," hissed the smallest of them. Intelligence was not an evolutionary strength of the reptilian races; among the liskash it was inversely proportional to size. "Yet you never did for them what you promised."

"Look about you." Khal waved a bejeweled webbed hand toward the chaos that was now Kazerclawm. "My agents promised your masters—our masters, that is, destruction of mrem. Have I kept my promise, or not?"

The slow reptilian minds of the liskash needed several moments to turn this over. Kazerclawm, heretofore an impregnable obstacle to conquest, had indeed been overthrown. And though they feared and hated Khal, just as they distrusted each other, none doubted the power of his magic.

"Promises work two ways," he continued, while they were still pondering his last words. "Were the promises made me by the Eastern Lords truly kept? Ask them yourselves. Would I have been thwarted the first time, had they supported me as they promised? They'll tell you I would not, if they are honest."

This needed more rumination by the liskash. First of all, the Eastern Lords were never honest about anything—else they would never have survived the reptilian struggles for power. Nor did underlings, under any circumstances, ever question their actions.

"Do not show your claws until I have opened for you the gates of Ar," Khal once more continued before their slow minds had quite caught up with him. "The mrem are an inferior race. So long as they can persuade themselves that this is but a raid by brigands and desert marauders, our superior cunning can negotiate them step by step toward annihilation. We must never let them unite. Besides," his voice assumed a low, insinuating rasp, "is it not fitting that we use mrem to destroy mrem?"

This time there was vigorous assent all around. Here was a principle instantly grasped by even the tallest liskash; a gangling reptilian nightmare, concealing a two-handed battle-ax beneath his cloak. Using mrem as screens or shock troops in battle was their regular tactic. They also grasped at once what it would mean to have the gates of Ar thrown open for them. Their claws flexed as if already seizing a furry victim; their jaws slackened hungrily, exposing rows of hideous teeth.

"Assure your masters," Khal said with false candor, "I mean our masters, of course, that I shall soon complete what I started years ago. But they must not be impatient this time. Above all, they must not interfere—until the hour comes for them, and for you as well, to reap the spoils."

"It shall be as you say, Kahl," replied the smallest liskash. "But be warned, the Eastern Lords have granted you a second chance. They will not grant you another."

Kahl nodded his acquiescence. He had no illusions about his position. The Eastern Lords also feared and hated him; they without doubt intended to dispose of him cruelly, once he had served their purpose. But he had intentions of his own, certainties about which would ultimately be the Master Race, about how the spoils would really be apportioned after the overthrow of the great city of Ar. He performed the farewell ritual with all his teeth showing.

Meanwhile Nizzam finished padding a nest for himself with armloads of dried grass. The gap in the ancient wall was now both snug and secure, and he scrambled over the rubble nearby for a last check on Kahl's whereabouts. He spotted him just taking leave of the mysterious hooded figures, no doubt regarded by him as his "servants." He seemed to regard all the world more or less as his servants. How had he coaxed so vast a horde to launch a *razzìa* at this precise moment? Or how had his agents found the Third Eye for him, or gained possession of a fragment of the Khavala?

Nizzam shrugged. This was hardly the time for abstruse questions, when his own safety and well-being were jeopardized. Then he was startled to find Kahl peering in his direction, and ducked back into the shadows. Had he been seen? In any case, he had better lie low for a while, and turned to slip back into the snug gap in the wall . . . and the stout wooden door opened before him, and he again found himself inside the mountain. Confused, he turned to leave; but the door was gone, and he stood alone in the middle of a palatial hall.

Then he became aware of a lovely young she-mrem beckoning to him from the shadows. Srana? What was she doing here? Or was it really Srana? He peered closer, but the shadows around her were too deep for him to be certain.

She beckoned, and he followed.

▲

Chapter 4
A Pounding at the Gates

▲━━━━━━━━━━━━━━━━━━━━━━━━━━━━━━━━━▲

A deathly silence hushed the last straggle of revelers at the Blue Dragon, as if the heavy thudding outside had stunned them. It was the rankers from the garrison who first realized what was happening, and they rushed and tumbled and staggered out into the street.

Leaderless, they at first only milled about in confusion, as the ominous *thud-thud-thud* continued to reverberate from the Watersmeet Gate. At last some hurried in that direction, while others ran toward the armory for weapons; a few old veterans merely shrugged and ambled back into the Blue Dragon for a nightcap.

Young Branwe had followed the rush into the street. Mamre had given him leave to turn in for the night, but he had prudently decided to stay on the job. Working overtime tonight might make Grujekh—who had glowered at him for returning late from school—more amenable tomorrow, when the time came to request leave to help Srana's grandfather.

He heard passing remarks that Kazerclawm was under attack, and his first thought was of Srana herself. Should the walls be breached, the garrison would fall back into the fortress; only those citizens prompt enough to slip inside before its gates closed would be safe. He knew that Srana would never leave home without her invalid grandfather, and doubted the help Nizzam would give her to carry him to safety. More and more people were now pouring into the streets and heading toward the fortress.

Branwe started to head back into the Blue Dragon but then hesitated, and circled to the kitchen door. Grujekh would need help to lug all his money and valuables to the fortress;

Mamre would probably want someone to carry her prize mirror there, even in its mutilated condition. Right now, he had more urgent tasks.

Scrambling up the ladder to the storeroom where he slept, he rummaged in the small locker at the foot of his pallet for the old practice sword Cajhet had salvaged for him from the armory trash can. He had had its cracked basket resoldered, and sewn a scabbard for it out of a pair of discarded leather leggings. It was a rude weapon, but all he had, and no garrison soldier had ever drilled with more heart.

A lone bugle sounded timidly from the direction of the fortress, as he feverishly buckled on the scabbard, dodged back through the congestion of kegs, bales, and grain sacks, and peered warily down into the kitchen. It was deserted, but the moment he started down the ladder, Mamre bustled into the room.

"Oh, there you are, Branwe! Hurry, lad, we need all the help we can get—" Then she noticed his rude sword and scabbard, and stared silently at him for several moments, before asking, "Srana? Yes, I should have thought of her myself."

"She needs help with her grandfather, and I didn't think Nizzam—"

He was interrupted by an impatient shout from Grujekh, but Mamre bustled back to the door and shouted him down—for the moment. "Do what you can for them, lad," she lowered her voice. "And don't bother about that Nizzam's helping anybody but himself. But first there's something I must tell you. Desert marauders, bandits, maybe the Eastern Lords themselves are trying to get at us. Who knows if we'll ever see each other again?" She took out a handkerchief and began dabbing at her eyes. "You were abandoned here as a kit. I've told you that, but there's more to the story, which I thought too wicked to bear repeating—though I meant to tell you someday. You see, the nurse that left you here was found murdered that same night, with another kit she'd picked up somehow or other. And not just murdered, lad," she whispered, glancing over her shoulder. "Tortured and mutilated, as if it was revenge . . . Yes, yes, I'm coming!"

She again went to the kitchen door, and exchanged more angry words with her husband, before hurrying back.

"The old screw's frantic about his money. I thought I knew all his hiding places, but he surprised me. As I was saying," she continued, "the nurse was murdered, and on her way to see the Sentinel—who was a fine figure of a mrem in those days, by the way. It seems she sent him a note, saying that she had something important to tell him. But whoever was after her got to her first, and she never saw the Sentinel at all. He retraced her steps back here to the Dragon, but no farther. Who she was—who you are, for that matter—or where she got that other poor kit, or what secret she was going to reveal, nobody knows to this day."

"Has Srana heard this?" His mind raced with wild romantic fancies, although none so strange as the truth.

Mamre shrugged. "Yes, yes, I said I was coming, didn't I?" she shouted out the kitchen door. Then she lowered her voice: "Do what you must, lad. Don't worry about me. There's plenty willing to turn a few coppers to move our goods to the fortress. Grujekh's just looking for somebody to do it for nothing, that's all. Now hurry before he spots you." She groomed him maternally. "You've been like a son to me, Branwe. May the All-Mother guide and protect you."

He had no chance to reply. They heard Grujekh approaching the kitchen, and she fairly shoved him out into the night.

The relentless *thud-thud-thud* continued to reverberate from the Watersmeet Gate, barricaded with carts, wagons, and futile heaps of lumber, but now came also the ominous crack and splinter of wood. Shouts and battle cries raged above; whole sections of the wall had already been abandoned; there were too many marauders clambering up too many scaling ladders for the surprised and out-numbered troops to repel, and they began falling back in confusion upon the fortress.

Mrem fled by the thousand, some trying to rescue valued possessions, most trying only to save their own hides; the streams of panic swelled into a roaring flood. Few who tripped or were knocked down ever rose again. Branwe was carried several streets beyond the stone dragon before he could at last—pushing, dodging, elbowing his way—break free into a crooked narrow lane.

Was he too late? Refugees from Srana's quarter pinned him again and again to the wall as they rushed past him in terror.

Hordes of enemies were already over the ramparts, looting, murdering, raping. The fortress was the last hope. Hurry! Where were the soldiers? The All-Mother protect us!

Then the sky began to redden. Fire! It came from the very direction of Srana's house.

Forcing his way anxiously into the street that led there, he found himself once more driven the opposite way. The armed mrem who now rushed at him were not panicky refugees. Bandits? Desert marauders? Shops and houses fell one after the other into their greedy hands. They seemed in fact greedier for loot than blood, but still butchered anyone in their path.

Branwe drew his sword and fell back into another crooked narrow lane, driven farther and farther from Srana's house. The sky over Kazerclawm now glowed like an evil dawn.

▲

Srana stared across her darkened bedroom in alarm. There was a mrem standing in the doorway. Why hadn't her danger sense awakened her sooner? Was she in fact in danger? The shadowy figure seemed to be listening for something.

Then she became aware of a muffled *thud-thud-thud* somewhere in the distance. Her danger sense was alerted as it never had been in all her young life—also by something in the distance. She sensed no danger from the direction of her doorway.

"Get up, dear," said her grandfather. "What we have feared for over two generations has now come to pass. A great evil flashed through my dreams like a shooting star."

"Khal?"

"He has the Third Eye," replied the old wizard. "Nothing else could explain so powerful a surge of evil."

Srana was out of bed and dressed in minutes. "We must escape while we can."

"There is no escape for me, dear. Khal's sole god is vengeance, his sole delight a sadistic cruelty. I must never fall into his hands alive."

"The fortress," she cried. "We'll be safe there, until the King of Ar sends reinforcements."

"It will be too late, even if he does send them. Those now attacking the city—renegades, bandits, desert marauders, whatever villainy Khal's agents have scraped together into a thieves' army—might have been resisted. But not if Khal abets them with the Third Eye."

"No, no," she insisted, "I'm sure we can escape together. Where is Nizzam? He can help us."

The old wizard shook his head. "No one can help us now but ourselves. Nizzam has not returned home. Nor does it matter any more, so far as I'm concerned. The potion that has given me the strength to rise from my sickbed will leave me more debilitated than ever, when its effects wear off. Perhaps too debilitated even to live. But by then it won't matter. All that matters now is your safety, and I know a way—"

They were both startled by a crash at the outer gate, then running footsteps. The old wizard reacted with a power that awed his granddaughter although she knew he had been the great wizard of his generation. The house door burst open and five armed mrem rushed into the vestibule, one of whom had a bandaged head. They expected to find only a sick old wizard, too feeble to resist capture. Instead they found themselves confronted by monstrous highland berserkers, armed with terrible claw-swords. Appalled, they froze in their tracks, then step by step began to retreat back down the corridor.

"They can't hurt you!" cried their leader, in the same gutteral accent with which he had earlier beguiled Nizzam. "They're only illusions. Charge boldly into them and they'll disappear. Remember who's waiting to reward or punish you."

This last was a forceful incentive, although the leader himself continued to hang back. He knew, as his henchmrem did not, how formidable the old wizard had been in his day, and was chary about what powers of magic he might still wield, redoubled as they would be by a fragment of the Khavala.

The first to charge down the corridor was the thug with the bandaged head, and sure enough the illusions vanished before him—until a shadowy figure leapt out of a bedroom doorway. And for the second time that night a stool cracked his skull.

Dazed, nursing his broken head, he retreated down the corridor, whimpering in pain. It was no illusion that had just brained him out of the shadows. He and his comrades bore only assassins' daggers, while the berserkers looming before them more vividly than ever brandished terrible claw-swords. They rushed from the house more resolutely than they had entered, their leader foremost.

"They'll be back with reinforcements," said the old wizard. "We have only minutes, so listen carefully and do everything I say. The very survival of our people may be at stake."

"I promise," said Srana, replacing the bedroom stool against the wall, and following him toward the rear of the house. She well understood the horrors awaiting either of them, should they fall into Khal's reptilian clutches. Nor was it likely that her grandfather could long survive the reaction to a potion that had given him such temporary strength. "An amulet?" she exclaimed, as he handed her the little leather pouch. "It's just like the one poor superstitious little Wilba wears around her neck."

"Yes, and here's her laundry bag. Wearing her shabby old dress—none too clean, I'm afraid—with this amulet around your neck, you'll pass for a scullery wench." He opened the pendant he wore around his own neck, and dropped the fragment of the Khavala into the pouch. "My powers of magic are strong enough by themselves to do what must be done. I regret that I can do nothing more for you, once you escape the house."

"I'll be brave, Grandfather." She fought back her tears. "Do you want me to get this fragment of the Khavala to The Three?"

He nodded. "Anything that reinforces their power to resist Khal is now important. Meanwhile the stone will redouble your own powers, but be very careful how you use it. Above all, you must never try to teleport yourself."

"That's one feat you've never taught me," she said.

"Just as well, for then you'd be vulnerable to Khal. Use concealment. You won't be captured if nobody looks at you." He noticed her grow tense, and listened. "Yes, I hear them too. Hurry! Into the front garden!"

She could no longer restrain her tears, and affectionately tried to embrace him, but he hurried her back up the corridor and out the front door. Then with all the forces of magic still at his command he braced himself to meet the onslaught he knew must soon come. His one great advantage was a knowledge of Khal's insane lust for vengeance. No matter how many reinforcements the first band of attackers recruited in the streets, they would do everything in their power to take him alive, for only thus would they be rewarded by their reptilian overlord. He positioned himself at the very center of the house.

Nor had he long to wait. With bloodthirsty cries and the brandishing of weapons, hundreds of desert marauders and bandits assailed the house from every entrance. But for some reason, not one of those pouring in through the smashed front gate looked toward a particular corner of the garden, and hence did not notice anyone standing there.

There were no illusions confronting them this time, nothing but an old man standing alone in the eerie candlelight of the parlor. Some began pillaging the house, but most crowded into the parlor and the corridors leading to it, to gawk at the legendary old wizard. He seemed too preoccupied with his own thoughts to heed them or their taunts.

Then all of a sudden he looked up, as if focusing his eyes upon a precise distance, and began very slowly—never relenting the fixed intensity of his gaze—to turn in a complete circle. The taunters fell silent; all now stared at him with superstitious wonder; even the looters hurried back into the corridors to see what was happening. But they all looked the wrong way. By the time they first smelled smoke, it was too late. The outer walls of the house behind them were already a sheet of flame.

Instinctively they pushed inward, jostling and shoving and crying out in alarm. All the while the old wizard continued to turn slowly round and round, and the inner walls, the very floor beneath them, spiraling ever inward, burst into flames. Then the roof overhead began to smoulder, and the pandemonium of the doomed erupted throughout the burning house. Round and round turned the old wizard. Death was his one escape from the ghastly torments awaiting him, but he would not die alone. Nor would any of the hundreds of enemies around him—screaming, choking, clawing, and trampling each other in panic—ever hunt his beloved granddaughter through the streets outside . . . .

Maglakh, the leader of the original band of five, was congratulating himself on his near escape at that very moment out in the street. The first repulse had shown him that he was dealing with no mere invalid, and this time he had not even entered the house. He was surprised that the Sentinel had used his last magic as a fire-starter, rather than to escape, as he himself would have done. Although he could understand why the old wizard might not want to risk being captured alive.

And where was Khal all this time? Why wasn't he abetting the conquest of the city with his invincible magic? For while the invading hordes were indulging themselves in plunder and rapine, someone, somehow, had rallied the garrison inside the fortress. If discipline were not reimposed soon, the whole timetable of invasion could bog down right here in Kazerclawm.

On second thought, Maglakh reconsidered, perhaps it was best for himself that the great sorcerer was not on the scene after all. Khal would be furious that his archenemy had escaped his vengeance, even through death, and might turn in reprisal upon the agents who had failed him . . . .

Flames shot explosively skyward, and he staggered back. Then he found himself looking down the street, away from the burning house, and minutes passed before he could bring himself to look back again. He doubted that anyone could have survived such an inferno, and started to look up the street to be sure—and found himself again looking down the street instead.

He had a suspicious mind to begin with, and a penchant for low life, and vicious habits. Such traits were more suitable to a bandit or renegade: the very epithets hurled after him by his former master, a grand wizard of The Three, while driving him from home after a brief and stormy apprenticeship. His successor's tenure had been briefer still. He was murdered only hours after his master had died and bequeathed to him a fragment of the Khavala, to be delivered to The Three in the great city of Ar. Maglakh had delivered it instead to a caitiff he knew from his low haunts as an agent of the Eastern Lords, but who had turned out to represent an even more sinister power.

Suspicious that some power of magic was compelling him, he exerted his utmost effort of will to look in the very direction he was least inclined to. He caught only a glimpse of a shabbily dressed servant girl hurrying up the street, before unaccountably looking once again down the street away from her. But he did not have to see anything more. He had heard that the Sentinel was being nursed by his granddaughter, a beautiful White dancer. It could only be she, exerting concealment magic; but it was a magic far too powerful for a mere female, unless multiplied by some occult force.

A cunning smile overspread his face, as he gazed into the raging inferno across the street, now spreading to neighboring houses. So that was the reason for the conflagration! The old wizard himself may have perished, along with hundreds of his enemies, but not his granddaughter—and not his precious fragment of the Khavala. Presenting them both to Khal—the one to enhance his power, the other to indulge his vengeance on—must surely redeem any remissness about capturing the old wizard alive.

Although it would not be prudent to challenge the Sentinel's granddaughter in person. Let others suffer from her claws and enchantments. He would concern himself solely with how best to exploit her capture. No amount of concealment magic would save the wench, once he surrounded her with enough pursuers.

A brawl had erupted just down the street, probably over drink or females or booty, perhaps all three. Ruffians were everywhere in this quarter of the city; he would have little trouble collecting a troupe along the way. Still disinclined to look up the street, he turned and hurried in that very direction.

▲

Branwe leapt out of range with an agility that caught his assailants off guard. Before they could respond, he returned to the attack, slashing one on the sword arm, hacking an ear off another. Then he leapt out of range again.

He had eluded his pursuers until they finally cornered him, just down the street from Srana's house. The flames he had seen were indeed coming from that direction, perhaps from her very house. Was he too late to save her? He had to know and soon, or it really would be too late. His frustration turned him into a leaping, dodging, slashing, jabbing fury. Too elusive to wound; too skilled to overmaster.

Too troublesome an opponent, in fact, to be worth the while of his assailants. All six were of the foulest type of desert marauder. They hated civilization in its every unfolding; they killed city folk for the sheer joy of killing. But there was no joy in having their ears hacked off by a swordsmrem who would not stand still and fight (six against one). Not when a whole city of easier prey lay prostrate before them. Cursing and brandishing their hook-bladed swords, they at last let Branwe dodge out of the trap.

He raced as fast as he could up the street—which was very fast indeed—his fears mounting with every step. It was her house on fire! The blaze reddened the night sky, one of many fires now raging across doomed Kazerclawm. The houses on either side of it were already burning, and flaming brands arched onto rooftops all around.

He staggered back from the heat and showers of sparks; he had never seen so explosive a fire. Then he realized that the street was no longer deserted. Timidly, their only choice now between certain death and the deadly perils of the city, people were creeping out of their hiding places before they were roasted alive or asphyxiated.

"Did anyone escape?" he pointed to the burning house.

"Hundreds went in, but not a soul ever came out again," said a shopkeeper. "Watched it all, peeking out my window up yonder. Poor old mrem, magician though he was! Poor little Srana! She was good to our children when they were sick."

Others confirmed his account; all were certain that nobody had escaped the blaze. The reek of burnt fur now tainted the air. But this was no time to waste in regret. Their chances of ever reaching the fortress alive—three of the she-mrem carried kits in their arms—lessened every moment they stood here.

Branwe's first impulse was to accompany them. The towering stone fortress had been built generations ago, over the old cisterns, so it would have a sure water supply in times of siege. It was the nucleus from which Kazerclawm had spread outward, ring upon ring, and still the citadel in times of emergency: the last refuge of the populace. But he was too overwhelmed by despair to go anywhere. Let the enemy corner him in the streets again. If he never lived to become a warrior, he could at least die like one—sword in hand, in mortal combat, valiant to the last.

He sat in the doorway across the street from Srana's house, and stared despondently into the flames.

▲

Srana was also becoming despondent. The fragment of the Khavala doubled her powers of concealment, but these were not infinite; not with so many mrem closing in on her from all sides. There were just too many of them, and they wanted her in particular. Somebody, somehow, knew who she was and what she carried in the amulet pouch around her neck. She had overheard one captain encourage his mrem with promises of reward, if she was captured alive. Another ordered his mrem to watch out for a "red jewel."

Had Khal himself set them after her? Her tail twitched nervously. Was she doomed to become the plaything of his vengeance after all? Even doubled by the fragment of the Khavala, her fire-starting magic reached no more than a few feet; else she might have escaped capture as heroically as had her grandfather. Her only resort now was concealment. Though with each alleyway, street, or plundered shop she dodged through there seemed to be more and more pursuers from whom to conceal herself. Too many, in fact.

"There she goes!" She heard a shout behind her.

She had been too occupied in concealing herself from the bandits who blocked the mouth of the narrow lane before her to deal effectively with the desert marauders behind her. She dodged into a looted pottery shop.

The potter himself lay sprawled on the floor, his throat cut, among shards of broken jars, vases, and glassware. The damage was wanton, senseless, as if the looters had merely avenged themselves for not finding anything here worth stealing. Just as they had wantonly murdered the harmless old potter.

There had been no escape for him, for his snug little shop was also his pottery, and had no rear exit. Srana's eyes, their irises opened full, seemed jet black in the feeble light; but one glance told her that there was no escape here for her either. Her chances of escaping at all were now too slight to risk the fragment of the Khavala's falling into Khal's hands any longer. But some sort of "red jewel" would have to be found on her person, or her brutal pursuers would torture her until she revealed where she had hidden it. She hurriedly began rummaging among the shards of broken glass and pottery. Shouts and running footsteps were converging in the lane outside.

Three times she had to risk approaching the moonlight at the doorway, before she was certain that she had a crystal of about the right size and color, originally part of the decoration of an oil lamp. Slipping it into the amulet pouch around her neck, she secreted the Khavala fragment in a broken pot, and focused such powers of concealment that remained to her on her pursuers.

These might have concealed her from a dozen mrem. But scores had converged in the lane, and she was seized only steps beyond the shop door, and her person roughly searched.

"Here it is," cried a captain, ripping open the leather pouch. "Thought she could fool me by disguising it as an amulet. There's a reward in this for all of us, lads."

Several villainous desert marauders had now joined the mob encompassing Srana, and they suggested another kind of reward they might take, before relinquishing her to whoever wanted her. Such beautiful females were never seen in the eastern deserts, not even those raped from caravans. A few others shouted agreement.

"Not this one, lads." The captain drew his dagger. He knew he could count on at least the renegade highlanders to back him, with their terrible claw-swords. "We'll take her straight to the fortress. It's either fallen already, or soon will. Somebody wants this wench in particular. Somebody who might not like it if she came to him damaged. Now let's go!"

There was no more opposition, for they all knew who that "somebody" was. Even the most brutal of the desert marauders was intimidated. Besides, there would be countless other chances for rapine, when the Eastern Lords launched their long-prepared invasion. Then all the land, all the hated cities and civilized peoples, would be left like their own homeland, a howling desert.

Srana marched unresisting among her savage captors, silent, her eyes cast down, her thoughts examining the contingencies that lay before her. She had still not abandoned hope. Even without the Khavala fragment, she wielded a powerful magic. All she needed was the right opportunity to use it—before she fell into the vindictive clutches from which there would be no escape. Where Khal was now, she had no idea. Nor, it seemed, had any of the scores of thugs and miscreants surrounding her.

Not even Maglakh himself, straggling unnoticed at the rear of the troop, as it marched through the plundered, burning city, could answer that question. The sky was graying with dawn. Soon many questions would have to be answered.

Chapter 5
Cajhet Disposes

▲————————————————————————————▲

"**T**astiest fish crisps I've ever ate, lads." Cajhet smacked his chops and belched. He had a special arrangement with the duty cook to get his breakfast on watch, rather than eating out like the other turnkeys. It was costly and against regulations, but the eyes of the prisoners, staring longingly out through the bars while he regaled himself, added a wonderful zest to his meals. Besides, he was a bachelor, and getting a decent breakfast hours before dawn was not easy. "Spicy batter, and done to a turn, just the way I like 'em. I'll just take this tray back to the kitchen myself, so's I can compliment the chef in person. Mighty tasty, mighty tasty." He strolled complacently toward the stone staircase, picking his teeth with the claw of his forefinger. "Now don't go away. I'll be right back."

Every cell was now occupied to capacity with thieves, hookpurses, and festival rowdies. Their only meal, hours ago, had been a bowl of rancid mush, and they glowered at Cajhet's back as he shuffled upward out of the deep underground prison. His complacent smile broadened as he climbed.

There had been a ruckus in the direction of the Watersmeet Gate, drowned by the garrison bugle, just as he came on duty. What it was all about, he still did not know, nor could anyone tell him. The cook had been on duty here all night, as had the alternate turnkey. Maybe somebody would know more about it now. It was probably just another festival brawl. The Blue Dragon was near the gate, and there had already been one brawl there, only hours ago.

He became cautious as he neared the top of the stairs. There was always the chance of some duty officer snooping around at this hour; remote, but possible. And any possibility, no matter how remote, of being hauled before Severakh was to be avoided at all cost. The military authority of the fierce old soldier may have been curtailed by the new governor, but he exercised what remained to him more vigorously than ever.

He heard voices and stopped. He prided himself on his acute hearing, especially for officers trying to nab him at derelictions of duty, but now he was not sure he could trust his own ears. Severakh? Here, at this hour? What really made him question his hearing was that somebody actually seemed to be arguing with the gruff old drillmaster. He tiptoed to the end of the corridor and peeked stealthily around the corner.

The tray at once began to tremble in his hands. It had been no audio illusion. There stood Severakh in the flesh, looking surlier than he had ever seen him (which was very surly indeed). The mrem arguing with him was the new governor: a sleek, beautifully groomed youth, garbed in the latest fashion of magenta silk, a cultured noble, accustomed to having mrem agree with him. He hardly bothered to disguise his snobbish distaste for the old soldier.

Cajhet also spotted his familiar nemesis, the watch officer. In fact, the entire staff was present, embarrassed by the argument between their superiors. He stealthily backed out of sight. Whatever they were arguing about, this was no place for him. There were plenty of corners in the old cisterns—sprawling endlessly, at varied levels—to secrete a tray until the coast was clear. Apprehensive about rescue attempts, he had explored the dank caverns until certain there was no way anybody could sneak up on him while on watch. All six possible entrances had been sealed; the two with doors were stoutly bolted on the inside.

The tray had stopped trembling in his hands by the time he returned to the lower dungeon, and he tried to assume his old swagger. But his prisoners were cunning rogues; they sensed that something was amiss. Every one of them was up from his bunk and watching him shrewdly through the bars when he returned from hiding his tray.

"What's wrong, Cajhet?" taunted the hookpurse Branwe

had witnessed against yesterday afternoon. "Nobody at home in the kitchen?"

"You'll be at home right here, and for a long time to come, Fefo," said Cajhet. He tried to compose himself by rattling his collection of extracted claws; but that only directed his attention to the sets of unextracted claws wrapped menacingly around the bars of every cell in the dungeon.

This made him unusually thoughtful, and he glanced every few seconds toward the stone staircase that wound down out of the upper levels of the fortress. The prisoners' taunts grew bolder in proportion to his growing uneasiness. Ordinarily a weak, foolish, self-indulgent rascal, his only keen sense was that of survival, and something told him that his immediate comfort and well-being were somehow threatened. Though he pricked his ears, he knew he was far too deep underground to catch a single word of the argument continuing upstairs in the fortress at that very moment.

▲

"I requested special patrols," Severakh insisted, "if nothing more, to protect villagers coming here for the festivals from bandits. But these were denied me. I trebled the number of sentinels on the walls, only to find my orders countermanded. And now I'm expected to defend an untenable position, with inadequate resources, and my hands tied?"

The elegant young governor sighed with boredom. "I've explained twice to you already why a sally would be inopportune. You've done a commendable job in getting so many villagers and townsfolk safely into the fortress. The way you withdrew the garrison under attack was masterful. I'm especially pleased that you've preserved the White Dancers from harm. But I must remind you again, Severakh, that I am governor of Kazerclawm, appointed by the king, and responsible to the king alone."

"Yes, my lord. But surely you must see—"

"I see that I'm wasting my time, if that's what you mean. Enough! I'm already late for breakfast. My guests will think me discourteous. Have my personal effects removed to my quarters, please. There are thousands of village menials and common soldiers at large in the fortress, and some of my belongings are priceless."

"Very good, sir," replied Severakh with the stoical obedience of an old soldier. "I'll do everything that must be done."

The young governor looked doubtfully at him for a moment, then turned and strode off in the direction of his private quarters, secluded to himself and his courtiers by a cordon of picked guards. The gray morning light made the hall somehow appear dingier than it had under torchlight; the very paintings, statuary, and fine furniture carried here from the palace now seemed tawdry.

Severakh knew they were in fact priceless, although his first impulse was to have the whole lot chucked from the battlements. Half the garrison, already undermanned, had been diverted from the defense of the city to saving the personal belongings of the governor and his courtiers. These belongings were the true reason, he was sure, behind the governor's refusal to attempt a breakout while there was still a chance. For then not only these darling works of art, but five great chests of treasure, hauled here by soldiers needed to defend the walls, would have to be left behind.

"All right, mrem," he ordered, "let's get this stuff to the governor's quarters. On the double! We haven't a moment to lose," he added to himself.

He had promised the governor he would do everything that had to be done, and so he would. This was no mere *razzia*. He was too old a soldier not to recognize the vanguard of an invasion. Nothing could now save Kazerclawm; all the artworks and treasure of the governor and his courtiers would fall to the looters as surely as if it had been left back in the palace. But things could be replaced, not people. The attack had been shrewdly conceived and executed, despite the general low quality of the enemy troops; but there was now an unexplained absence of leadership, and the force of the attack was being dissipated in rapine and looting. Had the enemy commander simply lost control of his army? Whatever the reason, so favorable an opportunity for a breakout could not last—perhaps no more than a few hours. Delay meant certain doom.

The governor was irresponsible if he was just waiting for the enemy to go away; naive if he thought they would negotiate. Why should they bargain for a part, when they had the power to seize the whole? Nor could the young King of Ar respond in time, if he responded at all. The only way out was to fight their way out; the only time was right now. Tomorrow would be too late.

"What have you got there, Ghenko?" he called to a junior officer.

"Prisoners, sir. They were caught trying to climb the wall. Desert marauders, by the look of 'em. Do you want to interrogate them, sir?"

One of the prisoners had been wounded slightly on the hand; the other had had his ragtag, evil-smelling garments— the plunder of caravans from many lands—ripped while trying to escape the claws of a sentry.

Severakh shook his head. "Not now. Just take them down to the dungeon. The rest of you mrem, over here. Now listen, and listen as if your lives depended on it."

In fact, they did. Sated, burdened with loot, addled with rapine and drunkenness, scattered in small bands all over the city, the enemy could hardly respond with effect against a well-organized and determined breakout. Neither could they pursue in force, until discipline had been reestablished. By then it would be too late. So long as the breakout caught them by surprise. Today. This morning. Now.

"I'll command the rear guard myself," he added. "Once past the ford of the Whitestone River you'll be safe. Pass the word for volunteers. A hundred good mrem and true will discourage this vermin from pursuit. You've got thousands of mrem and kits to organize, and an hour in which to do it. You'll travel light and fast, with three days' food. Scouts, wagons for the sick and wounded . . . you know what to do. I've trained you myself. Don't disappoint me."

"No, sir," they cried.

Each knew what their fierce old commander was doing for them; each knew why he was sacrificing himself with the rear guard. The queen mother never forgave insubordination toward her pet appointees, and it was she, not her son, the boy king of Ar, who had appointed the feckless young governor. Like all her appointees, his prime qualification for office was deference to her every whim. There were more volunteers than needed.

A veteran commander, Severakh wisely deployed whatever material he had at hand to best advantage. The mystique of the White Dancers transcended mere wealth or politics; certainly it transcended any military discipline he might have imposed on thousands of frightened civilians. Once instructed in what had to be done, the senior dancers, by gentler means, achieved wonders of order and dispatch, freeing him to marshal his garrison into a flying column.

The smoke from unchecked fires dimmed the morning into a sullen twilight, as thousands of soldiers and refugees burst without warning from the fortress. The undisciplined rabble of guards skulking outside were caught by surprise, and fled. The first band of pursuers were quickly driven off by Severakh and his rear guard, and the host of refugees continued unharrassed to the Watersmeet Gate with almost the precision of a martial dance. Once more a rabble of guards were surprised and routed, and the refugees passed safely from the city and out onto the western road.

The ford of the Whitestone River lay a good nine miles away, upriver from the juncture with the Mraal, where it bent toward the great city of Ar, many grueling days' march to the west. But once the ford was crossed, nothing less than an army would dare pursue them into the warrior domains beyond. That armies would soon come sweeping over those very domains, perhaps over the entire land, Severakh had no doubt. All he could do now was to ensure that no pursuit swept over the thousands of fleeing mrem before they reached safety, and he and his rear guard of volunteers took up their positions in the streets of the city.

The first assault was easily checked; the second only after a savage battle. Hundreds, eventually thousands, were now being rounded up in the streets, or roused from sodden slumbers, by their chiefs and captains. But they were not attacking superannuated caravan guards or benighted villagers now, and assault after assault was hurled back with grim casualties. The cries of the dying rent the smoky air, like a demon chorus to the clash of arms. Grudging every foot of ground, forestalling every attempt to outflank him, Severakh slowly fell back upon the Watersmeet Gate, leaving in his wake a trail of slaughter.

An hour passed, then another, and still the enemy hordes, though now swelled into a veritable army, could not pass him. Exhausted, bleeding from a dozen wounds, the old campaigner knew it could not go on much longer. He had already lost half his mrem and some of those still on their feet were wounded as grievously as himself. But he was expendable, and so were his troops, and every minute they held the enemy hordes at bay brought the refugees a minute closer to the Whitestone ford.

He took up his last stand inside the gate itself. Its tunnel-like arches would screen his surviving mrem from long-range missiles, and he had them erect a barricade from the lumber, carts, and wagons with which the citizens had tried futilely to erect a barricade of their own. This would not only shield them from missiles of shorter range, but shatter any concerted attack. He could do no more.

Scaling ladders still leaned against the walls outside. It would not take the enemy long to send enough skirmishers over the top to attack his rear. His position was hopeless. But neither could the swiftest army now hope to overtake the refugees before they reached the ford. His sole objective had been a delaying action, and he had already delayed pursuit longer than he could have expected. Nothing remained now but to die with honor.

He wondered what had become of the elegant young governor and his courtiers. He regretted disobeying the orders of a superior, but only on principle. He regretted nothing else. He had done his duty as he saw it.

Through the sullen twilight, down a smoky street befouled with the dead and the dying, he could just discern the enemy captains marshaling their brigands and marauders for a mass onslaught. That could only mean that those sent swarming over the walls were now ready to attack him from the rear . . . .

▲

Cajhet was tired of sitting dutifully at his post. Where was the watch officer? He should have made his rounds hours ago. The villainous crew peering out at him through the bars up and down the cell block made him nervous. The two desert marauders brought in earlier that morning had informed them that the city had fallen. What if the fortress should also fall? Thoughts of being turned over to his own prisoners made it hard to concentrate.

At last he could bear the suspense no longer. Assuming an

air of nonchalance, and humming a tune, he strolled casually toward the staircase. The dirty laughter behind his back made him suspect that he did not appear quite so nonchalant as he supposed. The hookpurse Fefo taunted him brazenly, as if he no longer feared reprisals.

Once out of sight, Cajhet tiptoed stealthily round and round the winding staircase, his ears cocked for any ominous sound. What he heard was ominous indeed. What he saw, peeking warily into the hall at the top of the stairs, made his very fur stand on end.

Precious artworks scattered like so much trash, noble silks tossed wantonly about, paintings slashed, exquisite furniture used like camp stools; shouts, curses, drunken laughter and brawling; the anger of brigands squabbling over loot. It could mean only one thing—the fortress had fallen. What had become of its hundreds of defenders, its thousands of refugees? More important, what would become of him, if he were turned over to his own prisoners?

An imminent possibility, for gangs of new prisoners—garrison troops, limping from wounds, some barely able to stand— were even now being marched in ranks into the fortress. Among them was a young female servant, about the loveliest he had ever seen, despite her shabby dress. He looked closer. It was Srana! The poor she-mrem had been taken captive. He wondered what had become of her old grandfather.

But not for long. The dungeons below ground were a vast congeries of cells, improvised originally to confine rioters, even prisoners of war; only the small central block was now in use. Prisoners of war, large numbers of them, were in fact about to be confined there, although not of the kind for which the dungeons were intended. Good thing he had come up into the fortress when he had. Even a few minutes later, and he himself would have been confined in one of those cells—if he were lucky.

He had been a dodger all his life; now was the time to dodge as he had never dodged before. Some of the apparel cast aside by the despoilers looked like the wardrobe of the governor himself. And one of the desert marauders had had both his shabby cloak and trousers ripped while trying to evade capture. Cajhet decided it was time to change clothes, and hastened back down the stairs.

"All right, my lad." He swaggered up to a barred cell. "Off with 'em. We treat our guests here like it was the Blue Dragon itself. Tailoring while you wait is our motto. Put these on while I get your own clothes repaired. The watch officer is going to inspect in a little while, and I can't have you disgracing me. No tramps wanted. Off with 'em, I say."

The scarred and villainous old marauder stared at him in wonder. But he was too crafty an opportunist to pass up a chance to dress in silks; it had been years since he had stolen anything so fine. The exchange needed only moments, and Cajhet strolled away with the bundle of rags—but not toward the staircase.

"I'll be right back, lads. Then we'll see about getting you some dinner. Now don't go away."

It was Cajhet who went away, silently but very fast, the moment he was out of sight. Lantern in hand, he scurried on tiptoes through the dank gloomy caverns of the old cistern, straight for the nearest of the two bolted doors. This exchange of clothes needed even less time than the last. The old villain had probably worn these smelly rags for years without changing them, but this was no time for sartorial fussiness. It was a time to blend inconspicuously into the environment—until he reached environs offering less risk of getting his throat cut.

Unbolting the door, he slipped into a circular pump-well; some of the chains and buckets of its primitive machinery were still intact.

"Whew!" He winced at the musty reek. "Something died down here. Let's hope that's not a bad omen."

The metal rungs extending at intervals from the crusted stone wall were badly corroded, but held his weight. The old pump house was familiar to him. The circular trapdoor which sealed the well had something on top of it, and he had to butt it with his head and shoulders several times before it at last yielded. He emerged into sweeter smelling air, but immediately began to sneeze. Four spice kegs had been stacked atop the trapdoor, and one of them had broken open when he butted them aside. Wiping his eyes, he hurried toward the outer door.

A wholesale contractor of fish sauce, condiments, general foodstuffs, and spices now used the old pump house as a warehouse. He was surprised the looters had not been here already.

Maybe because it was in so remote a quarter of the city. In any case, with so much to steal, it could not be long until the thieves did arrive. What he wanted now was some place where they had already been—and gone. The most plundered, ravaged, burned-out quarter in what remained of Kazerclawm. One of the poorer quarters, where there had been little to steal in the first place. There was not much time. Discipline was gradually being reimposed on the invaders; their captains would soon have patrols combing the ruins for survivors and hoards of valuables, if they had not done so already.

Only haphazard attempts to check the spread of fire were being made so far, but the frontier architecture of stone, glazed brick, and tile was not the material of conflagration, so the burning was still localized. Fortunately there was no wind. The pall of smoke hung denser and denser in the streets; the sun was but a dull red glow in the morning sky, the Kazerclaw only a vague shadow.

All the better, thought Cajhet, as he skulked down a deserted back alley. He was not comfortable with his apparel—especially its smell—and did not want to get too close to any real desert marauders. Those he spotted in the distance seemed mere phantoms, shadowy and faceless. They ignored him—if they saw him at all—and he avoided them.

When night came, he would find some means of lowering himself from the city wall, although he did not like the idea of traveling after dark. He had heard tales of nasty reptiles, some with weird magical powers, creeping out of their caves then, hungry for prey. But there were too many bandits and city criminals here in Kazerclawm who would recognize him, no matter how he was dressed. Those he had declawed over the years, on orders from the tribunal, would be especially happy to meet him now.

No, even liskash were a likelier prospect. There would be peril for only the first night or two on the road, in any case. Once ensconced inside the impregnable walls of Ar, it should not take him long to wrangle another snug berth for himself. He had been doing it since he first left the great port of Namakhazar, on the boundless Southern Sea, to join the army, when still a kit. The tales he had heard while growing up there—pirates, sea monsters, shipwreck, chartless islands ruled by magical reptiles or cannibals—had not encouraged him to follow the traditional calling of a seafarer. Nor had his peculiar home life. The farther inland, the better. Then, as now.

The bodies littering the streets prompted stealth. The fate of those still alive, who made the mistake of groaning or crying out in agony, was a dramatic lesson in silence. The torment of captives, especially those found wounded, was an art form among desert marauders, and bandits and renegade highlanders alike were merciless toward anybody they thought was withholding money or valuables from them. They too had strange ideas about entertainment.

At last Cajhet came to a neighborhood that seemed utterly deserted. The narrow winding streets led nowhere; a few shops had been broken into, a few burned-out houses still smoldered; but there was little here worth stealing, and the wily inhabitants seemed to have fled betimes. The only corpse he came upon sat hunched in a doorway, across the street from a house that had burned to the ground.

Or was it a corpse? In fact, it seemed familiar. He approached the doorway on tiptoe, and leaned over to get a better look at its face.

The next instant he had a sword at his throat, with barely presence of mind enough to howl, "Branwe, Branwe, Branwe," over and over again. "It's me, Cajhet."

Branwe pulled back his hood and examined him, before lowering his sword. "You caught me asleep, Cajhet. Not that it matters any more where I get my throat cut, or by whom." His eyes were bloodshot from weeping, his shoulders slumped, and his sword arm hung limply at his side, as he gazed forlornly across the street. "She never got out alive. How beautiful she was, Cajhet. How gentle and kind, even to a humble potboy at an inn. I suppose the Blue Dragon is gone now too. Grujekh and dear Mamre took me in as a kit, and raised me like their own. I know I should be concerned about them, and of course I pray they escaped in time, but right now I can't think of anything but poor Srana." He blinked at the tears welling in his eyes. "She never got out alive."

The soft-hearted Cajhet was so moved by the boy's distress

that he momentarily forgot even his own comfort and well-being. "She must have. I just saw her," he blurted out, and immediately regretted it. "That is, I mean, let's hope she escaped—"

"No, no," cried Branwe, "you said you just saw her. Where? You must tell me. Please."

Cajhet, old dodger that he was, saw all too well what was coming, and hedged and lied and concealed; but Branwe was relentless, and at last it all came out.

"You must help me rescue her," he cried, just as Cajhet knew he would. "Will they put her down in the dungeon? Or keep her somewhere else in the fortress? Wherever it is, we'll find her. Come, we must hurry!"

"We?"

Against his better judgment, Cajhet found himself being hurried back in the last direction in the world he wanted to go. Not for the first time had his soft-heartedness landed him in a mess. But how could he refuse to help Branwe, who had gotten him so many free drinks when he was broke, who had saved him from so many thrashings? Yes, he could get them back into the dungeons all right. But could he get himself out again? The question of questions.

He hoped to find looters in the old pump house, cutting off any means of descending unseen into the dungeons, and giving him a fair excuse for cutting out. But it was not so. There were in fact no stragglers at all in this quarter of the city.

"I heard sounds of battle near the Watersmeet Gate earlier this morning," said Branwe, as they picked their way through the crates, kegs, and bales of wholesale goods. "The garrison troops may have been making a last stand, or maybe a counterattack. I suppose the marauders were drawn from all over the city. That should make it easier for us to escape, after we rescue Srana."

Cajhet started to enlighten him about the difficulties ahead, but only sneezed, then sneezed again. Not all of the spice from the keg he had tipped over earlier had yet settled out of the air. Branwe also sneezed.

It was pitch black inside the old cistern; nor dared they light a lantern. Alone, Branwe might have wandered for hours through the vast artificial caverns, but Cajhet took him by the hand, and led the way unerringly through the blackness, until at last his eyes, their pupils dilated to the utmost, detected light.

"I don't know where she is down here," whispered Cajhet, "or even if she's down here at all. They might have locked her up somewhere else in the fortress."

▲

Chapter 6
Sneezes and Green Light

▲————————————————————————————▲

Srana would in fact probably have been lodged in special quarters elsewhere in the fortress, if the cunning Maglakh had not needed her so urgently down in the dungeons. Neither he nor anybody else knew what had become of Khal, but he had a vivid appreciation—so far only from hearsay—of what the liskash sorcerer was capable of in one of his blind vindictive rages. But that was vivid enough for him, and the forestalling of any such outburst was now his priority of priorities.

Maglakh could certainly not be blamed for the military strategem that had brought thousands of villagers and citizens, most of the garrison, and all the White Dancers safely out of the city. Nor could he be faulted for the brilliant rear guard action that had foiled pursuit until it was too late. But if he could present Khal with the granddaughter of the Sentinel —a White Dancer no less—his own failure to deliver the Sentinel himself for vengeance might be overlooked. After all, he was the one who got the Third Eye smuggled into Khal in the first place.

The trouble was that Severakh now lay in mortal danger of bleeding to death; he had not expected to be taken alive, and all his wounds were in front. Only because he had been clubbed down from behind was he alive at all. But for how much longer? Should Khal learn that Severakh too had escaped his vengeance, he might forget in his rage those who had helped him emerge from entombment.

"She's a healer," he explained to the captain of the guard. "Put her in the same dungeon with old Severakh. If his wounds can be stanched at all, she can do it. Should he die while in your hands, the escape of the garrison may be remembered."

The captain, a grisly old bandit chief, was already apprehensive about reprisals for that blunder, as well as for the grim number of casualties inflicted by a tiny rear guard—veritable hordes stymied for hours by a mere handful of regular troops—while thousands of prize captives escaped. The Eastern Lords would be merciless in affixing the blame. He agreed at once.

Srana recognized the old warrior lying on a cot the moment she entered his cell. The door clanged shut behind her, and they were alone. He had his eyes closed, but she saw that he was still conscious, although a shadow of the stout figure she was accustomed to seeing command the martial dances at festival time. The filthy blanket thrown over him was soaked through with blood.

"Let me die in peace," he muttered as she drew it back. "The cowards hit me from behind, or they never would have taken me alive. Don't bother, lass. Nothing can save me now. I don't want to be saved."

Ignoring his protests, she concentrated all the magic of her healing powers on dancing the flesh around his wounds, the gravest first, then one by one those less threatening. Twice he swooned from exhaustion; but at last the bleeding stopped, and she summoned the new turnkey.

This was none other than the hookpurse Fefo, the most villainous rogue she had ever seen. Bandages? Ointment? Clean water? Then she wanted a rich broth that the governor himself might have relished. Ordinarily her requests would have been met only with crude sarcasm; then threats and curses, if she persisted. But the captain of the guard had ordered him—with threats and curses of his own—to give her anything she wanted, and he complied.

"Thanks are due, lass," Severakh said weakly, when she had finished spooning him the last of the broth. "It would be mean-spirited to deny them. But I'm not sure my life is really worth saving. I've long known that a wizard of The Three resided here, on some special mission. You were pointed out to me one day as his nurse. You're his daughter, aren't you?"

"Granddaughter. He's dead now." She lowered her eyes.

Severakh did not comment. He knew what was in store for

both of them, for all the captives imprisoned down here. There were hundreds, mostly soldiers; they were now being marched up the stairs in batches to execution, and there was nothing he could do to save a single one of them. Any more than he could help himself, or this charming, lovely she-mrem who had preserved his life. They would be fortunate to die as easily as the soldiers, although he didn't tell her this. No point in frightening the poor child.

There was something sardonic in the way that their jailer, a common hookpurse, accomodated all their wishes. That could only mean that they were being reserved for special punishment, more terrible than mere execution. The reptilian minds of the Eastern Lords—there was no direct evidence, but he was sure they were ultimately behind the sack of Kazerclawm—were cruel and vindictive. It was their policy that none who offended them died easily.

What was their policy in this case? That he himself would be consigned to torment was a thing foredoomed. All that was left to him now was to hope that this innocent kit would not suffer a like fate. True, wizards were distrusted by the common folk; he knew of cases where they had been stoned to death, even burned alive. But such hatred seldom descended upon the wizard's family, and the female's only magical powers seemed to be those of a healer. Besides, she was a Dancer. Perhaps she had been brought here only to keep him alive. He hoped so. It was agony even to think about so lovely and innocent a child being subjected to torment.

▲

"What's the point in another load?" Cajhet protested, weary and out of breath. "And please don't ask me again. Do you think I'd break my back like this if there was any shorter way to the armory? These old cisterns weren't dug for our convenience, you know."

"These will have to do." Branwe silently unloaded the bundle of swords and pikes, the third they had hauled the long roundabout way through the cisterns. "The problem is still to find some way to get the soldiers out of their cells."

"Better solve it quick," whispered Cajhet, nervous at finding himself so close to the dungeons again, "or there won't be any more soldiers to get anywhere."

"That's at least the fourth batch they've marched upstairs." Branwe peered out of the dark cavern at the remotest cell in the entire block, now empty. "Where are they taking them?"

Cajhet silently drew a finger across his throat.

"But where have they taken Srana?" muttered Branwe. "You're sure this is the only way we can reach the fortress?"

"Unless you can figure out some way of opening the door at the top of the armory staircase. It's bolted on the outside, with a guard posted. There's no key."

"What about the keys to these cells?"

"Never let 'em out of my sight, when I was on duty. Somebody down here must have 'em, so's he can let these poor soldiers out of their cells, to get their throats cut."

"Does this tunnel lead to the main cell block? I'll try to get a look at who's got the keys—"

"Hold on, lad." Cajhet slipped off his boots. "This is more in my line. I've met some who could outfight me—quite a few, in fact—but none who could outsneak me. My own mother said I was a born sneak, and developed as I grew older. But let's not talk about Mother." He sighed. "Too many people used to do that. Wait here."

He was back within minutes, silent and thoughtful. "I never expected anything like this," he muttered. "Even flat on his back he looked mean."

"Who?"

Cajhet whispered, as if intimidated by the very name: "Severakh. I saw him in one of the cells."

"But that's wonderful. If anybody in the kingdom can get us into the fortress upstairs, it's old Severakh. It can't be very well guarded. He might even be able to recapture it. At least, long enough to find where Srana is being kept."

"No need, lad. She's being kept in the same cell with—" he lowered his voice again "—Severakh."

"How many guards are down here?" Branwe had trouble lowering his own voice, in excitement. "Which of them has the keys?"

"An old friend of yours. One who would dearly like to get his claws on both of us. Remember the hookpurse you witnessed against yesterday?"

"Fefo?"

"That's him."

"How many other guards are down here?"

"I saw only one more, another hookpurse called Toutou. There might be others, of course. But I think most of 'em went upstairs with that last batch of soldiers." Again he drew a silent finger across his throat.

Branwe gripped his sword. "Then we have to move fast."

"We?"

"I'll do the fighting. Once I get the keys, I'll hold whatever other guards are down here at bay, while you open the cells. Take a few swords with you. Maybe we can catch them napping."

He moved stealthily down the tunnel, with Cajhet a shadow behind him. But it is no easy matter to catch a hookpurse unawares, and he had no sooner leapt into the dim light than he found himself in mortal combat. A glimpse at Srana's lovely face behind bars distracted him only momentarily, and he dodged one sword thrust and parried another. He knew that he was fighting not just for his own life but hers as well.

The two hookpurses had armed themselves from the choice weapons of the garrison, and also brandished their own daggers. They were both strong and cunning, but neither had mastered technique as had Branwe, nor were they as agile. After the failure of their first murderous passes, they began shouting for help. Answering shouts echoed from the top of the staircase.

Then all at once Branwe faced only a single opponent. Somehow Cajhet had sneaked up behind Toutou, and stunned him with the flat of a sword. Fefo turned and raced for the staircase, but Branwe was there first, danced out of the way of a lunge, and drove his own sword into the hookpurse, once more splitting its mended basket.

Tossing the ring of keys to Cajhet, he turned to face the guards charging down the winding staircase. They had the advantage of numbers and momentum; but he knew that Srana's eyes were on him, and with a quickness and fury that intimidated the grisliest, he drove them back. By the time they rallied, he was no longer alone, and the garrison troops who now attacked them, if less quick, were more experienced fighters. They had seen their comrades driven up these very stairs to be slaughtered like herd-beasts. Not a single marauder escaped their fury.

Meanwhile Cajhet became alarmed that he might be mistaken for a real desert marauder, with fatal consequences, and hurriedly exchanged his smelly rags for his old uniform. One by one he unlocked all the remaining cells in the block, then tried to make himself inconspicuous—especially from Severakh.

"All right, all right." The old warrior impatiently shook off the hands trying to support him. "I can still stand on my own two feet. Over here, you. Now who are you, and how do you come to know so much about these dungeons?"

"I was the turnkey here, sir." Cajhet's voice quavered.

"One of the soldiers in my own garrison?" Severakh looked him up and down. "I make a point of knowing all my mrem in person, but I don't recall ever seeing you before. You can't have been here long. When were you first posted to my command?"

"Uh, eight years ago, sir."

"Eight years!" The old warrior literally staggered, and again proudly shoved away all helping hands. "What's your name, soldier?"

"Cajhet, sir."

"You're too sly by half, Cajhet."

"Yes, sir."

The scout Severakh had sent to reconnoiter came flying down the staircase. "Marauders and bandits, sir," he reported. "Looks like they've rallied the whole gang of looters, from inside the fortress and out, right at the top of these stairs. They'll be attacking down here any minute now. Although the first company to form was marched off in the opposite direction. Must be going down to the armory for weapons."

"What about it, Cajhet? You seem to know your way around down here. Can these dungeons be reached directly from the armory?"

"Only by a long way around, sir." Cajhet cringed each time the old warrior glowered at him. "Three trips I made lugging bundles of weapons, and my back still aches from it. The lad here helped some too," he added generously.

"Weapons? You idiot, why didn't you tell me at once?" Severakh looked faint for a moment, but forced himself erect by an effort of will. "Now where did you stash them?"

Cajhet was overjoyed to lead the soldiers to the hiding place; then he hid himself from Severakh. Every able-bodied soldier—less than half the total—was soon armed, with a few weapons to spare.

"Here, lad." Severakh beckoned to Branwe. "A fair exhibition you gave us with that little drill sword you've got there. But here's a true weapon for you. The sword of a true warrior."

"Thank you, sir."

It was the proudest moment of Branwe's young life, and he glanced self-consciously toward Srana. But she was busy cleansing and bandaging wounds, and did not notice. His disappointment was too evident to miss, and Severakh glanced shrewdly from one to the other, and his eyes narrowed with amusement.

Those shrewd old eyes, in fact, missed nothing around him. His captains knew this, and formed ranks as if they were on the drill field; those mrem unable to walk were carried. Meanwhile everything portable was heaped into a barricade across the staircase.

"There's a lantern, and there's another." Severakh pointed. "Light them, then dump this table lamp onto the barricade. Now where's that Cajhet?"

"Sir?"

"Don't sneak up on me like that!"

"No, sir."

"You got in here somehow. Can you get us out?"

"Yes, sir."

"Then do it!"

Still too proud to accept help, though Srana watched his every painful step with concern, the old warrior marched right along with his troops, up one level and down the next, through the vast artificial caverns. Gritting his teeth, he managed to pull himself, rung by rung, to the top of the old pump-well; though some younger mrem had to be carried.

"What is this place, some kind of warehouse? Is every mrem up? Then nail down that trapdoor. They won't be following us this way." He sneezed. In fact, everybody was now sneezing. "Now where did that Cajhet go this time?"

"Here, sir."

"I thought I told you not to sneak up on me like that."

"I'm sorry, sir." Cajhet sneezed, then grinned apologetically.

"I suspect you know everything here worth taking. They'll expect us to head straight for the Whitestone ford, so we're going to head south instead. Commissariat will be our biggest problem. We'll have to load all we can carry into packs, before going over the walls. Show my captains the most portable foodstuffs."

"Yes, sir."

"The rest of you gather around, and try to stop sneezing for a few minutes. That's all the time we've got. If we can get over the walls unseen, we'll have a good chance to beat them at their own game. I've hunted bandits all my life. I know the country, and I know their tricks better than they do. We're going to have to live like bandits ourselves. But never forget that you're soldiers. This is war, and we'll be doing our part the best we can. We have no choice, and no means of reaching the safety of Ar, or even telling them we're still alive. Do you understand me?"

"Yes, sir." The response was weak and dispirited.

"May I have a word with you?" said Srana, and she and Severakh drew out of earshot. "We may be able to communicate with Ar, but only if I recover something I hid before I was captured. Branwe has agreed to accompany me. Our only danger will be in reaching the hiding place. Afterward, we should be safe from attack. You needn't send any of your mrem. This risk will be ours alone."

Severakh nodded. He knew she was the granddaughter of a wizard, and suspected that magic of a darker kind had somehow conspired the overthrow of the city. There were forces at work here that he did not understand. Nor did he doubt that young Branwe was ready to accompany this lovely young she-mrem anywhere. Severakh beckoned to him.

"Do you know where the spur of the Kazerclaw narrows into Stonejar Valley, then bends back on itself like a fishhook? That's where we'll be holed up until nightfall. The All-Mother knows where we'll be after that, so don't dawdle. All right, mrem, pick up those stretchers, and not a peep out of any of you, or I'll know the reason why."

Still weak from loss of blood and painfully hobbled by wounds, the old warrior was nonetheless determined to set an example for his dispirited troops. After providing support for the wounded, inspecting his commissariat, and posting scouts, he led the way grimly out into the streets. The route he had chosen to the city wall seemed deserted.

Left alone, Branwe and Srana turned back toward the very heart of the city. Their route was anything but deserted. The streets they crept through were a charnal house of wanton butchery and horror; terrorism that warned all the cities of the land what lay in store for those which refused to throw open their gates to the Eastern Lords. And yet, to Branwe's dismay, they passed unnoticed. Though naturally inclined to duck for cover at the sight of roving thugs or scavengers, he found that these were invariably looking the other way. By the third time it happened he began to suspect that it was no coincidence.

He also suspected that Srana's concealment magic—there could be no other reason for their not being noticed—like his own swordsmanship, still lacked full technique. She could cause one, two, even small groups of thugs mysteriously to turn their heads, and not look at them as they passed. But whenever she spotted larger bands of thugs or marauders—too large for her limited powers to encompass—she prudently led the way down some detour street or alley. Branwe followed, ready to defend her with his life, should those powers ever fail. The sword old Severakh had given him was too magnificent for his homemade scabbard, so he carried it in his hand.

Then, through the acrid gloom of smoke and slaughter, they made out a lone figure skulking toward them, but this time Srana chose not to conceal them with magic. For she had seen this very figure lurking outside her grandfather's house when it was in flames, and again after she was captured. A wizard? One of Khal's agents? He might be able to resist concealment magic, or at least recognize its effects, and she drew Branwe into the ruins of a looted chandler's shop.

They did not emerge until the lone figure, skulking in the direction of the Sacred Gate, was nearly out of sight. Soon, to Branwe's amazement, they themselves appeared to vanish. In fact, from the moment Srana emerged from inside a certain pottery shop, nobody so much as glanced at them all the way to the city wall, even while they mounted the guard walk to the top.

The devastation of Kazarclawm was appalling. A valley breeze now wafted upward into the mountains, but seemed only to fan the smoldering fires, rather than carry away the smoke. How would the young king of Ar respond to such an outrage? This was no mere bandits' raid. The land was at war, the very survival of the mrem in jeopardy.

"We're going to have to live like bandits ourselves," said Branwe, when they had at last found one of the invader's scaling ladders propped against the outer wall. "The lands to the south are cruel and dangerous, but, well, you know I'd give, that is, you can rely on me to do everything in my power . . ." he ended shyly.

This time he was not disappointed. She did not reply, but there was a look of trust and gratitude in her eyes; a look for which any true warrior would dauntlessly battle to the death. And together they descended into the gloom below.

▲

Maglakh's feelings, as he slunk through the Sacred Gate, now unguarded, and began to ascend the mountain path, were a confusion of dread and delight. For though his poisoned soul still reveled in the scenes of horror through which he had just passed, he cringed before the personal horrors that might lay ahead. He had never actually seen Khal—no wizard of his generation could have—but had heard that the liskash sorcerer most resembled the Eastern Lords, although still more hideous and repulsive.

A stout wooden door studded with nails hung ajar; his pupils dilating, he stepped inside. The abandoned mine shaft had been crudely delved from the living rock by some prehistoric race. There was a greenish light in the distance, and from somewhere around the bend to the right, the echoes weirdly amplified, he heard groans, then whimpers of abject terror. Dark laughter seemed to reverberate out of the very heart of the mountain, so evil and reptilian that his fur stood on end.

But there was no turning back, no escape from Khal's vengeance any more, except by somehow appeasing it. Why was Khal still here in the mountain? Did he know yet that thousands of captives had successfully fled the conquered city? Maglakh approached the bend on tiptoe. The greenish light seemed to be coming from just ahead. Each burst of abject groans and whimpers was followed by evil laughter.

Maglakh's fur had begun to relent, but rose again as he peeked around the bend. Khal's alienness was beyond imagination; his iridescent robe, the array of shining rings too near the tips of his webbed fingers, only exaggerated it. He seemed indeed to have a third eye, glittering evilly between his own pair from a golden uraeus.

Nizzam groveled before Khal, his eyes bloodshot, his face writhing with horror. But it was not Khal himself he seemed to dread, though the reptilian sorcerer hovered only a few feet away, in the greenish light of a globe floating mysteriously in the air. Several minutes passed before Maglakh, baffled and appalled, at last understood what was happening.

Like some monstrous hybrid of ancient evil and childish self-indulgence, the sadistic torment of the weak, groveling fool seemed to absorb Khal more than the fall of cities. He knew exactly what so terrified the wretched Nizzam, for he was creating it, controlling it for his own delight . . . .

Had the terror no end? Over and over again Nizzam was deceived by appearances. First, the lovely Srana had led him shamelessly to a couch, but no sooner had he embraced her than he found himself embraced in turn by writhing tentacles. His bones were crushed, his flesh stripped away piece by piece, in an agony such as he had never known before . . . .

He must have swooned. He was not sure what had happened, only that he was still alive. When the pain and horror reached their utmost, when he knew he could endure no more, his mind whirled, and he found himself in a strange forest. Then in dark groping caverns. Then floating on a twilight sea. Childhood friends, his mother, his old master, recovered from his illness, came to lead him to safety. But each time he somehow ended up in torment.

Now he found himself in his childhood room; all his books and toys were just as he had left them, only there were no windows. Instead, each of the four walls had a door. He opened the first, and reeled backward in horror. Here was not the familiar landing, the carpeted staircase that led down to the comfortable old parlor, but a moonlit plain over which loped primitive mrem, like the prehistoric beings that had conquered the land from the Old Race. But these were clearly insane; their jaws slavered, their fanglike teeth chattered with rage, and there was madness in their eyes. They seemed to be waiting for him, as if they knew he must soon come out to them. He slammed the door, and rushed frantically to the next.

But each of the doors led to horrors grimmer than the last, more diabolical and cruel. Slamming the last of the four doors, Nizzam lay down to sleep on his familiar old bed. Here was his old refuge from neighborhood bullies; here was one place he would be safe.

He sensed rather than heard the dark laughter, and opened his eyes. The room was smaller now, the doors leading into various horrid landscapes closer than they had been. He began to tremble with fright as he realized that the doors were slowly moving inward toward him. That was what the creatures outside had been waiting for. That was why they knew he must soon come out to them . . . .

Then suddenly he found himself back in the prehistoric mineshaft, standing in the sickly greenish light of some mysterious globe that floated above him in the air. Khal stood only a few feet away, in the mouth of the cavern; but he now ignored Nizzam, diverted from play by more pressing interests. However, it was not Khal himself Nizzam now heard speaking:

". . . he would have died but for me," exclaimed Maglakh. "The commander of the garrison, who organized the escape which your own commanders were unable to check, the leader of the rear guard which beat back pursuit." He did not mention the terrible cost in lives, which he doubted would interest Khal in any case. "Severakh himself. The she-mrem used concealment magic, but I was not fooled. I had her put in the old warrior's cell, or he would have bled to death, and escaped your just vengeance."

"This kit is the granddaughter of the Sentinel, you say?" Khal spoke in a raspy hiss.

"A White Dancer, lord," said Maglakh.

"Ah, and is that in fact her true color?"

Maglakh was taken unawares, without the least idea why the sorcerer should be so interested in fur color. Nizzam was quicker to respond, so frazzled were his nerves that he instinctively sought a means to ingratiate himself with his tormentor.

"A flawless cream white, lord," he blurted out, not knowing either why Khal was so interested in fur color, only that he was. "I know this well, for I intend to honor her with marriage one day."

"And yet you betray her to me now." Khal examined him with a sardonic glitter in his eyes. "Perhaps you may serve as more than just a toy." He turned back to Maglakh. "Where are they now?"

"In the dungeons beneath the fortress, lord. The other captives—city trash, common soldiers, and the like—are being executed. But I left strict orders that Severakh and the Sentinel's granddaughter were to be kept isolated, to await your intentions for them, lord."

"It is well that you did. But you speak only of the Sentinel's granddaughter, and not of the Sentinel himself. It is he, above all others, that I desire. For years longer than you have been alive have I desired him. Where is he?"

"Alas, lord, your commanders also bungled his capture," said Maglakh, trembling under the intensity of the three ruby eyes glittering at him out of the darkness. "Hundreds surrounded the house, then entered, thinking foolishly they were dealing with just a sick old mrem, though I had warned them again and again to beware. All perished in a sudden fire, lord. Even the Sentinel himself."

"But the granddaughter escaped? A flawless cream white, you say? It is well that you captured her." The three ruby eyes now seemed to glitter with a weird hunger. "She will be the first of my collection, the first of many."

"She used concealment magic to escape the fire, lord," said Maglakh, uncertain what kind of "collection" Khal was talking about. "A magic too powerful for a mere girl. No doubt the Sentinel gave her his fragment of the Great Stone, like the one I had Nizzam here bring you."

Khal glanced sardonically at the wretched Nizzam, who at once began to smirk and kowtow. "Give me the fragment." He held out a webbed hand to Maglakh.

"Alas, lord, the girl substituted a worthless piece of glass for it, somewhere during her flight. My first thought was to force the secret from her, but then I thought you would rather do that yourself."

"A redeeming thought," said Khal. "A thought that redeems much of your other conduct. Yes, I shall enjoy drawing the secret from her. It may be long before I at last have her prepared for exhibit. Cragsclaw is said to be a great fortress. It needs be, to house the collection I have brooded upon for so many years in the darkness."

"Cragsclaw, lord? I thought it was Ar the Eastern Lords intended to overthrow."

"And so they shall—but not unless I first establish myself at Cragsclaw. The Three are still formidable. Their numbers and complicity must be reduced before an invasion can succeed. The Eastern Lords themselves know this, and there is no more strategic fortress than Cragsclaw for the purpose . . . ."

He continued to meditate out loud, as if he were alone—or soon would be. Maglakh wondered if even capturing Srana and preserving Severakh alive quite redeemed his failure to deliver the Sentinel. He saw that Nizzam also seemed uneasy, as if his doom were only minutes away. They were both startled by the muffled blast of a horn echoing through the mountain.

Khal looked questioningly at them.

"A parley horn, lord," explained Maglakh. "It sounds like it's coming from right outside the entrance into the mountain. Perhaps one of your commanders wishes to confer with you. The city has been overrun—"

"But its army and citizenry escaped." Khal silenced him, and turned and stalked up the mine shaft.

Maglakh and Nizzam crept after him, anxious to hear the news; more anxious still for a chance to slip away. Neither doubted that the reptilian sorcerer was on the verge of some evil tantrum.

His appearance before the troop of commanders outside on the mountain slope roused still more anxiety. The very desert chieftains seemed barely able to suppress their revulsion. The renegade highlanders were the most affected: their fur rose to a mrem.

Khal was sardonically delighted by this reaction; more delighted still with the smoke and gloom and ruin that lay beneath him; most delighted of all that the royal governor of

Kazerclawm and his lords and ladies, all dressed in court finery, now stood abjectly before him. He was only disappointed that none of the captive women was a flawless cream white: Srana evidently was not among them.

"And which of these nobles is Severakh?" he asked in a raspy hiss that caused still more fur to stand on end.

"Alas, lord," said a bandit chieftain, "there was a breakout from the fortress within the hour. It is believed that the captives have fled the city by now . . . ."

Maglakh, watching apprehensively from the mine doorway, did not wait to hear any more. Neither did the wretched Nizzam. They had both seen Khal begin to tremble with insane fury, and threw themselves blindly into the depths of the ancient mine. That they soon lost their way did not matter, only that they had taken themselves out of the way of his wrath.

From the cries of pain and horror reverberating through the mountain it seemed that others had not been so lucky. Hours passed before Khal's insane rage at again losing his prize captives had slaked itself. The silence that followed encouraged the frightened pair—antagonists only hours ago, but now clinging to each other in the groping blackness—to hope that Khal had left the mountain, or at least forgotten about them. Nizzam began to think about his empty stomach.

Then a burst of greenish light took away his appetite. Khal stood beneath the mysterious globe in all his liskash hideousness, his iridescent robe spattered with blood and tufts of fur. He seemed calm, as if his vengeance were momentarily appeased, although his ruby eyes still glittered with mad intensity.

"Come, my faithful servants." He beckoned Nizzam and Maglakh out of the shadows where they cringed with their arms around each other, their fur standing on end. "I have just received word that the cohorts promised by the Eastern Lords"—he sneered at their name, as if he considered them but an inferior breed of his own master race—"have at last arrived. We are now strong enough to march upon Cragsclaw, and still leave a garrison here. I want both of you with me. Yes, I have special plans for you there."

His dark laughter rang through the mountain like a shriek of madness.

▲

Chapter 7
The Walls of Ar

▲————————————————————————————————————▲

First under the glorious reign
of Talwe, then under the still more glorious reign of his son
Talwyn, Ar had aggrandized year by year in wealth and
power and splendor until it was now the great city of the
mrem, its mighty walls a wonder of the world. Nor were even
these its most formidable defense.

Centuries past, a market village had stood here at a crossing of the Mraal; that the greatest city in the land should arise
beside its grandest river seemed foreordained. But only through
wise policy had the channel of that river been so engineered
that Ar now stood on a veritable island, its walls rising sheer
out of the water, defying siege by even the most rapacious
hordes.

It was hordes of another kind that now burdened the
citizens of Ar. The thousands of refugees from Kazerclawm
had at first been welcomed; but then more thousands, fleeing
the doom of Cragsclaw, poured into the city, straining its
resources. The fall of the great fortresses had brought satisfaction to rival city-states, until they in turn were overrun,
further crowding the roads to Ar with miserable refugees.

Their misery was exploited to the full by the courtiers of
the dissolute young king, who saw the invasion as no more
than a chance for personal profit. By levying special taxes,
fees, licenses, customs duties, tariffs, assessments, and fines
that were virtual ransoms, they acquired the heirlooms and
other valuables of the refugees at desperation prices, leaving
many utterly destitute. And the pickings grew ever more
lucrative as more and more nobles, even kings, sought refuge
in Ar from the invading hordes.

A despicable trade, thought the venerable figure who stood alone upon the ramparts each evening at twilight, until the last refugees of the day—on foot, in carts, salvaging such valuables as they could from the debacle—straggled through the city gate below. For the first time since the erection of these mighty walls, the drawbridges were raised at nightfall from the two stone spans that arched across the bifurcated river, north and south.

As both queen of Ar and queen mother, Sruss had seen these mighty walls grow yearly until many thought them impregnable—especially her grandson's greedy courtiers, who troubled themselves about no welfare but their own. But she had known too much of warfare in her long lifetime to believe any ramparts truly impregnable, and knew too well the implacable hatred of the Eastern Lords for her people. Neither walls nor rivers would long protect a corrupt and disunited people against such malice.

She also knew the fierce independence of her people. Highlanders feuded eternally with lowlanders; some feuds between rival city-states were carried on from generation to generation; royal houses and nobles alike inherited old enmities with their coats of arms. Many resented the aggrandizement of Ar into the great city of the land, even some who now sought refuge within its walls.

She peered down the eastern road, flanked by rich farms and orchards, amber gold in the setting sun. The road was now deserted, as were the farmhouses themselves. There was no familiar form among the last stragglers of the day now crossing the bridge below, and she turned away with a sigh.

Was Srana still alive? All Sruss had discovered thus far, from those who had survived the fall of Kazerclawm, were rumors that the house of the Sentinel had been destroyed in flames. So reclusively had he lived that nobody she had questioned even knew he had a granddaughter. A few had known about a White Dancer residing there, but assumed she was just his nurse; for the single neighborhood she-mrem who had survived blessed Srana for healing her sick kit months ago.

That was just the problem in gaining information. The survivors were disproportionately made up of villagers who had come to Kazerclawm for its annual festival, and garrison troops; the citizens themselves had foolishly believed their own walls to be impregnable, and had perished in tragic numbers during the sack. Nor had the wizards of The Three been able to help her, even those possessing fragments of the Khavala. The mind was most receptive to contact during the dream state, but even then telepathy at such long distances was unreliable. Especially when it was not even known whether the subject was alive.

Besides, The Three were now trying frantically to summon all the powerful to Ar. Their failure to contact the Sentinel had made it all but certain that he at least was dead. What had become of his granddaughter, the favorite and most gifted pupil Sruss had ever had, none could say.

A long life brings many joys, and many sorrows. Sruss had known the love of a great warrior; she had seen their son ascend the throne of Ar, and preside over its rise to unrivaled splendor. Both had died tragically before their time. As queen mother her counsel had often been sought by her son, but she had never interfered in the everyday administration of his kingdom, not even in his choice of a queen. She wondered now if she had been too forbearing.

Rhenowla had indeed been beautiful. Her attractiveness was suspected to be magical; this had never been proven against her, though none doubted her ambition and love of power. Nor had she in turn any qualms about interfering in the administration of her own son, the young Tristwyn. He sat upon the throne, his word was law; but it was really she who spoke.

Hardly more than a boy, he was immature even for his years. His dissipations were a public scandal. It was rumored that his mother actually encouraged him to consort with none but the idle and dissolute, to indulge himself in riot and debauchery. There were even darker rumors about how the beautiful Rhenowla kept her hold on him; but like the suspicions about her magical attractiveness, these had never been proven.

As Sruss descended into the bustling streets below—teeming with bizarre costumes, the accents of far-flung peoples, and furs of many colors; redolent with the rich spicy smells of suppertime—she noticed two men turn and pretend to consider the wares in a peddler's cart. The Silent Ones followed her everywhere these days. Under her guidance, her late son had suppressed delation throughout the realm. But now spies and informers flourished as never before. It was no use trying to evade them; that would only make Rhenowla more suspicious. She probably knew already about tonight's meeting, and would certainly try to place one or more of her Silent Ones there.

Not much chance of that, thought Sruss, as the crowds parted deferentially before her; she-mrem curtseyed, mrem bowed and doffed their hats. She wore no royal trappings, only the robes of a senior White Dancer, but her moral authority in the land surpassed the might of kings. Many of those very kings—refugees from the marchlands, those whose small city-states lay helpless in the path of the invaders— would gather tonight in her gardens. Any spy would be conspicuous among them, and dealt with summarily. In that alone could the kings and refugee nobles be expected to act with unity.

Which was why she had agreed to such a conference in the first place. In peace, the fierce independence of the city-states was a glory to the land. In war, it was suicide. Nor was there any doubt that the agents of the Eastern Lords were everywhere fomenting the old feuds and rivalries. Their bloodthirsty hordes grew daily in numbers and ferocity, united in a common lust for vengeance and plunder. Unless the kings of the land also combined, they would fall one by one beneath the onslaught of relentless evil, never to rise.

Sruss paused and frowned, but then continued through the deferential crowds, parting everywhere before her.

Shamelessly, in the open air, prepared to go on haggling even after the light of day had faded into night, the street-corner auctions still drew crowds. The most shameless haggling, of course, took place behind closed doors. The prices involved, although so low in relation to the real worth of the goods as to constitute virtual theft, were still beyond the purses of street-corner idlers. Often the heirlooms salvaged by refugee nobles were all they had of value in the world, their sole means of keeping themselves and their families alive. The courtiers knew this, and acted in collusion to hold prices to a minimum, thus growing rich on the misery of the land.

Sruss did not have to glance over her shoulder to know she was being followed—if not by the pair she had spotted by the peddler's cart, then by others, everywhere she went these days. No matter. They could not harm her, and she ignored them. It may have rankled the jealous vanity of Rhenowla to see another more revered than herself, but she was too cunning to harrass a senior White Dancer, the legendary queen and queen mother during Ar's ascendency, in public. If she gnashed her teeth, she did it in private.

Sruss was more concerned for the wizards of The Three. They were not sacrosanct, certainly not revered, in a land where all magicians were distrusted. Especially now, when a confused and frightened people were beginning to look for scapegoats. She had already heard dark rumors about the fate of magicians in those borderlands threatened with invasion. It was well that The Three were now rallying to Ar—while they still could.

No thanks to Rhenowla, who was suspicious of any kind of unity as a challenge to her supremacy. There were other dark rumors that she was goading her son with hints about a plot to seize his throne. So far she had succeeded only in an official ban on all public and private meetings of wizards—at the very time when their unity was most desperately needed. She had also let it be known, unofficially, that any meeting with the old queen mother would offend her—and set spies to watch.

That these spies should still call themselves H'satie, the Silent Ones, was perhaps Rhenowla's most baleful perversion of all. Insidiously she had turned what was once the eyes and ears of justice, the first defense against wickedness, into her personal secret police. Those with scruples resigned; those unwilling to do her dirty work lost their jobs. Yet in so vast and teeming a city, if one had friends—the Silent Ones no longer had any—there were always ways of evading them. Not too obviously, though; for Rhenowla might have construed that as proof of conspiracies against the throne, a pretext for more stringent measures.

Turning a corner where yet another auction was in progress, she strolled through the deferential crowds into a mercer's shop, which she was long known to have patronized. In fact, she needed some precious silkwares, if she was going to don once more the regal trappings of a queen mother. But first things first, and she exchanged a meaningful look with the old mercer and his wife, and stepped through a sliding panel into the fitting room.

The seamstresses had been dismissed for the night; the shop itself would normally be closing at this hour, but Sruss was a very special customer, and she was here for a very special reason. The old wizard rose as she entered, and bowed.

"My lady." He came straight to the point. "The news is even worse than we anticipated. All that we have feared so long has come to pass. The Evil One has somehow regained possession of the Third Eye."

"Are you strong enough to challenge him?"

He frowned. "By uniting the powers of The Three we may just be able to neutralize him, but no more. As you well know, true wizards tend to be solitary. Getting a whole council of wizards to agree on any common purpose, without endless wrangling, is seldom easy. But it must be done, and done before our very deliberations become known. It was only by taking the Evil One unawares, while he indulged himself in insane orgies of vengeance, that we were able to overcome him the first time." He hesitated. "You seem troubled, my lady. Have I spoken too bluntly?"

"You were ever blunt, Dollavier," she said. "Ever forthright and worthy of trust, and I appreciate those qualities now more than ever. What troubles me is the vengeance of the Evil One, for one I love may have fallen into his hands."

"Indeed something to be troubled about, my lady. For all of us have friends and loved ones similarly endangered. It has become dangerous even to contact them."

"How so?"

"Long entombment has left the Evil One wary of our united power, although he surely knows that not one of us dares face him alone. Thus far he has avoided open confrontation. Instead he's placed himself strategically to probe our dreams, to interfere with all attempts at telepathy, perhaps to render teleportation a trap."

"Where?"

"Cragsclaw. Do you know it?"

Her reaction startled him, and for a moment he was afraid

she had been taken ill. She had no expression on her face, her mouth fell slack, and her eyes stared blankly past him as if in shock. Then she sighed and hung her head.

"Alas, I know Cragsclaw all too well. Too well to hear of its being so befouled without a wrench at my heart." With an effort, she at last regained her composure, and by a natural association of ideas turned to one who had shared many of her youthful adventures at Cragsclaw, even the very rebuilding of the city. "And what of dear Mithmid? Why hasn't he answered my summons?"

"He is even now on his way to Ar, my lady. But, as I say, teleportation would leave him dangerously vulnerable to the Evil One. His capture would incite an orgy of vengeance indeed, for no one was more decisive in entombing Khal beneath the Kazerclaw, or so vigorous in questing for the Third Eye. Alas, even he will be able to do little to unify us, when at last he arrives here."

"So I fear." She remained silent for the next several minutes, rapt in thought. The blunt old wizard was for once too tactful to interrupt. "It has long been my policy never to interfere in the administration of the kingdom," she said at last. "But there may soon be no kingdom, if I do not. Just as The Three must stand united against the Evil One, so too must all the kingdoms of the land unite before the hosts of the Eastern Lords. We have been accustomed to meet in this place every third day. Let our next meeting instead be on the fourth day from today, for on the third day hence I go to the palace."

"Very well, my lady. All the power I wield is at your disposal, even should you reclaim the throne."

"No, my good Dollavier," she said. "That is something I must never do. Though there were questions at the time about her true lineage, Rhenowla was accepted in law as a princess royal, and hence the king inherits his throne through her. Unity is all in all to us now, and few kings would form ranks behind a usurper. Difficult enough just to get them into the same room together . . . ."

It was in fact unlikely that anyone but Sruss herself could have done it. At least, not without brawls and challenges to combat.

Her gardens were all that remained of the old palace, in

the oldest quarter of the Old City. A small pavilion for herself, a few servants, and her pupils; an open space for dancing, a pleasance for tutelage and conversation; she had hoped to pass her final days here in peace and honor. All had changed with the emergence of the Evil One from entombment.

The gardens themselves were now too crowded with the tents of refugees—all the White Dancers who had fled Kazerclawm were here—for tonight's gathering. The humble pavilion, converted from the servants' wing of the old palace, hardly seemed adequate to contain so many kings. But not one of them felt his grandeur slighted, not one of them squabbled over rank or precedence, for the renown and moral authority of the legendary Sruss transcended even the vanity of kings. They stood deferentially before the armless wooden chair on which she sat facing them as if it were a jeweled throne, with their sons and chief retainers.

"My lords and gentlemrem," she addressed them, "you who have suffered invasion, and you whose realms now lie open to attack, know full well the evil that threatens us. Us, I say. All of us. For it is only through unity, only by leaguing personal interests in a common cause, for the common good, that we may hope to prevail. In peace, independence is a glory to the land. In war, it is folly. Old feuds must be resolved in a new spirit of cooperation. No matter who is to blame, or where the fault lies," she added quickly, as she noticed hostile looks being exchanged by two kings. "No matter what scores remain to be settled. We must all stand together, shoulder to shoulder, every sword pointed against the common enemy, or one by one we shall all perish. Be assured that, although the armies of the Eastern Lords seek only plunder and vengeance, the Eastern Lords themselves seek nothing less than our annihilation . . . ."

Resolving accusations, calming old hostilities, encouraging the withdrawal of challenges and the free return of hostages, she at last achieved what no other peacemaker in all the history of the mrem had ever been able to achieve. Even those who most resented the aggrandizement of Ar over their own kingdoms recognized its importance to their survival. All supplies and matériel must now be concentrated here, and the land scorched before the advancing enemy, denying him sustenance. That much was obvious.

Many decisions still had to be resolved; many concessions yielded, with varying degrees of reluctance; many sacrifices made. But the mighty walls of Ar were the one obstacle that could yet discourage such cruel and barbarous hordes—so long as they were vigorously defended. The city was a rich temptation to plunder, but such hordes were unlikely to endure the hardships of a prolonged siege. Once they began to straggle homeward with such booty as they had ravished elsewhere from the land, they would be vulnerable to counterattacks. Meanwhile Ar must be preserved, and that meant a sacred unity.

The All-Mother was the sole diety worshipped universally among the welter of cults, temples, priesthoods, and local gods and goddesses of the mrem. Her invocation in tonight's oath, consecrating the League of Ar, was thus symbolic of the vows of universal cooperation among the kings of the land. But Sruss knew that her work had only begun, for not a single king had mentioned The Three in regard to the invasion. A portentous omission, for nothing remained so urgently needed as the unity of The Three, both among themselves and with the warrior kings of the new League of Ar.

The evil that now looked down from Cragsclaw would seek by any means to shatter such unity, which it feared above all things. And its evil reached beyond this world, into dimensions that were themselves evil, whence sprang its ultimate source of power.

The refugee tents left little room for dancing in the gardens, but the White Dancers found space enough in which to celebrate tonight's consecration. Sruss herself joined in the complex figures with a grace and dignity that no king or princeling who witnessed it ever forgot.

These dances alone were visible to surrounding tenements, and hence all that could be reported to anyone keenly interested in everything that happened here.

▲

"The throne is yours, my darling," Rhenowla whispered in her son's ear, as she groomed him with sensual, comforting hands. "Yours by maternal right, and by law. Never forget that. You know she's jealous of your power, and would take the throne back if she could."

"I know you've often told me that, Mother," said young Tristwyn, soothed by the grooming that was more than maternal. He was in early adulthood, although small and immature for his years. His face would have been childishly innocent, except for a telltale slackness about the mouth and fevered eyes, which gave him at times, and particularly after one of the orgies that had lately become so notorious throughout the city, the look of a depraved kit. "Does anyone else know about this?"

"How could they? The H'sotie came straight to me with the news, and I naturally came straight to you. Within the hour."

In fact two whole days had passed since the meeting of kings, while Rhenowla brooded over the information. It could certainly be turned to account, but how she would use it and when—timing was everything with a mrem of her son's temperament—needed close calculation. She had been the great beauty of her generation, and was still sensually attractive; her high amber coloring was variegated in such a way that it accented the curves of her voluptuous figure, and her dark piercing eyes were bewitchingly slanted. Her beauty alone ravished beholders; enhanced by a magical attractiveness, she became irresistible.

"I couldn't very well have refused her, Mother," pleaded Tristwyn. "I mean, with so many kings, and everything. They're all coming here tomorrow. After all, it's a public audience day, so I could, well, hardly turn them away. You know how the people feel about Sruss." He felt his mother tense, and knew he had again said the wrong thing. "Besides, you have no idea how big and fierce-looking the retainers were who came to the palace, requesting the audience. I meant to follow your advice, Mother, really I did. But I just kind of blurted out yes, and now I can't very well go back on my word, can I?"

"A king can do anything he chooses, my darling." Rhenowla continued to groom him. Despite the feebleness of his protests, she sensed in him signs of independence. Had he granted the audience for reasons other than those he claimed? And what did Sruss really intend? Was it possible that she in fact wanted the throne? Everyone took as much power as he could, and the time might just be ripe for a popular uprising.

"Since you've disregarded my advice about granting an audience, at least have the audience chamber well guarded tomorrow."

"Yes, I certainly shall, Mother." He felt himself to be in a false position, as he always did with her; guilty about acting behind her back, uncomfortable about the very decor of his private quarters.

The drapes and furnishings of the secluded apartment were silkily voluptuous; the paintings and statuary crudely erotic. Incense burned in a copper thurible, perfuming the air with an aphrodisiac musk. His special friends would probably return here with him after tonight's orgy. He also felt guilty about his mother's exclusion from all such fun and indulgence, and listened obediently to her advice about how best to cope with Sruss and her entourage of kings tomorrow.

There was a spicing of old voluptuaries among the hundred or so wanton young mrem who crowded the banquet hall just after dark. The lighting was garish, the music wild and sensual, the dancing girls skilled and abandoned, their lasciviousness increasing with each garment they stripped away. But though the food and drink were lavish, the service was plain crockery, at least for the most dissolute of all the courtiers. That they were so served had become a mark of distinction among them. They were the courtiers who from time to time had been caught red-handed trying to steal jeweled goblets or service of precious metal. Their punishment was to dine at subsequent banquets from plain crockery. The "Crockercups," as they were sportingly called, were young Tristwyn's most influential courtiers, and the most active in enriching themselves at the auctions, or in buying priceless heirlooms from refugees for a fraction of their true value.

It was their common boast that if the war lasted just a few months longer they would all be rich for life.

They pressed the king tonight for a strict law against dueling within the city, with heavy fines levied against violators. It would not be difficult to foment duels among the refugee noblemrem, who carried old feuds and enmities to Ar with their few salvaged heirlooms. The fines would be a new source of revenue for the court—and the courtiers.

The king was unusually thoughtful as he suffered their blandishments, but for once did not succumb, merely putting them off with vague promises to consider the matter. To their wonder, he remained thoughtful for the rest of the night, sipping his wine with unusual temperance, scarcely nibbling the lavish fare set before him, course after course. His moodiness disappointed both his special friends and his favorite dancing she-mrem, for he left the banquet alone.

His balcony overlooked the New City, crowded as never before with thousands upon thousands of refugees. Two of the three moons shone in the night sky. His mother assured him that the danger would soon pass; his friends all told him to enjoy himself and not to worry. All had warned him against ever letting The Three become too powerful, and now he was also warned against plots to seize the throne. The possibility that this was true was as disturbing as the suspicion that it was not.

He had always trusted his mother in all things, but what if she now proved untrustworthy? That his own grandmother, the legendary Sruss, could ever mean him harm was inconceivable.

These thoughts, more than the prospect of facing angry kings tomorrow, caused him a sleepless night. Even more daunting was the likelihood of making his mother still angrier with him than she already was. But, really, how could he possibly have refused an audience to his grandmother? A senior White Dancer? Sruss? Dawn found him dull and headachy—with nothing resolved.

He felt still less than prepared, hours later, in the audience chamber. The Crockercups also looked dull and headachy, although for other reasons. They stood at a discreet distance from the throne, brilliant as always in their court regalia, useless as always regarding counsel or advice—except where it tended toward their personal profit or aggrandizement. Behind the throne and to its right hung a curtain, behind which stood his mother. She was never officially present at public audiences; although in fact she was always there, and—until today—the decisions were always hers.

He wished for once that she were even more prominent. After all, he was the one who had to face this terrifying assembly, with every king standing before the throne glaring at him like a dragon. They were unarmed, and outnumbered twenty to one by his personal bodyguard, but still he felt

uncomfortable. They looked so fierce! His mother often nagged
him about sitting up straight on the throne, but it was now an
effort to keep his shoulders from slumping, and himself from
sliding forward.

"Your Majesty." Sruss seemed to understand his plight,
and spoke with maternal kindness, as if to a beloved child,
something his real mother never did. "We are here today, by
your leave, to petition you to accept the leadership of a great
league to be formed for the defense of Ar." She outlined the
same arguments that had been so persuasive in the meeting
at her gardens, a few nights before. "All the resources that
can still be salvaged from the kingdoms of the land, and all
the mrempower, shall be concentrated here at Ar. All under
Your Majesty's leadership."

There was a narrowing of eyes among the assembled kings,
and more than one caught himself reaching unconsciously to
his side for a weapon he did not bear today, but such was the
influence of Sruss that even the most irascible held his peace.

The king braced himself, and sat up on the throne straighter
than he ever had in his life. "I accept!" he cried.

There was a strangled cry from behind the curtain to his
right, and again he felt himself sliding forward. But the
maternal kindness with which Sruss continued to address him
again stiffened his backbone. The wizards of The Three had
only bored or amused him in the past; he had issued the
mandate proscribing their free association within the walls
and territories of Ar to please his mother—the reason he
issued most mandates. Now he withdrew the mandate to
please his grandmother.

Then he immediately regretted it, for there was anger in
the second strangled cry behind the curtain. These public
audiences bored him more than wizards, but he decided to
string this one out as long as there was anybody in the
kingdom with a petition. If a stormy interview with his mother
was now unavoidable, he wanted to avoid it until she was
cooler.

How she could argue against a league of kings for the
defense of Ar, he did not know, or against a few old wizards
meeting at times. Except that it was not her idea . . . .

In his nervousness and indecision his fevered eyes swept
into every corner of the crowded audience chamber: armed

soldiers at attention along the brightly painted walls; courtiers straggling deferentially before them in brilliant regalia
(some of Crockercups were so shaky from last night's orgy
that they looked ready to keel over); flags, statuary, armorial
pennons, and glittering mosaics. And directly before him the
fierce warrior kings. At last, as if drawn by magic, he found
himself gazing hypnotically into the eyes of Sruss herself.

"Be the king you were born to be, Your Majesty," she said.
"Be true to yourself, and to the people who look to you for
protection and guidance. Nothing more is expected of you—
and nothing less."

Nor did he vacillate or go back on his word after she and
the kings had departed. There were whispered instructions
from behind the curtain, but for the first time in his life he
did not heed them. He showed unprecedented patience with
the weary parade of shopkeepers, farmers, merchants, and
craftsmren petitioning for the redress of wrongs, real or imagi-
nary. And if his decisions were sometimes callow, they were
at least his own decisions.

There was now only deathly silence behind the curtain.

▲

Sruss dreamed that night, at first with the usual confused
ramblings of images; then suddenly with a vividness she had
not experienced in years. She did not recognize the midnight
landscape—the foothills of a mountainous terrain, broken into
meadows and stands of forest—but she sensed that she was
not alone. Only a single moon glistened in the night sky. The
wild silvery meadow around her seemed deserted.

Still she had the feeling that someone was nearby; someone
she loved, someone who wanted urgently to speak with her.
Turning slowly around she discovered a shadowy figure standing before her, young and beautiful, though dressed in the
shabby garments of a servant.

"Beloved mistress." Srana spoke to her in a hollow anxious
voice. "I have tried again and again to contact you, but each
time some strange power has interfered. You must know
what happened to Kazerclawm by now. All that The Three
have so long feared has come to pass, and the very kingdom
of Ar is now in jeopardy. Some of us escaped the destruction

of the city, and now are fugitives, hunted relentlessly . . ." She paused, as if listening for something.

Then Sruss also became aware of an alien intelligence trying to probe their minds.

"Beware of Cragsclaw," she cautioned Srana. "Above all, do not reveal to me your place of refuge."

Then she sensed the intruder probing still deeper into her mind, and struggled against it, rousing herself from sleep like a swimmer fighting to reach the surface of the sea. It was in dreams that she was most vulnerable to the Evil One, and she awoke both relieved and disappointed.

How much she had wanted to tell her beloved pupil. How much she had wanted to learn from her. Still, she had gained the most heartening information she could have hoped for—Srana was still alive.

▲

Chapter 8
The Collection at Cragsclaw

It was too late for the hapless old charlatan, sprawling on the ground in the midst of an angry mob, to protest that he was no true magician. Charms, philters, love potions, elixirs for whatever ailed you; amulets to protect you from the malice of reptile-demons; predictions of the future. He had always made an easy living, and prudently never stopped long in any one town. He had been in this wretched village less than two days.

He was badly clawed and beaten; his left arm was numb, and he had trouble seeing out of his right eye. They had broken his legs so he couldn't run away. The glib patter that was his stock-in-trade now deserted him. It was hard to think with so many angry people screaming curses at him. Parts of his body were so benumbed that he could hardly feel them.

The riot had erupted so quickly, so unpredictably, that he had had no chance to bolt. That a mrem of his experience in reading the popular mood had been caught so unawares could only mean that he had an enemy here, stirring up the villagers against him, fanning their smoldering distrust of magicians into an explosion of hatred. Who was it? Why should he of all mrem have been singled out for vengeance? Or were magicians again being blamed for the ills of the land?

He had heard about the sack of Kazerclawm and the atrocities at Cragsclaw; the roads were thronged with refugees fleeing before the invaders. But why should magicians be blamed for the invasion? He wasn't a true magician, in any case.

He knew that the afternoon sky was cloudless, and yet was dully aware that a shadow had passed over him, and looked

97

up. Futilely he tried to cry out, to raise his battered arms in defense, to drag his broken body away; but he was helpless, doomed. Four husky mrem held a millstone between him and the sun, then dropped it. The mob shrieked its approval, and the four men hefted the great stone and dropped it again. There was no need to drop it a third time.

▲

In other villages, throughout the countryside, in the most populous cities, such incidents of harrassment and persecution were now being perpetrated all over the land. Nor were mere charlatans and bush magicians the sole victims.

The old mrem was a powerful wizard. Like most wizards he had led a solitary life, but as a matter of self-preservation had grown expert in reading the mood of crowds; his powers of concealment were formidable, and he could teleport himself short distances in emergencies. In his long lifetime he had seen other lynch mobs stirred up, even against himself, but never one stirred up so quickly, or to such a pitch of fury.

He had spotted the two agents who were rousing them, and fled the river city at nightfall. They had penetrated his disguise as a carpenter—a trade at which he was in fact adept—because they themselves were magicians; in whose employ he had no doubt. Everywhere he went these days, in walled cities or the humblest villages, he heard more and more of the common folk—frightened, dispossessed, plundered of all they owned by merciless invaders—blaming The Three for all the calamities that had befallen the land. There was little mystery about why the Evil One should disperse agents to foment hostility against wizards. More mysterious was what had become of the Evil One himself.

The last news of his whereabouts had come with the reports of the fall of Cragsclaw, amidst gruesome atrocities, but the armies of the Eastern Lords, swollen by renegade highlanders and bandits, had since moved on to ravage other strongholds. If he had meanwhile established himself at Cragsclaw—why? Some kind of command center? If he was in fact in command of the invasion, why hadn't he concentrated all the invading forces upon Ar? Once that great city fell, all the lesser strongholds of the mrem could be taken at discretion.

The sole encouraging report he had heard was that the land was being scorched before the invading hordes, denying them sustenance. Somebody at Ar had had at least that much sense of grand strategy. Perhaps the great city was not doomed after all. He knew that other wizards of The Three were rallying there, but so far he had been able to contact only Mithmid, by means of a coded message. Each time he tried telepathy, some probing intelligence interfered. A power of magic capable of such interference was dreadful.

There had been debates among The Three about just how much the Third Eye might remultiply the already formidable powers of the Evil One. More than the most timorous had feared, it seemed. Why he did not now focus that power upon the overthrow of Ar could only mean that he in turn feared something. The unified magic of The Three? That would explain his need to foment hostility everywhere against wizards. Unless it was just one more instance of his insane lust for vengeance . . . .

If his mere attempts to communicate with his fellow wizards were probed by an alien intelligence, he knew that teleportation could be risked only in cases of life or death. But dawn would soon force upon him just such a case. Did the agents who had roused the mob against him know that he was one of the original Seven, entrusted with a fragment of the Khavala? That would explain the relentlessness of their pursuit. Promises of rich donatives, in this time of ruin, would alone goad a mob to outrage.

Dawn was near. The eastern mountains were already silhouetted blackly against the horizon. Soon he would have no choice. But if he himself risked a desperate teleport, he had no right to risk having his fragment of the Khavala fall into the hands of the Evil One. Any increment of his already vast power tipped the scales that much further against The Three.

He waded across the shallow tributary of the Mraal, downstream from the bridge. His pursuers would not expect him to double back to the very place whence he had been driven last evening. The small river city was no refuge, of course. But if the servitors of the Evil One could exploit the general ruin, so could he. After the first hue and cry, nothing could have induced the bargemrem and his son to carry him downriver as a passenger. Only the guarantee of a rich prize, to be paid at Ar, had persuaded them to deliver even a message there—and a small packet.

He found them waiting anxiously for him in their riverfront hovel, surly and suspicious, as if they had had second thoughts. They both reexamined the written guarantee by candlelight, and again shrewdly weighed risk against reward. The latter still prevailed. Not a word was exchanged among them, only some earnest money and a packet. Then the old wizard crept invisibly back into the streets.

Without the fragment of the Khavala to redouble his magic, his powers of concealment were only strong enough to cause the few stragglers he encountered at this early hour to look the other way. But the bands of pursuers now converging on the small river city were far too numerous for such an effect; back and forth through the trees swept their lines, more and more visible, although they no longer brandished torches. The horizon was now a brightening rose-violet, dappled with fluffy pink clouds. It was dawn and he was trapped.

A teleport of a few miles was the most he could now manage. It might carry him out of danger, it might as easily carry him into horrors unimaginable; but in no event would it carry with him his fragment of the Khavala. Whether or not the bargemrem and his son fulfilled their commission, what to them would seem no more than a sliver of red glass was unlikely to fall into evil hands.

He wished he could say the same about himself. There were shouts and cries of anger, as his pursuers in their hundreds poured across the tributary bridge. These were answered from windows and doorways behind him. He had been recognized. The swarm converged from all sides, goaded to fury by the servitors of the Evil One.

Concentrating a lifetime of wizardry, in an inescapable situation of life or death, he disappeared before their eyes. He had directed his reemergence to a water meadow on the far side of the river, some four miles away. From there he might reach the walled city of Marbatan before nightfall.

He was disoriented momentarily when he instead reemerged into a place where it was already night. Slime-encrusted walls surrounded him; a carnal stench thickened the air, and he was terrified by a weird clittering sound, like scores of hungry reptiles grinding their teeth as they scuttled toward him out of the darkness.

He tried to teleport himself again, but was bereft of all magic. A still weirder sound echoed through the nightmarish halls and corridors. Whether it was dark laughter or a shriek of insanity, he knew he was doomed.

▲

Mithmid was careful not to betray any sympathy for the wretched old mrem chained to the stake. The sullen crowd thronging the marketplace certainly did not. Marbatan was not the haven he had expected. Nor could he reasonably expect any more that the last wizard of the Seven, the last bearer of a Khavala fragment still unaccounted for, would join him here as they had agreed. If he tarried here much longer, he might end up chained to a stake himself.

The priests of Marbat, the local nature god, hovered about the condemned mrem with rites and incantations so ancient that nobody in the crowd knew what they meant any more, perhaps not even the priests themselves. They finished just as the last faggots were heaped about the stake, and the public executioner stepped forward with a beaker of flaming oil.

As the smell of singed fur mingled in the air with cries of agony, Mithmid had to be more careful then ever not to betray his feelings. The pathetic old mrem had been a mere hedge wizard, half charlatan, half madmrem; a danger only to himself. But agents of the Evil One were provoking antipathy to magicians everywhere these days. This was the fifth public execution he had witnessed in the last fortnight. The condemned had all been elderly magicians, much like himself. Although none in fact had actually been a member of The Three, it was now clear that the wizards of that great order were the intended victims. In a way, this was heartening.

It could well mean that the Evil One was apprehensive about The Three combining against him. Indeed, its powers, redoubled by the concentrated fragments of the Khavala, and focused upon a common objective by a single mind, could be formidable. That they would be formidable enough to check the Evil One was improbable. He now seemed invincible, his overwhelming powers remultiplied overwhelmingly by the

Third Eye, and yet for some reason he hesitated—or so at least it appeared.

Why? Had his first defeat, followed by long entombment, induced in him a neurotic wariness toward The Three? Or were these the cold calculations of a master plan, aimed perhaps at the regained supremacy of the Old Race? His actions—sometimes brilliant, sometimes childish—were incomprehensible to any rational mind. Judged by the standards of mrem intelligence, Khal was insane.

Mithmid's own actions were now directed toward reaching Ar as swiftly as possible, with his own fragment of the Khavala intact. But he would be sure to attract suspicion if he left the marketplace before the pathetic old hedge wizard was utterly consumed by flames. All old mrem seemed suspect these days. While seeming to watch the execution with the rest of the crowd, he concentrated his thoughts elsewhere . . . .

Upon Ar, foremost of all, and the best means of reaching it safely. The invading hordes were now barely three days' march from Marabat, so it might be prudent, in view of the executions he had seen lately, just to straggle along with the growing stream of refugees, like any other old mrem fleeing west.

Meanwhile other thoughts disturbed his concentration, nebulous, unformed, only half-conscious. It was not now that the idea which was to expand this terrible war into another dimension first came to him, although ever afterwards he associated this day with the foreshadowings of that idea. True, the united fragments of the Khavala were still overmatched by the Third Eye. But there was a power in existence which overmatched even that evil stone . . . .

▲

Cragsclaw had been a mighty fortress, and courageously defended; but when its gates were blasted open by some mysterious force, the garrison was butchered without mercy, and the city itself given over to the atrocities of bandits and desert marauders. Khal reserved for himself only its governor, along with the elegant young governor of Kazerclawm, whom he had brought here with him; the bandit chieftain who had failed to keep its garrison and refugees from breaking out; and an old wizard of The Three he had somehow captured. Taking possession of the palace, he had indulged himself in an orgy of vengeance that lasted weeks.

"Sit here, my good Nizzam," he said one morning. "That's right. No need to tremble so, I'm just checking to see how your fur blends into the general color scheme. Hmmmmmmm, rather muddy, I'm afraid. The governor of Kazerclawm here is your best work." He now addressed his taxidermist, who had just finished arranging the hapless old wizard on a couch.

"I'm only as good as the materials I work with, my lord." The taxidermist fussily touched up the governor's ears with a fine comb. "This one took very good care of himself. You can see it in the glossiness of his fur. This other one"—he nodded toward the bandit chieftain, sitting on a plain camp stool— "was a job of work, I can tell you. I believe I caught his natural look—"

"Very natural, my friend," Khal murmured.

"But you see, my lord, he was such a tufty old rascal to begin with . . . ." He shrugged. "Looks rough beside these others."

"Variety is what we want here," said Khal. "You were recommended to me as the master of your craft, a true artist. Your first efforts prove this, although I realize it is new work for you. As my collection grows, so too will your artistry. There are several specimens already in the dungeons who will be given to you, eventually. As kingdom after kingdom falls, the great ones of the land will be brought here for my special attentions, and yours. My collection grows apace." He beckoned to Maglakh, who had just entered the stately chamber, and he hurried forward to report:

"The bandit chiefs have arrived, my lord."

"Very well, I'll receive them by this couch over here. Some of them may rejoice to see their old rival again, but all will understand the price of failure. You may wait by the door. Someone must hold their hats," he added with a sardonic glitter in his ruby eyes.

Maglakh did what he was told. After what he had witnessed of Khal's vengeance, and the bloodcurdling atrocities in the city below, he was fortunate to be still alive. He knew it, and no doubt Khal knew he knew it. In any case, he bowed the four grisly bandit chiefs into the chamber, and obediently remained by the door, holding their hats.

He caught only snatches of the conference, but knew exactly what it was about. Reinforced by stragglers and escaped soldiers, old Severakh had organized a guerrilla force so effective that the invasion of Ar had actually been stalled. Communications and supply lines were harrassed almost daily. Nor had the best-laid traps or ambushes caught him unawares. Someone in his band evidently had a danger sense so keen that it was magical, and Maglakh was pretty sure he knew who.

Khal himself appeared less concerned with the effects of the guerrilla raids than in recapturing Severakh and, above all, the beautiful Srana. He had had a settee crafted with shimmering white silk, where he intended to display her in all her creamy whiteness, as the cynosure of his collection. His craving for the granddaughter of the Sentinel now seemed to transcend his very interest in the war.

It certainly transcended all else for the four bandit chiefs. Maglakh could see both anxiety and determination in their cunning, ruthless eyes, as one by one he returned their hats at the door. Their fur was literally standing on end.

This amused Maglakh, as he knew it did Khal himself, who was well aware of the instinctive revulsion he caused those visiting him for the first time.

The emissaries from the Eastern Lords who soon arrived were more accustomed to liskash masters. Nor did Khal try in any way to intimidate them, holding their brief conference away from his budding collection of enemies, near the door. Maglakh was again relegated to holding hats, but now he could at least hear what was being said.

"Tell your masters that I have neutralized The Three with my superior magic," Khal boasted. "Tell them they may now proceed with the invasion."

"They have long awaited your personal guidance of this event, my lord," the eldest of the two emissaries said discreetly. "They believe that no consideration now transcends the overthrow of Ar."

Khal sensed that his conduct was being censured, that the Eastern Lords still considered him of no more importance than these two mrem turncoats standing so insolently before him. A useful servant, and no more. His three ruby eyes seemed to glitter with suppressed fury, although he spoke softly, like the hissing of serpents:

"Their will is my law. Let them know that I have established myself here at Cragsclaw the better to overwhelm any renewed efforts by The Three to hinder the invasion. Should they concert all their powers upon a single purpose, be aware that they could yet be formidable."

"That is well understood, my lord," said the elder emissary, again discreetly. "All the more important that your own powers must always be concerted against them . . . ."

Maglakh, holding their hats by the door, was no less discreet, although he missed not a word of the succeeding conference. It seemed that reports were coming in about something called the League of Ar, and that the invading hordes were finding it more and more difficult to live off the land. The boy King of Ar—or at least somebody there—was proving to be a more astute strategist than the Eastern Lords had reckoned on.

"Be assured that I will have ways of disheartening them, when the time comes," said Khal. "Ways that may surprise the mighty Eastern Lords themselves."

His dark laughter resounded through the chamber so insanely that even two such worldly mrem as the emissaries were disconcerted. Maglakh, watching avidly out of the corner of his eye, saw their fur rise in spite of themselves, and chuckled behind one of their hats.

He returned these courteously to them as they departed, but prudently remained by the door. The wretched Nizzam seemed to be thinking the same thing, and hung back inconspicuously in the corner where he had retreated at his first opportunity. Khal was angry, and they both knew it.

"The time will indeed come," he snarled in his raspy gutteral voice, pacing up and back with his curious stalking gait, as if searching for some victim to pounce on. "This land was once ours. This world was once ours, and shall be again. What are these Eastern Lords to me? Mere bastards and degenerates, who pretend affinity with the Old Race. They think I am useful to them, but we shall see who is really useful to whom. They think the war will end with the overthrow of Ar, but that will only be the beginning. I am the supreme power of this world, and there are powers in worlds beyond this which I shall also soon control. What indeed are these Eastern Lords to me?"

He had now worked himself into a rage, stalking angrily up and back, lapsing at times into a hissing gutteral language Maglakh did not understand, although his most furious raging seemed to be directed against The Three. Objects began to twitch and rattle mysteriously all over the chamber; then the stuffed wizard rose from his display couch, and was cruelly hurled back again. Where it might have led, had it not been interrupted at that moment, Maglakh did not like to think. Both he and Nizzam had retreated into the deepest shadows they could find and hugged each other in dread.

Maglakh sprang toward the door at the first knock, and threw it open with a sense of relief. Let somebody else feel the brunt of Khal's wrath. He was surprised to see standing there two carpenters, with a hand-carved settee, inlaid with bone, shell, and precious woods. Its dragon motif was so weird it could only have been designed by Khal himself.

The two carpenters fell back a step as the hideous liskash sorcerer stalked toward them like a ravening predator. Their fur rose and they trembled while he examined their handiwork.

"Excellent work," he pronounced at last, and handed them each a reward beyond their promised fee. "You have done well, and thus are well rewarded. Those who do not please me also receive their deserts." He nodded toward the couches near the head of the chamber.

The two carpenters also nodded, and their fur now stood completely on end. Gingerly they carried the settee to its appointed spot, adjusted it until Khal was satisfied with the arrangement, then nervously bowed their way out. It was grisly work, but most craftsmrem they knew had fared infinitely worse during the sack of Cragsclaw. They themselves were at least still alive . . . .

Khal sat at his secretary's desk, inscribed a few lines on tablets, and sealed them. "Here." He beckoned to Maglakh. "Take this down to the taxidermist Farwakh. He's expecting it. No need to hold hats at the door just now. You'll be holding them there for a long time to come," he added sardonically.

Maglakh could hear his insane laughter shrieking through the chamber behind him, as he hurried out the door with the tablets. A menial task, but at least one that took him away from Khal for a while, whose rage, he sensed, was ready at any pretext to erupt again into vindictive fury. It was best not to be around at such a time.

Nizzam felt the same way, but could only oblige when the liskash sorcerer beckoned him out of the shadows.

"A fine piece of furniture," said Khal. "Sit here, my good Nizzam, so I can see how it suits the other pieces of my collection. That's right. Now turn profile to your left, so you sit facing this other powerful magician, which you also claim yourself to be, I recall. Ah, the very pose. Don't move now." Nizzam was in fact now trembling so badly that the settee beneath him shook. "I want to be certain of the arrangement. For once the clever Farwakh completes his work, it can no longer be changed." Again his insane laughter rang through the grim chamber.

Farwakh was in fact busy mounting an enemy general he had just finished stuffing, with the help of his two brawny sons, into a martial pose, as Maglakh entered the shop. The general had had no great renown, but his fur was a peculiar colorpoint blue, and Khal was exacting about the color scheme of his growing collection. His favorite pastime nowadays was to stroll by the holding cells, while discussing the artistic possibilities of his varihued captives with his taxidermist. He was increasingly frustrated that he had as yet no captive of a flawless cream white.

Opening the sealed tablets and reading them, Farwakh looked the waiting Maglakh speculatively up and down. "Here's the one I told you about, lads," he addressed his sons. "We'll need reinforcing rods, perhaps a cantilever brace. Hold your hands out, please, palms up, fingers splayed. No, more bend in the elbow. That's right . . . ."

Maglakh had obeyed dumbly, but as he listened to the taxidermist explain for his two brawny sons the principles of cantilever bracing, a thought too horrible to contemplate forced itself upon his conscious mind. His pose was like that when he held the hats of visitors in the vestibule upstairs, and he recalled Khal's sardonic remark that he would be holding them there for a long time to come. As he glanced in panic around the cluttered shop, he found himself staring into rows of glass eyes, which stared mockingly back at him. Then he heard someone screaming, pleading, crying out in terror, and at last realized that it was himself. Powerful hands seized him.

"Easy, lads," cautioned the taxidermist. "Be careful of scuff marks."

It was not many days later that Maglakh was back at his old post, in the vestibule of the grand chamber, holding the hats of visitors. This was one job given him by Khal at which he would not fail.

▲

Chapter 9
The City of the Thieves

▲————————————————————————▲

It was now more by habit than expectation that Sruss stood each evening upon the ramparts of Ar, watching the refugees straggle across the stone bridge below into the city. She smiled to herself as she recalled Srana's cleverness. They now communicated regularly, defying entrapment by the Evil One, though Srana was in continual danger of being waylaid by the traps and ambushes of his servitors; bands of thugs and marauders, withdrawn in increasing numbers from the invasion force, concentrated upon her recapture. Their captains knew well the wages of failure, and yet were unsuccessful.

So successful, on the other hand, was the guerrilla army led by Severakh that the entire invasion had bogged down, the timetable for besieging Ar set back several precious days. Harrying supply trains, cutting off stragglers and reinforcements, raiding camps and depots where least expected, then vanishing again as if by conjury—the effect on enemy morale was more damaging than the actual harrassment. The ease with which the guerrillas evaded traps and ambushes, almost as if they were forewarned of danger, caused consternation and mutual suspicions among the captains detailed to the pursuit. There were rumors of torture, even executions, as they sought vainly to discover the traitors.

The guerrillas were in fact forewarned of every trap and ambush, but not by traitors. Without Srana's danger sense, they would long since have perished. As it was, they had become the salvation of Ar, granting the city time to consummate its defenses.

Stones, engines, catapults, moveable ramps, furnaces for

melting lead, cauldrons for boiling oil: never had the great
walls of Ar seemed more formidable. Well could Sruss look
upon them with pride, for she had seen them rise course by
course throughout the glorious reign of her son Talwyn, and
they had been well maintained until Rhenowla began divert-
ing state revenues to her own use. Few of the resources,
concentrated in haste from all lands still unconquered, were
thus wasted on repairs.

The kings of the new League of Ar were sanguine; the
morale of the regular troops, the armed retainers of refugee
nobles, and the motley of irregular militia was also high.
What it would be like when hordes of bandits, desert marauders, renegade highlanders, and cohorts of the Eastern
Lords swarmed the plains below could not be known.

No one did more to bolster this morale, to encourage and
unite the efforts of all the people toward the common welfare, than Sruss herself. She even heartened The Three, who
now met daily and without interference from the palace, to
believe in their ultimate victory—though every discussion
seemed to lead inevitably back to the Third Eye. Their magic
would be desperately needed once the siege began, but if its
total force was neutralized by the Evil One—what then?

Fortune was a goddess; her priests thrived these days. Her
temple in the river quarter of the Old City was cleaner and
better attended than Sruss could remember it ever having
been before. Two events happened that very night which
made her wonder if this primordial goddess had not heard
the prayers and supplications of her worshippers after all.

The first began with what she thought initially to be mere
impudence—common enough among the promiscuous mobs
of refugees she encountered daily in the streets. She noticed
a mrem waving his hat to her from the drawbridge below,
some drunken old rascal or vagabond, by the looks of him.
But this was no time to accept appearances, and she looked
closer. At last she smiled. It was none other than Mithmid.
Years had passed since she last saw him; generations since
they shared in the old dynastic upheavals of the city.

He watched her descend the masonry steps like a young
she-mrem. All the young mrem of his generation had been
hopelessly in love with her, and seeing her again evoked
pangs of longing and remembrance. But time was short; at

stake was the very survival of their people. He was among
the last stragglers to reach Ar, barely a day's march ahead of
the enemy vanguard. Tomorrow the great city would be
besieged in earnest.

"Scouts have been coming in since early this morning."
Sruss sensed his urgency, and came straight to the point.
They were old friends, old allies in other wars; there was no
need for the blandishments of the court, or even formal
courtesies. "You're fortunate to have arrived here today, dear
Mithmid."

He was indeed fortunate to be still alive; only because the
land had been scorched before the advancing hordes, forcing
them to depend on vulnerable supply lines, had he reached
Ar safely at all. Even so it had been a harrowing journey.
Others lacked his powers of concealment, and the atrocities
he had witnessed were a grim presage of the fate of Ar,
should its great walls be breached by the advancing hordes.

"Fortunate indeed, my lady," he said. The twilight streets
were thronged and chaotic; thousands had no other home,
and yet they parted deferentially before Sruss. He was gratified to be seen walking arm in arm with her, although the
curiosity of many, at seeing her in company with so shabby
an old vagabond, also annoyed him. His first purchase in Ar
would be a new suit of clothes. "Is the city prepared?"

She explained the formation of the League of Ar, and
described what had been done to resist assault. "The Three
are also united, and now meet openly each day," she added.
"Your arrival will hearten them."

They exchanged a meaningful look. There was no need to
explain why the great order of wizards should need to be
heartened at this hour. But Mithmid had pondered much
during his flight across country, and had reasons for both
greater optimism and more disheartening despair.

As he started to explain these, Sruss tactfully interrupted
and returned to the preparations for the coming siege. He
understood at once. Even during his long quest for the Third
Eye he had heard about the Silent Ones. One or more of
them were probably within earshot at this very moment.

Everything changed as they entered her gardens. He remembered well the old palace, and was amazed at the changes
wrought in what had once been no more than its servants'

wing. There were no Silent Ones here; all the other Dancers were soon lodged elsewhere for the night, the immediate neighborhood cleared of spies, and discreet messengers dispersed throughout the city. Rhenowla would of course learn about tonight's gathering of all the wizards of Ar, but the first sight tomorrow of enemy towers advancing upon the city walls like avenging giants would temper her thoughts of reprisal. When the battle started, she might even be glad The Three had united.

The last to arrive was blunt old Dollavier; only a single wizard of the original Seven was still missing, and Dollavier bluntly accounted for him.

"Khal has him by now," he said. "Whether dead or alive, I don't know. For his sake, better the former than the latter."

"Then Khal also has at least two fragments of the Khavala, in addition to the Third Eye," said Mithmid, and there were groans among the scores of wizards assembled in the pavilion.

"Only one," Dollavier contradicted him, and held out a second ruby fragment for all to see, along with his own. "Old Holclyn knew there was no escape for him, but managed to send this on to me before he was captured. A pair of bargemrem, father and son, delivered it to me within the hour. I had to pay them a stiff premium, but it was worth any price."

This was the second fortunate event today, and Sruss saw that the wizards were again encouraged. Whatever caused Mithmid to remain doubtful, he said nothing to dampen their spirits, at this time at least.

"Their plan is obviously to storm the walls," he said. "I've seen their towers. They'll mount catapults, and try to sweep the walls of defenders, while they barge their assault teams across the river. They may also launch grappling lines from the towers themselves, and pull themselves across hand over hand, covered by archers and slingers. You know how agile these desert marauders are."

"Costly tactics," said Dollavier, and there were nods throughout the pavilion. "Although the Eastern Lords won't consider mere loss of lives an obstacle."

"I doubt if they now consider Ar itself an obstacle," said Mithmid. "The campaign seems planned to overthrow an unprepared, demoralized city. That will be their first surprise, thanks to the League of Ar." All eyes turned gratefully toward Sruss. "They might still succeed," he continued, "if they are able to concentrate enough towers on any one section of the wall. An intensive missile barrage would make that section untenable. So it's there that we ourselves must be ready to concentrate all our own force."

Acclamation rang through the pavilion like a battle cry. They were not the legendary wizards who had first created the myth of The Three, generations ago; but they were many, a host, a veritable army of magicians recruited from all over the land. United, their individual powers focused by a single will upon a common objective, they might be truly formidable. Despite some peevish grumbling from Dollavier, a second acclamation nominated Mithmid their ringleader.

Every fragment of the Khavala in their possession, including the pair held by Dollavier, was at once forged into a bracelet. The Seven, scattered across the land in a futile search, were no more. It was now the One; capable of focusing through Mithmid, a wizard of wizards, all their united powers. He clasped the bracelet around his wrist in silent determination, and stood before them, a true leader. No harangue about the dangers they faced was needed, for these had been anticipated a full generation and more. Neither did he mention yet his apprehensions of dangers beyond those they had anticipated. For nothing mattered now but the concentration of all their powers on a single objective. Nothing would matter again—for himself, for the kingdom of Ar, perhaps for the very mrem—if the first furious assault upon the walls succeeded.

Without another word he retired to the apartment Sruss had allocated to him, while The Three filed silently out into the night. Through his strange rambling dreams he sensed an evil intelligence probing his mind, but he was too strong to be overcome. His bouts of sleeplessness were caused more by fears about whether the walls of Ar were equally too strong to be overcome. Once breached, nothing would stem the raging flood of marauders, not all the concentrated powers of The Three.

The dreams Sruss had that night were also disturbed by wild fears and premonitions. What had become of Srana? With their new means of communication they could evade the vigilance of the Evil One for minutes at a time. But this was the fourth consecutive night Srana had failed to contact her, and she worried that her very anxiety somehow hampered telepathy between them.

▲

Severakh could not blame anxiety for the plight of his guerrillas, only the unavoidable attrition of this kind of warfare. Any soldier killed in action meant a permanent loss of mrempower. Relentlessly harrassed and ambushed by bandit gangs, they had been driven farther and farther from sources of recruitment, into the remotest marchlands of any known kingdom. He now counted fewer than a hundred in his band, and many of these were crippled with wounds.

It was no longer an effective fighting force. His task was to harry the invaders, threaten their supply lines, cut off stragglers and foragers, and force them to divert as much of their resources as possible from the march upon Ar, to delay it by any means, and thus buy time for the defenders. It was galling that he could no longer do anything but just try to survive.

That was no excuse for slackness, however. There was continual grumbling over his drills and inspections—though not when he was believed to be within earshot—but that he considered a good sign. A bitching soldier is a happy soldier, the principle was universal. It was when troops were too silent, or too idle, that a commander had to worry. The martial dances of his own mrem might still have won prizes at any festival in Kazerclawm.

"No, no, lad," he groused. "A feint is always used to set up a thrust. Try it again. Now once more. You'll never be a true warrior until you master technique. And that means drill, drill, drill. Until every move is instinctive, until action precedes thought. Try it once more."

In fact he had never had so spirited a recruit as young Branwe. His youth and agility made him conspicuously the best martial dancer in the troop; his swordsmremship, despite flaws in his technique, was inspired, so inspired at times that the crusty old soldier could not help resenting it, in spite of himself. Not out of professional jealousy, but only at seeing such gifts born into a common potboy at an inn, the lowliest of the low.

Severakh's camp was as always well ordered; scouts were posted, and every entrance into the secluded mountain dell picketed with alert troops. They had been harried so far south that the snowy peak of the Kazerclaw was now barely visible above the horizon. Gray-bottomed clouds drifted across the afternoon sky. The five recruits taking part in the drill, including Branwe, lunged like specter swordsmrem in and out of the fleeting shadows.

Severakh sat on a lumpish boulder, grimly correcting every flaw he noticed—and he missed nothing. He had long recognized it as a flaw in his own composition that the danger sense of a mrem in his profession should be so dull. But he now sensed that something was wrong, and turned around.

"Cajhet!" he barked. "Come here this instant! Where have you been this last week? I thought we had lost you in the ambush down at Rushwater Cave."

"No, sir," said Cajhet, beginning to tremble. He had been tiptoeing around his commander's back, the only way he could reach the mess wagon unseen. He had in fact been unusually successful the last several days in skulking out of sight. "I was, uh, just on my way . . . that is . . ." He broke down and stared innocently off into space.

Severakh shook his head in disgust. "No loss if you hadn't come back from Rushwater." He started to turn around, then hesitated. "Say, aren't you on scout duty this week?"

"Yes, sir. That is, in a manner of speaking."

"Are you, or aren't you?"

"I am, sir. But I exchanged duty with a mrem in Blue Company, two watches for one."

"Why?"

"Well, sir, it's like this. I thought it would be more convenient all around, seeing that we've been on the run so long—"

"You've certainly been on the run." Severakh eyed him sternly. "It hasn't anything to do with liskash, has it?"

"Well, sir, in a manner of speaking, you might say it has."

"I thought so. We're in wild country now, so there are naturally more liskash, and they're naturally bolder. But their magic is defensive. It's for keeping you from hurting them, not the other way around. How many times have I told you that?"

"Well, sir, I believe fairly often."

Severakh rose to give him a thorough dressing-down, but again something behind his back made him uncomfortable. The graceful figure hurrying toward him had the keenest danger sense he had ever known; they would have been trapped fifty times over, had Srana not alerted them betimes. She pointed anxiously toward something behind her.

"A dragon," she cried. "I felt something was wrong, and went to investigate. It caught your scout with some kind of teleport maneuver, disappearing and reappearing from the opposite direction. It's still coming this way."

The scout was the very one Cajhet had exchanged duty with, and he was nodding smugly to himself, when he caught a fierce glare from Severakh, and immediately looked dutiful and concerned.

"Strange behavior," muttered the old warrior. "Dragons have been known to kill, but they always devour their prey on the spot. And you say it's still coming?"

"I climbed a tree for a better angle," said Srana, dressed like a common soldier, which only made her charming figure more enticing. "It was less than a mile away, and moving as if it knows we're here."

Severakh exchanged a meaningful look with her. Not just bandits, but every evil creature in the world had lately been converging on them, or so it seemed. The most dangerous were the wild liskash; semi-intelligent bipedal reptiles, they ranged in size from the squat carrion-eaters—the "kashies," as the troops called them—to the big, mean carnivores, half against the height of a mrem. The deadliest of these were the cave reptiles, and after the near disaster at Rushwater, he had avoided cave country. He was certain that at least some of the scouts reported missing had not just lost their way.

The tactics of the bandit gang in that ambush had been to drive them into the most dangerous caverns, perhaps knowing what lurked inside. Was this the opposite tactic—using a dragon to drive them into an ambush of lurking bandits? One thing was certain: They no longer dared remain at large in open country.

"Bring in the scouts." Severakh sent a trio of messengers

flying. "Cajhet, you're good at sneaking about. Sneak down to the head of this dell, and inform the men there what's happening. We're not going to be forced to run. Above all, we're not going to panic."

His strategy was a tactical withdrawal toward the sole inhabited place in this wild hill country. No city-state of the mrem was so resolutely independent as Ravarbal; none so predatory toward its neighbors. There was said to be a people called the Yozgat whom the very Ravarbalians dreaded, but whether these truly existed, or were merely the bugbears of legend, no man could say. The Ravarbalians were mysterious enough themselves.

Their walled city had been erected by slaves and war captives generations ago; to this day it was the final resort of all who shunned the law: the end of the civilized world—if Ravarbal could in fact be called civilized. Its depredations on travelers and caravans were tempered only by the fear of punitive expeditions. City-states as far away as Ar had proposed these again and again over the years, but the Ravarbalians had always been able to avert punishment with timely gifts and promises.

Severakh knew he too would have to make some timely gifts and promises, veiling the threat of the most vindictive punitive expedition ever launched, to get so large a band inside the city gates. The trouble was—he knew it, and the cunning Ravarbalians would also know it—that he was unsure of how much he had to back up such threats. What if the Eastern Lords conquered Ar? No city-state could then stand against them. They would launch their own punitive expeditions against all who had harbored their enemies . . . .

But first there was the dragon. They were ponderous, slow-moving creatures, and none too bright, but like all reptiles they wielded powers of magic, and could never be trusted. The mrem had ruthlessly hunted them from the settled land; they were now rare in the very wilderness.

It was not long before the monster lumbered into sight, its scaly head darting serpentlike from side to side in search of prey. Its scaly gray-green hide was scarred from old battles; its flared nostrils snorted anger and belligerence. At last spotting the armed mrem retreating in military order at the far side of the dell, it roared defiance. This was more strange

behavior in a dragon, which normally relied on reptile magic
and stealth to pounce on its victims. It confirmed Severakh's
judgment that the creature was not attacking alone.

The safest apparent retreat from the dell was northwest,
between a jutting volcanic tor and a wooded hillock, and the
dragon seemed to be herding them in that very direction.
The scouts Severakh sent out to reconnoiter were told what
to look for, and they found it.

"Must be hundreds of 'em, sir," reported the first scout to
return. "Armed to the whiskers, and all crouching behind
trees or rocks."

Severakh doubted the numbers were so great, or the bandits wouldn't have needed an ambush for their attack. But
probably great enough, should his mrem be taken by surprise, and forced to defend themselves on two fronts. He
ordered a clatter of swords against shields. The bandits knew
they were here; silence was wasted.

Strangely, the dragon was not fazed by the wild clatter, but
continued to lumber forward as if enchanted. The first javelin
was hurled from beyond effective range, and glanced harm-
lessly off its scaly hide. Bolder mrem ran forward to hurl their
javelins with better effect—but the dragon disappeared.

There were cries of pain and alarm as it reappeared and
seized a mrem in its terrible jaws, chewing the life out of
him. Twice more it repeated this maneuver, and Severakh
had no choice but to order a retreat in exactly the direction
he did not want to go.

The dragon at once ceased to attack, and again began to
lumber back and forth across the dell, herding them between
the volcanic tor and the wooded hillock, where the horde of
ambushers lay in wait. Twice it levitated to the treetops, as if
to assure itself that nobody was trying to hide from it there.
Several mrem tried through stealth or agility to outflank it,
but all were seized or driven back.

Severakh at last resigned himself to a mass attack upon the
creature; the loss of life could be appalling, but at least some
would escape. To be caught between a dragon and a horde of
bandits meant annihilation. He beckoned to his signalmrem,
but before he could order the charge he noticed Srana and
young Branwe striding directly at the creature from its left
side. The latter held his sword before him, a feeble weapon

against a monster more than twice his height at the shoulder,
with a hide like armor.

But for some reason the brute did not look in their direction, although twice they stopped to confer, the second time
almost close enough to be overheard. Then they backed away
a few paces. Still the dragon did not so much as glance at
them. Srana remained at that distance, the better to focus her
thoughts. Then Branwe suddenly darted forward, leapt with
amazing agility up the scaly hide, clawing and scrambling and
vaulted onto the dragon's neck. With both hands he plunged
his sword into its brain.

Writhing, screaming, viciously snapping its monstrous jaws,
it staggered forward, then all at once collapsed. Branwe leapt
free while it was actually falling to the ground, to save himself
from being crushed underneath. Srana hurried to him, but
fortunately he was not injured. A curt nod was his only
commendation from Severakh. The old commander was too
harried for time to squander it on idle praise or congratulations.

His first assessment, that there were not enough marauders lying in ambush for an open assault on his mrem, was
based on the flimsiest of scouting reports. He could well be
wrong. A superior force may also attack from ambush, if
conditions are favorable. Though it might be hours yet before
the ambushers learned that the dragon was dead, that their
trap had been sprung, they would not abandon pursuit. The
best strategy now was to try and steal a march on them.

Through wooded dells and barrens, across tumbling rills,
over foothills that rose steeper and steeper before them,
Severakh soon had his entire band marching in good order
toward the infamous mountain stronghold of Ravarbal.

Its walls were a dingy red-yellow in the evening sun; its
gates were already shut for the night by the time they reached
it. Nor were they welcomed. Scores of villainous faces glowered hostilely down at them from the ramparts. Generations
of those fleeing the law had found a ready sanctuary here. It
was otherwise with those fleeing the Eastern Lords, and it
was full night before Severakh—pleading, threatening, cajol-
ing, bribing, and haggling—at last got the poor remnant of
his guerrilla army into the city.

The narrow, crooked streets were as foul and villainous-
looking as the thousands of curious mrem and kits who lined

them. A few torches burned in cressets on the stone walls; but most of the light came from a peculiar type of lantern carried by individuals, which looked suspiciously like it had evolved from the dark lanterns used by thieves. The gawking of the younger Ravarbalians was shameless, their remarks rudely personal, and they did not seem to care who overheard them. The older mrem stared in astonishment—at Branwe.

A few actually came out into the street, and held up their lanterns so they could examine him closer. If anything, their astonishment seemed to increase. Soon there were so many people examining him, with uninhibited remarks about his fur and features, that he was quite surrounded.

He was dressed exactly like the rest of the guerrillas; obviously he had never been here before. Or had he?

He could only shrug in embarrassment.

▲

Chapter 10
Dragonneck Gorge

▲━━━━━━━━━━━━━━━━━━━━━━━━━━━━━━━▲

Plunder breeds plunderers; rap-
ine feeds on the ravished. The Eastern Lords had mobilized a
formidable host against the great city of Ar, but the spoils of
earlier conquests—towns, villages, city-states, whole kingdoms overrun—had recruited auxiliaries vaster still in number. The Mraal still flowed placidly between its banks, but
the plains beyond now flooded over with wild, seething,
numberless hordes of marauders. They had appeared in a
single night.

The wooden towers were larger, more complex, and certainly more numerous than Mithmid had reported. The clangor of axes—felling the groves, forests, and orchards around
the city for the timber to build still more engines and towers—
echoed from the great walls. The defenders ranged along the
ramparts were aghast at the spectacle below them. Few truly
believed that Ar was not doomed, certainly not the young
king, or the Crockercups hovering obsequiously around him
on the parapet above the Southland Gate. All were clad
resplendently in silken robes, but their jeweled daggers were
purely ornamental; none bore real weapons, or would have
known how to wield them if they had. Though the drawbridge
was up, never had the river seemed so narrow. Some of the
great wooden towers drawn up on the opposite shore overtopped the very parapet where they stood.

Rhenowla was conspicuous among the splendid regalia of
the courtiers. She had kept her seamstresses up half the night
finishing a new gown for the occasion, and it rankled her that
more attention was still paid to Sruss, attired modestly in a
simple white robe. However, she was too cunning to reveal

121

her displeasure, or interfere in the military dispositions worked out among the city prefects and the kings of the League of Ar.

She had never expected such hordes of enemies, such engines and towers arrayed before the walls. She now blamed her late husband for not raising them still higher, though at the time she had opposed his expenditure in building them at all.

While trying on her splendid new gown last night, she had had fancies about inspiring the defenders today with her radiant beauty, and had planned to stand supreme here on the parapet like their guiding star. And indeed she was radiant: Her high amber coloring glowed sensually in the morning sunlight, whose beams reflected from her priceless tiara, her costly array of brooches, earrings, bracelets, rings, and bangles with an electric glitter. But the furious activity on and around the towers facing her across the river—catapults being readied, files of slingers and archers pouring out onto some platforms, troops loading spring-swivels with grapnel lines on others, rafts being towed toward armed companies all along the shore—gave her second thoughts.

"The palace is the fit place for a king, my darling," she whispered intimately to her son. "You've done your duty by appearing here. Let's not interfere with theirs." Without waiting for him to reply, she ordered the retirement of the court entourage.

The Crockercups were the first down the stairs; they did not stop until safely ensconced within the palace, where a special banquet was immediately prepared for their delectation. They ordered the palace guards not to admit anyone who might be bringing bad news about the battle. If this was to be their last banquet, they were determined to enjoy it—whether the king presided or not.

Young Tristwyn in fact did not join them that day, and only rarely in the days that followed. He had obediently started down the stairway from the parapet with his entourage, but each downward step deepened his sense of guilt. His mother seemed to sense his vacillation, and took his hand and leaned affectionately against him. They reached the street together, but no farther, and she was vexed to feel him draw away from her. Concentrating all her infallible powers of attractiveness, she was still unable to impose her will on him.

Her slanted eyes narrowed, and she glanced vindictively up at the parapet above. Her failure could only mean that stronger powers of magic were being used to thwart her. Every wizard of The Three had gathered this morning upon the ramparts. There also stood Sruss herself. The battle lines were now drawn in more ways than one.

"Please return to the palace, Mother," said young Tristwyn. He did not look directly at her, but his dissipated, childishly innocent face wore an expression she had never seen there before. Not exactly defiance, but a kind of resolve—the look of a king. "The city is under attack. My place is on the ramparts, not hiding in the palace." He raised his eyes for an instant; then guiltily lowered them again. "Forgive me," he muttered, and he turned away and climbed the masonry steps back up to the parapet.

Rhenowla's beautiful face now also assumed a look of resolve, but it was not the look of a queen, or even a queen mother. She could hardly protest her son's action in public; she dared not castigate publicly so revered a figure as Sruss, for any attempt to discredit her with the people would probably rebound on her own head. The Three? She smiled cruelly to herself as she followed her honor guard through the streets, now silent and deserted, back to the palace.

Magicians were being stoned to death and burned at the stake throughout the land. Ar needed scapegoats as well, to appease the frightened multitude, whose ancient superstitions always overcame their good sense in times of trouble, and to assume the blame for the present calamity. Few things would so grieve Sruss as their destruction. Rhenowla scarcely heeded the thunderous uproar from outside the walls, as she contrived scheme after scheme for avenging this challenge to her power . . . .

The first attack was so tremendous that it nearly paralyzed the outnumbered defenders by its sheer vehemence. Boulders and pots of fire rained down upon the ramparts, amid clouds of slingstones and arrows; grapnel lines arched across the river and caught, and hand over hand with ferocious agility hordes of skirmishers poured from the towers. Down on the river below a crazy flotilla of rafts and captured barges

pushed off, laden with armed troops, scaling ladders, and
grappling lines. The noise of their wild battle cries echoed
from the walls like claps of thunder.

The very kings of the League of Ar fell back before the first
onslaught, but they rallied, and firmed their confused and
frightened troops by example. A troop of axmrem, armored
against the rain of sling-stones and arrows sweeping the ramparts, attacked the grapnel lines with powerful strokes, and
skirmishers plummeted into the waters below by the hundred. Boulders crashed down upon the defenders; fire pots
ignited their machines and catapults. New waves of grappling
lines now began to arc upwards from the approaching flotilla
below, too many for the harried axmrem to repel. Scaling
ladders were raised, ready to breast the walls the instant the
raft, barge, or riverboat supporting them was close enough.

The moveable ramps of the defenders now went into action, and boulder after boulder, with deadly aim, crushed
one vessel after the other in the crazy flotilla below. Then the
ramps themselves began to be crushed in turn, as the catapults across the river redirected their aim. Sling-stones and
arrows continued to take a fearful toll. So long as the great
wooden towers of the enemy overtopped the walls of Ar even
the most spirited defense was ultimately doomed.

The tallest of these was positioned near the foot of the
stone span, at the other end of which yawned the gap whence
the drawbridge had been raised. While its catapults swept
the parapet above the defenders, a team of sappers barged
unopposed across the river below, and began undermining
the gate.

At that moment occurred an event which turned the tide of
battle, today, and for months to come. Sruss and young
Tristwyn, driven from the parapet by the relentless catapult
barrage, had retired behind the shield wall protecting The
Three. The scores of assembled wizards stood in a compact
mass, their thoughts concentrated on freeing their minds of
all reserve or interference. Mithmid stood at the fore, a
lifetime of wizardry, remultiplied by the fragments of the
Khavala, directed against the great tower facing the gate.

Minutes passed in utter silence. If the attackers thought
about the strange assembly of old mrem at all, they probably
dismissed them as mere priests uselessly supplicating some

god or goddess for deliverance. Then all at once the great tower began to vibrate at its native resonance, more and more violently. The explosion shattered it to splinters.

Mithmid immediately raised his left hand, as if focusing the bracelet on his wrist, and again tapped the concentrated mindpower of The Three. Minutes later another tower vibrated to splinters. Then another. The attackers were thrown into confusion, their catapults unattended, and swarms of defenders surged back onto the ramparts in time to repel the scaling ladders with swords, poles, melted lead, pikes, and cauldrons of boiling oil. A tower with a triple deck crowded with archers shattered to the ground.

Renewed battle cries thundered into the morning air, but now these came from inside the city. Those moveable ramps not destroyed by the catapults were repositioned, and boulders again crashed down upon the flotilla below with deadly aim. Battle priests could now be seen moving authoritatively up and back among the hordes of marauders, rallying them for a second attack. It came, and was again beaten back. Then yet another attack, this time without any real spirit. At last the attackers fell back to regroup. The first assault upon the great city of Ar had successfully been repulsed.

Meanwhile Sruss was attending to The Three. The effort had exhausted them. Several old men had collapsed, and several more were teetering, supported bodily by their colleagues. Mithmid was still conscious, but seemed dazed by the tremendous effort of concentration. The shattering of but one more tower might also have shattered the mindpower of The Three. Those still capable of thinking clearly were happy indeed that the enemy had withdrawn for today.

What would tomorrow bring? That was the question of the hour, and few among the multitudes crowded into Ar slept soundly that night, so apprehensive were they about its answer.

The attack was launched just after dawn—if it could be called a real attack. It was more like a probe, or reconnaissance in force. New rafts had been built, new catapults remounted on the remaining towers; these were drawn up a full mile from the riverbank, and only a single one trundled forward with the advancing hordes. It was shattered while being positioned at the foot of the bridge.

The Three had recovered enough of their vitality overnight

to muster at least this much effort. How much more effort they could have exerted against another full-scale assault was doubtful; perhaps it was fortunate they were not tested.

But it was evident by now that so long as the enemy could not position towers on the opposite bank to sweep the ramparts of defenders, skirmishers trying to surmount them from rafts and barges or hand over hand across grappling lines were just too few and too vulnerable to succeed.

It was exactly one week later, while the populace joyously celebrated their deliverance, that a sentry reported that the Mraal was receding from its banks. The water level continued to drop slowly over the next several hours, then at an alarming rate. There were no more celebrations in Ar.

▲

"That's more like it," exclaimed Severakh. "I knew there had to be some reason for such natural ability. I've seen great soldiers rise from the commonest stations in life" —which was in fact exactly what he had done himself—"but you have to be born with such gifts. Not that your technique couldn't stand improvement," he added as a matter of principle. "Drill, drill, drill. It's the only way you'll ever become a great warrior, lad."

"Yes, sir," said Branwe, still dazed by the revelations of the past hour.

Could he really be the only living son of a noblemrem, though that noblemrem may have come to Ravarbal fleeing reprisals for some crime? He knew he had been abandoned at the Blue Dragon as a kit, and the Ravarbalians who now came from all over the city to inspect him, had without exception affirmed that he bore an uncanny resemblance, both in fur and feature, to a noblemrem known only as the Shadow Warrior. It was widely believed that he had been slain by some implacable enemy, along with his entire family, in revenge for some bygone transgression. Yet all knew the legend that the youngest son had escaped in the arms of a faithful nurse.

Could it be true? He hoped so, and not for his own sake alone. Rough living seemed only to enhance Srana's beauty. Some found her cold and aloof; but through their months together in camp and on the march, during skirmishes and flight, in all weathers, in hope and success and despair, he had come to appreciate as never before how warm and caring she really was. To have pressed his attentions on her at this time would have been unchivalrous, even contemptible. Enough to know that she was more open and trusting with him than with anybody else, and to seek in all things to be worthy of that trust. Besides, he was still awkward in her presence.

She had listened to the revelations of his possible ancestry as though sincerely glad for his sake; but also as if she knew more about the mysterious Shadow Warrior than the Ravarbalians themselves. The look with which she now regarded him combined both speculation and concern for his safety.

"Vengeance is Khal's only god," she said cryptically. "Nothing would save you, nothing would save any of us, should he learn what we've learned here tonight. What became of Mamre? She'll know the truth, if anyone does."

Branwe repeated everything she had told him about his infancy. That he had been abandoned by a nurse fleeing some kind of danger seemed to fit the legend of a surviving youngest kit of the Shadow Warrior. But what if there were things Mamre had not told him? And what indeed had become of the only mother he had ever known?

They were gathered in the common room of an inn that reminded him of the Blue Dragon only by default: slatternly servants, a villainous clientele, and greasy, overspiced fare that needed drafts of the heavy mountain wine to wash it down. Mamre would have made short work of everything disagreeable here, including the innkeeper himself, a tufty, broken-toothed old scoundrel who never showed his claws, rumor said, because he had had them extracted by a public executioner before fleeing here to Ravarbal.

"Mamre was preparing to flee to the citadel, the last time I saw her," said Branwe. "If she made it there safely, then she was probably among the refugees who escaped Kazerclawm. What would become of her then, I don't know."

"Headed straight for Ar," cried Severakh, "and didn't stop until she got there. At least, that's what she'd do if she had any sense."

"She was a sensible mrem." Srana looked more thoughtful than ever. "And a mrem of enterprise and courage."

Branwe nodded eagerly. "She must be alive. I'm sure of it."

Srana looked at him and smiled, pleased by this outburst of loyalty. But the issues here were too deep and uncertain for further comment, especially within earshot of so many uncertain mrem. Unconsciously she fingered the lavaliere around her neck. Using the code she had worked out for communicating with Sruss, through cryptic allusions to the secret lore of the White Dancers, was dangerous, though nothing was more dangerous now than inaction.

Enemies outside the walls, and treachery within: It was only a matter of time until tonight's revelations—whether true or not—reached the ears of the Evil One. If he had sent gangs of bandits, the very dragons of the hills, in pursuit of those who had merely thwarted him in Kazerclawm, he might launch armies to avenge himself on a son of the Shadow Warrior.

Her room was as noisome as the tavern below. By paying extra she had managed to get its wretched cot changed with fresh bedclothes, frayed, coarse, and grayish, but at least clean. A guard posted to sleep with his bedroll spread in front of her door out in the corridor insured her privacy. With her mindpower remultiplied by the fragment of the Khavala, she needed only moments to put herself into a trance, to probe the dreams of a mind conditioned to withstand any probing but hers . . . .

Sruss found herself in a mountain pass. It was uncannily familiar, and at last she recalled crossing it one chilly winter morning with her beloved Talwe, when she was young. She felt young now; dreams sometimes bequeathed that magic upon the elderly, and she strolled buoyantly across the silvery landscape through the light of double moons. Then she recalled that this very pass led to Cragsclaw, and her danger sense caused her to hesitate.

Black mountains loomed on either side of her; a raiding night-wind bit her cheek. As she turned to retrace her steps, she noticed a tent not far away; there was a light inside, and she cautiously approached. Who could possibly have spread his tent in this bleak mountain pass? She recalled hearing from refugees to Ar about the recent boldness of cave liskash.

She hesitated again, but this time was not disturbed by any sense of danger.

She drew back the flap, and peered inside. The figure standing in the shadows opposite her was indistinct, nebulous, like a vision not fully imagined. There were no candles, no lanterns, or campfire. She was unsure where the light came from as she slipped into the tent and dropped the flap behind her. The strange figure became even less distinct for a moment, hardly more vivid than the shadows it stood among, but then grew more and more lucid, more corporeal, and at last stepped radiantly forward into the light. It was Srana.

" 'Let out your breath before you bend your back,' " she quoted from the lore of the White Dancers. " 'The steps are never perfect, so you must adjust to the small mistakes . . . .' "

Only another White Dancer could have grasped the underlying significance of the recitation, but for once Sruss had difficulty constructing an intelligible picture from arcane hints and allusions, until at last she realized that the very shadows from which Srana had emerged also had meaning. That was the key which unlocked all the rest.

The Shadow Warrior? The first great enemy of the Evil One? She grasped the essence of what Srana was telling her, though some references remained obscure. The Three could perhaps elucidate these for her later. This contact had already been dangerously prolonged. She would ask Mithmid, first thing tomorrow . . . .

But Srana read her thoughts, and instead directed her by allusion to someone named Mamre, who may have been among the first refugees to reach Ar. More and more apprehensive about leaving themselves vulnerable so long, Sruss was determined nonetheless that there be no mistakes in what she recognized as of vital importance. But the first cryptic allusions were hardly out of her mouth, when her danger sense fairly caused her fur to stand on end, and she found herself alone in the tent.

She knew that she was dreaming. Srana must have awakened herself from sleep, or whatever kind of trance state she had assumed in order to communicate, believing that she herself would at once do the same. But at first she could not. They had gone undetected as long as it was Srana alone who spoke, which pointed to some concealing force exerted by the

Khavala fragment. Struggling and struggling, her own force was not enough to pull her upwards to the surface of consciousness. She could do nothing more than batten down the tent flap.

The sounds rumbling through the darkness outside grew ever closer and more ominous. They were like the low gutteral snarls of the liskash, but eerie and unreal.

She was startled by the ripping of canvas, and whirled around. Reptilian claws were tearing an opening, and she saw a face so hideous with malice that it might have belonged to the Evil One himself. Then more claws began to rend the canvas on the other side of her, then still more. At last the tent flap itself was attacked.

The situation was desperate, but she had known too many dangers in her long life to panic, too many adventures and tribulations, and concentrated all her will on awakening. The eerie liskash clawing at the tent seemed to sense her resistance, and their fury became that of demons. Reptile-demons. That was what they were. The Evil One must have succeeded at last in what The Three most feared of him.

To fall into their evil claws was a fate so ghastly that Sruss fairly hurled her soul across the ether of unconsciousness, as reptilian claws were actually grabbing for her. She lay upon her bed, exhausted and panting for breath, still so disoriented that she needed several minutes to reassure herself that she was really safe in her own room.

Most dreams are forgotten at the instant of awakening; this one must never be, and she concentrated with all the discipline of a White Dancer to reconstruct the message that had nearly cost her her soul.

Yes, she would indeed search out someone called Mamre. It seemed that some lad the female had raised as a son was in mortal peril. This was another matter that needed elucidation by The Three. Ar itself was imperiled by more than just the hordes swarming the plains outside. She dared not sleep again, and lay rapt in thought for the remaining hours of the night, impatient for dawn.

She dispatched a servant to Mithmid at first light, but he was already up and out. Then she sent for Dollavier, but he too was away from home. At last a messenger summoned her in turn. All the chief wizards of The Three, all the kings of the League of Ar, were again assembling on the ramparts. Another attack? Days had passed since the enemy hordes had withdrawn from the river bank, at first days of celebration, then days of increasing anxiety as the water level dropped. She dressed and hurried through the cold gray streets toward the Southland Gate.

The assemblage on the parapet was grim and silent. No words were necessary. Mithmid led her to the brink, and they gazed together down at the river, already shrunk several feet below its normal level. The first gray light of morning was now coloring into a lurid purple-rose, and across the plain they again saw the great wooden towers of the enemy, higher and more numerous than before, arrayed against them. Soon they could be trundled up to the very walls of the city, with whatever other siege engines had been constructed while the people of Ar celebrated their illusive deliverance.

"A dam?" she asked.

"Across Dragonneck Gorge," Mithmid replied. "Only one of our scouts has returned alive, but his report was conclusive, about both the barrage itself and the utter ruthlessness of the enemy. The way they defeated the rapids was with living chains across the river, and swimmers carrying great bundles of reeds. Hundreds were drowned, and their bodies just left to plug the dam that was thrown up, once the current was checked. The waters are backed up for miles, drowning Beacon Valley." He understood the question in her eyes, and shook his head. "Too far away. Not all the telekinetic powers of The Three, remultiplied by all our fragments of the Khavala, would be effective at such a distance."

She gazed thoughtfully across the dawning plain, where the numberless hordes of marauders, harried into ranks by their battle priests, were even now forming to haul their siege machines, their great wooden towers, up to the very walls of the city. In a matter of hours the riverbed would hold mere puddles. The Three might inflict terrible losses, but only at a terrible cost to themselves. They would be exhausted long before the engines and bloodlust of the enemy.

"We must summon the king," she said at last. There were other things she urgently had to discuss with Mithmid and The Three, but no urgency was now more imperative than the survival of Ar. Only when the city was again safe could

she dare return to the tribulations of her beloved Srana. She
was ultimately to learn that these were as important as the
great city itself. "Trethwen, Zeshmer." She beckoned two of
the most prominent kings of the League of Ar. "My lords, I
ask that you summon his majesty here into our presence.
Other messengers might be delayed, even turned away from
the palace door"—she did not have to say by whom—"but
not yourselves."

The two kings nodded shrewdly, and departed with their
armed retainers. It would be a bold palace functionary who
denied entrance to such mrem.

"My Lord Ortakh." She addressed another king of the
League of Ar. "Could the enemy somehow be prevented
from concentrating all his forces against a sally upstream?"

"A diversion downstream might accomplish that, my lady."
He glanced from her to the decrepit wizards of The Three
nearby, then back again. "If I guess its purpose aright, any
such diversion would have to be well downstream. There is a
boat-bridge some miles in that direction, built by the enemy
to carry troops and supplies across the Mraal. The dropping
water level renders it unnecessary, but it is nonetheless a
plausible target. Scouts have reported an armory and supply
depot there. Shall I prepare to march?"

"Such decisions must be made by the king," she said. "Just
as His Majesty should lead the sally against the barrage."

Ortakh ruled a wild highland realm, and had fought in
border wars for two generations. He knew that leadership
and morale decide more battles than mere numbers. A demoralized king could lead them to nothing but disaster.

"Just so, my lady." He nodded, a shrewd look in his eye.
"His Majesty should indeed take command."

What he himself took was a hint, and he at once began
mobilizing—upon his own initiative—the kind of raiding party
familiar to border wars. He would be ready to sally forth the
moment the king gave his official command.

The wizards of The Three were less ready to leave the
great walls of Ar. Some were appalled, and a few of the more
timid tried to slip away and hide, but they were spotted and
dragged back in embarrassment, if not disgrace. The promise
of riding in carts, requisitioned from city merchants, helped
mollify them. At least none of them tried to slip away again,

although that may have been because they were now more closely watched.

Sruss herself issued no commands, nor did she try to usurp authority that was not hers by right. She only counseled, as she had counseled her husband and their son, while they presided over the aggrandizement of Ar into the great city of the mrem; but her counsel was far-seeing and wise, and those who heard it invariably acted upon it.

The king himself, when he at last arrived upon the parapet—disheveled, blear-eyed from dissipation and lack of sleep, intimidated by so many grim-visaged warriors—accepted her counsel with relief, and was grateful for the tactful way she allowed him to issue all commands. His first reaction to leading the expedition against the Dragonneck barrage in person—outside the walls!—was like that of some of the wizards. But his grandmother so encouraged him that at last he buckled on a sword and unconsciously began to swagger.

Thousands of mrem now lined the ramparts, sullen and apprehensive. The purple-rose of dawn brightened into clear daylight, and cloud shadows loped monstrously across the plains below, where the great towers had begun to advance, hauled forward by straining teams of herd-beasts, to the crack of whips and savage curses, or swarms of barbarians, ravening for plunder. The marauding hordes seemed to reach the very horizon, while in patches the river barely reached a mrem's ankles. All eyes now turned toward the king.

For the first time in his young life he did not disappoint them. After a last conference with Sruss, he led the way down from the parapet, sword in hand. Trethwen and Zeshmer would lead the actual troops; Mithmid led the wizards of The Three, some of whom still looked tempted to slip away at the first opportunity. But the presence of the King of Ar did indeed revive morale—his own most of all.

What revived the morale of those lining the ramparts above—it seemed that half the population was there, with more straggling up to join them every minute—was the sudden eruption of conflict miles downstream. The advancing hordes seemed aware of it at the same instant, and thousands of brigands and desert marauders, with two full cohorts of renegade highlanders, were diverted from the battle to check it.

▲

There had been no means of judging from the report of a scout how resistant the barrage would be, or how much force might be needed to dislodge it, so Mithmid was chary of squandering the mindpower of his wizards in skirmishes or concealment. The lumbering train of market carts was led by a wily old herd bull, who never had drawn a cart in his life, but whose nerve kept the draft animals from panicking in emergencies. A thousand fighting mrem guarded the train, which had left the city through the still unbesieged North Gate, but no breach of silence betrayed its presence. By detouring through a forest, the approach to Dragonneck Gorge went undetected by a single enemy scout or sentry.

These had been posted with the casualness of thieves, and the sentries were caught napping and were overpowered. Mithmid and Zeshmer crept forward and peeked warily over the brink. The grim spectacle below both appalled and encouraged them.

Mrem were independent to the very neb of their claws; all political unity beyond the city-state, itself invariably a welter of feuds and factions, seemed alien to their nature; all regulation was opposed with fury. And yet hundreds drudged ceaselessly to shore up the crude barrage, from which the arms and legs of hundreds more—drowned in the first obstruction of the current—protruded at grisly intervals. Battle priests, rather than captains or chieftains, urged on the work. Whether driven by fear and superstition, or just greed for plunder, brigands and marauders drudged like slaves.

Zeshmer glanced at Mithmid, who nodded. Reed bundles, sandbags, timber pilings, fieldstone: the force of the backed-up waters was rising, but so was the object that resisted it. No engineering was needed; the barrage was only an expedient, built to last a few days at most, perhaps just a few hours. Ar could hardly withstand an onslaught directly upon its walls much longer than that.

The onslaught upon the barrage needed only minutes, and far less mindpower than anticipated, and not even the most decrepit wizard of The Three was left fatigued. This was because Mithmid had had the foresight to consult a master builder about engineering principles before leaving the city; the man had volunteered to accompany the expedition.

"The water will do your work for you," whispered the master builder, pointing to the timbers propping the center of the barrage. "Rotten work. Built it straight across the gorge, like the ignorant barbarians they are. Won't hold such pressure long, no matter how many timbers they prop it with."

"It won't have to," said Mithmid, as the wizards assembled around him on the brink. "Just long enough to overrun the walls of Ar. Should we attack the timber props at the center?"

"A waste of energy," said the master builder. "Just open up a trickle anywhere, and the water pressure will do your work for you."

Mithmid, tapping the telekinetic powers of The Three, focused on the reed bundles in front of tangle of pilings, sandbags, and propping poles just below. The reeds shattered, and a small stream of water hit the sandbags, whose upper courses were then shivered into rags and loose sand. Shouts and confusion erupted all over the riverbed below; hundreds ran to plug the tiny waterfall, which broadened within seconds into a cascade, whose rush carried away more timbers and sandbags, widening the gap further still. As the master builder had predicted, the water pressure did all the work, and hundreds now ran for their lives.

"We may now return to Ar," said young Tristwyn, patting the hilt of his sword—which in fact he had never drawn from its scabbard.

The attackers were once more balked by a rushing river; once more the populace of Ar indulged themselves in joyous celebration. Tristwyn suddenly found himself popular, even respected, for the first time in his life. It was a new feeling, and he liked it. Wild dissipations awaited him at the palace; but he listened to Sruss's counsel, and instead made public speeches—which to his surprise he rather enjoyed—and appeared among the worshippers at various temples whenever their particular god or goddess was feted.

Furious, his mother responded by implementing her plan to discredit The Three. But the decisive role they had played in twice delivering the city from disaster was known everywhere, and the insinuations of the Silent Ones were ignored.

This did not improve Rhenowla's temper. Her son increasingly tended to ignore her blandishments as well.

Not until the water level of the Mraal again began to drop, several days later, did her temper begin to improve. For the new barrage, scouts reported, was guarded by wooden towers, stone-throwing catapults, and a veritable army. The patent helplessness of The Three in the face of this new dilemma could be turned to their discredit, and once more the Silent Ones began to whisper among the people, more and more of whom began to listen to them.

▲

Chapter 11
The Army of Shadows

▲————————————————————————————————————▲

"**A** tragic story, my lady," said Mamre, dabbing at her eyes with a handkerchief. "Sad as you'd ever want to hear."

Once the new attack had been frustrated, Sruss had had no trouble locating the former proprietors of the Blue Dragon. This was because they were still the proprietors of the Blue Dragon, no longer a sprawling caravansary in Kazerclawm, but a little backstreet tavern for refugees here in Ar.

" 'Don't meddle where it's none of your business.' That's what my husband told me," Mamre continued. "But Branwe was always a good son to me, the son I was never blessed with myself. Anything I can do to help him, my lady. Anything at all. It's just like a tonic to me, to know he's still alive. I can't tell you how worried I've been. Now I wouldn't ask money to tell everything I know about him. Nor would I accept it, if offered," she added firmly, unwittingly implying that somebody close to her had in fact told her to get as much as she could for the information.

Sruss listened patiently to the good-hearted old she-mrem's stories and digressions, to her adventures since fleeing doomed Kazerclawm. She seemed proud of having salvaged her best furniture, including a handcrafted mirror that now hung in all its splendor over the bar of the new Blue Dragon, here in Ar. Her husband, it seemed, still nagged her about the expense of hiring fellow refugees to haul it, league upon league, all the way from Kazerclawm. But among these ramblings were hard facts, and Sruss was at last able to extract the confirmation she was looking for.

137

"And you say this mysterious nurse was murdered shortly after leaving the infant with you?" she asked.

Mamre began dabbing at her eyes again. "The very night, my lady. Her and another poor kit she'd found somewhere, bought or stolen, I never knew. Cut up terrible, they were. Nor were the wretches who did it ever caught."

Her account confirmed what Sruss already had learned from Srana about the mysterious nurse: that she had sent a cryptic message to the Sentinel, and was in fact on her way to see him the night she was murdered. Her substituting another infant for the one she sought so valiantly to save clearly indicated that she knew implacable enemies were in hot pursuit.

It also confirmed that the original infant had indeed been the son of the Shadow Warrior; the last kit of his exile, born when he himself was being pursued by implacable enemies. Sruss did not mention this to the old she-mrem—the gossipy proprietress of a tavern—who might not be able to resist boasting about it to her cronies. Who in turn might do some boasting of their own . . . .

It was a cloudless summer morning, and Sruss personally escorted old Mamre, still dabbing at her eyes with a handkerchief, to the garden gate. She did not insult her by offering money—although she suspected that her innkeeper husband was never insulted by such offers—but promised to keep her informed about the fate of young Branwe.

Only now was Sruss free to communicate her confirmation to Mithmid. He was still a houseguest, but Mamre had refused to say a word in his presence.

"I will have nothing to do with a wizard," she had insisted. "I believe I'm as tolerant as the next woman, but you have to draw the line somewhere. Nor would I serve one a drink, though he had the money in his hand. My husband is not so particular, but that's his business. I never meddle."

It was Mithmid who intended to meddle, as soon as he could, by any means, no matter what the danger. He had hardly rejoined Sruss in the garden when he was on his feet again, pacing anxiously back and forth.

"The ring closes," he muttered. "The world turns back on itself. Yes, why not? It's all clear now. Before it was just a notion . . . hardly that, really. Just the shadow of a notion . . . ."

Again Sruss listened patiently; although this time there seemed to be no hard facts she could grasp, until Mithmid at last stopped pacing, stared distractedly off into space for several minutes, then reseated himself on the garden bench beside her.

"The Khavala." He lowered his voice. The White Dancers had begun their morning exercises at the far side of the garden, and a flute droned melodically through the morning air; but still he was wary of being overheard. "The Evil One tried to get it, and that was the beginning of all our woes. He got only a fragment, but may try to get it all. In fact, I'm sure he will. He may be trying again even now. All-Mother, pray we are not too late! I blame myself for not foreseeing this peril sooner."

"What of the immediate peril to Ar?" Sruss asked.

He sighed, and wrung his hands, and started to rise again, but reseated himself at once.

"If only it were just a war! Army against army, sieges and battlefields, and so forth."

"The host besieging us seems to think only of plunder," Sruss exclaimed. "They've ravaged everything to the east of us, and should Ar fall as well, I doubt that any city-state of the west could long resist them. Certainly not without allying their forces, which they still seem unable to do. The disunity of the eastern kingdoms, and its inevitable consequences, has taught them nothing. The disunity of the land was, I believe, what the Eastern Lords counted on from the first. Now at least we have the League of Ar to oppose them."

"Thanks to you, my lady," added Mithmid. "But the Eastern Lords may have other forces opposing them, forces deadlier than our own."

"The Evil One himself?"

"I believe so." He frowned in perplexity. "There is no following a liskash mind, but I do indeed believe that he is trying to bend this war to his own purposes. Why, for instance, isn't he here now? Exactly how powerful the Third Eye makes him, I can't say for certain—"

"Can he say for certain how powerful The Three, your magic redoubled by other fragments of the Khavala, are in turn? The reports of your power have surely reached him by now."

"Perhaps." Mithmid frowned again. "But no warlord would want to admit failure to him, for his reactions are unpredictable, like those of a madmrem. I'm sure he's not really insane, at least not as we understand insanity. It's just that his mind is so alien to ours."

They were silent for several moments, each with his or her own thoughts. The melodic flute continued to drone; the White Dancers performed their exercises with a grace that seemed almost supernatural. Wispy clouds, like streamers of gauze, had begun to drift out of the west.

"I told you about my dream," Sruss said at last. "Were the reptile-demons trying to capture me real, or only illusions?"

Mithmid shrugged. "Who can say what is real, when we know that other dimensions exist? The reptile-demons belong to the same evil dimension as the Khavala itself. Our greatest fear from the beginning was that the Evil One would learn to summon them forth into our own dimension, to do his bidding. Some believe they are the spirits of the Old Race."

"Which he seeks to return to its old dominion over our world? The Eastern Lords, I'm told, are not of the same race?"

"Reptilian, but only distantly related. The Evil One no doubt considers them degenerate, to be annihilated in turn when they have served—" He stared blankly at her for a moment, as if thunderstruck. "That's it! You said illusions!"

Again he began pacing back and forth, muttering. Sruss watched him with a kind of maternal amusement, for despite his advanced years he was still boyish in his enthusiasms.

"Some mrem—I accuse no one by name—have been trying to discredit us with the citizens," he muttered. "But we're not after power, and we're not just foolish old mrem . . . . A few are, I'm afraid . . . . And by the All-Mother, we're certainly not helpless!"

He slammed his fist into his other hand, and cried so loud that some of the White Dancers glanced curiously at him across the garden. Self-conscious, he reseated himself on the bench beside Sruss, and lowered his voice:

"Illusions, my lady. Many of The Three despair over the new barrage being raised at Dragonneck. Mostly the foolish old mrem, which, I'm afraid . . . . In any case, I've questioned every scout who managed to return alive—alas, but a small percentage of those sent out—and have a pretty clear picture of what we're up against. Redoubtable, to be sure. Perhaps invincible by ordinary means. But not against the extraordinary powers given me to wield." He held up his left hand, and sunlight glitt%rd brilliance through the fragments of the Khavala that dangled like charms from his bracelet. "We too may have shadow warriors, my lady."

His wizened old face lighted up with such boyish enthusiasm that Sruss could not help smiling, though she knew full well the perils confronting them.

▲

It was a rare configuration of the night sky in which at least one of the planet's three moons did not shine. But the one now shining was still at a low angle, and would be in the eyes of the defenders. Anything approaching them from the direction of Ar must seem eerie to begin with, like an illusion.

Doubling the size of an army multiplies its effectiveness fourfold. That was an unchallengeable principle of military strategy, and Mithmid had been hard-pressed to convince the kings of the League of Ar that their best chance of success now lay in dividing their forces. It was the intervention of young Tristwyn, counseled by Sruss, that was at last decisive. Ultimately, in ways she had not foreseen; for the counsels of Rhenowla in this matter had been exactly the opposite, and her failure to wreak vengeance upon The Three was driving her to desperation.

Many of its wizards also resisted dividing their forces in the face of such overwhelming odds; some resisted the bare notion of dividing their persons from the protective walls of Ar, especially at night, with but a single moon low in the sky. But Mithmid—and Sruss—had at last prevailed, and a long file of wizards now found themselves tiptoeing apprehensively through a gloomy forest, without so much as a cart to ride in. Concealment magic had had to be used to leave the city this time, and some were already fatigued.

Surprise was everything. Once it was lost, so were they— and the great city of Ar along with them. For the new barrage was now complete, the riverbed again mere puddles; the enemy host, its numbers swelled by a new legion of desert marauders recruited by the Eastern Lords, was ready to attack at dawn. Torches and campfires, seeming more numerous than the very stars in the skies, covered the southern plains to the horizon. Only for a mile or two south of the puddled riverbed, the range of an effective sortie from inside the city, did darkness still prevail.

But tonight's sortie was of another kind, in another direction. Ortakh led a handpicked contingent of highlanders: those who had survived the diversion against the ford and supply depot downstream, when the barrage was first destroyed, recruited by highland soldiers from the regular army. They were freebooters by heritage; more cunning than the bandit hordes, more ruthless in battle than the very desert marauders. Those pockets of resistance in the land, still unconquered by the invaders, were mostly in the highlands. Ortakh had led this contingent in other sorties against enemy preparations.

The trees loomed unnaturally before the motley company of wizards and grim highlanders in the low angle of moonlight. The first sentries they encountered, posted haphazardly at checkpoints along the route, were drunk or asleep on watch, and quickly dispatched. Not until they were within a mile of Dragonneck Gorge did they run into their first real obstacle. A notorious bandit gang had occupied an old fortified manor, the seat of one of Ar's noblest families, which commanded a strategic road crossing. But scouts reported that the bandits were carousing drunkenly with a troupe of dancing girls, and either they had neglected to post sentries or the sentries had joined the carousal.

Ortakh decided prudently to bypass the manor. It was not the primary objective tonight, and even a surprise attack here might raise an alarm as far as Dragonneck. There was some grumbling among the highlanders over missing a golden chance to cut the throats of bandits, but he kept them firmly in hand, even when they divided their forces in an orchard less than a half mile downstream.

The wizards now also had reason to grumble among themselves. All had heard gruesome tales about the savaging of magicians by highland clans, and being left at the mercy of so many grim highlanders at night, in a deserted orchard, caused them to huddle apprehensively together. Many found it difficult to prepare their minds for the ordeal before them.

The key was Mithmid. He had to be almost literally in two places at once. With a third of the wizards and three fourths of the highlanders, he headed straight for the cordon of towers guarding this side of the river, impossible to infiltrate in force, and placed too far from the gorge for kinetic magic to operate effectively on the barrage now spanning it. Nor could enough towers be destroyed before The Three themselves were overwhelmed by cruel numbers. Somehow these numbers had to be equalized . . . .

A score of colossal towers loomed into the night sky, their size exaggerated by the weird angle of moonlight, every space between mounded with ramparts or fenced with logs or palings. The sentries here were many, and all awake, although the rising moon was directly in their eyes whenever they looked eastward, half blinding them to anything approaching from that direction. What they did see appalled them.

Mithmid assembled his wizards in a cornfield. Their own terror of what could happen to them should anything go wrong made a goodly number too nervous to concentrate properly at first. It took him several minutes of patient reassurances before he was at last able to tap their mindpower, to focus it, remultiplied by the fragments of the Khavala, upon the minds of the sentries, to create there terrifying illusions, monsters of the imagination . . . .

The first sentry to spot the nightmare dragon descending out of the moon was a chaw-eared old rogue, more accustomed to plundering villages than standing watch. He had been bored and sleepy, but now his eyes boggled in fright, and he raised the alarm with a wild howl, as he dived for cover. He had never seen a dragon like this before.

Neither had any of the other sentries, and they too howled and turned their heels on the ramparts. The crews up in the towers were all awake now, but only one was steady enough to fire its catapult at the flying dragon, and the shot somehow went awry. Then one of the terrible storm giants of ancient legend appeared suddenly out of the eerie moonlight, then another. The second dragon that descended upon the defensive cordon was even more menacing than the first.

The panic was complete; the whole camp was now in an uproar, running helter-skelter, howling in terror, ignoring the calls of their battle priests to rally.

Mithmid could do no more. The wizards he left assembled in the cornfield might sustain the illusions he had created, but without him to focus their powers through the fragments of the Khavala they could create no new ones. He left them in silent concentration, and scrambled over the deserted ramparts, with a helping hand from Ortakh.

His highlanders were now in their natural element, and bent back every attempt to rally against them, to block their path to the barrage. The rest of The Three were already assembled there according to plan. There were twice as many as in the cornfield, and Mithmid had only half the trouble concentrating their mindpower. And it had to be concentrated as never before, tapped if need be to exhaustion, for the new barrage was a far more massive structure than the first had been, and far better engineered.

It was difficult in the low-angled moonlight to pick out a weak point. The camp guarding the far side of the gorge was also up and moving, but in disciplined order; barges were already carrying troops across the pounded waters behind the barrage. They too could see the monstrous illusions, but seemed to recognize them as just that. There was no time to lose.

The center of the barrage, heavily buttressed, arched upstream against the miles of water pressure. There was no weak point there, and Mithmid focused his attack on the nearer side, where the barrage met the wall of the gorge. The hurried, makeshift construction was shoddiest here, and he first shattered a timber buttress, then began tumbling reed bundles and sandbags, and at last in one mighty explosion opened a sluiceway that quickly began to widen. But not quickly enough, and Mithmid continued to tap the mindpower of The Three, until the whole barrage collapsed and was swept away in a raging flood.

The barges ferrying troops across the river were swallowed by the foaming, chaotic rush of water; any cries for help were drowned by the thunderous roar that pounded and reverberated through the gorge. There would be no attack on the walls of Ar tomorrow, and as the divided bands of wizards and highlanders reunited for the weary trek home—some of the former, whose mindpower had been tapped to destroy the barrage, were so dazed and unsteady of gait that they had to be led by the hand like children—Mithmid drew Ortakh aside.

Tonight's sorties had gained only respite for Ar. Another barrage might be raised at Dragonneck Gorge; perhaps some other means found of getting the towers and siege engines up to the city walls. The only thing certain was that the siege itself would continue, the enemy more determined than ever upon rapine and plunder. The respite must not be wasted, and the conference between the wizard and the highland chief continued, with few distractions, all the way home.

▲

Sruss smiled maternally at the boyish delight of the old wizard, as she praised him. His deeds had once more preserved the city from ruin, and she had made certain that this was known everywhere. The defamations of the Silent One would themselves now be silenced. Rhenowla no doubt would find some new means of working her malice, but for the time being The Three were safe from public reprisals.

Since he had used his magic this time only to tap the mindpower of others, to focus and direct the concentrated force through himself, Mithmid was not at all depleted by the strains of last night's sortie. He could afford to swagger a bit before Sruss, and to revel in her praises.

They sat together once more in her garden. The White Dancers had already finished their morning exercises. It was a muggy overcast day; the noontide sun was hidden by lowering storm clouds, threatening rain.

"It must be risked," he said.

Sruss looked at him with concern. "A grave risk, perhaps foolhardy. I've told you of my own experiences. The very land of dreams has become dangerous."

"Only while the Evil One is vigilant," said Mithwid. "It is when his vigilance relaxes that I will make the attempt to teleport the sword. And I will assume the risk myself, grave as it is. No one with lesser powers could hope to succeed."

They both gazed thoughtfully at the ruby fragments dangling like charms from the bracelet on his left wrist. They seemed pathetically small compared to the evil magic concentrated against them.

"But how can you know when the Evil One relaxes his vigilance?" Sruss repressed a smile, knowing that the old wizard wanted her to ask that very question.

"Ah, but there is a way," he cried, as if expecting new praises for his cleverness. "The same way we overmastered him the first time. Vengeance is his god, his purpose in life, his fatal weakness. How will he react to the news that his latest plan of conquest has failed?"

"Yes." She was serious now. "He will indulge himself in beastly orgies of vengeance. But the timing will be critical. How can you know when the news reaches him—or if it does? The commanders of the enemy host also know the price of failure, and will be reluctant to report it to him."

"Ah, but they must. For if they don't, those seeking to supplant them in power will. Then would the wrath of the Evil One be implacable. No, they'll tell him what happened, naturally trying to blame others for their own blunders. But they will tell him."

"Do you plan to intercept the messenger?"

He shook his head. "That was my first idea too, but I've since learned it would be impossible. The runners who carry message pouches are just too swift, and more than one copy of the message would surely be sent over different routes, in any case. We must learn from the enemy warlords themselves when their reports are dispatched to the east. With the known speed of professional runners, we can estimate pretty closely the exact time it would take the reports to reach Cragsclaw."

"Then you will risk the teleport?"

He nodded. "It must be risked, for even the fall of Ar is not our gravest peril now. A son of the Shadow Warrior, at the very moment he is most needed. Who can now doubt the intervention of the All-Mother to protect her children from evil? But fear not, my lady," he reassured her. "Even should the worst befall me, I shall not be defenseless against the Evil One. His powers may be overwhelming in this dimension, but less so in any other. I have my left arm"—he held out the bracelet—"and my right, which will bear the Demon Sword we shall soon forge."

Carried away by his enthusiasm, he brandished this arm too—the spindly, flab-muscled arm of an old mrem, who even in youth had never borne arms—but quickly lowered it again in embarrassment. He glanced self-consciously at Sruss, but she was looking the other way, beckoning her lodge-keeper to approach.

"Ortakh, King of Maragadan," he announced.

"The mission I told you about, my lady," explained Mithmid.

"Very well," she said. "Please show His Majesty into the garden, Pepik. Have all the invitations been sent out?"

"Yes, my lady. I saw to it myself this morning." The tufty old lodge-keeper clearly disapproved of wizards coming and going at all hours, in a respectable house, but had been in service here too many years to question his mistress. "The preparations for tomorrow's assembly are nearly complete, and all the housemaids and kitchen wenches given the night off."

This last breach of household discipline seemed even more deplorable to him than the comings and goings of a lot of scoundrelly old wizards, but it was not his place to reason why, only to carry out his instructions with a good grace. The stiff dignity of his bearing, as he strode loftily from the garden, alone betrayed his disapproval.

"I don't think Pepik likes me," said Mithmid.

"The common mrem have always distrusted wizards." Sruss looked thoughtfully at him. "Not much is needed in times like these to provoke them to violence. You told me yourself about witnessing atrocities during your journey to Ar. Beware they don't happen here."

He too had heard of the insidious campaign being waged by Rhenowla's agents against The Three, but before he could reply, Ortakh entered the garden and approached them with the stolid gait of someone more accustomed to climbing up and down hills than walking on level ground. He greeted Sruss with his usual shy deference, but she soon put him at ease.

"I have learned the password," he said.

"Can the man who revealed it to you be trusted?" Mithmid asked. "Perhaps it's a trap."

"The man is a highlander," said Ortakh, as if no more were necessary to prove him trustworthy. "As you know, I sortied eastwards against an enemy supply depot, to divert attention from the attack on the first barrage. The flood waters cut off several of the defenders, and we put them to the sword. All but one. He drew in his claws, and begged for quarter. I granted it, on condition that he return the favor upon demand." He glanced at Sruss, then lowered his eyes. "Alas, my lady, there are all too many highlanders in the enemy host. Renegades in their own lands, to be sure. But highlanders nonetheless."

"So long as you are confident of this particular highlander," she said.

"I am," he replied without hesitation. "No true highlander, regardless of his crimes, would renege on his oath."

Thunder rumbled in the distance, and an ominous yellow-gray light glowered from the overcast sky, as if it were already dusk.

▲

Chapter 12
"The Bridge Has Wheels"

▲————————————————————————————————▲

Mithmid was not as confident about the fidelity of highlanders as was his guide through enemy lines; he depended rather on the bracelet encircling his left wrist. During his long unsuccessful quest after the Third Eye he had had various experiences with highlanders. Some could be nobly hospitable and just; some crafty, brutal, and treacherous. Often these traits commingled in the same highlander. Too often, in fact.

" 'Death to Ar,' " Ortakh boldly challenged a team of craftsmrem—most seemed to be carpenters—a couple of miles inland from the river.

" 'The bridge has wheels,' " their leader responded with the password.

"Carry on." Ortakh allowed them to pass.

Again Mithmid was impressed with his guide's cool resourcefulness, acquired through a lifetime of highland warfare. He himself would have been caught out at their first encounter, and this was at least their ninth. Despite the intermittent showers, the vast sprawling camp of the enemy was a hive of animation. Some great enterprise was afoot. The destruction of the barrage had only whetted the malice of the besieging hordes toward those who denied them rapine and plunder. Woe unto Ar, should its walls now be breached!

The camp followers seemed to Mithmid as vicious as the bandits, desert marauders, steppe rovers, highland renegades, and cutthroats on whom they battened. The dancing around the campfires was wild and lascivious; some of the dancers were village she-mrem, carried away by the invaders, or lured from home by natural lewdness or the promise of spoils, although most were obviously professionals. As they whirled and dipped and leapt, their shadows seemed to rage like demons at the fringes of the night. Drunken shouts and obscenities mingled with the rude music.

"The informer was vague about when the council was to be held," whispered Ortakh, as they passed between campfires. "It makes sense that the warlords should all meet tonight, to decide how to deal with the loss of the barrage. My informer heard rumors to that very effect. But we can't be sure, and I doubt if the password he gave me will get either of us into the council tent."

"I'll handle that part of it myself," said Mithmid. "Just get me to wherever the council is being held . . . . Oh, oh, looks like more rain."

Heavy raindrops began to patter around them as they joined the motley of thugs, cutthroats, and half-naked dancing girls scurrying for cover. Thunderbolts seemed to explode on top of them; lightning crackled; then the clouds burst in a drenching downpour. The evil-smelling tent in which they took refuge was too promiscuous for any risk of discovery. Ortakh looked like a highland renegade to his very whiskers, and Mithmid—long experienced in disguises—was dressed as a clan scribe. In any case, the shameless behavior of the dancing she-mrem, who made a rare show of drying out their wet garments, attracted all the attention.

The cloudburst did not last long, and the furious animation of the camp resumed at once, despite the mud and squalor.

Mithmid suspected by now that his guide had reasons of his own for infiltrating enemy lines, reasons shared by all the kings of the League of Ar. They were concerned only with military threats to the city. Were any new schemes afoot for rebuilding a barrage? How were the new towers, which could be seen from the city walls, armed and mounted? What was the meaning of the strange password, "The bridge was wheels"? These were the questions Ortakh and his fellow kings wanted answered. The ultimate peril to the race was still unknown to them.

"Ah, it *is* tonight." Ortakh nodded with grim satisfaction. "There's the council tent, there's one of the warlords and his staff just arriving, so you're on your own." He left Mithmid—standing where he fully expected to find him when he returned.

Reconnaissance was Ortakh's true purpose in slipping outside the walls tonight. No doubt The Three had interesting powers of magic—acting collectively, under the protection of others—but this was war, something magicians knew nothing about. The enemy hordes might be greedy for plunder, but their leaders had been handpicked for military acumen by the Eastern Lords. If a barrage upstream allowed them to trundle siege towers right up to the walls of Ar, well and good. But they would not be so foolish as to depend solely on that one strategem.

Whatever they were up to now, it was screened from the city by a dense concentration of towers. That's where reconnaissance would begin, and Ortakh strode openly in that direction with the swagger of a highland renegade. He knew the password; if there was any challenging to be done, he'd do it first.

Not that he was careless about Mithmid, who was amiable in his way; it was just a matter of priorities. He had known beforehand, as any experienced soldier must, that a council tent would naturally be so surrounded by armed guards, captains, battle priests, and the retinues of the various warlords as to be unapproachable by anything less than a battalion. But to have mentioned this, or refused to have guided the old wizard out here tonight, could have led to arguments and delays, just when some new enemy strategem was imminent.

He glanced back, to reassure his conscience that his charge was still in no danger, and froze.

"The old fool!" he muttered between his teeth.

He watched Mithmid walk straight toward the council tent, expecting at any moment to see him collared and dragged away in chains. But nothing happened. For some reason, nobody noticed him. The old wizard just walked right up to the tent and entered without a single person even glancing at him.

Perplexed, Ortakh turned and headed for the construction site he was sure he would find screened behind the massed towers. What he saw there made him more certain than ever that the magic of a handful of old wizards would not save Ar. The bridge indeed had wheels—three bridges, in fact, beside which no less than six of the great wooden towers stood ready to be mounted as counterweights. Their length indicated the northern branch of the Mraal, which was the narrower of the two. When completed, they would simply be rafted to the opposite bank of the river in sections, reassembled there, counterweighted with pairs of towers, and mounted on wheels.

An assault with towers and siege engines against the southern walls, like the first attempt to take Ar by storm, while bridges spanned the northern branch of the river? The Three had proven they could cope with one such attack; but a second would be beyond their endurance, if not their very powers. He had seen the dazed and exhausted condition of those whose mindpower Mithmid had tapped for the destruction of the barrage. No, force would have to be met with force, machines with machines.

He was favored by another downpour, which drove the construction crews inside the looming towers for shelter. He recognized some of the workers as highlanders; the type of renegade he had hunted down and punished all his life. Which meant that he in turn was in danger of being recognized, as the King of Maragadan. The few lanterns left burning shed a gloomy light, both on the massive constructions themselves and the hopes of Ar.

He slogged back through the mire and downpour, soaked to the pelt, his mind racing with battle plans.

Ar could not long withstand a two-pronged assault by such vast numbers. One of the prongs would somehow have to be bent back, delayed so that the entire resources of the city could be concentrated on each in turn. They had divided their forces to destroy the barrage; now they would have to unite them as never before. The land east of Ar had been scorched to retard the advancing hosts of the enemy; now they in turn were devastating the land north and south of the city, razing whole forests for the raw materials of their colossal towers and wheeled bridges. Ar would have to respond with constructions of its own, formidable new engines to mount the walls. Would there be time enough to build them? Could one prong of the attack truly be delayed long enough to beat back the other?

There was only one way. A fellowship of warriors, fighting together with berserker fury, qualities possessed only by his highlanders. Few would survive—he did not expect to live himself—but none would survive the fall of Ar. He had witnessed the terrible berserker ceremony only once, as a kit. But the priests of Maragadan would recall every detail of the ancient rite, for it was their god alone who granted berserker magic . . . .

Mithmid had kept himself dry and comfortable in the meantime. He sat in a shadowy corner of the council tent, his thoughts concentrated through the bracelet on his left wrist, and not once did his enemies so much as glance toward him. They were a grisly lot: cunning and battle-scarred, the survivors of malice, treachery, and unspeakable crimes. Their council was a pandemonium of threats, curses, and accusations; again and again they leapt to their feet, claws extended, teeth bared, eyes flashing mayhem. They agreed only in their mutual dread of the Evil One.

Not that they ever referred to him by that name, or any name at all, for that matter. Their references were always oblique, always deferential. There was no argument over the proposal that messengers not be sent to Cragsclaw until after the forthcoming assault, now scheduled for two days hence. Then surely they would carry only good news . . . .

The news Mithmid carried with him as he left the council tent—the armed guards outside all looked the other way as he emerged into the night—was not encouraging. He had had to concentrate much of his attention on concealment, and had grasped through the pandemonium only a sketch of the forthcoming assault, but he brought away a frighteningly clear picture of the effect it would have upon The Three, upon their ultimate struggle with the Evil One.

Forge the Demon Sword after the battle, so all the exhaustible mindpower of The Three could be focused on destroying the siege engines of the enemy? Or concentrate first upon the sword, at the risk of losing the battle? It was lucky the alert Ortakh caught up with him when he did, for the question so perplexed him that he tended to forget about concealment. Among so vast a host, this was unlikely to have gotten him safely home, in any case.

They found the boat waiting for them at the appointed place and time; two strapping highlanders at the oars, as soaked and miserable from the incessant rain as they now were themselves. As he looked up at the mighty walls of Ar,

looming nearer and nearer as they crossed the river, Mithmid
knew that even these might have to be sacrificed to the
forging of the Demon Sword. The fall of Ar would be a
disaster, but the Khavala in the hands of the Evil One could
mean the very annihilation of the mrem.

Was it even now in his hands? Had he already launched
another expedition to the Shadow Islands, to that remnant of
a lost continent where for a single night, at a single point, the
evil dimension conjoined the world? Had he launched an
entire fleet?

Mithmid's thoughts, as he climbed stiff and soaking wet
from the boat and entered the city, were as depressing as the
night around him.

▲

Young Tristwyn had often been awake until dawn; sometimes long into the next day. But on this particular night he
was not carousing. His companions, as he roamed the city,
were reputable captains, not Crockercups. His purpose was
to hearten his people, to encourage their utmost efforts both
tonight and on the morrow.

The revelations by Ortakh of Maragadan this morning,
before an assembly of the League of Ar, had brought consternation. The sight of towers, siege machines, and other massive constructions being rafted across the river this afternoon,
both upstream and down, had thrown the entire city into
panic.

It was to calm this, to direct the energies of the people into
readying constructions of their own, that Tristwyn moved—
albeit with frequent halts for refreshments—from rally to
rally, from workshop to workshop, all through the night.

As he encouraged the people, so his grandmother encouraged him. Sruss was too elderly now for such exertions; she
could not follow him everywhere, nor had she any wish to
lead. But her advice, when asked, was always profound and
to the point. Above all, it was always worthy of a king. For
the first time in his life he began to feel he was truly his
father's son.

Sruss herself meanwhile had other duties to perform.

Her faithful Pepik had ordered the household with faultless
efficiency and decorum; only in the cold formality of his

bearing was his disapproval of tonight's meeting evident. The first gathering of wizards here could be excused by the exigencies of war. But now they were making a habit of it: gorging and swilling brazenly, helping themselves to anything they found in his pantry, depleting the larder of edibles. This last was particularly galling, now that the city was completely invested, and its supply lines dangerously constricted.

Nonetheless he did his duty. After dismissing the last of the kitchen wenches for the night—he had little doubt how the bold minxes would spend it, with so many soldiers crowding the taverns—he bade a formal good night to his mistress, and took himself off as well.

As he left, he was surprised to find special watchmrem posted outside in the street. No one was allowed to loiter anywhere near the garden wall. All three moons now shone in the sky. Shaking his head, he turned in the direction of his married sister's house, where he would spend the night. What were the pack of scoundrelly wizards up to this time?

As it turned out, they did not know yet themselves. Only when Mithmid was assured by Sruss that there were no spies or interlopers anywhere in the vicinity of her gardens did he reveal their full peril.

Most had heard legends of the Shadow Warrior, how he had brought back some corner fragments of the Khavala from the Shadow Islands; all knew the power of the Third Eye, the largest and most powerful of these fragments. Nor did any doubt, when Mithwid at last finished his narration, that the Evil One would grasp the first opportunity to increase that power, to renew his quest for the entire Khavala: to unleash all the evils of its dark dimension upon the mrem.

"The Eastern Lords seek only plunder and slaves and empire," he added. "Khal wants nothing less than the restoration of the Old Race to world supremacy."

Silence hung shroudlike over the assembly. Not a wizard present had to be told that the restoration of the Old Race meant the annihilation of their own. The question about why the Evil One had not used all his power thus far in the overthrow of Ar was now answered. He wanted besieged and besiegers alike mutually exterminated.

"Be sure he hasn't got the Khavala yet," old Dollavier said

bluntly, "or he'd have used it against us by now. But what if he's already sent out another expedition, led by some new Shadow Warrior, to get it? We may be too late."

"We have no choice but to believe we're not," said Mithmid. "Besides, we have a Shadow Warrior of our own. His last living son, and a formidable swordsmrem."

"Do we know that for certain?" asked Dollavier.

"We know for certain that the young man is with Severakh," said Mithmid.

There were grins and nods and chortles among the The Three, a few outright guffaws. Severakh's reputation as a drillmaster—when not overruled by foolish superiors—was known throughout the land, and wizards, as a matter of survival among a people hostile to magic, were alert for all such knowledge. Nothing more needed to be said, and the wizards joined hands in seven concentric circles.

The sword itself had been furnished by Sruss. It was an heirloom, the renowned sword of Talwe, tested in scores of battles, over many years. The ceremonial blade worn by the present king was shinier, and encrusted with a treasury of gemstones, but this was the sword of a true warrior.

Chanting in counterpoint, the concentric circles rotated slowly in alternate directions; round and round, their chant rising and falling, their mindpower tapped and concentrated, the wizards drifted into a ceremonial trance. Mithmid stood at the focus of the circles, his left hand extended toward the sword at his feet like a mystical lightning rod. The tempered steel did not actually glow, but all who saw it afterwards knew that it was somehow different from any other sword.

Mithmid at last picked it up; its weight strained his spindly arm as he brandished it in shadow passes. Appropriate, for the magic of its new temper girded it against shadows; against the phantoms of an evil dimension; against reptile-demons.

Sruss smiled maternally as she watched Mithmid brandishing the sword, for she knew what he was thinking. However, she was also concerned about the exhausted condition of some of the elder wizards, and served refreshments with her own hands. Would The Three be able to wield their powers effectively tomorrow? At the moment they just looked like tired old mrem.

▲

Another ceremony, in another quarter of the city. No watchmrem were needed to discourage curiosity here. The legends of highland berserkers were all the more terrible to city dwellers because theirs was a form of magic—if it was indeed magic, and not some form of insanity—alien to their experience. They wanted no part of the hundred or so high-landers gathered in the courtyard of an abandoned hostelry—abandoned when the owner and clientele saw the highlanders coming—near the Northland Gate.

Kegs of mountain wine stacked the cellar, but they went unbroached; for the drunkenness the highlanders sought was of another kind. The chant of their priests was in an older, more primitive tongue than the incantations of the wizards now forging the Demon Sword. Wilder and more gutteral, the words less and less intelligible, the primal meaning of the chant was yet increasingly manic and possessive; each was in his soul drawn back through time, reminded of prehistoric savagery, of cruel ages when their bestial ancestors hunted the night on four paws. Then was combat total; then was all the power of tooth and claw and muscle concentrated utterly upon the kill; then did they drive the Old Race into caves and desert haunts; then did they conquer the world.

Hour after hour, throbbing like the primitive cadences that with the passing of time had become true music, the chant of the highlanders echoed the litany of their priests, echoed the hunting madness, the blood fury, of their ancestors. The passion did not exhaust them, but only made them stronger, more savage. None remembered now that it would be a mere hundred highlanders against thousands upon thousands of enemies, veritable nations. Fear had become as meaningless as time itself, and at dawn they were led forth by the mighty Ortakh through the deserted streets of the city—deserted by the first rumor of berserkers at large.

Towers and siege machines lumbered out of the north like avenging giants, ominous and fell in the rose-purple light glimmering behind the dark mountains of the east. Closer and closer, the shrill of grinding wheels sounded to the thousands watching hopelessly from the ramparts above like cries of agony, the crack of whips like omens of eternal bondage. News of an even more terrible host advancing upon the south walls made their plight more desperate still.

The hastily constructed machines now being winched up to the ramparts seemed pitifully few and inadaquate, the defenders vastly outnumbered.

Then, to the astonishment of all, the colossal machines and towers ceased to advance; the shrill of wheels, the ominous cracking of whips, fell silent; an inexplicable hush fell upon the morning. All that was visible in the rose-purple light was a commotion around the towers nearest the Northland Gate. The cries of agony were now genuine, the crash of arms beat like the tattoo of metal drums; enemy platoons rushed forward—and were at once driven back, littering the field with casualties. The commotion spread outward to the flanking towers and machines, one after the other, until the entire host weltered in confusion.

A cheer rang from the walls, and every highlander there—no matter what his clan, forgetting old feuds and enmities—swelled with pride. It was madness, suicide; glory that would never be forgotten. Wielding their great two-handed claw-swords, the berserkers, a mere hundred strong, had in their fury checked a horde numbering tens of thousands. The colossal wheeled bridges could not approach near enough to the river to extend their spans across to the walls.

Magic? Insanity? No matter which, so long as the berserkers held back the enemy hordes from overrunning the northern walls, the strength of the city could be concentrated on throwing back the still vaster hordes menacing from the south.

▲

The Three again assembled upon the ramparts above the Southland Gate, their mindpower concentrated through Mithmid upon the advancing towers of the enemy. The one nearest the bridge shattered into sawdust; then the one beside it, being trundled ponderously forward by a train of herd-beasts; then a huge mounted catapult. Screens of hide had been erected to shield the wizards from the rain of missiles sweeping the ramparts, but nothing could protect them from exhaustion. The towers advancing upon them were too many and too huge, their own resources of mindpower too quickly exhausted. They could not check the enemy alone.

The young king had, to his mother's shrill displeasure, opened all the shops of the palace, all its storerooms and all its hoards of treasure, to the city's master builders. His authority had also provided them with all the manpower they needed, and a prodigious array of machines was now mounted along the southern wall. He directed their fire—literally fire—in person.

Sruss did not meddle with the directives of her grandson, even when his boyish enthusiasm carried him too far. She only saw that this enthusiasm did not foolishly endanger his life, and a pair of stolid shield-bearers paralleled his every move along the ramparts, screening him from the rain of missiles.

The missiles arcing down from the walls were fewer in number, but more effective. Fire-spears riddled the great wooden towers, igniting them, delaying their advance. Brigades of skirmishers had to be diverted to bucketing water from the river, to extinguish the fires, further delaying the advance. This gave The Three what they most needed: time. Time to bring their flagging mindpower to bear upon shattering every great siege tower within range, one after the other.

The rafts and barges on the river below, crammed to the gunnels with marauders, grappling hooks, and scaling ladders, were now deprived of missile cover from the towers. Boulders crashed down on all that drifted too near the walls, and the current bore downstream a ghastly flotsam of wreckage and bodies.

Dreading the consequences of failure, the enemy warlords pressed their merciless attack, and casualties mounted until the very battle priests began to rebel. Resistance was furious, terrible, unanticipated. But though their own attack had stalled, the expectation that soon the northern wall of the city would be overrun encouraged them to persist.

Then messengers brought the grim tidings that that attack had also stalled. The thousands of defenders atop the walls could no longer restrain their cheers and taunts, as one after the other, minutes apart, the towers of the enemy continued to shatter into sawdust. The hail of missiles sweeping the ramparts momentarily slackened into a mere nuisance, while the barrage of fire-spears and boulders hurtling down from those ramparts grew ever more terrible. So dense became the smoke that at first the defenders did not perceive the new menace trundling toward them across the plains.

Maddened by anger and the dread of failure, the enemy warlords threw all their remaining strength into one last desperate assault. While a giant catapult hurled boulders directly at The Three, massed on the parapet above the gate, with a force that mere hide screens could not deflect, a pair of strange machines were hauled to the riverbank facing the remote ends of the wall. Through the billowing smoke, their purpose was not immediately apparent.

Though the tallest of all the siege machines yet thrown against Ar, they mounted neither catapults nor archers; no sling-stones or pots of fire rained down from their lofty turrets; no grapnels arced across the river. They were shaped like monstrous T's, with crossbars longer than their stems, crossbars that lengthened farther and farther, once the machines were anchored on the riverbank, until they overswept the walls. Only then was it realized that the machines were nothing but giant cranes, whose deadly claws began to pluck defenders from the ramparts—five and six at a clutch—and swing them back across the river to their doom.

The Three could not at first resist them. Mithmid was now too hard pressed just to keep his wizards from bolting, while at the same time tapping their mindpower to deflect the boulders hurtling down at them out of the sky. He was unable to concentrate long enough to destroy even the catapult pinning them down, let alone the giant cranes.

It was now that young Tristwyn first truly showed his mettle. Through the renewed hail of arrows and sling-stones, he had three of his own siege engines mounted on the parapet, and their barrage of fire-spears soon ignited the towering catapult facing them, hampering its crew with blinding swirls of smoke. Moments later, it exploded into sawdust and ashes.

Then thousands of enemy troops could be seen retreating through the smoke and reek of battle; neither their battle priests nor their captains could rally them, nor did they dare try.

A thundering cheer rang from the walls. But the battle was not over yet, and The Three, moving along the ramparts beneath a roof of shields like some monstrous shelled reptile, made their way toward the western battlements.

The few defenders still alive here had taken cover; the huge crane, having plucked scores from the walls, was even now being repositioned along the riverbank to put hundreds more within clutching range of its deadly claw. Mithmid positioned The Three just beyond that range, and pointed his left hand at the crane. Minutes passed. Then a new explosion of sawdust and ashes sent the enemy into retreat here as well.

It was over a mile back along the wall to reach the other crane, but word arrived that it was already in flames. Then word that the northern wall, even farther away, was threatened. Brain-weary, stumbling with exhaustion, the scores of wizards descended into the city. They were cheered to find carts waiting for them, thanks to the foresight of Sruss, and crawled gratefully inside. But there was no chance for the nap many so dearly cherished. The draft animals were whipped to a lather, to rush through the streets with all haste, and they had to hang on with both hands.

Fewer than half the berserkers were still alive, but they fought on with the same magic-insane fury, as oblivious of danger as they were of the siege machines that now began to explode around them. The wheeled bridges were Mithmid's first targets. They were too colossal for the enfeebled powers of The Three to destroy utterly, but he so crippled their undercarriages that they were immobilized. Barrages of fire-spears did the rest, and soon the enemy hordes were in full retreat here as well.

The mightiest cheer yet now rang from the walls. Highland trumpets recalled the berserkers, but for all save a few it was too late. So deep had they regressed into primordial fury that they could no longer be brought forth again. Savages they had become, and savages they would die; cutting their way into the enemy hordes with their great two-handed claw-swords, in the throes of blood madness. As dangerous now to friend as to foe, Ortakh had to abandon them to their fate, and save those whose minds were not utterly lost in fury. A bare quarter of those who had gone forth with him at dawn ever returned, and all, including himself, were bloodied.

Nor could their wounds be tended until they were safely

disarmed. But such was their berserker madness that hours passed in manic victory dances, sword dances, wild shouting and singing, and boisterous carousing, as they quaffed flagon after flagon of heady mountain wine, before anyone dared approach them. Only when they began to drop from loss of blood or sheer exhaustion could they at last be nursed.

Sruss tended them in person with a few Dancers, who reminded her vividly of her beloved Srana, whose powers as a healer were truly magical. Where was she now? Why had it been so long since she had last contacted her? The All-Mother preserve her from the Evil One . . . .

Many other gods and goddesses were also invoked that day, and far into the night, and every temple throughout the city resounded with the joyous prayers and choruses of thanksgiving. Ar had been delivered. The most virulent assault ever mounted against it, in all its long history, had gloriously been thrown back. The enemy hordes were in retreat. Praise be to the All-Mother, or Jubala, or Poon, or Kabib-Izama! Religious celebrations at this hour of deliverance were natural, and to be condoned, no matter which diety was praised.

More sinister were the rumors about dark invocations of Narlock, the primordial war god of Ar, whose cruel sacrifices had long been forbidden. For mysterious reasons, the Silent Ones had begun stirring up the vilest superstitions of the people. At whose behest, Sruss had no doubt, and she pondered deep into the night the possible reasons for so unexpected a maneuver, the purpose of which eluded her. In fact, none of Rhenowla's machinations had ever so troubled her before, although as yet she had only vague premonitions of the evil that would not manifest itself for months to come.

Meanwhile, despite all the thanksgivings and celebrations, Ar still lay in deadly peril. For the Eastern Lords had yet to exert their full might, to concentrate the scattered bands of desert marauders and bandits now ravaging the land, or to recall the troops assigned to the transport of slaves and treasure back to the east. Neither had the Evil One yet focused all the vast powers of the Third Eye upon the city. The silence from Cragsclaw grew daily more ominous. All that could be known for certain was that the punishment waiting there for those who had again failed to conquer Ar would be terrible even to behold, let alone experience.

▲

It was in fact an experience every warlord gathered in the council tent that night sought by any means to forgo. All had ordered executions for insubordination and cowardice, appointed new captains, and suppressed ruthlessly the least shadow of mutiny. Deserters were even now being hunted down. But no matter how effectively they restored discipline, it still would not win today's battle, and they dared withhold the news from Cragsclaw no longer.

Finding messengers to carry such news faithfully to the present occupant of Cragsclaw—they avoided naming him more superstitiously than ever—was a problem in itself. For all knew by now the fate of those who displeased that nameless occupant. After so costly an enterprise, no prudent mrem would want to bear the ill tidings.

Threats, curses, and accusations rang through the tent, but no one leapt to his feet now, claws extended, ready to back up his words. Their situation was too grim; the problem without any apparent solution.

No messenger was in fact sent to Cragsclaw that night. A messenger arrived instead *from* Cragsclaw—and all problems were instantly resolved. A new blockage would be raised, across a valley too many miles upstream for any sortie of wizards from Ar to destroy it; new towers and siege machines would be constructed, new catapults, cranes, and wheeled bridges; all bands marauding the countryside would be brought in to reinforce the final assault; all supply lines to the city would be cut. These preparations might need months to consummate, but they could not fail. Every warlord seated in the council tent was assured about that.

Only when the messenger issued a summons to Cragsclaw, for the purpose of "clarifying authority," did the warlords again look apprehensive. Though scarred and grisly rogues, the survivors of unspeakable crimes and treachery, here was an evil so alien and malicious that even they were appalled.

The *generalissimo* and the warlord of the army recruited by the Eastern Lords were to leave tonight. The others were to follow in a few days, after all the new dispositions had been set in motion.

There was no choice but to obey, and the two mrem

ordered to depart at once sent body slaves flying to their respective tents, to arrange their baggage and transportation. Meanwhile each pondered ways of casting the blame for today's fiasco on the other. Not in their innermost thought did they mention the dweller at Cragsclaw by name.

▲

Chapter 13
Kizzlecosh

▲ ————————————————————————————————————— ▲

Never in his life had Cajhet entered a scuzzier den of thieves, but he was a veteran of low life, too experienced certainly to enter alone. The five brawny highlanders with him were insurance against a cosh on the back of the head, or something other than wine in his goblet—or worse. He had heard dark rumors about what became of strangers who entered such dens alone: The young ones ended up in pies, the old ones in stews. But he dearly needed a drink, and music, and dancing, and perhaps some game of chance, although the gambling here looked rough.

All the inhabitants of Ravarbal in fact looked rough. The last refuge of pariahs and outlaws for generations, at the outermost reaches of the eastern marchlands, smuggling and banditry were still the mainstays of the economy. Severakh had spent a full week fortifying himself against treachery, both from within the city and without, before granting a single night's liberty—with everything more than three blocks from their fortified caravansary off limits.

This particular den was exactly three blocks away (or perhaps a bit beyond), and the only one Cajhet had discovered that promised any real fun. He smacked his chops over a heady goblet of mountain wine, and called for another.

The wood-block floor was two steps below street level, and may have been swept within the last month or so; the plaster walls were so grimy that it was impossible to determine their original color in such dim light. Lute, pipes, drums, and scrapers—the musicians continued to play lascivious dance rhythms, though the last of the dancing she-mrem had just retired through a beaded curtain, leading a drunken cus-

165

tomer to be fleeced elsewhere on the premises. The villainous bartender looked like his true calling should have been a bandit chief, and perhaps it was. On a display board behind him hung what looked from the main room like dried fruit.

Snacks? Cajhet wrinkled his nose in distaste. Whatever they were, they did not look very appetizing. Neither did the forty-some mrem, in varying states of drunkenness and debauchery, crowded into the dim, squalid, reeking, low-ceilinged room about him. The attraction at the moment was a game being played by three rogues. Cajhet would gladly have joined in the wagering, but at first was unable to figure out the object of the game. The three rogues—all more or less drunk—seemed to be trying to stab each other's hands with daggers. Shouts encouraged them, wagers were called back and forth, money was exchanged.

So much attention now focused on the game that it was a natural opportunity for a hookpurse, and Cajhet instinctively clapped a hand over his money.

One of the players suddenly shrieked in pain as a dagger pinned his left hand to the table. Laughter mingled with curses, wagers were paid off and collected, then the game resumed between the remaining two mrem. The excitement mounted; the stakes redoubled. Cajhet kept a firm grip on his own money.

Out of the corner of his eye he noticed that one of the highlanders who had accompanied him was not as prudent, and that a hookpurse—a rather clumsy hookpurse, it seemed—was in the act of robbing him. Shout a warning? But that might have ended in a brawl, and he was too far from the street door. He looked around for the bouncer.

This turned out to be a female, a strapping, fierce-eyed she-mrem who wore a mean-looking cosh dangling from a strap around her wrist. Cajhet caught her eye, and glanced meaningfully toward the hookpurse, whose apparent clumsiness, he now saw, was due to the fact that he had in fact nothing to hook purses with. A declawed criminal, if he had ever seen one.

Given the hint, the female bouncer now saw the thief too—and pounced. But instead of leveling him with her cosh, she seized him by the ear with her teeth. He at once went limp, as tame and docile as a sleepy child. Guffaws and shouts of laughter—the two players left off their game to enjoy the fun—followed the collared thief all the way to the street door. He seemed very anxious not to show the least resistance, despite a barrage of ribald advice on how he should fight back, for the bouncer still had his ear in her teeth.

An expectant silence fell on the crowd the moment the pair disappeared out into the street. Sharp curses accompanied the thudding of some blunt object against flesh and bone. At last the strapping female bouncer strode back through the door alone, cosh in hand. A burst of ribald applause greeted her, but her look was so fierce that attention immediately refocused on the gambling game.

Cajhet also looked prudently the other way. Moments later he sensed someone hovering beside him, and turned his head. The female bouncer looked even more imposing up close. She jerked her thumb toward the bar, and he obediently followed her there.

"Good work, laddie," she said in a deep hoarse voice. "I take it kinda personal when anybody thinks he can steal on me. Outside is one thing, in here's another. Ain't that right, Haggie?"

"Right, Kizz," said the bartender, who was obviously afraid of her. "Spotted a hookpurse, did he? Well, he's earned a drink on the house."

"Thanks." Cajhet sipped from the brimming goblet. "But he wasn't really a hookpurse. No hooks. I used to be chief lockup at the fortress in Kazerclawm, you see. Had my own collection of claws in a metal beaker, which I would rattle now and then when the lads acted up. Nothing personal. I was sorry to see 'em lose their claws, but if your job is to keep order, then you've got to do it."

"Same goes with me, laddie. They know better than to fight back when Kizzlecosh has got 'em by the ear." She jerked a thumb at her own mountainous bosom. "Claws, you say? Why you're a mrem after my own heart. I got a collection of my own. Out of the way, Haggie, so's I can show him."

Cajhet suddenly felt queasy. It was not dried fruit on display behind the bar; certainly not snacks. Nailed in rows were ears of various colors, bitten off by sharp, powerful teeth.

"That's my collection," she continued, "and everybody knows it's here. But I'm always fair. If they behave themselves when I take 'em by the ear, why then I just lead 'em out into the street, and give 'em a tap or two to remember me by. If they don't . . ." She finished by jerking her thumb at the rows of ears.

Cajhet swallowed hard. "Very, uh, impressive I'm sure." He noticed the bartender dodging glances from one to the other, and chuckling slyly to himself. "Much more impressive than my own poor collection."

He turned back to her. The fierce look in her eyes had softened into something almost tender, and he began to feel uneasy for he sensed that the look could become fierce again in a hurry, if she were rebuffed. She edged closer. Her smile revealed rows of sharp, powerful teeth, and he could feel his ears tingle. She began tenderly to groom him, with hands he was sure could spring sharp, powerful claws.

The next thing he knew they were slipping arm in arm through the beaded curtain. He glanced back, and saw the bartender shaking with silent laughter.

▲

Out in the street, the battered hookpurse was also shaking himself, but not with laughter. He had been coshed about the head and shoulders, and as consciousness slowly returned he could feel lumps already rising in several places; his nose was sore, and one eye was swollen shut. He could also feel both ears, which was a relief, considering the circumstances.

Gingerly, he tried to rise, fell back with a groan, then tried again. This time he succeeded, and began feeling for broken bones. Happily, he found only more lumps and bruises. Kizzlecosh must have been in a good mood. Life had been much easier for him when he still had claws, and he squinted warily up and down the street in search of enemies. One beating tonight was enough.

The street was deserted—then all at once an old man appeared out of thin air. An old wizard with a big shiny sword stood not five yards away. He seemed disoriented, as if not yet sure where he was. Then he relaxed, and nodded a greeting.

"Could you direct me to the Anglock Inn, my good man?" asked Mithmid. He was dressed in the cap and gown of a master wizard, but wore armor on his sword arm, a scabbard, and stout leggings, as if girded for battle, although even the startled hookpurse doubted his martial prowess. He pointed.

"Two blocks down, and turn left. A little over one more block after that. You can't miss it."

He deftly caught the coin tossed him, and watched the old wizard stride off brandishing his big shiny sword, as if he had recently been taking fencing lessons. The blade itself looked formidable, although not the scrawny arm that brandished it . . . .

Severakh was even less charitable. He had a low opinion of wizards in general. But he knew that Srana was a White Dancer, and twice in his long life he had seen the legendary Sruss in person; the last time, during an investiture ceremony in Ar, at a distance of no more than a hundred feet. But was this ridiculous old mrem telling the truth? Srana appeared satisfied with the signs brought her from Sruss.

"Then Branwe is truly the son of the Shadow Warrior," she said thoughtfully. "The tale you've related to us here tonight is both tragic and dreadful. The All-Mother pray that the Evil One has not anticipated us."

"Amen," murmured all those gathered in the refectory of the Anglock Inn.

It was sometimes chilly at night, this high in the mountains, and a fresh log had just been laid in the fireplace. Srana gazed down at it, rapt in thought. She seemed, in her youth and beauty, so charmingly like what Mithmid recalled of the young Sruss that his whiskery old face softened with nostalgia.

Severakh snorted impatiently. "If you've brought that sword for Branwe, give it to him before you cut yourself with it." He did not add, "you silly old fool," but it was implied in the tone of his voice. "Now gather around and listen, all of you. Our duty is clear, and we're going to do it, or by the All-Mother I'll know the reason why." He glanced sternly from face to face, but none demurred. "We've long since resigned ourselves to being cut off from Ar. Nor would it be a refuge for us any longer, even if we could reach it. Mithmid here has given us a full military appraisal of the situation, and told us about all his tribulations, worries, trials, fears, dangers, and rare swordsmanship." His captains glanced sardonically at the old wizard.

Mithmid failed to detect the irony in this, and assumed so proud a bearing that the captains now laughed outright. But another stern look from Severakh quickly brought them to order.

"Where's Cajhet?" he asked. "On liberty? Then send out a platoon to fetch him. At once!"

"Yes, sir." A captain hurried out the door, returning in time to hear Mithmid detail all the dangers, real or legendary, they might have to face.

"I'm not a seaman," exclaimed Severakh at last. "None of us is. But if this Khavala is as important to our survival as we've just heard"—he glanced at Srana, rather than Mithmid, as if trusting her confirmation more than what the old wizard had told them in the first place—"then we must not let it fall into the hands of the Evil One. If we can't bring it back, we can at least destroy it. Wherever these Shadow Islands are, we'll find them first. Somehow, some way, no matter what it costs. We'll leave at dawn—"

He was interrupted by a commotion out in the corridor; the door opened, and a pair of stout sentries hauled Cajhet into the room by the elbows. He grinned ingratiatingly at Severakh.

"Caught him trying to sneak in the back door, sir," reported one of the sentries. "He dodged the platoon out searching for him, but not us."

"Wipe that silly smirk off your face!" Severakh growled. "You're a disgrace to the army."

"Yes, sir." Cajhet rocked unsteadily on his heels, a sleepy dissipated look in his eyes. His futile efforts to stand at attention really were disgraceful.

"Pinch him and pull his whiskers," cried Severakh. "If that doesn't work, drag him out and hold his head under the pump."

"Yipe!" Cajhet squealed as he was pinched, but steadied himself enough to stand at ease, if not attention. "You wanted to see me, sir?"

"I never want to see you, you scoundrel, and in fact I

seldom do. But right now we need your services. You're from the port city of Namakhazar, I believe?"

"Yes, sir."

"Well, that's where we're going—some of us, at least—and you're the one who's going to get us a ship, once we get there . . . ." He was silent for several moments, a frown wrinkling his forehead. "The first problem is getting there at all."

Mithmid alone failed to understand what he meant. The bandit gangs that had harried them for weeks past now invested the city; to get by them, or evade their pursuit afterwards, now seemed impossible. Fight their way through them? Even if successful, so determined a movement in the direction of Namakhazar would surely alert the Evil One to their objective.

"Oh, uh, sir," Cajhet began self-consciously. "I've made, shall we say, a friend here in town. She, I mean, this friend seems to know a lot of bandits. Perhaps, uh, this friend I've made could arrange some kind of safe passage for us . . . ." He fell silent as he sensed the fierce old warrior glowering at him.

"Who could have believed that it would someday come to this?" Severakh shook his head. "Two generations a soldier, and I end up haggling with bandits for our salvation. And I have no doubt who this friend is, or at least what she is. All right, scoundrel, see what kind of passage you can wrangle for us. There's money if you need it—and you probably will—but hurry! The very appearance of a wizard here in Ravarbal may be reported to the Evil One." He glanced toward Mithmid, but found he had retired into a corner with Srana. He turned to one of his captains: "Accompany this wretch wherever he wants to go, or the platoon I sent out may just pick him up and drag him back here again."

The conversation between Mithmid and Srana was brief—and disappointing to the former. He had brought her a message from Sruss, for her ears only, and was again touched with nostalgia at the way her lovely eyes shone with courage and determination. But while he was thus softened, her reaction was exactly the reverse.

"No." She declined his request firmly. "I must keep the fragment of the Khavala bequeathed to me by my grandfather. Not for my own sake, but for that of this entire band of

refugees. Without it, we would long since have been surprised by our pursuers and destroyed. I realize that it would
further multiply the power of The Three to defend Ar from
ruin, but you yourself have just said that the recovery—or
destruction, if need be—of the Khavala is ultimately more
important."

"But anything that now multiplies our power is critical," he
protested. "If Ar falls, what then could stand against the
onslaught of the Eastern Lords? Half the land is already laid
waste, and each city-state of the other half now foolishly arms
to defend itself only. Independence is the strength of the
mrem, but it can also be a weakness. In this case, a fatal
weakness. The final assault upon Ar may not be launched for
months yet, but this time the Evil One himself will direct it,
with all the force of the Third Eye. We must somehow
remultiply our powers against him."

"Another sliver of magic will make little impact," she said.
"Only the Khavala itself can do that. Which means, in the
event we recover it, that it must somehow be transported to
Ar. Your teleportation here was a grave risk. It must never be
chanced with the Khavala, which would then be vulnerable
to the Evil One."

"But its powers would overwhelm those of the Third Eye,"
he said. "At least, wielded by a magician."

"Exactly my point. According to my grandfather, the Khavala
has no powers of its own, but only multiplies a force of magic.
No magic, no power. For you may multiply nothing as many
times as you please, and the result will always be naught. I
possess only the knowledge my grandfather was able to im-
part to me in the weeks before his death, but it is a real
quantity, and hence can be multiplied. Perhaps not enough
to challenge so mighty a sorcerer as the Evil One, but suffi-
cient to transport the Khavala to Ar—should it be recovered."

He bowed acquiescence, then gazed fondly at her. "You
have not only her beauty, but her wisdom as well. It shall be
as you wish. But will you be safe here until the expedition
returns?"

"One more reason why I must retain my fragment," she
said.

He bowed again, and again gazed fondly at her. Then he
realized that young Branwe was also looking at her, and felt a

twinge of jealousy, both for his youth and good looks and for the shining Demon Sword he now wore in his scabbard.

▲

The two largest moons were now in the sky, dimmed alternately by scudding clouds, and the crooked narrow streets seemed to throb with silvery light. Wild music throbbed from the doorway of the thieves' den—nameless, for anything Cajhet ever learned—outside which sat a ragged young thug, groggily nursing his right ear, or rather the side of his head where his right ear should have been.

Cajhet found Kizzlecosh nailing it up along the bottom row of her collection, behind the bar.

"He'll know better next time," She bit the air menacingly with her sharp, powerful teeth, and Cajhet felt his own ears tingle. Then her fierce look melted into the fondness of love, and she laid down her hammer and tenderly began to groom him. "I'm glad you came back. Some mrem tell me there can be too much of a good thing."

"Never for me." He tweaked her whiskers playfully, and she exploded with ribald laughter, and hugged him to her massive bosom. After a moment to catch his breath, he explained why he had come. "Can you do anything for us, love?" He again tweaked her whiskers.

"Haggie owes me a couple of favors," she said, "and people owe him, and so forth. He's as treacherous as a liskash, but knows what he'll get if he tries any tricks with me. Namakhazar, you say?"

"I was born there."

"Ah, that's the reason," she cried. "Peculiar color, you are. Seen it mostly in southern ports, among sailors. Know who yer pa is? No, I thought not. Does yer ma?" She again exploded with ribald laughter, and gave him an affectionate hug. "Anyways, I think I can get your people there safe and sound. About thirty of 'em, you say? I'll do it, and it'll be a nice vacation for me too."

"Oh, that's too much trouble. I couldn't think of imposing—"

"No trouble at all—unless you don't want me to come." Her eyes narrowed, and her lips began to draw back from her sharp, powerful teeth, and he unconsciously began to cover

his ears with his hands. But he recovered his presence of
mind, and winked lecherously and poked a playful finger into
her bosom.

"If you don't go," he said, "I won't go myself. This is my
lucky night."

"And it ain't over yet," she added, and he found himself
being swept once more through the beaded curtain, to the
silent delight of the bartender. "You're sure I'm not, well, too
exuberant in bed? Some mrem think I am, and never come
back, and that hurts my feelings."

"You're exactly the kind of woman I've always dreamed
about meeting," Cajhet said tactfully, with a desperate look
in his eye.

▲

There were many desparate looks among the thirty men
gathered in the barroom of the Anglock Inn, two nights later.
Impatient as he was to march, Severakh was too experienced
a soldier to plunge rashly into the unknown, when a strategem
might achieve the same ends.

More bandit gangs turned out to be hovering in the vicinity of Ravarbal than he had realized, almost as if this city too
were under siege. Spies now lurked in the neighborhood of
the inn itself, probably with the connivance of city officials. It
was unlikely that the rogue population would ever allow them
to surrender anyone who sought refuge here from any kind of
authority. Nonetheless, the two days of waiting had been
anxious.

"All arranged, sir." Cajhet sauntered into the room with
Kizzlecosh on his arm. Or perhaps the other way around,
since he stood barely to her shoulder. "This is the lovely
young lady I told you about, who's been helping us. Isn't she
a wonder?"

Severakh wasn't sure what she was, and there was some
rude guffawing across the barroom. But a glance from the
hulking Kizzlecosh silenced this, and there was no more
rudeness that night.

"We'd better shake a leg," she said, "if we're going to be
out of sight before dawn. We have to make a long detour to
the north, before heading south, 'cause it's a gang there I've
made the deal with. The only one I could, which started me

thinking." She eyed Severakh suspiciously. "There's something going on I ain't been told about. Cajhet here don't know, or I'd have had it out of him by now. Who's after you, and why? Bandits are usually easy folk to deal with, if you meet their price. But something's got 'em scared."

Severakh explained to her as much as he thought she needed to know. About Khal, at least. Only his most trusted captains knew about the Khavala.

"All right." Kizzlecosh was satisfied. "That's good enough for me, though I suspect you could tell me more if you had a mind to it. It's a good long hike to Namakhazar, and we'll have to carry all our own food. Due south, except for a detour about three days out. We don't want to come anywheres near Yozgat country. Are you ready? I am, so's the gatekeeper."

"And so are the spies watching the inn," said Severakh. "I'll send out a platoon—"

"Don't bother, old darling," said Kizzlecosh. "When I do a job, I do it right. There were four spies posted tonight, but it seems they all suffered a mysterious accident about the same time. Got their heads busted when they wasn't looking. Split up, keep the noise down, and meet again at the north gate. We got a long march tonight, so say your goodbyes, and make 'em quick."

Severakh repressed his vexation at being treated so familiarly, at having anybody give orders but himself, and got everything ready for departure. The entrance of Srana and Branwe, followed by Mithmid, caused a brief delay. But for Cajhet's adroitness, the delay might have been serious. First of all, Kizzlecosh did not like magicians, which was why she had so willingly assented to help them elude the vengeance of a sorcerer; secondly, her dislike of beautiful young she-mrem could sometimes turn violent. But Cajhet so humored, distracted, and jollied her that Srana was able to conclude her final interview with Severakh without incident.

Srana was to remain with the bulk of the refugees, to camouflage the departure of the others for Namakhazar as long as possible. Once these put to sea, not all the magic of the Evil One could impede them; for they would soon sail beyond the range of even the Third Eye.

"It is a brave thing you do." She addressed Branwe. "A quest that shall never be forgotten, an adventure that may someday be recorded in the *Dragon Book* itself, so schoolkits for generations to come might be inspired by your exploits. I know you will succeed, Branwe. May the All-Mother guide and protect you."

Branwe clasped the hilt of the Demon Sword; his eyes sparkling, his nostrils flared. He would succeed if he had to cut his way to Namakhazar and back again single-handed. Srana's words may have sounded to the others present like no more than formal leave-taking; he alone saw the deep concern for his safety—and perhaps something more intimate— sparkling in her eyes. Never had she seemed to him so beautiful.

This beauty caused Kizzlecosh's nostrils to flare also, but her eyes glowered, rather than sparkled, and the deeds she was inspired to were not at all noble. But Cajhet nudged her from the barroom, and the others, in silent threes and fours, dispersed by different routes toward the north gate.

Srana was left alone with Mithmid. She had already given the old wizard a message for Sruss—perhaps their last for months to come, for any other form of communication now left them too vulnerable to the Evil One—and bade him farewell. Then she was alone in the barroom of the Anglock Inn.

Mithmid had kept his growing apprehensions over the delay here in Ravarbal to himself. He had expected his sojourn to last only hours, not days, and no longer had the Demon Sword to defend himself with. His timing for the teleport here had been perfect. He had expected messengers to bring word to Cragsclaw of the failure to carry Ar by assault, but was informed by scouts that the very *generalissimo* himself had been summoned there. A canvass of merchants had given him a close estimate on how long the journey would last; he knew himself how soon the Evil One would be thrown into a blind orgy of vengeance at the news—although not how long that orgy would last. This teleport was a far graver risk.

He rematerialized, and waited for the strange sense of disorientation to resolve. But it did not. Dark reptilian creatures lumbered toward him across a tortured landscape of volcanic fires, smoke, and skeletal trees. An eternal crimson twilight made everything around him lurid and hideous.

Then from near and far, seeming to echo across the crimson skies, a sardonic laugh resounded all about him. And he knew he had delayed his departure too long.

▲

Chapter 14
The Zanira

▲———————————————————————————▲

The palace gardens in Cragsclaw had long been renowned for their luxuriant splendor. They were now a reeking hellhole of liskash nastiness. This seemed to delight Khal, as he gazed down upon them from the royal balcony on the morning of a gloomy overcast day. Most of the foulness below had been perpetrated by the monstrous dragon chained securely by its left rear leg.

"He's a mighty levitator," Khal explained to the eight mrem reluctantly gathered around him, the commanders of the hordes besieging Ar. "The mightiest I have yet discovered. He is being tamed by me, so that I may ride a fitting mount when I lead the final conquest over my enemies." His eyes swept over the eight mrem as if he included them in the designation.

None of them noticed, for they could not meet Khal's eyes—any of the three, which glittered like rubies with an alien madness. They were rogues who practiced deceit as naturally as they breathed. But if they succeeded outwardly in disguising their revulsion, their fur—rising instinctively again and again—betrayed them. Khal noticed, and in some insane fashion it seemed to please him.

He had taken special measures to appall them, to flaunt his alienness for its full shock value. His fantastic robe glittered with an iridescence that seemed electrical; the rings he wore too near the tips of every digit made the webbing of his hands all the more grotesque.

"Have you any questions, gentlemrem?" he asked in a guttural rasp like the hissing of serpents. "Anybody in particular you wish to know about?"

All assured him there was nothing at all they were curious about, self-conscious that their fur was again rising in abhorrence.

"You're quite certain?" Khal's two ruby eyes gleamed with malice; the Third Eye shone between them with an evil greater still.

No, they were quite certain there was nothing they wanted to know, nobody they were the least bit curious about, especially the two warlords who had preceded them here to Cragsclaw, several days ago, with their personal entourages.

"Very well, then." Khal signaled to one of his liskash servitors, with which, as they were recruited from caves and desert fastnesses, he was replacing the original palace staff. "We'll enjoy the feeding of my pet below, then adjourn for our own dinner. Unless any of you has other plans?"

No, they had no other plans; certainly not. Nothing in the world they would rather be doing at this minute than standing here with him on this very balcony, as he fed his dragon.

Then their fur truly stood on end, as they saw what he was feeding it with. All recognized the mrem shoved naked into the garden as the personal steward of their *generalissimo*. The dragon recognized him only as a meal, vanished, then reappeared beside him, and caught him in its terrible jaws. The steward's screams died at a snap, as he was literally bitten in half and devoured.

"Have no fears, gentlemrem," Khal said mockingly. "He's fastened by a chain of my own creation. Not all his magic will loose him, only mine. But I see my pet is still hungry. He's grown quite sleek on his new diet since I brought him here. I indulge him, you see, for he must one day render me a valuable service. It's wonderful how much more efficient my slaves have become since I first stabled him here."

His dark laughter echoed across the gardens below, and the dragon raised its head and looked at him. Khal pointed toward the overcast sky, and the dragon at once began to levitate, rising until it was level with the balcony. Khal then pointed toward the gate below, and the dragon looked downward as another naked mrem was shoved into the garden.

The dragon's chain had faded into a smokelike wisp, hardly visible, and the mrem glanced apprehensively into every corner of the garden, in fact in every direction but up. Warily he crept forward, his head moving from side to side as he advanced—until he was directly below the dragon. He never saw it; never even cried out. It dropped on him out of the sky like an avalanche, crushing him in an instant.

"He could levitate half again as high, as if I let him." Khal looked on with satisfaction at the wretched mrem being devoured below, and with still more satisfaction at the undisguiseable horror reflected by the fur and features of the eight commanders around him. "How many more?" he called down to his liskash servitor.

"Just one, master," he hissed in a raspy voice.

"Bring him forth, while I decide."

The last to be dragged between two liskash into the garden was none other than the wretched Nizzam, stripped pathetically naked, half dead with fright. The dragon glanced evilly at him, but continued its meal, with a hideous slavering and the crackle of bone and cartilage.

"No, perhaps we'll save this one for another day," Khal said, reconsidering. "I mustn't overfeed my pet. It could spoil him and ruin his digestion. Give this one back his clothes, and send him up to my special chamber."

Nizzam fairly sobbed with relief, as he was half-carried out of the garden, although this same charade had been performed every few days for the last month, ever since the dragon was first brought here. No servant in the palace now groveled more abjectly. As he hurried to his master's side, he hardly noticed the stuffed hat rack, once the magician Maglakh, or the other stuffed effigies of mrem kings and queens, lords, ladies, priests and generals, arranged in a tasteful color scheme on exquisite pieces of furniture all around the hall.

Khal ignored him at first, as he introduced his collection of stuffed enemies, figure by figure, with the pride of a connoisseur, to the eight horrified commanders. These had been the famous and powerful of the land before the invasion; their names the commanders knew like legends. All of them had taken part in the surprise attack on Kazerclawm, and recognized the effigy of the elegant young governor.

They murmured their appreciation as they moved about the chamber. Then they were truly horrified, for posed in martial array were none other than their quondam *generalis-*

simo and the commander of the pursuit forces who had let the refugees escape.

"My taxidermists finished mounting them only late last night." Khal examined the figures. "This is my own first look at them. I was busy with another enemy, one who foolishly thought he could elude my vigilance. He too will one day find a place here, but not just yet. Greed and haste must never be allowed to mar the delights of vengeance. I was certainly not hasty with these two, yet as you see there is no evidence of my passion. Rare workmanship! I must provide such artists new material to work with." The eight commanders glanced nervously at each other. "Ah, here's my good Nizzam. Have you learned your lesson about filling my goblet from the left side, and not the right? Perhaps next time I won't be so generous."

"It will never happen again, master. Never, I promise. I swear it to you." Nizzam abjectly kissed the hem of his robe. "Thank you for your generosity."

"Be seated here." Khal pointed to the most beautiful piece of furniture in the entire room, a small dainty couch of inlaid precious woods, silken upholstery, and gemstones. "Assume the pose I showed you. That's right. A poor substitute for the one who will shortly repose here, gentlemrem. A young she-mrem of rare beauty, a flawless cream white. A White Dancer, in fact. Nizzam here knows her, and will help me bring her here, the crowning jewel in my entire collection. Won't you?"

"Yes, yes, anything, master."

Khal's ruby eyes glittered down at him. "Your response seemed slow. Have you any reservations?"

No. Nizzam groveled. He had no reservations. Nor had any of the eight commanders who now seated themselves nervously at the dinner table, although normally they squabbled like curs over every scrap of preference or advantage. Neither the service nor the delectable viands set before them left anything to be desired; the wine was a famous vintage. But they had little appetite. Perhaps it was their silent audience, perhaps the disgusting food devoured greedily by Khal, or the liskash servitor who waited personally on him, perhaps they had secret suspicions about what might be in their own food and drink. In any case, they only sipped and nibbled at what was for them a lavish banquet.

Nizzam was not invited to sit down; he never was. He was merely a factotum of the lowest degree, in continual terror of his life, and scurried discreetly to the vestibule the instant he noticed a messenger enter. Another mistake today could cost him his hide—literally.

Relays of professional runners had brought the message fifty leagues in a single day, a service for which a goodly reward might normally be expected. But the messenger did not wait. Weary and still breathing hard from running, he was nonetheless able to put a couple of miles between himself and Cragsclaw, within minutes after delivering his message at the door.

Nizzam's first wild fancy was to try and match him stride for stride, over hill and dale. He had never heard of a marchland fastness called Ravarbal, but knew the report of events there would not please his master, who was already displeased with him today. Dragging his feet, he slowly returned to the dinner table, whispered the message—then very quickly dived for cover, behind the effigies of the king and queen of Dobaragh.

"Fools! Idiots!" Khal shrieked so maniacally that all eight commanders fairly bounced in their chairs. "This vengeance is mine by right. Mine! Mine! Mine! A flawless cream white! Why haven't my orders been carried out?" He sent his liskash servitor flying from the hall, and stalked back and forth through his collection of effigies raving like a madman.

Then all at once he stopped in his tracks. His ruby eyes glittered with frenzy, and his webbed fingers groped unconsciously for the Third Eye, as if some new development threatened its power, as if the true meaning of what he had just heard had suddenly penetrated his mind. His hissing scream exploded through the hall like a volcanic bomb:

"They must be stopped! At all costs, they must be stopped! Now I know what they're after!"

The legate from the Eastern Lords, one of the smaller, more intelligent liskash, who entered the hall at that moment with Khal's servitor, was startled by the outburst. He both feared and hated Kahl, for he sensed that he was despised.

"Call off the siege of Ar!" Kahl shrieked at him. "We march

at once! All available troops. I know what they're after. They must be stopped. At once, at all costs . . . ."

Though the legate could not understand what the all-powerful sorcerer was ranting about, and suspected at first that this time he really had lost his mind, he was certainly not going to call off the siege of Ar on any pretext. Not with victory almost within their grasp. His sole loyalty was to the aggrandizement of the Eastern Lords and, though he dreaded the wrath of the raging figure before him, he stood firm.

Khal startled them all again by suddenly ceasing to rave. Cold, rational, again in full command of his evil faculties, he gazed at the legate with icy malice.

"It will be remembered," he hissed, and stalked from the chamber to make arrangements of his own.

▲

"Three days lost dodging spooks and legends," grumbled Severakh. It was morning, and the port of Namakhazar sprawled about its haven in the coastal valley like a toy city. The ships at anchor certainly appeared like toys at this distance; too tiny and fragile ever to survive out on the vast shining sea beyond. "Where's that Cajhet?"

"Here, sir."

"Didn't I tell you not to sneak up on me like that?"

"I'm sorry, sir. I was just, uh, I mean—"

"Just trying to get back to your tent for more disgraceful behavior, without my seeing you? I'm ashamed to be in the same army with you."

Cajhet stood at attention, without daring to look his gruff old commander in the eye. He knew he was in trouble; in normal times he would probably have landed in one of his own dungeon cells. But what else could he do? Kizzlecosh had gotten them safely through bandit country, and no matter what the regulations said, if he didn't sleep in her tent every night—he got very little sleep, in fact—her feelings might be hurt. His ears tingled at the very thought . . . .

"This is your hometown." Severakh continued to glower disgustedly at him. "You should have contacts here, at least a few relatives who could help us. I want you back here by sundown with a good report, or I'll know the reason why.

We're already behind schedule. Well, why are you still standing there?"

"Uh, it's like this, sir. Kizzlecosh says she wants to meet my mother, so I thought—"

The explosion of curses startled him. Then he found himself seized by the throat and shaken. But Severakh was too canny an old soldier not to exploit any given opportunity, by any means.

"All right," he sighed, releasing Cajhet. "Take the wench down to the harbor and drown her, for all I care. Just be back here by sundown with a good report. Remember, there's more places you can be drowned than the sea."

"Yes, sir."

As it turned out, Severakh could have marched his whole contingent straight into Namakhazar as bravely as Kizzlecosh herself. Gatemen, sailors, sea captains, innkeepers, waterfront idlers—she had a way of making any inquiry a confrontation, and quickly got whatever information she wanted. She also got a job.

"I'll be here waiting for you when you get back, love," she promised. "You're so brave, I'm proud of you." And she hugged him to her massive bosom. "Now let's go find your mother."

Fabulous riches dwelt cheek by jowl with squalid poverty; outside of the palace quarter, the only law was that of tooth and claw. Everybody carried weapons, and knew how to use them. There was in fact relatively little crime or violence, since retaliation was too swift and certain, and even the drunken brawls along the waterfront were seen as just part of the night's entertainment for the sailors involved.

It was in a notoriously low dive, part of which overhung the very water on pilings, that Kizzlecosh got her job. Bouncers seldom lasted long in the Tangletide, so she had been hired on the spot.

It had been many years since Cajhet had last seen his raunchy old mother, and he was not sure he would still recognize her. Following the directions of her neighbors, he found her in the Temple of Attapran, the patron goddess of sailors. It seemed his mother now sat in some temple or other, every morning of her life, with the notion that she was thereby expiating old sins. Her worship of gods and goddesses was as promiscuous as her earlier life had been.

"Hello, Cajhet." She recognized her son at once. "You look like you need feeding up. A bit of heft looks good on a mrem."

She was then introduced to Kizzlecosh, and the two females, after a few suspicious moments, recognized in each other kindred spirits. They shared a bawdy conspiratorial laugh that made Cajhet nervous, although he didn't know why.

His mother's real name was Bastanza, although he alone seemed to remember that. She was familiarly called "Buppy"; very familiarly, it turned out. He felt all the old pangs of his youth as they returned through the narrow squalid lanes of the waterfront to her dwelling, for the male half of the neighborhood greeted her with sly endearments, while the female half was as bawdily conspiratorial with her as she had been with Kizzlecosh. The few rivals and enemies she had among the latter were no match for her in obscene repartee.

Cajhet recalled only two of the extraordinary number of half-brothers and -sisters he was introduced to along the way, although they all seemed to know his name. What extravagant tales his mother must have told them about him, he could only guess. For they all seemed to think he was a military hero, intimate with kings.

The briny tang of the air, overladen with the tarry-fishy smells of the docks, reminded him vividly of the many nights he had spent sleeping on doorsteps or wandering the noisome streets, while his mother entertained a friend, sometimes several friends. More than once he had come home to find strange mrem seated up and down the stairs, waiting to get in to see her.

She now dwelled in more spacious quarters—the entire upper two stories of an apartment house—so she had evidently prospered during the intervening years, by one means or another. The furnishings reflected her own tawdry opulence. She had a pair of slatternly servants, and five children still living at home.

"Make yourselves comfortable, dears," she said. "I always do." She exchanged another bawdy conspiratorial laugh with

Kizzlecosh, and the two she-mrem withdrew to a plush window seat for some real conspiracy.

Cajhet had been personally warned by Severakh himself not to reveal anything about their enterprise, but of course Kizzlecosh had gotten every detail out of him the first night. She seemed to get every detail she needed out of Buppy as well—they were already pals—and soon the kits were sent running on mysterious errands. One by one Cajhet's half-brothers entered the dwelling, conferred with the two females, and departed.

In the days that followed, Severakh took part in the conferences, while the kits were sent on other mysterious errands, to fetch other half-brothers from all over the city. It became quite embarrassing for Cajhet, after a while. He was excluded from the conferences; soon he was excluded from the very apartment. Some nights, at least. It seemed that his mother, despite her age and opulent figure, had enticed yet another lover. Once more he found himself sitting on doorsteps, or wandering the crowded, brawling, noisome streets of the waterfront, as if he were a kit again.

He sometimes fell in with his comrades, alone or in twos and threes; like himself they were relegated to the streets, although for other reasons.

Severakh had imposed on them a discipline which recalled their Kazerclawn drills; in addition, he placed the waterfront taverns off limits, so no careless word could betray their mission to a spy or informer. Their only recreation now was walking the streets after sundown, in inconspicuous groups of no more than two or three. They understood the perils of the expedition before them, if not its true purpose; nonetheless it grew harder with each passing night to walk by the open door of a tavern.

It was even worse by day, when they had nothing to do but skulk out of sight, in the scattered tenement rooms where they were lodged. But the outfitting of their ship was best accomplished by Cajhet's half-brothers, who were already within a day or two of completing their work. In addition to shipfitters, these included merchants, sea captains, wharfingers, harbor officials, and common seamrem; the few who had even heard of the Shadow Islands believed them to be mythical. There were no charts. The search for a trustworthy pilot had to be carried out with hermetic secrecy.

The sole pretender to any real knowledge about the islands turned out to be a waterfront lounger known only as Shimsham, and considered half mad. Miserably poor, declawed for theft years ago, and laughed at for his wild ideas, the grisly, scrounging, drunken old sailor claimed to have been shipwrecked in the Shadow Islands as a youth. For a drink or two he'd spin yarns by the skein about monsters and demons, pirates, storms, shipwreck, and beautiful island she-mrem. And if you didn't like one tale, he'd spin you another.

Cajhet happened to be present the first time Shimsham was brought in to tell his story. "Three claws above the horizon, and due west," was all the navigation he could remember from his youthful adventure. Since he had no claws himself any more, and was obviously drunk, even this vague reference seemed implausible. Severakh had him kicked down the stairs.

Kizzlecosh was meanwhile making inquiries of her own. The Tangletide sat at the foot of a notorious smugglers' wharf; she had already earned a reputation for ferocity, and began a new collection of ears. But any mention of the Shadow Islands only provoked jibes and laughter. "Ask Shimsham," was the invariable response. "He escaped on a raft, but had to leave his wits behind. Not enough room aboard." Then laughter and coarse badinage.

Cajhet himself, at least for the first few nights after Kizzlecosh got her new job, managed to sneak a drink or two at the alley door of the Tangletide. It was always accompanied by breath-crushing hugs and intimate grooming, and tonight he wondered if he was really that thirsty after all. Even a desperate voyage into uncharted seas would be a reprieve from his usual labors . . . .

Then he realized that a little she-kit was standing in front of the doorstep where he sat, head in hands, looking curiously down at him. He was about to shoo her away, when he recognized her as a half-sister.

"Kizzlecosh said I should run and fetch you," she lisped. "She's anxious to see you about something, she didn't say what," the girl added with a sly giggle. "Better hurry. She just bit somebody's ear off."

With tingling ears, Cajhet at once rose and followed her. Kizzlecosh had intimated that she was making special arrangements with the tavernkeeper for afternoon and evening visits. Was that why she had summoned him? He noticed that his half-sister was still watching him with precocious curiosity, and he glared sternly at her.

She responded with an impudent grimace that squelched any ideas he might have had about fraternal authority.

It was still an hour before midnight, but the Tangletide was already crowded with ruffians. The sea ballads here were lilting, and the musicians seemed able to play any tune called for—which was probably lucky for them. Cajhet found Kizzlecosh behind the bar, nailing up a tufty, grizzled ear; the third already in her new collection, though she been here less than a week.

"Recognize it?"

Cajhet shook his head. "But it looks very nice beside the others, love," he added quickly, afraid he may have hurt her feelings. "You'll have a collection bigger than your last, in no time."

"Maybe, maybe not. Right now, I have to establish my reputation, so I'm being extra strict." She bit the air with her sharp, powerful teeth, then gave him an affectionate hug. "Won't have time for many more of those for a while, my little Cajie-wajie. Not after what I just heard."

He winked lecherously, and poked a sly finger into her massive bosom. "Then we'd better not lose a minute, love."

She exploded with bawdy laughter, and gave him so passionate a hug that his eyes rolled in his head. When his vision at last restabilized, he found that she had drawn him into the deserted passageway to the kitchen.

"That's Haggie's ear I just nailed up." She lowered her voice. "I spotted him skulking through the streets on my way here tonight, and pounced. Held him by the ear till he told me everything. The slimy liskash sold us out to an even slimier reptile. One at Cragsclaw. His first skulkers are already here, and a horde of bandits and desert marauders not far behind 'em. Why these think you're so important, I still don't know. But it don't matter now. All ships have been restricted to port, unless cleared personally by the governor himself, and a whole big flotilla has been ordered fitted out for some big voyage, somewheres to the west. The same place you're heading, is my guess."

"Don't look like we're heading anywhere right now." Cajhet frowned.

"You'd better—and dragon-quick. Haggie sold the big liskash all your names, and when the army gets here you'll all be hunted down, then dragged off to Cragsclaw for you-know-what. Tell old Severakh right now. Even tomorrow morning might be too late."

"You're right, love. I'll check with one of the officers—"

"Just go home and check with your mother. She'll know where to find Severakh at this hour," she added drily.

Cajhet looked bewilderedly at her for a moment; then a new thought struck him. "Say, won't you be in danger? Even without an ear, Haggie could sell you out. You're mean and tough, love, but you can't take on an entire army by yourself. If they'd hunt us down, you know they'd also hunt down anybody who helped us. No," he said firmly, "I'm not budging till I know you're safe. Don't ask me to do it, because I won't."

She gazed fondly down at him, her big jowly face melting with tenderness. "Oh, Cajie-wajie, you really do love me. But don't worry, pet. I'll be all right." She led him past the kitchen to a secluded room set on pilings directly over the water, and pointed to a trapdoor. "Haggie's always been a back-stabber. I didn't like the questions he was asking before we left Ravarbal, so I told him I was only going with you a couple of days' march, to show you the way. That gave us near a week's start, because he had to be sure I wasn't coming back before he dared sell us out." She savagely bit the air with her sharp, powerful teeth.

Cajhet started instinctively to cover his own ears, but disguised the gesture by pointing to the trapdoor. "Haggie?"

She nodded. "No telling where he'll end up. They got something here called tangletides. A sailor told me it has something to do with the three moons acting at different angles. I don't know about that, but I checked and found out that we're getting bad tangletides tomorrow, starting just before dawn. Nothing will be able to get out of the harbor until late afternoon. So better get moving, and tell Severakh everything. The folks you left back at Ravarbal are in a bad

way—the big reptile's sent a whole army after them—but
there's nothing you can do for them now. They're on their
own, and you'd better be on your way."

This time it was Cajhet who did the hugging. "I'll be back,
love, and then I'll never go away again."

She chuckled. "No, you won't, my little Cajie-wajie. I'll
see to that. We'll have a lot of nights to make up for when
you get back." If her return hug was an earnest for those
nights, Cajhet had good reason for the sense of apprehension
that overcame him—when he at last caught his breath, and
his eyes stopped rolling in his head.

"Where are we going now?" lisped his half-sister, who had
waited for him in a doorway across the lane from the Tangletide.

"Home, and fast. I have to talk to Mother."

"Better wait till morning." The kit spoke with the voice of
experience. "Mama don't like us to walk in on her when she's
entertaining."

"Can't be helped this time. I've got to find old Severakh
quick, and I'm told Mother knows where he is."

"Oh, she knows that, all right," the kit said drily.

But the first person Cajhet encountered as he burst into
the apartment was not his mother. It was Severakh himself,
clad in nothing but one of her fluffy pink dressing gowns.
There was a look on his face that Cajhet had never seen there
before, a look that quickly hardened from embarrassment
into his old drillmaster's glower. Arms akimbo, he seemed to
defy his subordinate to make a single impertinent remark.

Cajhet instead reported dutifully all he had just learned
from Kizzlecosh. His mother entered the room at that moment, wearing a flouncy lavender nightgown, with a tray
holding twin goblets and a carafe of wine. Her eyes twinkled
merrily at the scene.

Forgetting his effeminate garment, Severakh began pacing
sternly back and forth. "They haven't arrested us so far," he
muttered, "because they're not sure yet who will win the
siege of Ar. Damned fools! Can't they see that if Ar falls, then
all the city-states of the mrem are doomed, including
Namakhazar? Perhaps the very existence of the mrem . . . ."

Buppy saw only that all the fun in life would be doomed,
and while Severakh sent Cajhet flying with orders to assem-
ble the mrem at once, she sent her other children with

messages to their older half-brothers and -sisters, to help with the escape, but cover their tracks. For if the great city of Ar was in fact doomed, there would certainly be reprisals afterwards against all who in any way aided its partisans.

As Cajhet hurried through the streets, he thought about the last words his fierce old commander had given him: "Do not mention to anyone, and especially to young Branwe, anything about Ravarbal. He can't help those we left there now, but he might foolishly risk his life—and our mission—to try." He also thought about the last look Severakh had given him. It said clearly: "One word to anybody about pink dressing gowns, and I'll have you pitched overboard."

▲

A single moon shone low in the sky, as thirty armed mrem crept along a deserted wharf, where they were soon joined by teams of stevedores wheeling barrows and handcarts laden with provisions. The wharfinger was Cajhet's half-brother.

"See that magnificent argosy out at the very center of the harbor?" He pointed. "It's the finest ship afloat. Here are the seamrem who have enlisted for your voyage. They didn't expect to leave so soon, and you may have to carry some of 'em aboard. But they'll do their jobs—once they sober up."

"I'm sober already," said Shimsham. This was obviously untrue, and whether his wild tales had any basis was still unknown. But no one else who even pretended knowledge of the Shadow Islands had been discovered. If they were to have a pilot at all, he was it. "And I'm ready to go. If somebody could just give me a hand with my navigational gear . . . Careful! Don't drop the box. What's inside is precious."

The wharfinger shrugged. "Anyway, you might as well pirate the argosy. In your situation, the law doesn't mean much anymore. So forget about the ship we were outfitting for you."

"I can't forget about a whole fleet lying at anchor," said Severakh, while his mrem descended silently into a pair of squat barges. "My mrem aren't sailors. It's going to take them a few days to learn the ropes. What if we're pursued?"

"So long as you leave before the second moon rises, there will be no hot pursuit all of tomorrow. Just be sure you leave before then—or you'll be trapped in port. The tides are nasty all along this coast. As for being hunted down by this flotilla now being outfitted, they won't know which way to go. A number of witnesses—fishermrem, sailors, dock hands—are going to come forward and testify to having seen your ship head east along the coast. It's the best we can do for you. May the All-Mother guide and protect you."

"Amen," said Severakh. "And may she watch over your own mother. Many thanks for all you've done for us."

Zanira was the polestar; it was also the name of the magnificent argosy they were approaching across the midnight harbor. Shimsham, sitting protectively on his box of navigational gear, found this a good omen.

"It's Zanira we've got to watch," he said. "Keep it three claws above the horizon, and sail due west. Trouble is, I'll need somebody else's claws."

"You'll get mine, if you don't shut up," growled Severakh. "Easy now, lads. We don't want any commotion. Even with these sailors telling us what to do, it's going to take hours to get the ship ready to sail."

Branwe sat beside him, the Demon Sword in his hand. "Have you heard anything more from Ravarbal, sir? I can't help worrying about, well, those we left behind."

"Srana, you mean? Are you saying that she can't take care of herself?"

"No, of course not. She's as courageous as she is beautiful."

"Then what are you worried about? Didn't I leave her twice as many mrem as we've got here? Well, then?" Severakh looked him straight in the eye. "We're depending on you, lad. That sword was forged for a warrior as daring and able as your father."

"I won't fail," said Branwe, without noticing that his question had never been answered.

As the most agile aboard either of the two barges, he led the scramble up the side of the *Zanira*. The two watchmrem on deck were swarmed over; the small crew below decks were mostly asleep in their bunks. They offered no resistance, and willingly helped unload the barges. They too had heard about the invasion of the Eastern Lords, and had been waiting only for the first voyage out—under anybody's command, the longer the better. They rigged the ship to sail in remarkably short order.

"Three hands and more above the horizon now," Shimsham remarked, seated comfortably in the stern beside the huge steering oar, on his box of navigational gear. "That means a long voyage south, before it sinks to just three claws."

Severakh gazed thoughtfully out to sea, as the sails caught the offshore breeze, as the masts groaned under the strain, and the argosy hove faster and faster across the harbor. The second moon was just rising, and the tides were beginning to tumble chaotically in from the sea. Not for weeks to come would a conjunction of all three moons focus on one particular spot, in the major island of the Shadows, somewhere in the chartless western seas.

Exactly how this peculiar focus of moonlight caused an evil dimension to conjoin their world was wizard's business, not his. All he knew was that they had to be ashore on that island of islands, on that night of nights, or their voyage would be in vain, and the great city of Ar—perhaps their very race—lost forever.

▲

Chapter 15
The Yozgat

▲————————————————————————————————————▲

Not since her arrival in Kazer-
clawm, to tend her dying grandfather, had Srana's danger
sense so disquieted her. Not even during the weeks of pursuit and flight that had brought her at last to this remote
pariah city, deep in the mountains. Was it something she had
dreamed?

The evil presence that seemed to lurk like a predator at the
borderlands of her unconscious mind, as if waiting to pounce
when she was most vulnerable, had lately not troubled her.
Now she felt evil converging from all directions.

She sat up in bed and listened. There was nothing but the
settling noises of an old building. Her door was bolted on the
inside; grilles covered every window; an armed guard slept
on a bedroll across her threshold out in the corridor. The
danger was not immediate, but the trap was closing. They
had to flee at once.

She pondered over the fragment of the Khavala for a moment, then shook her head. Attempting contact was too great
a risk. Perhaps not for her, but for Sruss. After all, her
strange disquiet might just be some insidious new snare
contrived by the Evil One. Was she in fact in any real
danger? Or was the probing intelligence now just trying to
entice her with false warnings into doing something foolish,
something that would leave her vulnerable to entrapment?

Again she shook her head. No, her danger sense was too
vivid. This was no phantom, and she rose and dressed and
woke the guard sleeping outside across her threshold.

The danger seemed less menacing to the south, in the
direction that Branwe and the others had departed, toward

the port of Namakhazar. They had in fact discussed the contingency of repairing there en masse, but in the end decided that so large a band could not possibly elude detection by the bandit gangs lurking outside the walls—perhaps tipped off by agents inside the walls. Nor was a dash for Ar feasible; it never had been. Troops of marauders ravaged the country between, and the city itself was reported to be now completely invested.

The number of spies lurking in the streets around the Anglock Inn had quadrupled since Severakh's departure for Namakhazar. There were also the bandit gangs outside the city to elude; probably dragons and other nasty reptiles as well. Was it her fragment of the Khavala the Evil One so desperately sought? Ever more power to work evil? To bring down the walls of Ar? She wondered now if she had been wise to keep it after all.

Severakh had encharged the remnant of his guerrilla army to capable lieutenants. They well recalled how her danger sense had saved them again and again from being cut off or surrounded while harrassing enemy camps and supply lines, and now heard her warning with apprehension. In minutes the Anglock Inn was a hive of activity, with scores of soldiers silently arming, packing, and provisioning for immediate flight.

The spies lurking in the neighborhood had grown wary since Severakh's escape; nonetheless they were taken unawares—all except one. But that one was enough to alert corrupt city officials that their guests were flying by night. Fortunately these officials dared not make their collusion with the bandit gangs hovering outside the walls too public, and had to be circumspect about alerting them in turn. This granted the fugitives a few critical hours' head start on their pursuers.

Over barren ridges, through mountain defiles, valleys, and dark forests, guided unerringly by Srana's danger sense, they maintained their lead all that day, and increased it in the days that followed. A misty drizzle, and streamers of fog seeping down from the heights, helped conceal them; but they drew ahead mostly because their pursuers—scouts reported them a thousand strong, and increasing daily in number—were more and more reluctant to close on them. Not even when reinforced by regular troops, and enjoined by the magic of battle priests, could they be driven any nearer a particular range of mountains.

Severakh's lieutenants naturally took advantage of this strange reluctance. The land through which they now marched was so devoid of civilization that they feared dragons. But none appeared, and soon the various nasty lizards that had until now assailed them nightly also disappeared. It was a wilderness such as none of them had ever seen before, and through wooded valleys, up slopes and down, in mist and rain and sunshine, through dark silent forests and flowering meadows, they marched unharrassed all the fourth day.

It was just when the most optimistic among them had begun to picture themselves snugly ensconced within the walls of some southern haven, that Srana sensed danger approaching from that direction too. Scouts were sent forward, and soon reported that a cohort of regular troops, with auxiliaries of bandits and desert marauders, were indeed marching toward them—although not directly toward them. Like those who had pursued them for the last week, these new enemies also seemed chary of entering this strange silent realm.

Srana's danger sense now so disquieted her that she could no longer determine whence they were most threatened. Danger seemed to be all around them, lurking in every shadow like the alien intelligence that again sought nightly to penetrate her subconscious. At her request, Severakh's lieutenants and all sixty-some mrem were interrogated. Three mrem only stepped forward from the ranks.

All had heard old wives' tales about this particular region. Something called a Yozgat, or perhaps *the* Yozgat, was or were supposed to dwell somewhere in the depths of the mountains. Two of the three believed it to be a monstrous dragon that had depopulated the countryside; the third had heard stories about a mysterious lost race, whether of mrem or liskash origin he did not know, that only came out at night, when there was no moon in the sky.

"I've heard two versions, my lady," he added. "That these Yozgat are cannibals, which means they're probably some nasty type of cave liskash, or that they skin their victims alive just for sport. One mrem I met years ago, a caravan teamster by trade, swore to me on oath that he'd actually seen a flayed carcass hereabouts. Twice, in fact. So he always gave the Yozgat plenty of room after that. He'd heard whispers about whole caravans that had just disappeared and were never heard of again, like they were swallowed up by the ground. Might be some kind of cave reptile at that," he concluded.

Two moons hung in near conjunction, one full and the other gibbous, directly overhead. Campfires burned arrogantly on a hilltop, visible from miles away—also miles away from the real encampment. Severakh himself could hardly have chosen a better defensive position, or posted his sentries more effectively.

Hour after hour the scouts reported in, snatched refreshments on the fly, and slipped back into the midnight forest.

"That's the third squabble reported in an enemy camp, and they've blocked us in three directions," one lieutenant commented, as the conference settled down in the shadows at the edge of a clearing silver with moonlight. "Seems their battle priests are getting pressure from Cragsclaw to round us up—at any cost—and right now."

"But for some reason the bandits and other ragtag are hanging back," added another lieutenant. "That might give us enough leeway to wriggle out of the trap."

There was no agreement about this. The consensus was that the regular troops, at least, would soon begin tightening the noose. Perhaps tomorrow; certainly no later than the day after. There were so many of these now in the field that it no longer mattered whether the bandits and desert marauders superstitiously hung back.

"We had better hang back ourselves until morning," decided the acting commander, after all the scouting reports had been evaluated. "Whether this Yozgat really is a species of monstrous dragon, or flesh-eating liskash, or horrors that prowl only at night, we'd better wait right here until dawn. By ascending into the mountains, we might be able to slip past the troops to the south, and outrun them to Namakhazar. In any case, we have to move eastward tomorrow. We're blocked in all other directions."

This was unanimously agreed to, and as the morning peaks first silhouetted blackly against the eastern sky, the sixty-some fugitives were already on the march. The first scout to

rejoin them reported that the decoy campsite had been attacked just before dawn by hundreds of regular troops. Soon
other scouts were reporting a great pincers fanning out across
the lower slopes; by noon the last scouts to come in reported
that the pincers had begun to close. Their trail had been
picked up; the jaws of the trap were shutting.

A barren defile, carrying icy meltwater down from the
snow-capped peaks, ran due east like a highway. Bogs and
debris cones made the going rough in places, but they had no
choice except to follow as far as it led—which turned out to
be not far enough. With a thousand troops closing in from
below, concealment was no longer possible, and they clambered helter-skelter up the slopes toward what looked like a
pass or saddle through the first towering range of mountains.

There was still no sign of habitation, although more and
more frequently they came upon strange animal tracks. What
made these tracks so mysterious was that they began and
ended abruptly, as if some large powerful creature had appeared out of nowhere, run a short distance, and then disappeared again. There were whispers about dragons, although
the footprints were clearly not reptilian.

The whispers among the lieutenants were now about finding some defensive position where they could make a last
stand. They had been seen by the enemy; a dense column of
regular troops—followed by a rabble of desert marauders and
bandits—marched up the wooded slopes behind them, while
the pincers closed upon them from north and south. Their
only hope was to find some natural rampart where they could
defend themselves until sunset, then slip away in the dark.

Even that desperate hope seemed to vanish, as they scrambled onto a broad flat-topped hill less than a square mile in
area. There was little vegetation, and no cover at all. Nothing
but rock and scrub and patches of barren soil. There were
also more of the strange footprints that appeared suddenly
and led nowhere. In the distance they could see what looked
like a natural gateway, and began to run for it as hard as they
could—until they saw it was no use. The arms of the pincers
were closing in too fast. They would be cut off before they
were halfway there, and they halted.

Then the pincer arms also halted, although no order seemed
to have been given. Mass dissension now began to seethe all

through the enemy ranks; those nearest the mountain gateway could be seen pointing at something while their captains and battle priests raged among them, trying futilely to drive them forward. The angry cracking of whips echoed through the mountains.

The fugitives, continuing to straggle forward out of mere inertia, looked about them in dismay. Then their acting captain also pointed to something, although not at whatever was now so intimidating their pursuers. South of the mountain gateway, a cascade of volcanic rock ascended like a giant's stairway. Not the ideal spot for a last stand, but the best within reach.

Srana's vision was the keenest of them all. Row upon row of white objects lined the rocky cascade, or sat atop posts, and she was the first to recognize these as skulls. Soon others around her also realized what they were, and pointed and hung back as superstitiously as the enemy pincers.

"Keep moving!" barked one lieutenant after the other, rallying them. "If you don't like what's in front of you, take a look at what's coming up behind."

The main column of the enemy, a thousand regular troops, had just climbed onto the broad flat-topped hill, and continued to march relentlessly forward, weapons at the ready. But not all the whipping and cursing and shouting of the captains and battle priests could yet drive the pincer arms a foot nearer the gateway, and the fugitives, their desperation overcoming their own fears, reached it first.

Then there was a moment of indecision. They had their defensive position for making a stand, but perhaps they should plunge straight through the gateway instead, hoping their superstitious enemies would be too irresolute to follow. All they could see through it was another broad flat-topped hill, some three times the extent of the one on which they now stood. Then the decision was made for them.

Once more it was Srana's keen vision that first perceived the new danger, and her warning sent them all scrambling frantically for safety, up the volcanic blocks and ledges.

What exactly was approaching, she did not know; only that there were a lot of them, moving swiftly with long gliding leaps, and obviously hostile. Both the column of regular troops and the pincer arms—which had at last resumed closing—were still moving blindly forward. They seemed to outnumber the approaching forces a good four to one, although only the roughest estimate was as yet possible; for there were at least two or three riders mounted on each of the strange animals running and leaping unseen toward them. Nor did these riders seem very big.

"Shield wall!" cried the acting captain, as darts and missiles began to arc upward from below. "Take cover where you can!"

The wall of shields that went up like the shield of some great shelled animal might not have met Severakh's exacting standards, but it succeeded in repelling the first barrage. There were no serious casualties—and no second barrage. For their pursuers suddenly became the pursued; their attackers the attacked. They looked down in wonder as those who had sought to overwhelm them were now in turn overwhelmed; a fate that would surely have befallen themselves as well, had they not taken refuge high up the cascade of rocks. The rows of skulls lining the mountain gateway were no idle warning.

Through the gateway, like a living avalanche, ran and leapt and sailed a weird cavalry of dwarfish warriors, mounted in twos and threes upon huge two-legged animals that would run a short distance, leap into the air, spread flaps of skin along their sides, and glide incredible distances forward, a scant few feet above the ground. The wall of shields went down again, and the fugitives stared down in wonder at the most bizarre means of warfare they had ever witnessed.

Srana had decided to use concealment magic long enough to secrete her fragment of the Khavala where it could never be found. Even if she died here—like her grandfather she knew better than to let herself be captured alive by the Evil One—at least his power would not be augmented. But she now recognized magic of other kinds.

Surely the weird two-legged animals possessed at least rudimentary powers of levitation, to prolong glides only a few feet off the ground such incredible distances. The battle empathy of the dwarfish warriors who rode them also seemed magical.

The true odds against the newcomers turned out to be about five to one; but in any actual combat these odds were proportionately reversed. Wherever there was weakness or confusion, wherever a flank was exposed or a line extended too far, an avalanche of the weird animals would drop out of the air as if drawn magnetically to the spot; hundreds of the dwarfish warriors would pour from their backs, swarm over every exposed enemy, then as quickly remount and bound out of range of any counterattack. No orders were given; none were needed.

Wielding broad-bladed curved swords as tall as themselves, each little warrior seemed to know empathetically what he was supposed to do, and what each of his comrades was doing or expected of him at any given moment.

Their larger and more powerful foes were unable to either advance or retreat. Wherever they rallied as a disciplined mass, they found that it was only those who had not rallied that were attacked. They formed a solid phalanx, and were at once attacked from the rear; they formed a battle square, an impenetrable mass of spears, swords, and javelins pointed outward, and were attacked from the inside. As the absolute odds dropped toward equality, the relative odds swung heavier and heavier in favor of the dwarfish warriors. Eight, nine, ten of them at once would now swarm over every solitary foe. They wore peculiar cloaks over their armor, dramatically blended from pelts of many colors, which they twirled so deftly in the faces of any helpless wretch they attacked that he could only lunge blindly into whirlwinds of fur, before being swarmed over and cut to pieces.

Then began the rout. So long as they massed together, the regular troops could at least stave off the inevitable, although they were never able to fight back with effect. Their swarming attackers either were out of range of their darts and missiles, or deflected them with their broad-bladed curved swords with an astounding deftness. But the instant they bolted, every mrem for himself, every last one of them was lost. There was no quarter asked or given; no prisoners taken; not a single survivor.

Seated upon their strange mounts, twirling their blades as they glided through the air, just as they had twirled their fur cloaks in battle, the dwarfish little warriors lopped off head after head from behind. The pursuit was swift and inexorable.

The bandits had been the first to bolt, and hence the last to be overtaken, but none escaped.

Meanwhile Srana descended unseen down the rocky ledges to the battlefield below. Nobody looked in her direction, neither friend nor foe; she could easily have used concealment magic at this moment to escape, perhaps to make her way eventually all the way to Ar. But that would have doomed her companions to certain death, and probably rendered the quest for the Khavala futile. For the mystic stone was of no use to anyone without magical powers, and there were no magicians among those now seeking it—except the Evil One himself, the greatest magician of them all.

The mass levies he had recently dispatched to Namakhazar could only mean that he had somehow discovered that others now sought the Khavala. Merely destroying it to keep it out of his hands would no longer be enough. At least, not enough to save the great city of Ar from destruction.

As she started across the mountain gateway she noticed three troops of mrem, dressed humbly and trotting in martial step, approaching from the same direction as had the dwarfish warriors. But these mrem were not at all dwarfish; if anything, they were exceptionally tall. So humble and obedient were they, however, that a single warrior was enough to keep them in drill-field order.

Srana wondered who they could be, but did not lose her concentration. Nobody looked in her direction. She had picked out the leader of the dwarfish host by his overbearing demeanor and the jeweled coronet on his brow. He stood waiting the arrival of the three troops of exceptionally tall mrem, while the pair of riders who had shared his mount with him throughout the battle now joined in the pursuit. He never saw Srana approach.

"Bravely done, my lord," she whispered. "But how long could even so valiant a people as yours withstand the Eastern Lords, once the mrem have been overrun?"

Startled, he turned around—but in the wrong direction. There was nobody near him.

"You have defeated odds of five to one," she continued, from the direction he was not looking. "How would your warriors fare against a hundred to one, a thousand, against all the hordes of the steppes and deserts?"

Again he turned in the wrong direction. "Parvatta? Is it you who counsels me, goddess?" he whispered with superstitious awe. "I know what you tell me is true, but your own High Priestess opposes me. You know that the Yozgat have dwelt in isolation from other peoples for many centuries. You also know that our sacred traditions are inflexible, that from birth until death they rule every moment of our lives, that to deviate from them is to perish. For only through adhering to these sacred traditions have we prevailed over peoples larger than ourselves. Any deviation could provoke our very Mamlocks to revolt."

"But dare you remain aloof, when all the world is in turmoil? Would you be allowed to, even if you so desired? Would the enemies who surround you stand against the Eastern Lords to defend you, or join them in your destruction? I see that you know the answer."

He groaned. "I have known it since the first reports of the invasion, goddess. That is why we were so well prepared this morning. I knew an attack must come eventually, and kept the bambarongs saddled night and day. Making an example of their first attack may discourage a second."

"For how long? Your warriors are now returning, and troops of mrem approach from inside your own land, so we have only minutes. Listen carefully."

There was no possibility of such a people allying themselves with the Evil One, or with anybody who might encroach upon their fierce independence, perhaps with anybody at all. But Srana related why she was here, who was after her, and even an intimation about the quest for the Khavala. She desperately needed allies, or at least a refuge until she knew whether Branwe and his companions had succeeded or failed.

"Though your people and mine can never be true friends, my lord," she concluded, relenting her concealment magic, "we have common enemies. Should they prevail, neither of us will survive."

This time he turned in the right direction, but was again startled. "Parvatta, it is you," he muttered with awe. But at last he realized that it was only a she-mrem standing before him, although a she-mrem so beautiful compared to the squat tufty ugliness of his own people that she indeed seemed truly a goddess. "Say not another word," he cautioned her. "My warriors are already demanding the pelts of your companions as trophies of honor, which is their sacred right. If I fail, my own pelt will be among them."

But he did not fail. His name was Changavar, Prince Warrior of the Yozgat, an authority that was neither hereditary nor elective—at least, not formally so—but earned both in council and in war. Another sacred tradition was that the decisions of a Prince Warrior were infallible during a battle; they could be questioned only in council afterwards.

There were fierce looks, and some demonstrative pointing toward the fugitives, who had again raised their shield wall on the rocky ledges above, but no open mutiny. Perhaps it was the number of trophies already claimed, perhaps Changavar's sword prowess, but he succeeded in preserving the lives of the fugitives—at least, for now.

Getting them to descend from the ledges and surrender their arms needed still rarer diplomacy, and this time it was Srana who was the diplomat.

The Yozgat warriors were hardly more than waist-high to their Mamlock bondmrem, who also turned out to be significantly more numerous. Yet so humbled and browbeaten were they that they servilely performed all the menial tasks in the land, freeing their overlords to perfect the very martial skills which domineered them in the first place. At any other time the swagger and arrogance with which the fierce little warriors bullied their towering menials might have seemed comic. But as the Mamlocks abjectly set to work, flaying the "trophies of honor" from the corpses of the enemy, scattered by the thousand across the broad flat-topped hill, the fugitives, at last coaxed down from the ledges by Srana, looked tempted to scramble back up again out of sheer horror. Not one of them but half expected to lose his own pelt.

It was the superstitious awe for Srana's beauty, which they saw reflected on the ugly, tufty faces of the Yozgat, that at last reassured them. Also, they no longer had anything to lose. For even the boldest among them now realized that they could not prevail against such doughty warriors; neither could they escape them. Their strange mounts could easily overtake them up the very ledges of the mountainside. They naturally felt uncomfortable at the way certain Yozgat openly appraised the quality of their fur, but so far at least they were not molested.

In fact, most of the Yozgat were now too busy pressing claims for battle trophies to bother about them. Swaggering on their short little legs, cursing, posturing arrogantly, kicking laggard or clumsy Mamlocks, they settled conflicting claims by what looked like a martial dance, but was really a means of sortition. There were no open squabbles, although there were sometimes seven or eight claimants for the same pelt because of the swarming-attack method of the Yozgat. Stolidly the Mamlocks continued their grim work.

They would remain behind to cremate the flayed corpses, add more warning skulls to the mountain gateway, and lug the trophies back to the communal barracks, with only a single mounted warrior left to supervise them. The fugitives were meanwhile formed into ranks and marched away. Srana alone was honored with a mount, seated behind Changavar himself at the head of his weird cavalry.

No Yozgat had been killed in the battle, few even seriously wounded. Twirling their swords and fur cloaks as they rode, they chanted a resounding victory song, which the running, leaping, and gliding of their bambarongs caused to quaver eerily across the broadening mountain valley.

Since every glide covered a hundred yards and more, Srana was able to answer most of Changavar's questions—which was why, she suspected, he had seated her alone behind him. She appreciated more fully now just how dangerous was his break with tradition. He in turn appreciated more fully the dangers besetting his people. Run, leap, glide; a few terse words of conversation; then run and leap again. The glides became progressively longer and longer, as the land sloped downward and the valley continued to broaden.

Miles and miles of orderly farms, paddocks, and orchards centered upon two clusters of barracks—each a veritable city—which in turn centered upon a sprawling stone edifice, the Temple of Parvatta. There was no ornament. The architecture was perfectly functional. It was a military encampment, a society of little soldiers and big orderlies, with the latter forbidden weapons upon pain of death.

As she approached the Temple of Parvatta, Srana's keen ears perceived, mingling with the quavering victory song of the warriors, a paean of welcome by female voices. Over a hundred dwarfish, tufty little she-mrem in green robes formed a chorus upon the temple stairs. Leading them was the oldest and tuftiest of all, the High Priestess of Parvatta.

The plaza before the temple looked more suitable for martial drills and parades than religious worship. It was now thronged with thousands of Yozgat mrem, and kits. There were murmurs of astonishment as Srana dismounted; many glanced toward the inner temple, where stood the eidolon of Parvatta. Then her danger sense warned her of hostility, and she glanced toward the High Priestess.

Never before had she seen such malice concentrated in mrem eyes. Khal himself could scarcely have fixed more vindictive hatred upon her. She also sensed other concentrations, as if this ugly, tufty old priestess did more than direct the singing of the chorus behind her, as if she were already tapping their mindpower: using it as a force, a probe, a weapon.

There was a shimmering clarity in the mountain air; the morning sky was blue and cloudless. Srana did not yet know if she had any friends here, but she clearly saw her enemy.

▲

Chapter 16
The Judgment of Parvatta

▲──▲

Most of the news these days was bad, and Nizzam had learned his lesson about delivering it in person. Let the messengers themselves bear the consequences. The legate of the Eastern Lords, after being closeted for hours with Khal, had at last emerged content that the siege of Ar would end victoriously, that soon the entire realm of the mrem would lay open to plunder and enslavement. But Khal himself was not content, and Nizzam had also learned to read his moods with the acuteness of a survivor.

How much longer he would survive was the question of the day, every day. From the woeful looks of the two messengers he ushered through the door, he probably would not have lasted the afternoon, had he been so foolish as to announce their bad news for them.

He had discovered that his master's reptilian eyes were not keen at distinguishing stationary objects. There were now over a hundred stuffed effigies ranged about the hall, and the mountings for a dozen more each awaiting the capture of some mighty personage of the mrem, and he had survived several outbursts of insane rage lately by posing among them until Khal stopped shrieking and gnashing his teeth. But he did not trust even that expedient now. So enraging was today's news that the first words were hardly spoken, when he prudently ducked behind a stuffed *generalissimo*, and crawled on his hands and knees out the door.

Nor did he stop in the dim corridor outside. Not until he had reached an abandoned tower of the palace, remote from Khal's grisly chamber, did he feel safe. For the moment, at least. There was no escape, of course, should Khal really want to get his repulsive webbed hands on him; but out of sight, out of mind. Perhaps when Khal thought about him again, his insane rage at the news that Srana had again eluded capture—evidently the whole army sent to pursue her had mysteriously been annihilated—would have cooled.

The tower overlooked the befouled palace gardens. The chained dragon was restless, and it was not long before Nizzam discovered why. It was feeding time. The gate was opened, and the two hapless messengers thrust into the garden. The dragon at once vanished, reappeared behind its victims, and pounced. While it devoured one of them, it evilly watched the futile panic of the other out of the corner of its eye.

Nizzam watched only long enough to be certain of his own fate today, should his hiding place be discovered. Khal had not even bothered to appear on the balcony to enjoy the torment below as he usually did. Had his rage truly driven him insane this time? Perhaps too insane to remember the existence of his wretched servant . . .

But soon this hope too was dashed. The palace servants—a staff decimated by Khal's wrath—were now out in force, searching the rooms and corridors for something, and he was pretty sure that something was himself. He glanced down into the garden. The dragon had now devoured its second victim, but still looked hungry. Or had Khal some more insidious torment waiting for him? He dared not wait to find out.

The servants, as fellow sufferers, had shared their intimate knowledge of the palace and its neighborhood with him. He had long cherished wild fancies about using this knowledge to escape, but until now had always lacked the courage to try. Courage still did not inspire him—it was sheer despair. For those same servants, in fear of their own lives, would not hesitate to betray him to Khal. Just as he would have done to them, had their positions been reversed.

There was only one wing of the palace that these mrem servants never entered, where the staff was exclusively liskash, handpicked by Khal. At least, none entered who ever returned to tell the tale. But despair breeds desperate measures, and he sneaked and crept, slunk, dodged, and tiptoed, up stairs and down, hiding in empty rooms, skulking through deserted corridors, until he reached a particular closet.

"These liskash ain't so smart as they think they are," an old wine steward had boasted to him one day. "I've been here forty-three years, and could tell them a thing or two about this palace."

Among the things he had revealed to Nizzam was that a secret passageway led from a closet in the consort's bedroom to another closet in the old guest wing of the palace, the very wing from which all mrem were now excluded. The secret of this passageway had supposedly been passed down from generation to generation by the reigning mistresses of Cragsclaw. But of course every servant in the palace, down to the meanest scullery wench, knew about it, just as they gossiped freely about every tryst secretly indulged in the night before by their betters.

Lighting a candle, Nizzam slid the panel shut and, hardly daring to breathe, tiptoed down the narrow, musty passageway. For how many generations had the secret lovers of the queens of Cragsclaw tiptoed through this very darkness? Would there ever be kings and queens here again? For the first time in all his dreadful months of groveling before an alien sorcerer he thought of something nobler than saving his own hide.

But it was the sight of the eggs that really brought home to him his role in unleashing so many evils upon the mrem. Emerging from the closet in the old guest wing, he crept warily down a winding staircase to what had once been a dungeon block, now sealed off from the vast cavelike cellarage. Moldering stone walls, rough hewn from the living rock, he had expected to find here the ideal hideout, repulsively dank and nasty, but the last place anybody would think of looking for him. What he found instead was a teeming broodery. In dungeon after dungeon, like caverns beneath a mountain, hundreds of sickly-green eggs nestled in beds of plant mold, warm with decay: the nucleus of a master race.

This explained some things that had recently puzzled him. Twice he had come upon Khal in the presence of strange cave reptiles, surly, ugly, and suspicious-natured, but physically like the warlord. Much more like Khal, certainly, than the legate of the Eastern Lords. It was apparent now that whole families of liskash must have been brought here for selective breeding. No doubt the remote fastnesses of the planet were even now being combed for the most likely specimens of Khal's lost race.

Then he came upon something more ominous still. Hatchlings barely knee-high crouched in the cavelike dimness of an old dungeon cell, while a hideous liskash nurse recited to them in some hissing, gutteral language: perhaps the first incantations of their training as sorcerers. An entire planet dominated by a race of Khals? Nizzam shuddered, and tiptoed away.

This was definitely not the hideout he had expected. He knew what the dragon was fed up in the garden. He did not want to find out what these gruesome little hatchlings ate down here. But as he crept back toward the winding staircase, he heard footsteps descending, and ducked behind a slime-encrusted stone pillar.

Peeking out, he felt his fur stand on end. It was Khal! Had the sorcerer followed him down here? Trembling with panic, he turned and plunged down the nearest corridor, seeking the blackest shadow he could find. But turn where he might, he could not elude the sinister footsteps, and the dim, flickering light of Khal's lantern drove all concealing shadows away before him.

Then he reeled with terror, and nearly swooned. It was a dead end! The corridor opened into a dungeon, or perhaps a natural cave; it was difficult to judge exactly what it was in the gloom, only that there seemed to be no exit. And even the concealing gloom was now deserting him! And the footsteps were drawing closer and closer! Half paralyzed with fright, he backed into a stone block or altar at the very center of the cavern, and barely kept himself from howling in despair. The footsteps now whispered in the corridor just outside.

Frantically, Nizzam groped over the stone block, hoping he might at least hide behind it. Then he realized that it could be nothing other than the marble slab relieved to fit a reptilian shape, on which Khal had lain for so many years beneath the Kazerclaw. Did he still lie brooding upon it, as he had all those years, seeking to extend his powers further and further into the evil dimension? Whyever it was here, it was growing more visible by the moment, as were the drank, scraggy walls around it.

The brightening light confirmed that there was indeed no

exit, but he spotted an alcove and dived into it just as the footsteps reached the door. Hunkering down in its gloomiest corner, Nizzam shut both eyes and clapped both hands over his mouth, to muffle the chattering of his teeth. His fur and ears standing on end, he cringed as if expecting the first scream of rage to strike him like a blow.

But it never came. He heard only the whisper of a reptilian body stretching out on the marble slab. Minutes passed in deathly silence. Then more minutes. At last he began to hope against hope that Khal had not followed him down here after all, and was unaware of his presence. Tentatively Nizzam opened his eyes.

He was startled by a ghastly shape that vanished the instant he looked at it; time enough only to sense its consummate evil. Still more minutes passed in silence. Then the ghastly shape reappeared, more vivid and hideous with evil; just when it had nearly incarnated into a living being, it suddenly vanished again. The next time it reappeared it was not alone.

Shutting his eyes tight, Nizzam tried to pretend it was only his imagination, that he was hallucinating out of sheer fright. But it was no use. He knew that the evil shapes were real, that Khal had succeeded in exorcising reptile-demons from the evil dimension to which they belonged. More tentatively than ever, he reopened his eyes—and instantly shut them again. Reptile-demons, at various stages of incarnation, were all around him now. Each time he squinted his eyes open, he found more of them glaring down at him with vindictive malice. They knew he was here; soon Khal himself would know.

There remained only one possible chance to escape, a desperate chance, whose possible consequences were so horrible that he had scarcely dared contemplate it before. But the consequences of remaining where he was were now certain, and perhaps even more horrible. Khal belittled Nizzam's powers of magic with relentless sarcasm; nonetheless he was a true magician. He realized by now that he would never rank among the great wizards of The Three—so much had his sufferings humbled him—but he really had studied diligently, and knew at least by rote the principles of teleportation.

He now regretted that he had not made a practical trial of

his book learning when he first encountered Khal beneath the Kazerclaw. True, his wits were so befuddled at the time that he could hardly remember his own name, let alone complex incantations; but he should at least have tried . . . .

Since then Khal had intimidated Nizzam with boasts about how many powerful wizards had fallen into his clutches when they attempted that very means of escape. Hence no wild fancies about his own escape had ever included teleportation. But this was it. Though more terrified than he had ever been in his life, terror seemed this time to clear his wits rather than befuddle them. To remain where he was even a few minutes longer meant certain doom. Still, he hesitated longer than he should have, hampered from facing the inevitable by a lifetime of cowardice.

At last, gritting his teeth as if plunging into an icy stream, he concentrated on his book-learned incantations. Perhaps Khal's own concentration on exorcising reptile-demons was too intense to notice a teleport of a bare few hundred yards or so, to an open field beside the road to Ar. Overcoming a final jolt of panic, he hurled himself into nothingness.

Nizzam's first thought upon rematerializing was that he had miscalculated. It was night. Had he teleported himself through time as well as space? And what spatial region was this? Certainly not anywhere near the road to Ar. Volcanic fires, smoke, and skeletal trees: a tortured landscape made lurid by an eternal crimson twilight, over which brooded a lurking evil. In the distance he could see dark reptilian shapes, more hideous even than those he had just escaped; for some reason they hung back from charging ravenously at him. No, he had not miscalculated—except in believing he could elude Khal's vigilance.

He felt like just sitting down on one of the volcanic boulders and bawling. Then he realized that someone was already sitting on a boulder not far away, with his back to him, and Nizzam approached him warily from behind. Just as he reached him, the man turned around. It was of all people the master wizard Mithmid. Nizzam recognized him at once from his visit to the Sentinel, some four years ago, although his face—gaunt, starving, demon-haunted, and weary to exhaustion—had aged dramatically.

"Hello, Nizzam," he said in a parched voice. "You haven't

brought anything to eat or drink, have you? Ah, too bad. Although sleep is what I need even more. I don't think I can hold them off much longer." He nodded toward the dark liskash shapes. "They probably wouldn't kill me right away, though. Us, I should say. Looks like you've fallen into Khal's clutches, too."

"Out of them, really," said Nizzam. "At least, for a while. What do you think he'll do to me here? Us, I mean?"

Mithmid shrugged wearily. "He's been trying for what seems like weeks to subject me to the most fiendish torments he can devise. The illusions are the worst, although he isn't really very imaginative. Just cunning and vindictive. Exactly what he plans to do with me in the end, I don't know."

"Have you stuffed and mounted on a hand-carved wizard's chair, between the governor of Kazerclawm and the king and queen of Casmara," Nizzam blurted out. "He's boasted about it."

Mithmid stared at him in wonder. "How in three moons could you possibly know that?"

Nizzam started to posture and prevaricate, according to his old custom, but the look in the great wizard's eyes, and the bracelet he flourished on his left wrist, glimmering with fragments of the Khavala, extracted the truth from him. Most of it, at least. He still withheld his role in the events at Kazerclawm.

"You're despicable, Nizzam." Mithmid frowned at him. "But I shouldn't be surprised, after what your late master, the Sentinel, told me about you. Srana told me some things too, indirectly. We'll get to the bottom of this later, though I'd just as soon leave you here. I will, too, if you don't do everything I say. Understand?"

Nizzam nodded his head abjectly.

"All right, then," Mithmid continued. "Tell me all you know about Cragsclaw. But be warned. I know the place intimately."

This time Nizzam withheld nothing; he detailed all the changes Khal had wrought in the ancient fortress. The dark liskash shapes appeared closer now, as if they were edging up for an attack. Mithmid noticed this too, and rose wearily to his feet, and raised his left hand, aglimmer with fragments of the Khavala. The reptilian shapes scattered for cover.

At that moment Nizzam caught another kind of reptilian shape out of the corner of his eye: hideous, ghostly, evanescent. Then it was gone. Moments later it reappeared—or one like it—just as in the subterranean vaults beneath the palace of Cragsclaw.

"He's coming," he cried. "Look! He's becoming stronger and stronger at conjuring up reptile-demons. For months, maybe years. And now that he has the Third Eye—"

"Oh, stop whining, Nizzam," Mithmid said with weary impatience. "Of course he's coming—and we're going. Now that I know how his force image is directed, we need only ride its counterforce back to the place from which he teleported himself."

"Not there!" Nizzam started to protest.

"Stay if you like," said Mithmid. "I'm too tired and hungry and thirsty to argue. In fact, it might be better if you did stay."

"No, no, I'm sorry. Anywhere you want to go is just fine with me. Even back to Cragsclaw." He lowered his voice, and looked nervously around at the hideous shapes incarnating around them. "Soon, I hope. He's coming—"

After a moment's disorientation, Nizzam found himself seated on the very marble slab from which Khal must have just teleported himself. Mithmid sat beside him, his head in his hands, as if the effort of riding the counterforce back here had exhausted his last strength.

"Shall I help you, master?" whispered Nizzam. "I know a way to the palace gate, so nobody will see us."

"I know it better than you do. I also know the way to the kitchen." His weak, parched voice was barely audible. "And right now I'm so famished I don't care who sees us."

For such a scrawny old man, Mithmid tucked into an amazing spread of trenchers and goblets. The cooks who served him whispered anxiously among themselves, as if wagering on the precise moment he would burst. But the repast only strengthened him—enough at least to be well clear of the neighborhood of Cragsclaw by nightfall. The soft, plump Nizzam now seemed the more exhausted of the two.

"I was on the road for many, many years," explained Mithmid, "in search of the Third Eye. A quest that was, alas, unsuccessful."

Nizzam lowered his eyes so guiltily that the old wizard watched him with curious attention. But it was late, and he really was exhausted from his long sleepless ordeal. They would be on the roads and rivers together for many days yet. Time enough to elicit the rest of Nizzam's history.

Devastation was everywhere, but it was haphazard, the work of marauders rather than armies. That would come with the fall of Ar. Towns with formidable defenses were still allowed to buy their safety; those without were simply plundered, on the old barbarian principle that one only bargains where he lacks the power to seize.

Wizards were now more hated than ever, and it was as an itinerant housepainter and his apprentice that Mithmid and Nizzam took lodgings at an inn. They were up and on the road betimes the next morning, the former much refreshed, the latter footsore from so much unaccustomed walking. Two days later they found themselves in a river city, its people impoverished by tribute, but its walls still intact. It took Mithmid less than an hour to find a particular bargemrem and his son, who had not long ago delivered one of the very fragments of the Khavala on his wrist downstream to Ar.

"Can't get you closer than, say, five miles from the city, master," said the bargemrem, who suspected that he was not bargaining with any common housepainter. "I was well paid the last time, and expect to be again."

This was no time to haggle, and the arrangements were soon concluded. How soon the new barrage being erected across the river would be complete—and the final assault on Ar launched—the bargemrem did not know.

"Level hasn't dropped yet." He shrugged. "Last two times it did nearly put me out of business. Remember, five miles is as close as I'll come, and it's for cash, not promises."

That night Nizzam had a strange dream. He again sat at his mother's knee like a schoolboy, confessing all his adventures and transgressions, knowing that as always she would coddle and forgive him. Even after he had told her every last detail of the events at Kazarclawm . . . .

He awoke to find Mithmid scowling down at him, and knew that it had been no ordinary dream; nor had it been to his mother he had confessed all his wrongdoing.

"You're even more despicable than I thought, Nizzam."

Mithmid shook his head disgustedly. "It's fortunate Srana escaped the Evil One—no thanks to you—or I'd send you back to him. She seems as beautiful and courageous as, well, someone I once knew when I was young. May the All-Mother guide and protect her, and those now questing beyond the sea." He glanced expectantly at Nizzam.

"Amen!" he blurted out.

▲

Weeks passed without any decision being reached. They were cut off from the rest of the world as if the valley of the Yozgat alone still withstood conquest by the Eastern Lords, while the colossal barrage that was to doom Ar was being constructed, while Severakh and his gallant argonauts quested unknown seas. But if the decision that could well determine the very survival of the mrem was not yet even being debated in public, decisions with consequences no less far-reaching were being resolved in private.

Traditionally, the High Priestess of Parvatta alone had the power to chastise; she alone determined when a Yozgat warrior received the sword of adulthood; she alone punished with death any cowardice or lack of empathy in battle. But all decisions were made in full council, where voting was by the raising or lowering of swords, which from adulthood until death no Yozgat warrior was ever without. No council, no decisions.

It was the High Priestess who also summoned these councils to meet, and thus far she had not done so. For the Prince Warrior presided, not she, and Changavar's authority was still paramount. After his mighty victory at the very gates of their realm, a mighty array of swords could be expected to sustain his every proposal.

That scores of outlanders had entered the land as living prisoners, rather than just their pelts as trophies of honor, flouted all tradition. Under the persuasive assertions of Changavar—in the communal refectory, during martial drill, on the very steps of the temple—to small groups of warriors, even the demand for pelts had begun to subside. So persuasive had he been that there was now actually talk about aiding the resistance to the Eastern Lords.

And who in turn had beguiled Changavar? The High Priestess had foreseen all that had since come to pass, the moment she first laid eyes on the bambarongs returning with prisoners rather than pelts. At least, she had now convinced herself of this. Her brooding hatred for Srana now blinded her to the very safety of the Yozgat. Not only was this outland female treacherous and as beautiful as the eidolon or Parvatta herself, but she was also powerful. Efforts to probe her mind had been rebuffed like the foolery of children. A sorceress? She seemed young to wield such powers of magic.

But could the blandishments which had so beguiled the Prince Warrior have been other than magical? Had this treacherous outland she-mrem been insinuated here by the enemies of the Yozgat to sap their martial vigor, to lure them into destruction? The longer the High Priestess brooded over Srana, the more convinced she became that it was her sacred duty to destroy her at the first opportunity.

The longer she contemplated her beauty, the more certain she was that Srana must be evil. Yozgat females granted their favors only to proven warriors, and only when those favors had been earned. But Srana looked as if she would grant her favors to any man who asked; perhaps do the asking herself. The fact that she was the only female among scores of virile young soldiers spoke for itself. No, any she-mrem that beautiful must surely be evil . . . .

The city of Parvat was unwalled, openly defying the world to attack it. Swords and battle empathy were the only walls needed by the Yozgat. They were warriors or the consorts of warriors; their very childhood games were contests in martial dancing, endurance, and agility. Youths were seen daily standing erect, holding a weighty battle sword at arm's length, for minutes and at last hours at a time, until their whole bodies were palsied with the strain. The biting ridicule of the maidens, for those who lowered their sword arms too soon, was a powerful incentive to persevere.

The two sexes dwelt in separate barracks complexes, each with its own characteristic training grounds and regimen, each with its own characteristic weapons. For in all-out war the females also fought, and their battle empathy was said to be keener than the males'. Trained from infancy to be ambidextrous, they wore sets of razor-honed steel claws on both hands, with shield armor on both forearms. They scavenged the battlefield in the wake of their males, and woe unto any straggler they came upon. Only those who met rigorous training standards by day were allowed to meet sexually at night.

"Lot of work for an ugly she-mrem," quipped a ranker as the band of fugitives marched toward the sprawling stone plaza before the Temple of Parvatta. "I think I'd rather stay home nights myself."

His lieutenant shushed him, and stared down any others inclined to mock. The squat, tufty little Yozgat females were certainly not prepossessing, but he had observed their martial drills, and seen the Yozgat males in battle. He had also heard that wardrobes lined the communal barracks of both sexes, hung with trophies of honor, and that a few of these wardrobes were still vacant.

The fugitives all assumed that the ceremony they had been summoned to attend by the High Priestess Parvatala had something to do with the summoning of the council, where their fate would at last be decided. Since the fate of the servile Mamlocks, who farmed the surrounding countryside, tended the herds and orchards, and built and maintained their own dwellings and those of the Yozgat, had been decided centuries ago, they were left to drudge through their daily tasks. Thus only Yozgat crowded the stone-flagged plaza, thousands strong, female as well as male.

Their mountain valley was surrounded on all sides by looming blue peaks, the highest snow-capped, the lowest like the crowns of bald heads above the shaggily forested slopes below. The air was crisp and clean and invigorating; only a few gauzy wisps of clouds mottled the blue morning sky. An idyllic setting for a ceremony.

Srana alone was not beguiled. The green-copper doors of the temple had been opened to display its sacred interior, and she noticed that the great eidolon of Parvatta, despite the idealized beauty of the goddess, had extended claws. She also noticed that the High Priestess Parvatala had assembled an extraordinarily large chorus of maidens on the temple stairs. It reminded her of Mithmid's description of how he had concentrated the mindpower of The Three in the defense of Ar.

The chanting of the chorus went on for over an hour. The

songs had little religious significance, but tended to unify the chanters in a common purpose, opening their minds to external suggestion. The effect was hypnotic, soothing, lulling. Thus the sudden halt was all the more dramatic; the silence that followed all the more ominous.

Then the shrill voice of Parvatala resounded eerily with cries of accusation, cries that echoed and reechoed from the stone pavement and the stone barracks and stone refectory buildings around it; cries that demanded the Judgment of Parvatta.

Srana had no idea what that meant, only that she herself was the one to be judged by the goddess, for the malicious old priestess now pointed an accusing claw directly at her.

She glanced at Changavar, but saw no help there. He too had been caught by surprise. In fact, it was he, as Prince Warrior, who had to lead her forward into the center of the plaza, and leave her standing alone in a position where the eidolon of Parvatta seemed to gaze directly down on her from inside the temple.

"I'm sorry," he whispered. "There's nothing I can do. The Judgment of Parvatta is the most sacred of all our rites. I had no idea she was so angry. Be careful!"

Then Srana was alone. She did not face the temple eidolon for judgment; her sentence had already been passed, and now awaited only its execution. Instead she met the eyes of the High Priestess, glaring balefully at her across the open plaza. The contest had begun.

Once more the chorus of maidens began to chant, this time like an incantation, unified and hypnotic, and Srana detected an intrusive will probing her mind for control. More and more intrusive grew the probing, more spiteful and determined; the High Priestess was somehow tapping the mindpower of the hundreds of green-robed maidens chanting behind her on the temple stairs, and concentrating the force through her own malice. But it was soon evident that she wielded no true magic; nothing that Srana, her powers redoubled by the fragment of the Khavala, could not overmatch.

Although it was not a great contest, and quickly forgotten, she gained from it the confidence to meet challenges to come; challenges that would one day be recorded in the *Dragon Book*.

She was distracted momentarily by the collapse of one of the chorus maidens, whose mindpower had been ruthlessly tapped to exhaustion. The moment's loss of concentration opened her own mind to the phantoms being created in the minds of the spectators by Parvatala, through a kind of mass hypnosis. Thereafter Srana kept herself simultaneously aware of both illusion and reality. What she saw were two High Priestesses: one standing piously before the chanting chorus— the illusion no doubt seen by the thousands of Yozgat around her, listening glassy-eyed to the hypnotic chant—and another donning a pair of steel battle claws, claws like those on the eidolon of Parvatta.

She wondered if the Yozgat also saw only a false image of herself. The strategem of the High Priestess was now evident. When clarity was restored to their eyes, they would see only that the arraigned had mysteriously been clawed to death, that the Goddess Parvatta had rendered judgment. Not even the shrewd Changavar seemed to suspect trickery.

Another chorus maiden collapsed from the strain; then another. From the way Parvatala brandished her steel claws as she advanced, her eyes glittering with malice, Srana had no doubt that she had been a cruel and ruthless warrior in her youth. Three more chorus maidens collapsed on the temple stairs. Gloating, a snarl of triumph twisting her mouth, the High Priestess slashed at Srana's face—and missed altogether.

Staggering off balance, she righted herself and slashed again, then again, and yet again. Still nothing, though the maddeningly beautiful she-mrem stood directly before her without so much as flinching. Then all at once the chanting chorus fell silent, Parvatala's camouflage of illusions dropped away, and she found herself exposed at the very center of the plaza, wearing telltale steel claws. All eyes were on her— some surprised, some puzzled—but more and more awakening to her deceit, more and more aflash with anger.

Meanwhile what had become of Srana? No one in the plaza was more mystified by her disappearance than the High Priestess herself, who in embarrassment tried awkwardly to conceal her steel claws beneath her robe. Srana had never left her view, from the moment she descended the temple stairs until she futilely slashed at her face. And yet she was gone.

At last she was seen kneeling on the temple stairs, tending the poor dwarfish maidens who had collapsed. All she had done in fact was reinforce the false image of herself, hypnotically created in the onlookers by Parvatala, and walk right past her. Being no true magician, the High Priestess was unaware of the effects of concealment magic, and had simply not looked in her direction.

Now an increasing number of eyes turned toward Srana. How she had exchanged places with Parvatala still bewildered the Yozgat, and they looked on in wonder at the gentleness with which she revived the stricken maidens. They were ashamed of displaying such weakness in public and, despite her prudent advice that they return to their barracks and rest, stubbornly insisted on resuming their places in the chorus, though they staggered from exhaustion, barely able to stand.

All the chorus maidens in fact had been badly depleted of vitality by Parvatala's ruthless exploitation of their mindpower. But that only made them more determined to show themselves strong. Chins up, shoulders back, not one of them deserted her post on the temple stairs.

It was at that moment, while Srana had her back turned to the plaza, that the High Priestess made her fatal blunder. It was only a small gesture, but enough to condemn her forever in the eyes of the Yozgat. Letting her blind hatred get the better of her judgment, she drew her claws from under her robe and started for Srana. She had taken barely two steps before she caught herself and again concealed her claws. But it was too late. The battle empathy of the Yozgat made them sensitive to the least nuance of a gesture, let alone one as blatant as this.

The warning shout—several Yozgat warriors, including Changavar himself, leapt between the two, swords drawn—resounded in Parvatala's ears like a death knell. To be shunned and banished beyond the mountains, or executed—in the end it amounted to the same punishment—were the only alternatives now before her, and she unbattened the steel claws and dropped them to the ground. Her first humiliation would be confinement in some Mamlock hovel, as if no longer worthy of dwelling among the Yozgat, until her fate was decided in council. A guard of twelve warriors escorted her from the plaza.

Changavar meanwhile seized the moment. The shouts of anger against Parvatala had hardly abated when he transmuted her special ceremony into a special war council of his own. Though his proposals were ambiguous, each one in turn was acclaimed by an exuberant raising of swords. There was no dissent, no discussion. Within the hour, Mamlock runners were sent to a neighboring valley, whose dwellers had an old accommodation with the Yozgat. By nightfall, Mamlock messengers were dispersing through the foothills—south toward Namakhazar, west toward Ar—in search of news, rather than conveying it.

"A new High Priestess must be selected," said Changavar, as he and Srana stood together in the moonlight, outside her quarters in the female barracks. Though he barely stood as high as her elbow, she treated him with the respect due a great warrior. "Every candidate will oppose our flouting of sacred tradition. At least two, possibly three of them that I know of, would move to have me deposed. They are the guardians of Parvatta, whose laws are forever. Were our valley the entire world, I too would oppose any deviation from these laws. But as you have said, we may defeat odds of five to one, perhaps ten, but not hundreds or thousands to one."

"Can't you postpone the selection?" asked Srana.

"I have already done so, in the only possible way—by reviving an ancient tradition. High Priestesses once could not be selected until the night when the three moons triangulate in a peculiar way, as if focusing on the planet, had safely passed. Why this night of all nights was considered evil, no mrem knows today. But that it once was so believed can be found in sacred records."

Srana gazed thoughtfully up at the night sky. "I know that night well. It occurs in exactly one month less three days. Much will be determined on that night, elsewhere. How long after that could you delay the selection?"

"Two months, perhaps three." He looked curiously up at her. "What is to be determined on that night?"

"Our future—if we have one," she replied. "Can you trust the messengers you sent by different routes to Namakhazar?"

"Their people exist only at our discretion, which is the best insurance of good faith. They often act as our go-betweens to the outland world, and are always faithful. That is how I first learned about the siege of Ar, and what its fall would eventually mean to my own people." He shook his head wryly. "If only I could make them understand that themselves."

"So long as you can delay the selection of a new High Priestess at least two months," said Srana. "If we do not receive favorable news from Namakhazar by then . . ." She shrugged, and continued to gaze upward at the configuration of the three moons in the night sky.

▲

Chapter 17
Three Claws Above The Horizon

"**Z**anira's the big shiny blue star over there, lad." Shimsham squinted across the rolling waters of the sea, glowing like liquid metal in the threefold moonlight, as he directed Branwe's observation. "Can't miss it. My eyes ain't what they used to be, but I don't care how many moons there are upstairs, I can always spot old Zanira right off. First thing I look for every night."

They stood together at the rail, on the squarish afterdeck of the argosy, opposite the great steering oar. The vessel had been at sea just a few weeks, with only a small cadre of real sailors, but was trim and shipshape. If Severakh had been a stern drillmaster on land, he was doubly so on board ship. Regular military drills had continued while his men were learning their ropes. They had outrun pursuit from Nama-khazar, but were now entering pirate waters.

"Your claws are just the size mine were as a lad," he continued. "None of them other noddies Severakh wanted me to learn how to navigate had the claws for it, and guesswork ain't good enough in these waters. Now hold the string in your teeth where I got it knotted. That's right. Now hold the little board out arm's length, and line its bottom edge square along the horizon. Has to be exact, remember. Now what do you measure?"

"A little over three claws," said Branwe through clenched teeth.

The navigation device consisted of a rectangular board the size of a mrem's hand, with a string fastened precisely at its center. By clamping the string in his teeth at a fixed distance from the board, held at arm's length with its bottom edge aligned with the horizon, the observer could judge accurately just how high the polestar stood in the sky. Thus the relative latitude could be measured each night, and the ship's course adjusted accordingly. Once an experienced navigator knew how many claws the polestar stood at night above his destination, he needed only sail to that latitude and follow it, due east or due west, until he reached port—if one existed.

There were no known ports in the Shadow Islands; it was not even known for certain where the islands lay, or if they existed at all. Shimsham could not be relied on as a navigator—not after Severakh discovered the true nature of his "navigation gear."

Shimsham had at first kept the mysterious crate he had brought with him securely locked below decks in the hold. But his increasing mellowness throughout each day—by nightfall he was often so mellow that he could hardly talk—and his headachy nervousness each morning became more and more suspicious, until at last Severakh had the crate broken open. It turned out to be packed with nothing but wine flasks.

His first impulse was to have the lot tossed overboard, along with Shimsham himself. But that would have left them without a navigator, on a desperate voyage, and he decided instead to bide his time until others mastered all Shimsham knew—or pretended to know—about navigation to the Shadow Islands. There would be plenty of opportunities later to jettison wine and wine-bibber alike . . . .

Keen-eyed, with a steady hand and a proper set of claws, Branwe was Shimsham's prize pupil, although the old wharf skulker began each lesson as if he had already forgotten everything he had said the night before. On some nights his memory was better than on others. Tonight he was in a mood to sentimentalize over old stories—very familiar old stories by now.

Branwe's years as a potboy had taught him to cope patiently with the situation, although at the Blue Dragon it had been easier to avoid a drunkard's foul breath being huffed in his face.

"There's one!" cried Shimsham, his right elbow on the railing as if it were the bar in a tavern, his left arm dangling around Branwe's neck. "They're coming out late tonight. First one I've seen."

Branwe had already spotted several of the long-necked marine reptiles, which sometimes followed the ship for miles, as if hoping somebody would fall overboard. They seemed not to possess the magical powers of land reptiles. He tried to ease himself further down the rail.

"Used to try and snatch me from the raft I built to escape the Shadow Islands." Shimsham was beginning to slur his speech, and would probably fall asleep soon. "Ever tell you the story? I did? Well, that's all right. I'll tell it better this time . . . ."

Branwe sighed, and pretended to listen to the tired old story, while his eyes drifted heavenward. The sky was cloudless, and so bright with threefold moonlight that only Zanira and a few other stars of the first magnitude were visible. Faint, distant haloes encircled the moons; at two points their arcs seemed actually to touch.

"Bad sign, lad." Shimsham startled him. " 'When moon rings meet, Woe to the fleet.' " He quoted the old sailor's adage, momentarily sobered. "A little over three claws, you say? Better set our course while we've got the chance. We're in for a blow tomorrow. Maybe tonight. I'll wait right here for you."

Glancing back, Branwe saw the old rascal slip something out of a nearby coil of rope and lift it to his lips.

The sea was calm; its long swells hardly disturbed the moonlight pointing across its liquid-metal surface like giant fingers. All sails were set to catch the fickle easterly breeze, and the magnificent argosy glided smoothly through the water. Branwe reported the new course to the helmsmrem, who personally helped his crew of four reset the great steering oar and batten it down.

Cajhet was among them, but as Branwe started to address him, he held a finger to his lips and nodded amidships. Severakh had just been summoned up from his cabin, and stood conversing with the lookout, while they peered southward over the port railing. Curious, Branwe followed their eyes.

His first thought was that the dark mass on the horizon was a cloud bank, perhaps the frontal lobe of the storm Shimsham had warned him about. But if it was a cloud bank, it was a very small one. An island? Shimsham had told them about how his raft had at last carried him to an island, where he was picked up by a merchant ship, and allowed to work his passage homeward to Namakhazar. There were variants of the story—one including a romance with a beautiful island she-mrem, another about how he almost married the captain's daughter, who was also beautiful—but that was its essence.

As Branwe started back across the afterdeck toward Shimsham, he noticed Severakh heading in the same direction. Then Shimsham also noticed him, and quickly bent over the coil of rope again. He was leaning innocently against the railing, a bland smile on his face, by the time the fierce old warrior finally reached him.

"The lookout just reported an island far to the south." Severakh looked him suspiciously up and down. "Is that the one you told me about, where you were picked up by the merchant ship?"

"Right smack on course." Shimsham nodded his head sagely, and hiccuped.

"Then why is the island so far south of us?" Severakh demanded.

"I've already made tonight's course correction, sir," said Branwe. "The steering oar has been reset."

"Good lad, good lad," mumbled Shimsham. "I once had eyes like his, and claws too. I'll never forget when I first was here. I was just Branwe's age, and a beautiful island she-mrem came to my cabin one night—"

"Shut up," said Severkh. "The only story I want from you now is about the Shadow Islands. And it had better be the truth."

"Or better than the truth?" Shimsham winked archly at him. "Some stories you have to tell a few times before they start to sound good." His elbow slipped from the railing, and he staggered and would have fallen, had Branwe not caught him.

"Good lad, good lad," he mumbled. "Rough seas tonight. 'When moon rings meet, Woe to the fleet.' Keep that in mind, and you'll never regret it."

"I regret ever laying eyes on you, you scoundrel." Severakh lowered at him. "But I won't much longer. You say Branwe here has been making all the course corrections?"

"Used to have eyes like his, and claws too. I was innocent, but they declawed me anyway. A victim of injustice, that's what I am. But nobody cares." A sentimental tear glistened in Shimsham's eye. "Buy me another drink, and I'll tell you the story. Saddest thing you've ever heard." He staggered, and again Branwe caught him.

Severakh dived past him and pulled a nearly empty flask out of the coiled rope nearby. "That did it! Lieutenant!" he cried over his shoulder. "I need two mrem for a special detail. Branwe, are you confident about how to set our course?"

"Yes, sir. I've been doing it every night for the last week."

"Good lad, good lad," mumbled Shimsham. "My eyes used to be just as sharp, maybe a little sharper even. So were my claws, when I had 'em. Rank injustice! I was innocent, and always have been."

"Lieutenant!" Severakh cried impatiently, and started to turn around. He was surprised to find two mrem standing at his elbow. "Cajhet! How many times have I told you not to sneak up on me like that?"

"Several, I believe, sir."

"Then don't do it again."

"No, sir."

"There's a big crate down in the hold," said Severakh. "This wretch here says it's filled with his navigation gear. Wipe that grin off your face!"

"Yes, sir," said Cajhet.

"Over the side with it, and right now. I've looked the other way for the last time. Meanwhile I'll decide what else is going overboard tonight." He glowered at Shimsham, who began maudlinly to weep and groan and wring his clawless hands. "Now what?"

"A ship, sir," reported the lookout, running up. "Approaching from the direction of the island."

"A merchant vessel?"

"No, sir. It's a galley. Only pirates ever move that fast."

Severakh turned on Shimsham again. "You've been telling us you were picked up by honest merchants. It was really a pirate ship, wasn't it? What else have you withheld, you scoundrel? Were you a pirate yourself? Did you lure us out here for your old pals to rob?"

Shimsham wept and wrung his hands. "I'm a victim of

injustice and nobody cares. They made me do it. 'Be a pirate like us,' they said, 'or it's back on your raft with you.' See that reptile out there with the long neck? And there's another. They were just waiting to gobble me up."

"They've waited long enough!" cried Severak. He seized Shimsham by the scruff of the neck and dragged him to the railing, but then had second thoughts. "Throw him in the brig! Lieutenant, sound quarters! All hands on deck! A single galley against a ship this size? These wretches must think they're attacking a lot of milk-livered merchants."

"Shall I ready the catapults, sir?" cried the lieutenant, as a horn sounded and armed mrem poured out on deck, and scurried helter-skelter for their battle stations.

"Not yet," said Severakh. "This lone galley is in for a surprise, but pirates usually hunt in packs. We don't want to show them our full strength until we have to. Branwe!"

"Yes, sir."

"That's the Demon Sword in your hand, isn't it? Well, whatever magic it possesses, we don't need it now. These are pirates, not demons, no matter how wild they fight. No sense in risking its being shattered or lost in battle. Take it down to my cabin, and exchange it for one of my own blades."

By the time Branwe clambered back up on deck, he found the pirate galley racing as if to cut across the bow. Then at the last instant it swerved broadside, and a terrifying shout rose from below, as grappling lines arced by the score over the railing and into the masts and sails aloft.

The agility and savage vigor of the pirates often carried a merchant ship at the first rush. But merchant seamrem were rarely mrem-at-arms; nor were they ever drilled by so exacting a drillmaster as Severakh. Hacking, clawing, shrieking like madmrem, the first wave of swashbucklers poured over the side of the ship—and broke against a rock wall of swords and pikes. The second wave was more tentative, but made no more impression, and fell back amidst a backwash of dead and wounded.

Branwe was at least as agile as any of the grisly ruffians attacking the ship. Some of these, scrambling hand over hand up grappling lines into the masts, had ideas about taking the defenders in the rear. None succeeded. From shrouds to stays to yardarms, up the masts and down, into the very sails,

Branwe scrambled wherever a grapnel took hold. Like all Severakh's weapons his sword was honed razor sharp, and he slashed through grappling line after grappling line. Cursing and shrieking as they fell, pirate after pirate crashed to the deck below, where they were immediately dispatched and their carcasses pitched over the side. Only twice did Branwe arrive too late to cut away a line, but not too late to cut down the pirates themselves.

Swinging onto the mainsail, he met the first swashbuckling assault with uncanny agility, parrying a barrage of wild and savage blows until he at last found an opening, and the pirate fell screaming to the deck below.

The second contest was more perilous, not so much because this opponent was more skilled—although he was certainly heavier and stronger—but because the footing was becoming increasingly more treacherous. The breeze had freshened, and the huge argosy was beginning to heave in the rising swell. Branwe had to cling to the stays with one hand, while parrying savage hacks and slashes with his sword. His fatal thrust only grazed the pirate's ribcage, but caused him to lose his footing. The fall broke his neck with a sickening crunch.

There were no more grappling lines to cut, but as Branwe clambered down from the riggings he saw that the pirate galley, though it had already lost half its crew, was still greedy for plunder. It now stood off the port bow, and in the bright moonlight he could see the pirate captain toss a handful of powder into a fire which had just been laid in a pottery urn amidships. Crimson flames shot heavenward, and were soon answered with beacon flares from the island. It was not long before three more galleys were visible, swiftly approaching across the silvery sea.

A heavy sea now. A blanket of storm clouds drew ominously across the eastern moon, and the first galley, its crew decimated, had to struggle against the choppy waters to keep pace with the *Zanira*, flying full-sail before the wind. The pirates had been unprepared for such stiff resistance and were badly mauled, while Severakh in turn had suffered few casualties. He kept his mrem at their battle stations.

He had anticipated this second assault, but not the storm. The accuracy of the catapults he had held in reserve would be much reduced. On the other hand, the rough sea would make boarding the *Zanira* that much more difficult, although the pirates would not be surprised a second time by hard-fought resistance.

He roved continuously from battle station to battle station, inspecting, encouraging, haranguing. Mrem for mrem his troops were more than a match for such undisciplined cut-throats, but they would soon be dangerously outnumbered. The ship would almost certainly be boarded from all sides; even a defensive square would be vulnerable as it never was in land battles, since here it could also be attacked from above.

"Branwe!" He called him aside. "You did good work aloft. Pick out six or seven of the younger mrem—the most agile you can find, maybe the regular sailors—and take 'em up with you. I don't want our lads dropped on or taken from the rear."

"Yes, sir." Branwe saluted.

The footing aloft was more treacherous now. The masts bent and groaned; the sails snapped like explosions in the gusting winds; the yardarms swung dizzily back and forth, as if trying to shake loose all those trying to cling to them. That the pirates would attack in such weather proved that they had let their anger get the better of their judgment. There would be no quarter.

As it turned out, there was almost no battle. Severakh did not uncover his catapults until the last of the approaching galleys hove within range. He ordered his catapulters to concentrate their first barrage on the galley struggling to keep alongside, off the port bow. It was the nearest and, because of its decimated crew, the least mobile. Even so, with the deck rocking beneath them, the catapulters were unable to sink it with a clean shot. At last a glancing missile shattered eight of its starboard oars, and it began at once to lag behind the *Zanira*, flying faster and faster before the wind.

The other three galleys, seeing this, began to zigzag as they raced to surround the great argosy, and not a single catapult missile struck them. Then grapnels began to arc from all directions, while axmrem aboard ship scampered up and down the railing, chopping feverishly to cut away the lines.

But there were too many lines, too many savage pirates clambering up them too agilely, and several of the axmrem themselves were cut down.

Battening their galleys to the sides of the argosy, scores of angry, shrieking pirates poured over the starboard, over the port, over the very bow and stern. It had been many years since so rich a prize had ventured so near their island, and they attacked with greedy abandon, hungry for plunder and vengeance. They were not accustomed to even one of their galleys meeting such fierce resistance.

What they met this time, instead of terrified seamrem throwing down arms they wielded clumsily at best, was a defensive square formed by steady, well-drilled professional soldiers. Mere fury did not avail against such disciplined ranks, nor shrieking, nor the tactics of wild onslaught and terrorism. Slashing swords were parried; leaping swordsmrem hurled back. The blood fury of the pirates at first blinded them to their mounting casualties. Dead and dying littered a deck now slobbered with gore, but still they hurled themselves savagely at the firm ranks of the defenders.

Severakh himself commanded the troop of veterans he held in reserve at the center of the square, leading them in support of whichever side appeared most hard-pressed. Had the pirates united their forces in one concentrated attack, they would certainly have broken the square, overwhelming its ranks from the inside out. But undisciplined fury was all they knew, and a thirst for blood and plunder. Higher and higher mounted their casualties.

If the pirates found themselves overmatched with weapons on deck, their fabled agility was even less a match for Branwe and his small troupe of sailors in the masts and shrouds, on the yardarms and stays, aloft. The sails continued to snap like explosions in the wildly gusting winds; only a single moon now lit the sky, as black storm clouds flashing with thunderbolts massed out of the east. Higher and higher tossed the storm waves; foam and spindrift pattered down like rain. Grapnels were kicked loose, grappling lines cut away. None who saw young Branwe that night, leaping through space, his sword flashing as he hurled back pirate after pirate, ever forgot his valor.

The battle ended as abruptly as it had begun. The pirates

were boldest in attacking the defenseless, and their bloodthirsty greed for plunder at last awakened to the terrible
casualties they were suffering. Howling threats and curses,
they suddenly broke and ran for their galleys, hurtling themselves over the bulwarks, slashing mooring lines before all
their comrades were safely aboard. Several plunged into the
sea and were drowned. So swiftly was the *Zanira* now flying
before the wind that the pirate galleys were soon lost from
sight.

Now began an even graver battle for those aboard. The
dead pirates were tossed overboard, perhaps also a few who
were merely stunned or dying, but Severakh saw his new
peril too clearly to be nice about the matter. Neither did he
have the seventeen pirates who were captured alive—mean,
grisly, and treacherous as they looked—chained in the brig,
but impressed them at once into his own crew. The storm
was their common enemy, and his own casualties had somehow to be replaced if the *Zanira* was to survive the night.

It did—but just barely. Two mrem fell from the riggings;
no fewer than five were washed overboard. The moons were
swallowed in blackness; crackling, exploding bolts of electric-
ity, again and again hurtling down out of the boiling storm
clouds, were the only light. The mainsail tore loose before it
could be reefed, and flapped so violently in the wind that it
threatened to tear away the mainmast as well. Once more
Branwe was called on to go aloft. Scrambling, clutching,
dangling by one hand, sometimes over the ocean, sometimes
over the deck, he at last cut the mainsail away, and scrambled back down out of the riggings.

Not to the safety of the deck; there was no safety anywhere
tonight. Even when morning came, the blackness of the sky
only faded into a sullen yellow-gray; the terrors of the sea
were now more visible, the exhausted crew more terrified.
But Severakh was relentless. Never sleeping, never seeming
to tire, he continued to make his rounds, inspecting, encouraging, haranguing, reprimanding where necessary.

The rains came and went in violent downpours; the winds
abated, then burst out again with gale force; the sky shaded
from black into yellow-gray, then back again. For three days
and three nights the storm continued to rage. The pirates,
unused to such rigorous labor, grumbled and protested and at

last refused to work at all. Severakh had them marched to the starboard rail.

"Which is it, lads," he demanded, pointing over the side, "work or swim?"

They muttered and glowered and cursed under their breath—then returned to work.

Not until the afternoon of the fourth day did the overcast sky begin to patch and tatter; not until that night did the sky itself break through. Shimsham, with the loss of his "navigation gear," had in fact ceased to navigate. He lay groaning on his bunk, often delirious, sometimes shrieking that liskash were all around him. Branwe was now their only hope.

How far they had been blown off course was unknown. Shimsham was too wretched to care. The pirates merely shrugged. Not until the polestar was again visible could Branwe himself determine their latitude. For all anybody knew, they had already been blown past the Shadow Islands, to die of thirst somewhere at the ends of the world.

"Up with you, lad." Branwe found himself shaken from a sound sleep. "There's a break in the clouds."

"Cajhet?" He sat on the edge of his bunk, yawning and rubbing his eyes.

"Hurry, lad." Cajhet shook him again. "The old man himself sent me down here, and if we're not back on deck in two minutes, he said he'd kick me overboard. And he'd do it too. I think he's just waiting for the chance."

Branwe found the grim old warrior pacing the afterdeck. Cajhet hung back, uncertain whether the two minutes had elapsed or not. The wretched Shimsham, looking more dead than alive, sprawled with his back against a coil of rope.

"Didn't save me a drop," he groaned. "The liskash have been at me for days."

"Some reptiles with long necks really will be at you, if you don't shut up," Severakh growled at him. "It's only because of my good nature that you're still aboard. Come here, lad." He beckoned to Branwe. "I understand your navigation has something to do with the polestar. Zanira was visible when I sent for you, but now it's behind the clouds again. You'll have to be ready the next time it peeks out. Here, you two." This time he beckoned to Cajhet and one of the steering crew.

"Take hold of this scoundrel and toss him"—Shimsham howled and clutched the coil of rope—"back into his bunk."

Shimsham relaxed his grip, and allowed himself to be carried down the nearest hatch below decks. Meanwhile Branwe, his simple navigation gear in hand, braced himself against the starboard rail, and waited. And waited. The stormwaves had subsided, but the seas were still heavy, the heavens still overcast. Pillars of moonlight burst through the tattering clouds, then as abruptly disappeared again. It was barely an hour before dawn before he at last got his chance.

Even in his best shape it was unlikely that Shimsham could have taken an accurate reading tonight. Two hands were needed—one to hold the little board at arm's length, one to measure with—which left no means of support on the rolling deck. Just aligning the bottom edge of the board along the horizon needed rare coordination, and the break in the clouds lasted only minutes.

"Looks good, sir," Branwe reported. "We're almost right on course. Only needed a small correction of the steering oar."

"The storm's abating," said Severakh. "You're on the night watch from now on, lad. No other duties. Keep a sharp eye on Zanira, and also on the three moons—when they're all visible again, that is. I'll show you what we're looking for tomorrow." He gazed thoughtfully out across the dark, choppy sea. "I don't know how much time we've got before they triangulate, but we've got to put in somewhere—and soon—or we'll never get there at all. We've tattered some canvas, lost the mainsail entirely, split the foretopmast, and I've got half the watch section pumping and baling below decks. Just keep us on course, lad. The Shadows are an archipelago. There's bound to be somewhere we can put in for repairs, before sailing on to the main island." He now gazed thoughtfully up at the overcast sky. "If only I could see the position of the moons . . . ."

It was a gaunt and miserable Shimsham who dragged himself up on deck two days later. Liskash no longer troubled him, but he was still nervous that they were lurking somewhere out of sight, ready to pounce the moment he turned his back. He had finally been able to hold down a few morsels of food and drink, although the latter was not the kind he really needed.

"Does that look familiar?" Severakh pointed to a low-lying mass on the horizon. It was a sultry morning, only the bottoms of the fluffy masses of clouds were tinged with gray, and a fresh breeze hissed through the riggings. Most of the sails were reefed, so no undue strain would widen the rifts in the hull or the damaged foretopmast. "Can you even see it, you wretched little squint?"

Shimsham was indeed squinting across the white-capped seas. "My eyes ain't what they used to be, but if that's the first island you spotted, we still got a ways to go. Shadow Island is what we're after, which gave its name to the whole group. It was on one of these small islands that me and the other two was marooned, and where we built ourselves a raft."

"You said you were alone on the raft."

"Uh, well, I was. Most of the time, leastways. We had short supplies, and a long way to go. I awoke one morning and found myself alone. The other two must have accidently fallen overboard in the night."

Severkh eyed him suspiciously, his fingers twitching as if tempted to seize him by the throat. "Yes, I think I can guess what kind of accident that was, and why you were marooned here in the first place. Now get out of my sight!"

The island turned out to be more extensive than they had supposed; its rugged southern coast indicated that it was probably just a remnant of a once far more extensive land mass, perhaps a continent. Harborage was poor—a mere roadstead sheltered by a rocky headland—but the sea was calm now, and Severakh immediately set most of his crew to work on repairs.

The remainder, including all the pirates, he marshaled into a foraging party, which he would lead in person. All empty water kegs were loaded aboard the ship's four longboats.

"Down to my cabin, lad." He drew Branwe aside. "Now's the time you might need that sword given you by the old wizard."

Frothy waves washed over a beach of coarse gravel, glistening pinkish-red in the noontide sun. The vegetation was exotic; in the distance, on the middle slopes of the mountain range which divided the lush island like a spine, rose ancient

ruins. Or was it a natural formation? Not even Branwe's keen
eyes could really distinguish from so far away.

The pirates unloaded the empty kegs as sullenly as they
had manned their oars. Why had they all been brought
ashore? Did the old warrior intend to maroon them here? Or
was he just cautious about leaving too many of them aboard
ship? Severakh did not betray his motives; neither did he
allow the pirates to remain near the longboats once the water
kegs had been replenished at a nearby stream.

"It's paradise, sir," the first scout reported in. "Never saw
anything so beautiful as the valley yonder. Makes you just
want to lie down in the shade, and never go away."

"We need supplies, not naps," Severakh growled at him.
"Anything to eat?"

"Just like a big garden, sir. In patches, at least. The rest of
the valley's pretty much like it is here."

"Only in patches?" Severakh looked curiously at him. "Why
not the whole valley?"

The scout shrugged. "It is kind of strange, now that you
mention it, sir."

▲

Chapter 18
The Lurkers in the Mirage

▲──▲

Branwe was certain that the shrewd old Severakh had noticed the pirates whispering secretively among themselves—huddling together in small groups, flickering mutinous glances at anybody who came near them—although he appeared to be looking the other way. Were they in fact plotting a mutiny? Or, more likely, a mass escape into the trees? The regular sailors were now enough to crew the *Zanira*. Had Severakh brought the pirates ashore just so they could run away—and good riddance?

He had assigned all the necessary mrem and resources to ship repairs, which would take a good two days to complete. Exploring the mountainside ruins—if indeed they were ruins—would keep both the pirates and idle crewmrem from hampering the work. His mrem all bore weapons, and well outnumbered the disarmed pirates.

As the column marched inland, Branwe noticed the pirates stealthily edging to the front, their eyes darting furtively back and forth, as if scanning the trees and underbrush for a gap to shoot through. He doubted that any obstacle would be thrown in their path—as soon as they found one. Again Severakh appeared to be looking the other way.

In the morning sunlight the valley seemed even more of a paradise than the scout had reported it. Certain patches were so lush and enticing that they appeared artificial; too similar and perfect to be natural. Gardens? Was the island inhabited? The pirates exchanged sly glances. If they somehow managed to escape, they would at least not starve to death.

Severakh's mrem also hankered after some relief from shipboard rations, and never in their lives had they seen such cool rippling pools, abounding in fresh fish, such succulent fruits and berries. To a mrem they were tempted to rush straight into the nearest garden and begin the feast.

Branwe alone stood aghast. Clutching the Demon Sword in his right hand, he saw before him only a valley of horror. He could not understand why the others were not falling back in loathing and disgust; rather than gazing before them with longing anticipation. At last he suspected some evil magic at work, and laid the Demon Sword on a rock.

Instantly the valley of horror was transformed into a paradise, its garden patches enticing and beautiful. Snatching up the sword, he saw once more only horror and loathsomeness. Where the others saw mirages of paradise, his own eyes, unclouded by the power of the Demon Sword, saw only flattish multilegged reptiles. There were no cool rippling fish ponds around them, nothing but gnawed bones and excrement. Nor did the bones look reptilian. They looked, in fact, exactly like the bones those around him would leave here, were they too enticed into a mirage. Anxiously he beckoned to Severakh.

"Hold this sword, and take another look around the valley, sir."

"Reptile magic!" Severakh sneered. "Never used for any higher purpose than getting a meal."

With the eye of an old commander, scrutinizing every rise and declivity within sight, as if searching for some advantage in an impending battle, or trying to detect signs of a lurking enemy, he examined the terrain in detail. He then passed the sword back to Branwe, and once more examined everything around them; then he took the sword back again. Thrice he repeated the exchange, until confident he knew what was illusion and what was not.

"Halt!" he cried, and beckoned the entire company around him. "Now listen, and listen carefully. Don't be fooled by the garden patches that seem to be all around you, and don't let me see you even thinking about going near them. They're deadly traps. Understand? They might be why some of our scouts haven't returned yet."

That he was not more explicit about the danger was curious to Branwe. Severakh's own men would obey his orders as a matter of course; but the pirates seemed more mutinous than ever, whispering secretively amongst themselves at every opportunity—especially after one of the missing scouts did return.

"They're ruins all right, sir," he reported. "Oldest I've ever seen. Looks like they were built thousands of years ago, and not by mrem." He lowered his voice: "But there are mrem here, or leastways something like mrem. Only saw footprints, though."

"You mean to tell me that one of my scouts isn't sure whether footprints are mrem or not?" Severakh looked him up and down.

"Yes, sir." The scout now lowered his voice to a whisper. "They're mrem footprints—and handprints, too. Looks like they sometimes walk on all fours."

Severakh gazed thoughtfully toward the mountains and the ancient ruins. "Perhaps the Shadow Islands really are remnants of a lost continent," he said at last. "Maybe this is how it was in the beginning."

Meanwhile Branwe had noticed consternation among the pirates; they had been watching something out of the corners of their eyes, careful not to stare openly at it. Looking in the same direction, he at last spotted two pirates creeping up on one of the flattish, multilegged reptiles, as if they were going to pounce on it, instead of the other way around. It was evident that they could not see it yet.

But what did they see? Or their perplexed comrades? He was now reluctant to put down the Demon Sword, even for an instant, and beckoned to Cajhet.

"Do you see those two pirates trying to sneak away?"

"Sure," he said, "and between you and me, good riddance. I spotted 'em crawling off into the underbrush, but where they're now hiding I can't say. Funny the way they just kind of disappeared, like into a mist. Except it's morning, and the sun is shining."

Branwe started to reply, then froze in horror. So did the pirates, but it was too late for them. The multilegged reptile hit them with poisoned fangs, and in seconds they were both truly frozen, unable to stir. Then out of hiding scuttled five little multilegged reptiles, evidently at some signal from their mother. Maternally she began to tear gobbets of flesh from one of her paralyzed victims, and to feed her young. The second pirate would furnish her own dinner.

Like Cajhet, the other pirates had lost sight of their two comrades in what seemed like a strange kind of mist, and could not see what was happening to them. They were warier and more suspicious than ever, though their eyes still watched furtively for opportunities to escape, as the column resumed its march toward the ruins. They seemed leery for the moment about further attempts.

Due to Severakh's vigilance there were no further incidents of any kind, all the way to the foothills of the spine of mountains. Only then did he call a halt. While rations of food and water were being distributed, Cajhet sidled up to Branwe and whispered:

"There was something funny going on back in the valley, wasn't there? Something you didn't tell me about? But old Severakh knows, don't he?"

Branwe had not been cautioned to silence by his commander, and saw no reason not to inform Cajhet about the true nature of the mirages they had seen, and what lurked inside them.

"Whew, glad I didn't try it then." Cajhet was shaken by the account. "No thanks to the old mrem. I can't tell you how sick I am of ship biscuit and salt fish, so I was kinda sneaking over to one of them gardens, thinking I might improve my diet, when I caught him watching me. But he didn't bark, or chew me out, like I expected. Just turned away and pretended he hadn't noticed. And now I know why." He glanced over his shoulder and whispered: "It's the fluffy pink dressing gown. Bet on it! He's worried somebody else might hear about it, and he'd never live it down."

"What are you talking about?"

Cajhet put a sly finger beside his nose and winked, but said nothing more.

It did not take long to explore the ruins, which had clearly lain uninhabited for millennia. Nor was there any doubt they were of liskash, or at least not of mrem, construction, although the use of pointed arches seemed to be in crude imitation of early mrem architecture. The ruined structures were more indicative of magic than intelligence.

Of the mrem themselves, only barefoot tracks were found,

the tracks of creatures that walked on two legs but still ran on four.

It was on two legs, both walking and running, that the pirates at last made their escape. There was no pursuit. In fact, had they been bolder, they might have slipped away any time they chose, these last few hours. Severakh merely shrugged when they were reported missing, and remained thoughtful all the way back to the longboats.

"This must be how it all began," he muttered to himself. "For thousands of generations, forgotten in the mists of years, the struggle for supremacy between liskash size and magic, and the evolving intelligence of our own ancestors, must have continued relentlessly, just as it still does here today. Just as it still does in the world at large. Especially around the walls of Ar—if they still stand. Forget about the pirates," were the first words he cried aloud, as he and what remained of his foraging party at last boarded the *Zanira*. "They've got their struggle to survive, and we've got ours. You've done good work while I was gone, troops. But now let's concentrate more on the hull. We can always repair sail under way."

There was little more he could do now, and for once he indulged himself in an afternoon nap. Despite his age and the exertions of the past months, he looked a lot sprier than Shimsham that night, when they appeared together on deck. Certainly he looked a lot sterner.

"None of your lies or stories now." Severakh glowered at him. "You've held out on me for the last time, scoundrel. Oh, now don't start whimpering again! I'll put you ashore, and the pirates will really give you something to howl about. And nobody's going to feel sorry for you, so don't try that old dodge either. All three moons will be visible in an hour or so, and it looks like they're getting close to focusing a perfect triangle on these islands. That rocky headland shelters us from the worst tangletides here, but what about Shadow Island itself? And what about the triangulation of the moons? Can the phenomenon be judged more accurately than by the naked eye?"

"Two questions, one answer," said Shimsham, who was beginning to recover both his health and his impudence. "Meanest tangletides I ever seen, around the big island. There was a nice quiet cove, but with the water rushing this way and that, I never thought we'd get snug inside. How we did it, I don't know exactly. You see, they kept me working below decks most of the time. It was a well-run ship."

"Must have been, if they kept you below decks. Now what's the one answer to my two questions?"

"When the moons focus, then so do the tides. Round and round the island they go, like they was trying to swallow it in a giant whirlpool. No more tangletides then, just this one big swirl. Only lasts a few hours, though. Just like whatever you're after on the island. Glad I wasn't ashore that night, 'cause most of those who were never came back to tell the tale. Turns out I was lucky, too, in being marooned. Maybe you heard about what happened to those who made it back to Namakhazar?"

"We won't talk about that now." Severakh gave him a meaningful look. "And we won't talk about that later. Understand? All right, then. It's time you started pulling your own weight. I'm assigning you to the night watch on the steering crew. Tomorrow night or the next the moons will focus. So tell the lieutenant about the tides and anything else you remember about navigating the waters around Shadow Island. Now move!"

Severakh's next interview was with Branwe. He knew there was nothing more he could do to help the young mrem. He had taught him all the sword technique he could; he had never drilled anyone with more inborn talent, so willing to learn, so determined to be a warrior. But how could any swordsmrem truly be prepared to fight shadows?

Severakh himself was now more and more oppressed by a sense of futility. He was an old soldier, and did his duty, although he felt that he too had been sent off to fight shadows. A lifetime of martial experience frittered away, not as a commanding general of armies, but as the led captain of magicians, whom he had always distrusted in any case. There was something distastefully reptilian about magic . . . .

"So far, so good, lad." He clapped Branwe encouragingly on the shoulder. "We know that these legendary islands really exist. We must assume that the rest of the legend is also true. You're not less a warrior than your father was. You know how much depends on your success, and you know how much Srana depends on you. Do your duty, lad. I can't say more than that."

"Will it be tomorrow night, sir?" asked Branwe.

"Yes, or the night after, at the very latest." Severakh examined him, and he knew he was no longer looking at a kit. He could hardly imagine the terrors that concentrated upon Shadow Island at the focus of the moons, but his martial instincts assured him that, if they could be overcome at all, this resolute young warrior standing before him could do it.

Every couple of hours throughout the night, Severakh summoned Shimsham down from the afterdeck to quiz him further about their destination, and to assure himself that the three moons in the sky had not yet triangulated. Sometimes they seemed to form a perfect equilateral triangle; sometimes it was obvious that one of the legs was out of alignment. Shimsham found all these questions trivial, even annoying. The third time he was summoned he actually cheeked Severakh—but he never did it again.

"Land ho!" cried the lookout, about an hour after dawn.

Once again Shimsham, who was now thinking fondly about a nice hot breakfast and crawling into his nice soft bunk, found himself summoned down from the afterdeck. His ears still rang from the last interview, and he was very careful not to make any more impertinent remarks.

"That's it, sir," he swore. "Not a doubt about it. Shadow Island, if I ever laid eyes on it. I remember like it was yesterday, coming up from below decks—"

"Get below decks again," Severakh growled at him, and he was gone. "You'd better get some rest too, lad," he said more gently to Branwe. "I don't know if the moons will focus tonight, but we have to be ready if they do."

By nightfall the *Zanira* was coasting the shores of a dark, barren island, whose towering cliffs had been undercut by violent wave action, whose offshore pillars of rock pointed like giant fingers toward the direction from which the waves attacked them. They were not under attack now; the rolling swell washed barely halfway up the small pebbly beaches at the foot of the cliffs.

Everything began to change after sunset. The first moon rose, and with it the tides, tides that became more complex with the rising of the second moon. Then the third and largest moon appeared in the night sky, and the tangletides so rushed and leaped and plummeted along the coast that Severakh ordered his helmsmrem to draw farther out to sea.

"There it is!" Shimsham cried the moment he popped out of the hatch. "The cove. You're going to pass it. Then you'll have to sail clear around the island—if tonight's the night." He studied the alignment of the moons. "We'll know in a couple of hours."

Meanwhile Severakh reversed course, tacking back in the direction pointed to by the offshore stacks, never far from the sheltered cove, which seemed in the silvery moonlight to have been bitten from the cliffs around it by giant teeth. The scalene triangle of moons gradually became obtuse, then more and more symmetrical, until the naked eye could judge no variation in the length of its legs.

"The tide's turning!" cried the lookout from aloft.

"Then so are we!" Severakh ordered his helmsmrem.

The great steering oar was shifted, the sails reset, and once more the *Zanira* reversed course. By the time it came around again the waters offshore were swirling like a millrace, round and round the island.

"Fetch your sword, lad," cried Severakh. "Things are moving fast." He wanted to say more, but knew that words no longer mattered; his or anybody else's. Sword technique, courage, and—luck. One lone kit pitted against an evil dimension for supremacy over an entire planet. What words would now avail him?

Sending mrem aloft to tie down the last unreefed sails, dispatching five of his brawniest soldiers to throw their weight against the steering oar, he brought the *Zanira* through the swirling current and into the sheltered cove.

Beetling cliffs overhung its northern shore; down the southern slopes, like ribbons of silver, wound a trellis of streams. The threefold moonlight was eerie and unreal, like the twilight of a dying world.

"Looks like the moons have nearly focused, lad," said Severakh, clambering into the longboat as briskly as any of his mrem, despite his age. "Nothing but rock, as far as I can see. Not even ruins. If there's a temple here, like the old wizard said, I can't see it."

Branwe stood beside him in the bow, the Demon Sword

clutched firmly in his right hand. The spectral shapes he saw
looming in the distance may have been an effect of the eerie
moonlight. Whatever they were, he did not mention them.
No one else could see them, and he knew he had to face
them alone.

"We'll be waiting for you, lad," said Severakh, as two of his
mrem beached the longboat. "No matter what. I know that
my words are unimportant. I can only repeat what a certain
lovely young she-mrem would have told you now: 'The All-
Mother guide and protect you, Branwe. I'm depending on
you.' "

If Branwe's hand tightened on his sword, if his jaw muscles
set firmer with determination, no one noticed. Springing
agilely over the bow without looking back, he picked his way
up the trellis of glistening streams to the top of the slope.

Wiry shrubs and a scattering of low trees, windswept and
nearly bereft of foliage; it was a weird symmetry, as if the
barren landscape was arrayed artificially—or had been thousands of years ago. The spectral shapes, which he alone saw,
loomed some two or three miles inland; they seemed more
real now, and he headed directly toward them.

Everything in fact seemed more real now—except reality
itself. Branwe glanced back toward the cove. The slopes
screened him from the waiting longboat, but the *Zanira* now
seemed to him like a ghost ship, hazy and insubstantial. He
followed a narrow road inland—or a leveling that had once
been a road—and he suddenly had the feeling that he had
seen this all before, that he had once walked this very road,
in this same eldritch moonlight. The shapes looming in the
distance were no longer spectral.

If it was a temple, it was that of no god or goddess he
knew. Its architecture was crude and repulsive; its single
opening like a giant liskash eye, aglow with ruby light. He
could not determine yet whether it had a roof or lay open to
the skies. As he approached, he became aware of other
shapes looming out of the weird twilight, living shapes, and
he sensed that they were also aware of him. Some appeared
to bear weapons, and began to range themselves between
him and the temple entrance.

Branwe did not hesitate. The threefold moons now trained
on him like the light through a magnifying glass. All of

time—past, present, and future—seemed to focus on this very moment. He could now distinguish the three figures that barred his way. They wore dark robes emblazoned with occult figures and designs; the swords they brandished appeared now more ornamental than military, and they did not know how to wield them with effect. Their greenish-white faces were gauntly reptilian: hideous and evil.

Thrust, parry, thrust, parry, slash, parry, parry, and thrust again. A minute, no more than two, and it was all over. Wiping his sword on the robe of one of the loathsome carcasses sprawled in the road, the young warrior continued resolutely forward. The ruby glow before him seemed to watch his every movement.

Glancing back, he was surprised to find that nothing now lay in the road behind him. However, more and more reptilian figures, robed and unrobed, armed and unarmed, but all of demonic hideousness, seemed to be drawn from nothingness by the power of the focused moonlight.

Branwe entered the crude, repulsive temple, and again had the feeling he had been here before. There was indeed no roof, and yet the moonlight did not penetrate to the slime-encrusted floor, as if the ruby glow somehow repelled its beams with a light pressure of its own.

Pillars of dark stone, crudely engraved with the same occult figures and designs as adorned the robes of the guardians he had slain outside—Had he in fact slain them? Did they die in any true sense of the word?—rose before him in ponderous files, as if supporting a roof that did not exist, in this dimension at least. Warily, sword in hand, he strode between them toward the source of the ruby light.

A foreboding of evil weighed down upon him, impalpable and unseen and yet with as powerful a force as that which repelled the threefold moonlight. His steps began to lag; he seemed now to be pushing against some current of repulsion, as if wading through an invisible sea. Heavier and heavier weighed the burden of evil, the sense of foreboding.

Parry, slip, parry, and thrust. The hideous robed figure had leapt out at him from behind a pillar without warning. Warily, sword poised for another attack, Branwe stepped over the sprawled body. The moons overhead were now barely visible, as if he looked up at them from the bottom of the sea, as if the conjunction of the evil dimension with his world was becoming ever more substantial, more real, as if more and more of the hideous robed guardians were now gaining the power to materialize around him.

He had the uncanny feeling of something creeping up on him from behind, and glanced over his shoulder. But there was nothing. Not even a body sprawled on the floor.

The next attack was more determined, the odds more formidable. The sword technique he had mastered under the exacting eye of Severakh now served him well—up to a point. No drill had ever pitted him against three antagonists at once, much less the six he now faced. Quickness and agility were here more valuable than technique. Dodge, parry, leap, thrust; then duck and spin out of the way. They tried clumsily to surround him, to corner him against a pillar; but instead he used that very pillar to his own advantage, circling behind it and reemerging on the other side, decapitating two enemies before they were aware he had reappeared.

Without the Demon Sword his attackers might not have been visible to him; no ordinary weapon could have killed them. Or did its power just drive them back into the evil dimension whence they sprang? A last thrust at the last of the robed figures, and Branwe broke free and waded onward against the repulsion of the ruby light.

It was too late now for caution. More robed figures, along with still more sinister creatures, naked in all their demonic hideousness, were now pouring through the entrance into the temple. He had seen them incorporating out of nothingness in the moonlight outside. He now saw them in all their liskash evil, surging after him; their angry cries were like the hissing of vipers. They realized now why he had come.

Every step closer to the ruby light called for more effort, more resolve, as if he were now wading through invisible quicksands, as if the light itself knew why he had come, and was exerting all its evil brilliance to drive him back. He did not have the strength to run; mere walking exhausted him; the angry reptilian horde, surging through the temple entrance, seemed actually to be gaining on him. Step by wearying step, the young warrior drove himself forward.

Nothing could discourage him now; no power in this dimension or any other could daunt him, no force drive him back. Too much was at stake: the great city of Ar, the very survival of his race, Srana. Clutching the Demon Sword, his jaws clenched determinedly with the strain, Branwe continued to slog his way against the invisible pressure into the innermost recesses of the temple.

So intense became the ruby light as he approached it that he was nearly blinded. Its source was now directly ahead, and he squinted his eyes against the painful brilliance. Then all at once he seemed to remember things about the Khavala that no one had ever told him, things unknown about his father's incursion here. He had the uncanny feeling that this was not the first time he had penetrated the crude temple, or fought its hideous guardians.

Ever more brilliant became the light, ever more painful to his eyes. Whether he actually saw the stone altar first, or through some uncanny remembrance just knew it would be there, he was suddenly cognizant of what lay directly ahead. For the first time Branwe truly appreciated the epic magnitude of his quest, and the awe of what he had undertaken, more than any sense of dread, momentarily disoriented him.

Recovering, he slogged his way the last few feet to the stone altar. Everything was just as he remembered it would be. The Khavala protruded from the altar like the naval of an entire world: a world alien to the one he knew. Its ruby phosphorescence glowed like a sentient light, as if the very elements from which it had crystalized were alien to his known world. It was the size of a clenched fist; one corner was scarred by an old wound.

This reminded Branwe of the most disturbing thing he had been told about the first incursion here: how his father was so pressed by the demon guardians that, in the midst of fighting for his life, he had time enough only to hack a few fragments off a corner of the mystic stone—and that his sword had shattered.

Still awed by what he was doing, Branwe tried to use his own sword to pry the stone loose.

Escape from the evil horde now rushing toward him would be a challenge even to one wielding the Demon Sword; without it he would never leave this evil dimension alive. How his father, the legendary Shadow Warrior, had escaped this very temple with a shattered sword, Branwe did not know. Perhaps its stub retained enough magic? More likely there were not so many reptile-demons on guard here then, and the Shadow Warrior's incursion had taken those few by surprise.

The liskash were prepared now for any second incursion, scores of them, perhaps hundreds. How many more were still incorporating in the eerie moonlight outside, Branwe could not know. All his mind and soul were concentrated on prying loose the Khavala. But it was no use. The horde of reptile-demons were almost upon him. He might battle his way through them, even escape back to the ship. Then what? Return home in disgrace, confess his failure to Srana, and together wait for the Eastern Lords—or the Evil One himself—to come and get them? Better to die right here, if he must.

Gripping the Demon Sword in both hands, he measured his strength, and hacked down at the mystic stone with all his might. If he could not abscond with it himself, he might at least damage it, lessen its power for wreaking evil; perhaps destroy it utterly. The shock jolted his entire body. His hands were numb, his arms and shoulders tingled, but the Demon Sword was still intact, its magic—concentrated by fragments of the Khavala itself—greater than that imbued into his father's sword by the Evil One.

Ruby phosphorescence glistened all around him. He had cleft the mystic stone in twain, but was still unable to pry the larger half from its setting, and now had more urgent use for his sword. Pocketing the loosened half, he dodged around the crude altar, leapt past the onrushing horde, and doubled back through the flanking rows of pillars. A gutteral shriek rent the air as the hideous robed guardians discovered the sacrilege to their precious Khavala. No moonlight at all now penetrated from above, and their cries of fury resounded through the crimson gloom.

But not all the fury of an evil dimension could compensate for their reptilian slowness, and Branwe—dodging where he could, fighting when he had to—doubled back again through the occult pillars toward the entrance, ahead of the returning horde. The ruby light was dimmer now, so dim that when he at last fought his way back out into the open, he was momentarily blinded by the threefold moonlight.

Reptile-demons seemed to be everywhere, but whatever evil magic they assailed him with, it was neutralized by the Demon Sword.

They at last realized this themselves, and began to run, slither, lope, scuttle—no two were alike in their liskash hideousness, nor in their means of locomotion—toward him. Nothing could better have served his purposes, and he lingered near the temple entrance until just before the raging horde inside burst through it in pursuit. The only hope of those outside was to cut him off from the waiting longboat, but for the moment at least he had them all moving in the wrong direction.

At the last instant, just as one horde of reptile-demons burst out of the temple, he dodged through the second horde—slithering, loping, and scuttling toward him from the opposite direction—as if they were standing still. Their cries of rage and frustration were otherworldly, like echoes reverberating out of an abyss. Everything around him in fact now seemed to belong to another world. And though his fleetness soon carried him beyond the reach of his laggard pursuers, he felt more and more insecure, nagged by increasing fears that something was wrong.

Doubts now burdened his flying footsteps like leaden weights. A growing sense of helplessness oppressed him, seeming to whisper ever more insistently that escape was impossible, that he would never leave Shadow Island alive. Certainly he would never leave it if meanwhile something had happened to the *Zanira*. But what harm could possibly have come to the great ship, which he had left riding peacefully at anchor in a quiet cove? He knew such fears were irrational, and yet they oppressed him nonetheless, as he neared the trellis of silver-bright streams.

The longboat awaited him at the base of the slope, so his angle of approach meant that the *Zanira* itself, anchored well out in the middle of the cove, was the first thing he would see. What he saw staggered him with horror. Giant marine reptiles, their long necks bobbing hungrily up and down as they tore away great chunks of wood and canvas, were attacking the ship from all sides. It was already too damaged to survive out at sea; there was no escape from Shadow Island, just as he had feared. He continued to stumble forward, more from inertia than with any clear intent, until he reached the top of the slope.

And there below was the longboat, its crew calmly awaiting his return. Couldn't they see what was happening to the *Zanira*? He glanced back across the eerie moon-washed landscape. The reptile-demons had given up the chase. Were they now trying to capture him by other means? Hundreds of them, in all shapes of hideousness, massed unmovingly about a mile inland, as if concentrating their malice on him alone. Even at this distance he could sense their eyes focused evilly upon him.

Then he realized that other eyes had also spotted him, as he stood amidst the trellis of streams, at the very top of the slope. The longboat crew at once took to their oars, and Severakh beckoned urgently to him. Yet all the while he could see the giant marine reptiles tearing the *Zanira* to wreckage, out in the cove behind them.

Illusion; an illusion meant to paralyze his will. That had to be the answer. Nor was it really a convincing illusion, now that he looked closer. An argosy being torn to pieces by monstrous jaws would create some noise, probably a lot of noise. But only a ghostly silence reigned below.

He hesitated. The risk was great, but he had to know. Very gingerly he laid the Demon Sword on the ground, and released his grip, his fingers poised hardly an inch from its hilt. In an instant the world was transformed, and he reeled and almost fell beneath the weight of evil assailing him. The hideous crunching of monstrous jaws, destroying his sole means of escape from Shadow Island, plunged him into such depths of despair that he nearly surrendered himself out of sheer hopelessness.

Then he had the Demon Sword in his hand once more, and the evil magic was again neutralized. Had he moved his hand even a few inches farther from the hilt, he might not have had the will to grasp it again. Only now did he truly appreciate the power vested in his sword, though he himself was no magician.

What then of the force inherent in the object in his pocket?

He could barely imagine its potential for withstanding evil—or creating it, in the wrong hands. Although, as he was no magician, it was nothing but a big shiny stone to him. Were Srana here, the whole pack of reptile-demons would surely have been sent howling back to their own dimension by now. Perhaps the Evil One was not invincible after all; nor the war against the Eastern Lords as hopeless as it had once seemed.

But the battle was still only half won; the Khavala was not yet in the hands of someone capable of wielding its power for good. Scrambling, sliding, leaping over silver-bright streams, he descended the slope to the longboat.

He patted his pocket, in answer to Severkh's questioning look. The old warrior nodded a "well done," and they scrambled aboard the longboat, and pushed off from shore.

Ghostly illusions still assailed him, but he now recognized them as such. The only damage to the *Zanira* was that wreaked by the storm and the pirate attack, most of which had already been repaired, though there remained some concern about the hull.

Coursing the millrace waters still swirling offshore, they were carried many miles to the south before they at last broke forth into the open sea. The breeze was easterly, but they could not have retraced their course home even had the wind been more favorable. Three claws above the horizon would not give them the longitude of Namakhazar, and they set sail and headed due north. What lay there, far west of the realm of the mrem, was as legendary as the Shadow Islands themselves. But only a coasting voyage would now get them home.

Would it get them home in time? Was Srana still safe at Ravarbal? Had the great city of Ar fallen? Branwe fretted all the next day, and for several days thereafter; never for a moment did he succeed in curbing his impatience, and volunteered for all the most vexing jobs, below deck or aloft, as if that would somehow get them home sooner.

Severakh was no less anxious, but he had fought too many campaigns over too many years to fret needlessly about events over which he had no control.

Also, he had a sounder grasp of grand strategy. The three moons would not triangulate again for nearly two years. Until that time, whatever remained of the Khavala would be out of reach of the Evil One, and the war won and lost with whatever powers of magic now existed in the world.

He himself was more concerned about the marshaling of armies—the true concern of a warrior—and about the deteriorating condition of the hull.

▲

Chapter 19
Flames and Shadows

"**O**f course there's a blockade, you idiots!" snapped Severakh. "Why in three moons do you think I anchored so far from the city? We stole the biggest ship in Namakhazar right out from under their noses. Don't you think it's been missed by now? Or that the murdering fiend who sent everything from dragons to bandit gangs to kill us just may have guessed where we've gone, and why?" He looked disgustedly from Cajhet to Shimsham, then back again. "Why is it that whenever I need the best mrem for a job, I have to send the worst?"

Only a single moon stood in the night sky; the second would rise just before morning; the third had already set. Not a glimmer of light shone aboard the *Zanira*. Its sails were patched, its stays spliced and respliced; and though its hull wallowed dangerously low in the water, Severakh had at last called his pumping crews, who had so valiantly kept them afloat on rough seas and calm, back up on deck. His catapults, which again and again had repelled attacks by wreckers and shore pirates during the long coasting voyage home, would not avail him against the entire enemy fleet, should they discover him here, he had also relieved his catapulters of duty. A new ordeal awaited them all, and his crew needed as much rest as they could get before facing it.

He had in effect beached his ship in this rocky inlet where even a scout ship would hardly dare to follow him, the mouth of which was guarded by treacherous reefs and breakers, agitating the surf to froth. The *Zanira*, daughter of the polestar, had sailed her last glorious voyage.

"Now listen to me, the pair of you." Severakh gave Cajhet

and Shimsham each in turn a meaningful look. "The tangletides are at ebb, and the breeze favorable, so the longboat I'm sending you in should reach port well before morning. Shimsham here knows the city—"

"Know it like the fur on the back of my own hand."

"—so he'll be able to get you safely through the streets. Your mother—" he searched Cajhet's face, but found no hint of fluffy pink dressing gowns, "—should be able to give you the latest news. Or contact whichever of your half-brothers or -sisters is most likely to have the information we want. Ample moneys were left on deposit with them. I believe they can be trusted to organize and supply an expedition back to Ravarbal. Just bring me the news." He gazed thoughtfully across the rocky inlet, its dark waters mottled with foam. "If Ar has fallen, we may have to make other arrangements. Guerrilla resistance; perhaps try to rally the western city-states, if they too haven't been overrun by now. But there's really no point in speculating without data. Bring me the news."

"Yes, sir." They both saluted, each with his own secret plans for indulging himself in the licentious port city of Namakhazar.

"I couldn't eat another salt fish if I was starving," whispered Cajhet, as he and Shimsham clambered aboard the waiting longboat.

"The very thought makes me thirsty," added the latter with a grin of anticipation. "I've seen some demons of my own, this trip. I've earned me a good fling."

The sailors piloting the longboat also seemed to anticipate a spree. But the fact that they had not yet received their wages, and wouldn't until Severakh and his men were beyond the reach of reprisals, ensured their good behavior—and discretion. They knew the coastal waters, the peculiar tides and hazards, and slipped unseen into the harbor of Namakhazar before the second moon rose.

The ships at anchor, or moored along the docks, were only small merchant or fishing vessels, and surprisingly few in so commodious a harbor. Somebody was indeed determined to intercept the returning *Zanira*, perhaps even desperate, to pay the costs of so massive a blockade. Every ship of significant tonnage in Namakhazar seemed to be out at sea.

"All the better for us, eh, lads?" whispered Shimsham, and there was laughter up and down the thwarts.

"Our first stop is the Tangletide," said Cajhet, "and maybe our last—tonight." And there was more laughter. "There it is now, on stilts over the water. Hear the music, lads? You know what that means."

The dancing she-mrem and regular female patrons at the Tangletide also knew what it meant to greet sailors returning from a long voyage, and soon they had all vanished into neighborhood bedrooms. Shimsham alone never left the bar, where he presided for the rest of the night—and many, many nights thereafter—with a goblet in each hand.

"Never thought I'd make it," he was heard to mutter over and over again. "Twice to the Shadow Islands and back again. Did I ever tell you about the beautiful island she-mrem I met on my way home? Here, youngster, I believe it's your turn to buy the drinks. Now gather around, and I'll tell you about the night I first met Tamani . . . ."

Meanwhile Cajhet was being hugged and groomed until he was dizzy by the overjoyed Kizzlecosh, to the delight of the grisly patrons she usually terrorized. The first thing he had noticed upon entering the Tangletide was how much her new collection of ears, tacked up in neat rows behind the bar, had prospered since his departure.

"Oh, my little Cajie-wajie, I'm so happy to see you safe and sound," she cried again and again, hugging him passionately.

She had evidently thrived here at the Tangletide, if her increased robustness was any indication. But there was also a tender look in her eyes, and Cajhet too had been at sea a long time. He poked a playful finger into her massive bosom, and winked lecherously. Her bawdy laughter rang through the tavern, and soon they too had vanished for the night. A bedroom is as good a place as any for getting the latest news . . . .

"I've kept my ears open for you, you dear little Cajie-wajie," Kizzlecosh said affectionately at the breakfast table the next morning.

Cajhet winced, afraid she was going to hug him again. Her unflagging exuberance all through the night—hour after hour after hour—had left him nearly delirious; his eyes were puffed and bloodshot, his fingers trembled, and he had trouble

concentrating. But she certainly had prepared a savory breakfast for him; the table fairly groaned with bowls, platters,
cups, trenchers, and chafing-dishes of rich and succulent
delicacies. Despite his soreness and love fatigue, he soon
found his strength returning. In fact, he began to wonder
with apprehension if that was exactly why she was feeding
him up with such gusto.

"They escaped Ravarbal just in time, no thanks to Haggie."
She bit the air with her sharp, powerful teeth. "He won't stab
me in the back again, but there are other spies lurking all
over Namakhazar these days. They even tried to quiz me, but
I set 'em in their place right off, so now they steer clear.
Maybe you noticed the ear with the white tuft at the tip,
fourth from the right, in the bottom row?"

"It looked beautiful, love," said Cajhet, "and it does you
proud."

"Yes, I must say myself it does look nice there," she
conceded. "Anyways, they don't bother me no more, or even
stick their noses inside the Tangletide."

"Or their ears?" he winked.

She bellowed with laughter. "Oh, Cajie-wajie, you are a
darling. But I know you're on a serious mission—I'm so
proud of you—and I found out all I could. Messengers were
sent from the Yozgat, believe it or not. Remember what I
told you about them, and got you to detour around their
territory? Well, it seems your folk have actually taken refuge
there. How they managed it, I don't know, but they couldn't
be safer."

Cajhet was meanwhile wondering how he himself might
remain safe here in Namakhazar, for the duration of the
ensuing conflict. Ar had not fallen, and he knew what that
meant for all those under the command of the redoubtable
Severakh. Some snug berth well behind the lines, perhaps
something like his old job in Kazerclawm, with regular hours,
not too much work, and plenty to eat and drink. That's what
he really hoped for right now. He was wondering how much
influence his mother still had with Severakh, when Kizzlecosh
said:

"I've already sent for the messengers from the Yozgat. You
looked so cute this morning—snoring and drooling on your

pillow—that I didn't want to wake you. I know you had a long voyage. You must have been tired."

"Yes," he said drily, "riding the billows can be exhausting. But what's to become of you, love? It looks like there's a lot of hard work and danger ahead of me," he added, hoping it was in fact all behind him.

"I'm coming with you," she cried. Then, seeing his startled look: "Unless you don't want me any more."

"If you're not coming, I'm not going." He made the best of the unexpected development. "We wouldn't be here at all, without you. I don't care that much"—he snapped his fingers— "for what old Severakh himself says about it. Let him court-martial me for desertion. You go, or I stay. That's my final word on the matter, and I'll stand by it, whatever the consequences."

The fond look in her eye reminded him of the many fond looks she had given him last night, but he was reprieved by a jangle at the front door.

He naturally believed that the two messengers who now entered the apartment were Yozgat, as did Kizzlecosh herself—to their later dismay. The Mamlock messengers had been given certain questions to ask, which only those really under the command of Severakh could possibly answer, and Cajhet had no trouble satisfying them about his identity. After some probing questions of his own, he informed them in turn about the successful voyage to the Shadow Islands, and they left Namakhazar inside an hour with the news.

Nor did it take Cajhet much longer to conclude arrangements with influential half-brothers and -sisters for supplies; even a shady deal to salvage the *Zanira*, before it was discovered by scout ships. All the arrangements had in fact been concluded—and paid for in advance—by Severakh, before his first departure from Namakhazar. Cajhet had only to give the word.

The second departure from the neighborhood of the licentious port city was as clandestine as the first. Kizzlecosh did not bother to give notice at the Tangletide; she just failed to show up for work one night, and a full week passed before anybody could be certain that she was not coming back again. Then the barkeeper found himself vexed once more by nightly brawls and disorder, as his grisly clientele lost all concern for their ears, and it was not long before the Tangletide had regained its old reputation as the scuzziest dive on the waterfront.

▲

Srana opened her eyes. Though quartered in the strange seclusion of the female barracks, in a remote mountain valley, among the warrior Yozgat, she had been sleeping with all the soundness of youth and good health—until something alerted her danger sense, which never slept. But what? The Eastern Lords, the Evil One himself, would not dare attack so bellicose a folk, at least until they could marshal overwhelming force against them—something they would be unable to do so long as the great city of Ar still stood.

No, the danger was nearer at hand, more individual, more sinister. Like all the dwellings of the Yozgat, her quarters were sparsely furnished and without adornment; privacy was the only concession granted her. She listened, but could hear nothing ominous. Without stirring her bedclothes, she slowly turned her head.

For an instant she had the uncanny feeling that she was reliving the night when all her troubles began, the night when her grandfather died so valiantly in flames so that she might live. Once more a shadowy figure stood in the doorway of her room, but this time her danger sense warned her that it was an enemy. It was hooded; its dwarfish stature alone revealed it as a Yozgat.

Then she realized that the hooded figure was creeping slowly toward her. Only one moon now stood in the sky; a lone pallid beam slanted down through the single window at the far side of the room. All else lay in shadow. But her eyes were keen, even in the dark, and she saw clearly the steel claws the figure wore strapped to its wrists.

Concealment magic was now useless, perhaps dangerous. It might alert the clawed figure that she was awake, and was unlikely to cause so intense a gaze to turn away from her in any case. She heard sounds of commotion outside her window, but faint and far away, too far away for sentries somewhere out in the city to reach her in time, were she to cry out. The she-mrem in this very barracks could no longer help her.

The advancing figure raised its steel claws as maliciously as if they were its own; its intense hatred concentrated upon the head of the cot, as if it did not just want to kill Srana but to claw her beautiful face to ruins.

Srana also concentrated. If the shadowy figure in the doorway had reminded her of the night her grandfather died, it also reminded her of the manner of his death. Even redoubled by her fragment of the Khavala, her fire-starting magic was limited compared to his. But if she could not bring an entire house down in flames, she should at least be able to ignite a piece of cloth—the hooded dark cloak worn by the assassin.

The first waft of smoke only caused Srana to focus her magic more intently; the first glow of fire to redouble her concentration. But so intent was the malice of the approaching figure that its cloak was actually in flames before it even hesitated.

The commotion outside in the streets seemed to be drawing nearer, but was now drowned by the wild commotion that erupted inside the room.

Srana leapt out of bed. She did not have to cry for help; the shrieks of the small hooded figure, evidently female, had already awakened the barracks. There were answering cries outside the corridor; the sounds of running feet. Srana herself was cut off from the door by the shrieking, writhing, flaming horror; she slipped into the darkest corner of the room, and used concealment magic to elude observation.

The running footsteps were now right outside her door, the shouts of converging sentries right outside her window. But she was still in deadly peril. The pounding at the door meant that its inner clasp had somehow been jammed so it would not open. The assassin at last writhed free of the burning cloak. The reek of singed fur tainted the air; the firelight rose brighter and brighter, the smoke and heat became more and more oppressive as the bedclothes were ignited.

Srana at last recognized the assassin. It was the High Priestess Parvatala, somehow escaped from the Mamlock dwelling where she had been confined. Her guards had been reinforced after her condemnation: every sword in full council had been raised against her. Had this merely provided her with more mindpower to tap, used to cloud the very minds she was tapping? Whether by this means or one more violent, she had somehow broken from confinement. Not to escape the land of the Yozgat—with bambarongs to pursue her, that was impossible—but to wreak vengeance.

Half blinded, in agony, with no hope, perhaps no desire anymore, to escape, Parvatala slashed the smoke and shadows around her, still trying to claw the beautiful face of her enemy to ruins. The pounding at the door grew more desperate as smoke seeped out into the corridor; the shouts of the sentries now resounded from inside the barracks.

Slashing, clawing, shrieking unintelligible curses, Parvatala now began to work systematically back and forth across the small room, as if in her cunning she had guessed that some manner of concealment magic was being practiced on her. Her ugly dwarfish figure was like the phantom of a nightmare— illuminated by the flaming bedclothes, veiled in billows of smoke—as she drew ever nearer the corner where Srana had concealed herself.

The pounding at the door was now succeeded by heavy thudding crashes. A bench, used as a battering ram? A beam? Srana could hardy breathe in the choking heat and smoke, her eyes burned, and yet she dared not move.

So frenzied now was Parvatala's wild slashing and clawing that it seemed impossible to slip past her. If the intruder herself was no magician, she understood at least the workings of magic. With the door locked, and the single window a mere slit, her enemy must still be somewhere in the room. Srana could not escape her vengeance. Parvatala's shrieks sounded more and more like cries of triumph.

Srana was desperate. Concealment magic could not hide her much longer from someone who knew she was there. And what if she fainted from smoke inhalation? Nothing would then conceal her from the vindictive razor claws of the High Priestess. Parvatala was old now, but she was a Yozgat, with all a Yozgat's almost supernatural battle empathy. She would respond with lightning reflexes to any movement around her. The timing had to be perfect.

Now literally cornered, Srana's own reflexes told her when to move—with the agility and muscular coordination unique to a White Dancer. Even so, the slashing razor claws hooked the skirt of her nightgown, but their very sharpness saved her as they cut through the cloth like air.

A wild scream of rage, and the High Priestess was after her. Srana reached the door just as it burst open, with a splintering crash. She had a confused experience of dwarfish warriors rushing past her, of the crazed High Priestess being swarmed over from all sides at once, then a dizzy, half-conscious awareness that she was out in the corridor, supported by a score of anxious little females, none standing much above her elbow.

Her next awareness was of lying on an unmattressed cot in the dormitory. Changavar himself looked down at her with concern.

"She'll be all right," he said. "Swallowed too much smoke, that's all. A day's rest, and she'll be fine."

Srana looked up at the tufty faces around her, and smiled. They responded with satisfaction, and a few homely smiles of their own, but never quite lost their expressions of awe. Though they had just brought down the wicked High Priestess Parvatala, their reverence for the goddess herself was undiminished, and Srana still seemed to them her very incarnation.

"The first thing I'm going to find out," said Changavar, "is how the treacherous old hag got the news."

"News?" Srana sat up.

"The Mamlock messengers to Namakhazar have at last returned," he said. "As is our law, they were questioned in full council. Somehow the news leaked out, or Parvatala had some illicit arrangement with the Mamlock family on whom we quartered her. I'll find out, and when I do, somebody's going to hop for it," he added, and an impromptu council began to discuss the ways and means for discovering the traitor.

Srana was soon so impatient that she felt like hopping herself. "What news?" she cried at last. "Are my friends safe? Did they accomplish their mission? Please tell me. It's important for all of us."

"They'll tell you themselves in a few days," said Changavar. "Exactly what they set out to accomplish, you've never fully explained. Only that it's important, and I believed you." Though Srana sat on the edge of the cot, while he stood,

their eyes were on a level. He looked thoughtfully at her for a
moment. "It will have to be very important indeed, for other
messengers have brought grim tidings from Ar. No, it still
stands. But for how much longer, I don't know. The troops of
marauders who have ravaged the land are now rejoining the
besieging army, along with reinforcements from the Eastern
Lords. It seems that a river somehow protects Ar—I care
nothing for those who hide behind walls—but now has been
damned."

"There are still powerful defenses there," replied Srana.
"Defenses that have nothing to do with walls."

"Magic?" Changavar guessed. "Yes, I felt there must be
other reasons why Ar still stood. The Yozgat need no walls.
Nor would walls avail any people we went forth to chastise."

A sizeable crowd of male and female warriors had now
gathered around the cot. They too had only scorn for walls.

"Even magic may be overcome by stronger magic," continued Changavar. "Which may already have happened at Ar."

"What do you mean?" Srana stared at him in alarm.

"The last messenger to arrive reported that a great sorcerer
has just taken command of the besieging armies. It seems
even they are terrified of him. The messenger swears he
actually saw him riding through the camps on a monstrous
dragon. Can this be the Evil One you told me about?"

Srana nodded, an anxious look in her eyes. She could
understand now why the High Priestess had tried to assassi-
nate her tonight. The old she-mrem had somehow learned
the news brought back by the messengers from Namakhazar,
and realized that she must strike now, or forever lose her
chance. There would be more outlanders allowed into the
land of the Yozgat; more flouting of sacred traditions. Perhaps
her twisted mind had seen the assassination of the person she
held responsible for it all as justice, rather than personal
vengeance. Or perhaps she anticipated what Srana now requested of Changavar:

"It is a long distance to Ar. You all know what will become
of the Yozgat if the great city of Ar falls to the Eastern Lords.
And if I don't return there in time, with what my friends are
bringing me from beyond the sea, then it must surely fall.
Will you help me?"

"By Parvatta, I will!" cried Changavar. Then, sensing an

ominous silence in the crowd around him, he added, "I will present all the facts before a full council, as is our law. They alone must decide the matter, but I'm sure that decision will be favorable."

The crowd nodded their approval, both of the issue and of Changavar himself. The blatant treachery of the High Priestess had once more brought about the opposite effect she had intended. Changavar had been Prince Warrior of the Yozgat for nearly seventeen years now, an unusually long term, and was too canny to push this advantage too far. He knew what had to be done, but the decision would have to be made officially by a majority of lifted swords, and many believed he had already gone too far in profaning the sacred traditions of the people. What he proposed was nothing short of revolutionary.

Shrewdly, he named the very Temple of Parvatta for the standing of the full council—the Yozgat considered sitting in council nearly as effete as living behind walls—and dressed Srana in a peculiar robe of copper green, identical in fashion to that worn by the eidolon, at whose feet she stood throughout the proceedings. He made not a single reference to her during his long harangue, nor did she herself utter a word; but the impression that an incarnation of the goddess herself sanctioned these violations of custom had a powerful effect on the council, and carried many swords aloft at the final vote—enough to carry the day.

"When your children's children wonder at so many trophies of honor—so many, my fellow warriors, that many of you, male and female alike, may have to get Mamlocks to build new presses to hold them all—your names will be remembered with awe." The question of trophies was still a sore point with the council, and Changavar sought craftily to allay it with the promise of new opportunities. The last show of swords was out of sheer enthusiasm.

Nonetheless there were some evil looks four days later, even some grumbling, when Severakh's band marched smartly into Parvat, but at least there were no open demands for pelts. Not even for Kizzlecosh's, though grim jokes wondered if hers would fill an entire press by itself. The military smartness of the new arrivals was another point in their favor, a very important point. Severakh took personal charge of their drills. His guerrilla army—what was left of it—was again united, and he immediately set to work drilling out any tendencies toward slackness.

Meanwhile Changavar personally drilled his own warriors, in competition with the outlanders, whose military posturing was an old object of derision among the Yozgat.

Although contrary in size, and from adverse traditions, the two leaders instinctively recognized in each other true soldiers. No matter what the past, though in years to come they might again be hostile, both realized they must now stand together, side by side, might and main, against the common foe. They drilled morning and afternoon, and conferred with their captains and each other long into the night; neither slept much for the next few days. Nor did they scamp their preparations, despite Srana's urging and impatience.

Her first meeting with Branwe, upon his return, had been public. To the warriors of both Severakh and Changavar it had seemed like no more than the formal report of an emissary; his presentation to her of the cloven section of the Khavala like no more than a royal gift. But the Yozgat shemrem were not beguiled. The pair of tall and beautiful outlanders were in love, and their possible relations, their every exchange of look and gesture, became in the barracks and on the drill field an exhaustless subject of gossip—though this did not keep the females from drilling with their own particular weapons as staunchly as the males did with theirs. In addition, they had charge of the bambarongs.

Most of the delay in departing for Ar was due to these bizarre creatures. It was a sacred law of the Yozgat to keep as many of them ready for war as there were warriors to ride them. But it had been generations since so mighty a host had ridden forth to battle, and from upland meadows, from Mamlock farms and pastures, from neighboring valleys, the huge two-legged animals were still being brought in. Some had grown half wild with freedom, and had to be rebroken to the saddle.

The Yozgat females were more adept at this art than the males, and from dawn until late afternoon bambarongs could be seen running, leaping, and gliding back and forth across the countryside surrounding Parvat, each with three little riders—the normal complement when riding forth to battle—

saddled on its back. Many had been out to pasture for months, even years, and were unusually strong and vigorous. It was these bambarongs that were reserved to carry one of the heavy outlanders along with two of the smaller Yozgat.

Kizzlecosh was a special problem, as well as an object of wonder to the Yozgat, over whom she towered. They thought her too ponderous and slow to be effective in battle—until they saw her out on the drill field one morning. From years of keeping order among crowds of drunken thugs and bandits she had acquired a battle empathy of her own. Nor was a cosh the only weapon she was capable of wielding. The broad curved sword of the Yozgat—as long as the Yozgat themselves, and honed like a razor—was like a wand in her big powerful hands. Also, there were her teeth . . . .

"All settled, love." Cajhet trotted gingerly out to her on the she-mrem's drill field one sunny morning. The steel claws worn by the dwarfish females still made him nervous. "I stayed after them till they gave me the right answer, and I never gave in. You'll ride when we do, or I'll know the reason why. We leave at dawn."

She dropped the spiked mace she had been practicing with, and hugged him possessively to her massive bosom, to the delight of the little Yozgat she-mrem nearby. "Oh, Cajie-wajie, I'm so happy. I don't know what I would have done if I had had to stay behind."

The difficulty of leaving her had in fact been the principal consideration in finding some means of transporting her to Ar. Priestesses and superannuated veterans alone would remain in Parvat, and many of these had voiced concern about being left in her company—especially since the subject Mamlocks would outnumber them fifty to one, with only the fear of reprisals keeping them in order. Cajhet tactfully omitted to mention this, or refer to the hunt for the strongest and most vigorous bambarong in the entire valley. Mamlocks were even now crafting a special saddle for her.

Other craftsmrem, under continuous guard and allowed only naps at their workbenches, had been working for days on a far more grandiose project. Copper was the most precious of all metals, and the Mamlock smiths who worked it could verdigris even their freshest engravings. The scepter on which they mounted the ruby Khavala stone was as green as the eidolon of Parvatta, and as exquisitely carved: a scepter that could be held forth like a beacon for all to see—including the enemy. Not until it was in the hands of Srana herself were the artisans allowed to leave their workshop.

The entire host left Parvat the following morning. No new High Priestess had yet been appointed, and no incident marred the sacred battle formulary. The green-copper doors of the temple hung open, but it was just dawn, and the eidolon of Parvatta inside was only a shadowy presence, barely visible in the cold gray light. It was on Srana rather that thousands of Yozgat eyes were now fixed with awe.

She stood alone on the temple stairs, wearing the goddess robes she had worn the day of the great council. Exactly how much power the engraved scepter in her hand granted her, she did not know. Enough, she hoped, for her to carry it safely to Ar. Mithmid and The Three, their formidable powers thus remultiplied, should then at least be able to neutralize the evil magic of Khal. While she herself would again be with Sruss, her beloved teacher and friend, comforted and safe.

The martial chanting of the chorus on the steps below her had the opposite effect of the last time she heard them. Then it had been soothing, lulling, hypnotic; now it stirred the valor and patriotism of the Yozgat warriors—females and males armed with their respective weapons—assembled in ranks in the square below. The very bambarongs, saddled and held ready by Mamlock handlers, appeared stirred.

Srana wondered if the strange beasts really could surmount the ramparts of Ar, as Changavar had assured her. She was certain now that their long glides, sometimes hundreds of yards at a bound, were aided by some unevolved form of levitation magic, for neither their running leaps nor the skin flaps they spread while in the air alone could possibly sustain them aloft for such distances. But she had never seen them leap more than a few feet off the ground, and though, according to Changavar, the Yozgat had often carried enemy towns by simply leaping over the walls, he could have no real conception of how imposing were the ramparts of Ar, the loftiest ever raised by the mrem. She would know for certain only when they got there.

Meanwhile she had somehow to communicate the arrival of

friends. Even if Changavar was right about the powers of his bambarongs, they could not just leap blindly into a besieged city. But with the Evil One now surely more vigilant than ever, she might bring Sruss into deadly peril by trying to contact her telepathically. The sole means she could devise for signaling her that friends were coming—else the garrison might think they were being attacked, and resist—was to don the unique garb of a White Dancer, when the time came, and ride in the lead. She had it packed across her saddle.

As the martial chanting continued, she saw Changavar confer with old Severakh, who leaned down to exchange whispers with him. Apparently they were going to share the same bambarong, in a way unifying command. And there was Branwe. His eyes were on her, as she knew they would be until she was safely inside the walls of Ar. She felt a stirring of tenderness toward him, and for the first time in her young life had second thoughts about the restrictions of the White Dancers.

With no dissident voice to interfere, the sacred battle formulary—the chanting of little green-robed maidens, the ranks of armed warriors, the hundreds of imposing bambarongs, crimson dawn reaching across the isolated mountain valley—was inspiring and beautiful. It concluded with a welter of activity.

Srana descended the temple stairs, as Yozgat warriors, with a few score of her own people, raced for their bambarongs. Branwe met her at the foot of the stairs, and escorted her to where a group of dwarfish she-mrem awaited with her battle costume, an enlarged version of their own. They raised a screen of fur cloaks, the trophies of honor flayed from bygone enemies, while she changed.

Branwe thought she looked even more charming in the quaint battle costume than wearing the copper-green robes of a goddess. The scepter crafted to mount the Khavala stone made her seem regal, and the fierce little Yozgat females around her instinctively treated her with deference.

She and Branwe gazed into each other's eyes. Each understood the dangers before them, the fatefulness of defeat; there was no need for speeches.

"May the All-Mother guide and protect you," was all they said.

Then they were mounted upon their respective bambarongs, ready to begin the long journey to Ar. So were all the Yozgat; their uncanny battle empathy seemed to extend even to preparations for war, and no parade could have been more precise and orderly than their mounting of the hundreds of bambarongs, three to a saddle. The only incident that was not their fault, and it was a comic incident, was one that lightened their mood and sent waves of laughter through the ranks.

The sumpter bambarongs were generally the sturdiest animals; the exception was the one assigned especially for Kizzlecosh. Only one other rider was to share its special saddle with her, but the dwarfish male was so disconcerted by her bulk—the very bambarong looked rebellious—that he was not sure what to do next. There were grins at this, but not until they were actually mounted, Kizzlecosh behind the Yozgat, did outright laughter erupt. Their contrast in sizes was truly comical.

Kizzlecosh did not seem to notice, and stared straight before her. But Cajhet, mounted on a bambarong nearby, could see that her feelings were hurt. Woe unto the ears of the little warrior mounted in front of her, should he make a single unlucky remark.

The remarks came from others, safely out of range of her sharp powerful teeth, when it was noticed that her bambarong—as huge and vigorous as it was, with but two riders—neither leapt as high into the air nor glided as far between runs as any of the others.

Twirling their swords and fur cloaks as they rode into the dawn, the Yozgat chanted their ancient war song, and the morning air quavered with the rising and falling of their voices, as the bambarongs they rode ran and leapt and glided down the valley, westward toward Ar.

▲

Chapter 20
The Last Battle Begins

▲————————————————————————————▲

The dark ceremony being enacted upon the midnight plains, miles beyond catapult range from the walls of Ar, was neither inspiring nor beautiful. It was terrible to behold; its purpose was to terrorize.

There were no gods or goddesses worshipped here, no eidolon or chanting priestesses; only Khal, hideous and evil, his three ruby eyes glittering with malice in the trembling firelight. Tomorrow the great city of Ar would finally be his—though his reveries tonight were less about the deployments of the last battle than the vengeance which would follow.

He would have vengeance not only against the conquered inhabitants of the city, but cunningly against their conquerors as well; eventually against the Eastern Lords themselves. Their contingents of liskash, with the enslaved mrem they deployed in battle as screens and shock troops, had just encamped down river. Only now had they joined the besieging armies in force, thinking that tomorrow would indeed see the last battle, and hungering for the spoils. Their warlords possibly—nay, almost certainly—had secret instructions for making sure of him, once The Three were no longer an obstacle, and the mighty walls of Ar finally breached. They would soon learn the folly of their treachery; they and the Eastern Lords, who foolishly presumed that conquest of the mrem meant their own supremacy.

Eggs were now hatching daily at Cragsclaw, and the hatchlings being prepared to reassume their lost heritage. Every step had been meticulously worked out to the last detail, as he lay brooding in darkness, year upon year, in his vault of

enchantment beneath the Kazerclaw. Power and vengeance.
His reptilian mind had been cleansed of any other thoughts
but the means to achieve these, to revel in them, to trample
underfoot all his enemies. His very daydreams were about
the torments he would inflict upon The Three, now that they
were as good as in his hands.

Let these mrem barbarians sate themselves with rapine
and plunder; let these lesser breeds of liskash delight in their
own crudities of torment and beastliness. The seeds of dis-
cord had already been sown. Little more was needed to goad
the inevitable squabbles over booty and females, the rivalries
and distrust natural among so incongruous a host of bandits,
desert marauders, and renegade highlanders, into open conflict.

Mutual antipathy always lurked just beneath the surface of
any seeming concord among the races of liskash. His claws
fairly tingled to scratch that surface. Even at tonight's dark
ceremony the mrem warlords sat mistrustfully apart from
those of the liskash. Squabbles goaded, old feuds rekindled,
instinctive fears and hatreds inflamed, racial hostilities enraged;
then open war, a war to the death, internecine and without
quarter.

Yes, the eggs were hatching, the hatchlings maturing far
more swiftly than the offspring of these wretched mrem.
Soon the Old Race would again rule the planet. Soon would
power and vengeance be his.

The great barrage, spanning an entire valley, was a stupen-
dous feat of engineering. Not just the Mraal, but the conflu-
ent of another major river, which had its source in the same
watershed, had been impounded for weeks now in a vast
artificial lake. The riverbed bifurcating around Ar was cracked
and dusty, and the warlords had long clamored to renew the
assault, this time directly against the walls. But Khal was not
to be hurried with the unfolding of his master plan. A failure
with himself in personal command, and the Eastern Lords
might try to supplant him before he was ready to challenge
them for supremacy. There must be no mistakes this time.

The Three were still powerful—no doubt they would wreak
vast destruction upon the attacking hordes—but the effort
would soon exhaust them. By nightfall they would all be in
his hands. He had issued strict orders that no wizard of Ar
was to be killed.

Weeks? Months? Years perhaps? They would not die soon, nor easily. And in the end they would all die with him—or at least their stuffed effigies would, reposing in various postures around his banquet hall forevermore. So intense were these reveries that for long minutes he was oblivious of all else.

The lesser vengeance being ritually enacted before him, and before a picked assembly of battle priests and warlords, was of only passing interest. War captives, slackers, those who had failed in their assigned tasks; their torment and execution tonight would ensure the valor of the attackers tomorrow, but there were no kings or queens here, not a single great personage of the mrem. It was a mere object lesson to the beholders.

From a throne plundered from a king of the mrem, Khal seemed to look down upon the firelit arena, but his thoughts—alien, drifting in and out of reveries of vengeance, coldly reptilian—were elsewhere. The steps of his master plan must be taken in natural order, never forced, never hastened. So long had he brooded upon them that they were now a second instinct, and yet again and again, as he pondered their unfolding, something at the very outreaches of his mind made him uneasy.

He was alert to detect enemies trying to project their thoughts telepathically, or any wizard still so foolish as to attempt teleportation. But it was a feebler sort of magic that now disturbed him. Some new enchantment by The Three? No, still, feebler than that; more individual.

Focusing his powers through the Third Eye, he was surprised to discover that it was no more than concealment magic, a trick any shabby bush wizard could perform.

Had he become too skittish about magic practiced against him? Too leery of The Three? Rationally—if indeed his liskash mind was ever truly rational—he knew he was more powerful than them all. But so had he been years ago, when he first acquired the Third Eye, and still they had taken him unawares and entombed him in a vault of enchantment. He might have been there yet, had the Eastern Lords not decided that the time was ripe for invasion, that they needed his powers of magic.

No, he could never be too vigilant where The Three were

concerned, never too cautious. After all, their most powerful wizard had recently escaped him, in a manner still unexplained . . . . He gazed down at the cruel execution of a war captive, his mind tending to wander off again among reveries of torment and vengeance. But the uneasy feeling continued to disturb him.

Concealment magic? No mere bush wizard could have exerted so powerful an enchantment over the minds—With a hissing snarl of rage he leapt to his feet. All eyes were on him; executioner and victim alike, ghastly in the trembling firelight, turned toward him. His hideous liskash face writhed with fury, as it had when he first discovered that the most powerful wizard of The Three, Mithmid himself, had escaped his trap, denying him many more days, perhaps weeks, of delight. The couch he had had especially designed for Mithmid still stood empty in his banquet hall at Cragsclaw.

Battle priests and warlords parted deferentially before him as he stalked off in the direction of the old quarry at the edge of the forest. It had become a place of dread for the assembled armies, as he had intended it should. All knew that this dragon had a mighty appetite, a knowledge which had wonderfully improved efficiency throughout the camps.

▲

"I've lost everything," moaned the bargemrem.

"You still have your life." Mithmid hushed him. "But if you don't be quiet you'll lose that too, and our lives along with it. I told you you'd be compensated for your barge. Now shut up, or by the All-Mother I'll have the gates closed in your face."

There was not another word from either the bargemrem or his son. They had sensed that the old wizard was no businessmrem, and had both cunningly wheedled him for higher rates—and higher and higher and higher. But if they knew he was no businessmrem, they were also aware that he was a powerful wizard. In all the miles they had traveled upriver since their barge was stranded by the receding waters, not a single watchmrem, sentry, or patrol had looked in their direction, though twice patrols had passed within a few feet of them. It was magic, powerful magic.

"All right," whispered Mithmid, "down the riverbank. Watch out for pockets of mud and quicksand."

There were no arguments. Nizzam was still apprehensive about the judgment of The Three, when they learned of his conduct at both Kazerclawm and Cragsclaw. He knew he had a lot of explaining to do, and could hardly have been more servile to Khal himself.

The ramparts loomed above them in the dual moonlight, as they picked their way the length of the city, through cracked mud, dust, remnant pools of water, war wreckage, rotting fish, and the skeletons of sunken boats, toward the Southland Gate. This was one night that Nizzam would have welcomed an overcast sky, but there was not a cloud. Magic alone concealed them, a magic that in his new humility he had to admit surpassed any he himself would ever wield.

As he trudged miserably along, his nose wrinkling at the fishy stench, deathly afraid of stepping into a pool of quicksand, he wondered why everything had suddenly grown so dark. The night was cloudless, and yet he was now engulfed in shadow.

He looked up—and fell straight back into a pool he had carefully just stepped around, soaking himself through. The cold water revived him from his swoon, but it was not the coldness that now made him shiver or his teeth chatter. He had not realized that the great dragon could levitate so high; it hovered between him and the lesser moon, in the sky above, as high as the very ramparts of Ar. On its monstrous neck sat Khal himself, his ruby eyes boring down at him with a malice that paralyzed any thought of resistance.

Yet even in his terror he knew why Khal had not already blasted them all into smoke: He wanted them alive—in Mithmid's case so he could resume his interrupted torments, in his own so they could begin. There was nowhere to hide, no use in running. Mithmid himself seemed to realize this, and stood stock-still, gazing fixedly up at the dragon and its rider. Then he raised his left hand, whether in challenge or a plead for mercy, Nizzam did not know. He knew only that either gesture would avail him nothing with Khal.

The reptilian sorcerer made no move, issued no command. He seemed intent merely on prolonging his delight in the helplessness of his victims, in their dismay at the torments awaiting them. He himself was invincible, and he only grinned sardonically at Mithmid's gesture. Too late he realized that in his triumph he had protected himself only.

With a hissing scream of anger the dragon dropped straight to the ground, flames shooting from beneath its colossal tail, its long neck snaking back and forth as if seeking its attacker, its terrible jaws snapping savagely at the air. For several minutes Khal could do nothing but cling to the saddle, in danger of being bucked from the monster's writhing back and smashed to a pulp by its lashing tail. The screams of pain and anger echoed against the city walls with redoubled fury.

Concentrating his power through the Third Eye, he at last brought the dragon under control and healed its singed flesh. Then it was aroused anew by a catapult dart, shot down from the ramparts across the riverbed. Once more he had to soothe and protect it, screening them both from the rain of darts and missiles now being fired with deadly accuracy down from the walls.

He was invincible! He was Khal the Great! His outrage momentarily unhinged his mind. Vengeance against all who dared oppose him! Vengeance against Ar! Remultiplying the natural levitation magic of the dragon, he would raise it up onto the very ramparts of the city. Then would the city reel beneath his vengeance! Mithmid and the wretched Nizzam had used his discomfiture to slip inside the gate. They would not escape him long! None would escape him! Kings and queens had fled here from all over the land, the great personages of the mrem, like ripe fruits ready for plucking. Now would he glean his harvest! Now would vengeance be his! What need had he of armies, of the Eastern Lords themselves? He was Khal the Invincible!

"Up, my pet!" he urged the dragon, now calmed, its wounds healed and soothed. "Up, up on the ramparts, whence these barbarians seek to torment you. Up!"

Magically screened from the catapult barrage, the dragon began to levitate, at first without resistance, higher and higher, its natural power multiplied by its strange rider. It had been kept hungry so it would not be sluggish during the battle tomorrow, and now saw hundreds of mrem defenders—succulent and juicy—furiously working their catapults. Fire-spears were added to the barrage, but were deflected as magically as all the other missiles. Higher and higher rose the dragon.

Then its dull mind sensed resistance, not only to its own primitive magic, but to the force remultiplying it. On the highest rampart, directly over the Southland Gate, stood scores of old mrem, motionless amid the furious bustle all around them. There, it sensed, was the focus of resistance. That was where it should attack, and its terrible jaws opened with an angry hiss. But the resistance stiffened, and it levitated no higher, nor was it able to move across the riverbed below toward the walls.

Had its wits been keener, it would have sensed the tremendous struggle now being waged in silence between Khal and The Three, hurriedly assembled on the ramparts by Mithmid. The barrage of darts, fire-spears, and missiles continued to arc through the moonlight; thousands of defenders had now gathered on the walls. More and more of Khal's force had to be diverted to screening himself and his mount from injury. Nor did his inflexible reptilian mind function effectively on more than one object at a time. Nonetheless he persisted; such was his fury, his insane lust for vengeance.

Half the city was now roused against him. Volcanic streams of lanterns and torches flowed toward the walls below; the catapult barrage intensified in violence and accuracy. In the instinctual recesses of his mind Khal had until this moment still been leery of The Three. But he now realized exultantly that the force resisting him was already beginning to tire, like an old one who has exerted himself beyond his strength. Even at its strongest this force had barely neutralized a fraction of his own divided powers.

Tomorrow, when he would again be able to concentrate all his overwhelming might against them, he would reduce this assemblage of foolish old mrem to groveling helplessness. That would free him to realize more perfectly than he had expected all the sinister workings of his master plan; to ensure that besiegers and besieged alike suffered the most terrible possible casualties, while the great city of Ar at last fell into his hands.

An exultant cheer rang through the night as he and the dragon retreated from the riverbank. With his back turned to them, the thousands cheering upon the moonlit ramparts above were unaware that his own face gloated with a dark exultation. Nevermore would the mrem laugh or cheer or congratulate each other on their deliverance in Ar, after he returned there tomorrow.

▲

Mithmid did not have to see the sorcerer's hideous gloating to realize how desperate the situation had become. All the united powers of The Three, allied with all the armed forces of the League of Ar, had been needed to repel the last major assault upon the city, months ago. And it had been a near thing, even after an heroic foray had destroyed the barrage impounding the waters of the Mraal.

This new blockage was far beyond their reach. There were more enemies now, many more towers and machines, which for weeks now—while he himself was slogging his way upriver, after his barge had been stranded—could have been trundled right up to the city walls. It seemed that the assault had been delayed until the Evil One himself took command, when all preparations were complete, and victory a dead certainty. All the combined powers of The Three would have to be diverted from the battle itself just to neutralize him—if they could even do that.

"We need a miracle." Mithmid lowered his voice so Sruss alone could hear him. They sat on a bench together in her garden the following morning. What had changed most in the city since his departure was its morale. The White Dancers went through the motions of their daily exercises without their usual verve and dedication—with Sruss herself looking on! "You haven't heard anything more from Srana? No, neither have I. But I never expected the people to become so demoralized."

"Blame Rhenowla for that," said Sruss. "She has used the intervening months to renew her hold on young Tristwyn. Not directly, but through the Crockercups, who work insidiously to renew their own power and luxury by leading him back to his old dissipations. They know I'm their enemy. They also know that the worst thing which could befall them is the reign of a strong and just king."

"But why would the king close the Temple of the All-Mother, especially at a time like this?"

"He hasn't. Nor is it ever done officially. The Crockercups —no doubt at the behest of Rhenowla—merely interrupt every ceremony, barring the Dancers from even entering the temple."

"Can't someone help you?" asked Mithmid. "The king? The League of Ar?"

Sruss shook her head. "I dare not ask. The Silent Ones are more insidious than ever, spreading rumors, misleading the people with false accusations. Rhenowla is behind it all, of course. She seeks only a provocation, something she can use to discredit the Dancers." She lowered her voice. "I fear for their very lives."

Mithmid looked at her aghast, as if he could not believe what he had just heard.

"It's true," she assured him. "Recall her campaign to discredit The Three. It failed because even the most ignorant and superstitious realized that you are needed for the defense of the city. Not so with the White Dancers. For weeks now the Silent Ones have been spreading rumors that they care nothing for the safety of Ar, hinting darkly that they may be working in collusion with the enemy, or have already sold the gates. You have heard of the god Narlock?"

Mithmid's jaw dropped. "The ancient war god? But no temple of Narlock has existed for centuries, only old superstitions. His cruel rites were suppressed when Ar was hardly more than a market village."

"But never forgotten," Sruss added. "Rhenowla has uncovered an engraved oracle, and the H'satie are showing it everywhere. In time of utmost need, when Ar seems doomed, the city can be saved only by sacrificing the Chosen."

"The White Dancers?"

She nodded. "That is exactly the interpretation Rhenowla is spreading among the people. Few believed it at first, but now more and more seem to every day. Especially since the Dancers have not participated in a single ceremony for weeks now. The people do not know the reason, only the fact."

"You don't have to tell me any more." He sighed. "Narlock was the first god worshipped in Ar. The city is being punished for turning to foreign gods and ways. And so on and so forth. It's really you that Rhenowla is trying to punish—if she has to destroy the city to do so, and herself along with it.

Something that now seems inevitable, no matter what she does. Unless," a new thought struck him. "she's in collusion with the Eastern Lords herself. They might make her absolute ruler here, in return for services rendered. Is that what's behind her attacks on you?"

"For power, Rhenowla would do anything. Nor do I doubt she would ally herself with the very Eastern Lords to get it, if that were the only way. But I have no evidence of this."

They were silent and thoughtful for the next several minutes, each with his or her own peculiar cares. Sruss watched the dispirited exercises of the White Dancers with a heavy heart. Mithmid kept one ear cocked for the call to the ramparts, to the last doomed stand of the enemy. The great towers and siege engines were at this very moment trundling across the plains beyond the dry riverbed, converging at last upon the city, evidence that the Evil One was now utterly certain of victory.

"If Ar falls," he said, although both understood that there was no longer any "if" about it, "we must at all costs save the Dancers. Only through their moral authority, through their preservation of the culture and history of our nation, can the mrem remain united, or even hope to survive. The magic of The Three may not be powerful enough to save Ar, but the enemy will know they were in a fight. Our defensive strategy now must be aimed at opening some means for the Dancers to escape. Perhaps in the confusion of battle, concealment magic may get them away unseen. Perhaps King Ortakh can once more rally his berserkers, and cut an opening through the enemy hordes, who may in any case be greedier for plunder than captives."

"And Rhenowla?" Sruss turned to him. "Don't forget that the Dancers' most virulent enemy is inside the city, not outside. While we seek opportunities, so will she. The people themselves, in their fear and anguish, will also seek someone to blame for their miseries. The traditional sanctity of the White Dancers may actually be turned against them, when all traditions fail, when the very priests of the city, perhaps young Tristwyn himself, demand that the ancient oracle be fulfilled, and the Chosen sacrificed to Narlock."

"She won't get away with it," cried Mithmid. "We won't let her. A public worship of the All-Mother, the more public the better; spread the word through the city. Let the Crockercups again try to bar the White Dancers from the temple, and the people will then know who's really abetting the enemy. So public a confrontation must surely disconcert the whispering campaign of the Silent Ones, perhaps long enough for us to get the Dancers safely out of the city. Can you spread the word in time?"

"No, but I know someone who can." They paused and listened; the White Dancers froze in the middle of a figure. "There's the trumpet. The attack has begun. You'll be on the south rampart? I'll send word to you the moment I've arranged the ceremony. The All-Mother guide and protect you."

He repeated the blessing, and hurried from the garden.

"Any news of the lad yet, my lady?" was the first question Mamre asked upon entering the garden soon afterwards. "Ah, poor, poor lad. I've kept a room special for him, just like in Kazerclawm. My husband says he needs the space for better things—you see, we're more crowded here than at the old Blue Dragon—but I tell him there's no better use for it than to give a home to my dear Branwe. He always was a good lad, my lady, and a hard worker. Ah, me. Such times as we live in . . ."

She began a rambling account of how she was packed up to flee to yet another city, and how much trouble she had had selecting what to take and what to leave behind, and how her husband had abused her over a prized mirror she insisted on taking along. But Sruss tactfully interrupted, and explained the problem.

Mamre's eyes narrowed. "You leave it to me, my lady, Why, the liskash! Desecrating a holy temple with their tricks! There's some that drinks regular at the Dragon, highlanders and soldiers even, that would make the fur of these Crockercups stand on end, just to see 'em. Oh, yes, my lady, I'll spread the word for you all right. You can depend on me."

She was as good as she said, and by midmorning it was known in every quarter of the city that the White Dancers would lead high worship at the Temple of the All-Mother. It was known even sooner to Rhenowla.

"My son is on the ramparts, where a true king belongs." She did not hover behind a curtain now, but sat brazenly on the very throne, as if she believed that that was where she belonged. "His friends must act for him. Can I depend on you, my loyal subjects?"

Never in all the long history of Ar had so many dissipated, fawning, cowardly, self-serving rascals been gathered together in one place. The Crockercups exploited the king's bounty, and cunningly encouraged his dissipations, but it was from the queen mother that they took their orders. She was their last best hope of saving their lives and their riches. The city itself was now clearly doomed; it might last the day, but certainly not another. It was more profitable to answer the summons of Rhenowla than the call to the ramparts.

"Arrangements have been made for emigrating to Hurakh Tam," she said, and the Crockercups nodded their satisfaction. They all knew of the secret amassing of royal treasure for transshipment, of course, but were gratified at her confiding in them. "But I cannot leave the city with scores unsettled. I wish to travel only with friends, and the next few hours will determine who are my true friends, and who are not."

Scores of heads nodded their understanding. Every Crockercup in the throne room had at one time or another done Rhenowla's dirty work for her. This was the dirtiest job of all, but she had made clear the alternatives. Obsequiously they bowed their way from her presence.

The instant the last of them had disappeared, she clapped her hands, and a trio of rogues that made even the Crockercups seem wholesome appeared through the curtain behind which she herself was wont to eavesdrop. Retaliation upon the White Dancers was only an indirect means of punishing her most implacable enemy, an enemy too powerful and beloved to assail—until now. But anything might happen amidst the turmoil of a conquered city, and she beckoned the three rogues to draw closer, and exchanged whispers and purses with them.

▲

Like an army of giants the towers advanced upon the southern walls. Harrassed relentlessly by fire-spears and missiles, they were slowed, but not stopped. Every few minutes the closest or most threatening tower exploded into ashes and splinters; but these intervals grew longer and longer, the towers closer and more threatening, the vitality of The Three ever less potent. At either end of the wall, colossal booms now swung back and forth, plucking defenders from the ramparts and dropping them to their destruction in the dry riverbed below.

Another tower shattered, then another, but ten more were drawn forward by teams of uxen to replace them. And in the distance, a monstrous dragon could be seen moving ominously through the enemy hordes, which swarmed the plains without number, rapacious and greedy for plunder. On its back sat the Evil One himself, gloating sardonically at the internecine course of the battle. Soon The Three would exhaust themselves, expending their last reserves in a futile effort to save a doomed city. Then he could pluck them up as deftly as the colossal booms plucked other helpless defenders from atop the walls.

The besieged had not wasted the intervening months; they too had constructed machines. Until the Mraal ceased to flow, some weeks past, they had been able to boat a wealth of supplies and matériel into the city, and the kings of the League of Ar had drilled soldiers and civilians alike into a keen readiness. Ar had not been built in a day; it would not fall in a day. Although Mithmid could see already that it would not last much longer than that.

The bulk of the siege machines were concentrated atop the northern wall, and opposing towers had been erected inside the walls to increase firepower. Rocks and quicksands precluded assaults from east or west by anything but small commando teams, and these were easily repulsed. Since the major attack came from the south, it was there that Mithmid had again concentrated The Three. But he had not expected such suicidal fury in the attackers. It was as if every one of them felt himself to be personally under the eyes of the Evil One.

Then Mithmid realized that those eyes were in fact turned away from the battle, toward a hilltop miles to the east. His own eyes were no longer keen enough to discern what was gathered there. Multiple riders seemed to be mounted atop a veritable herd of weird two-legged creatures. Through his long years of questing after the Third Eye, he had heard

many strange legends. He had an inkling of what he was
seeing, but needed younger eyes to be sure.

King Ortakh of Maragadan answered his summons. "Yes, I
see them clearly," he said, "but can hardly believe my eyes.
The Yozgat never leave their mountain valley, except to
punish those who would infringe their independence."

"Are they for us, or against us?" wondered Mithmid, still
naive in military matters.

"The Yozgat have no allies, nor have ever needed them.
Look, the Evil One himself gives you your answer. He hesi-
tates. He has seen seen something that makes him unsure of
himself. The very dragon he rides seems confused."

Mithmid squinted, trying vainly to see better. "All I can
make out is a figure in white, mounted on one of the strange
creatures, holding forth some object for all to see. Who is it,
do you suppose, and what is the object?"

Even Ortakh's keen eyes had to squint at such a distance.
"The object appears to be a scepter, held forth by none other
than a White Dancer. Yes, it must be the scepter that has
made Khal so unsure."

"Now I understand," cried Mithmid, fairly dancing with
excitement. "I know what the scepter is, and who is holding
it. They are indeed allies."

"Then they need our help. Here, Ingol, Finakh." Ortakh
summoned his captains, "Prepare for a sally! Summon the
highlanders! All is not yet lost!"

▲

Changavar gazed across the swarming plain to the walls of
Ar, and was chagrined. The neighboring peoples of the Yozgat
had to be chastised from time to time, and no walled village
or even city-state had during his lifetime ever held out against
the bambarongs. But these walls were colossal, as sheer as
cliffs, towering—insurmountable. The bambarongs would enter the city through its gates, or not at all.

Nor had he ever beheld such vast hordes of enemies. It
was some consolation that he had been right in at least that
respect, and saw that those around him on the swelling
hilltop realized it as well. Not even Yozgat valor and battle
empathy could hope to prevail against such odds.

Only minutes ago he had noticed a score of Yozgat she-mrem dismount and hold up their fur cloaks as a screen. Srana had emerged from inside the circle dressed in the costume of a White Dancer. She had remounted her bambarong alone, where she now sat gazing down upon the swarming plains below.

This gesture had further chagrined him. She would not have brought the costume if she had trusted his assurances. But then he felt a tap on the shoulder, and Severakh, mounted behind him on his bambarong, pointed down to those very plains. He had noticed the dragon and its rider, of course, but now understood that this was the Evil One. Had Srana's costume then only something to do with magic? It was more comforting to believe that.

Changavar felt another tap on the shoulder. This time Severakh pointed toward the city gate. The enemy forces were being driven back by a furious sortie of highlanders; although taken by surprise, such overwhelming numbers would soon rally. Changavar was now in his own element. The military situation was crystal clear, and he signaled the charge.

Running, leaping, gliding over the heads of the astonished enemy, the hundreds of bambarongs raced at incredible speed over the plains. A cheer rose from the beleaguered walls above; the Yozgat twirled their swords and fur cloaks in defiance, as they plunged triumphantly through the gate.

Branwe alone would have turned back, but he sat between two Yozgat warriors and had no control of their bambarong. He glanced behind him from the bridge. Srana had never moved. She still sat alone upon her bambarong, scepter in hand, at the crest of the hill, while down in the plains below the dragon and its rider stood facing her. Branwe had seen many duels in the garrison city of Kazerclawm, and this was how they always began, with the two opponents sizing each other up, each trying to gauge their respective strengths and weaknesses, searching for some advantage before beginning the actual combat.

Then they were lost from sight, as Branwe was carried through the open portal and into the great city of Ar.

▲

Chapter 21
The Wall of Death

▲ ─── ▲

Whatever the outcome of the duel, Mithmid knew that for a time the Evil One would be neutralized. Enough time? The weird running, leaping, gliding creatures could only be the bambarongs he had heard of in travelers' tales, and for once the tale did not exceed the reality. Even without evil magic to aid them, the hordes besieging Ar must soon overrun the walls. How soon? The great barrage damming back the Mraal was too many miles upstream to have been reached by any possible sortie against it—until now.

He reached the bottom of the stairs just as the city gates closed. Ortakh, as befitting a highland king, was the last mrem inside. And there was Severakh! Mithmid hurried toward him, disconcerted at first by the dwarfish size of the warriors climbing down from their strange mounts. He also noticed Sruss, standing beside a blowsy old she-mrem who was tearfully hugging young Branwe. But there was no time for that now, and he immediately summoned the rest of The Three, many of whom already looked weary and dispirited, down from the walls.

"More magic!" snorted Changavar, when Mithmid had explained his plan. "The Yozgat are warriors, not liskash. I didn't lead my people here to be jockeys for a lot of scoundrelly old wizards."

"No, no," Mithmid assured him, overlooking the insult, "we need you in battle. Desperately, and at once. Only you can relieve the pressure on the walls long enough for us to reach the dam in time. Sorties and more sorties. You're our only hope now, Changavar."

The dwarfish warrior continued to snort and stomp up and back before the gate, but was clearly mollified.

"I'll take only fifty or so of your, uh, bambarongs I believe they're called," Mithmid continued. "With a wizard riding on each one—"

"Two on each," decided Changavar, "and if they fall off we can't stop for 'em. She-mrem are best at this kind of thing. They'll jockey you there as fast as you want. Meanwhile, there's fighting to do."

"That's what we came for," added Severakh, and the two old soldiers strode off and started issuing commands for battle.

Mithmid sighed at the obtuseness of the military mind, but had to be satisfied with whatever logistics it determined. There was no time to contest anything. While Changavar told the she-mrem who would guide and defend the sortie, he himself selected fifty wizards to accompany it, a selection that necessarily had to be a compromise. The youngest would be the surest riders, but they lacked the mindpower of the eldest. All had accompanied him in the sortie against Dragonneck Gorge, and knew what had to be done. He felt like a schoolmaster lecturing children as he explained the enterprise to the Yozgat she-mrem:

"It's only a small river gate, so you'll have to get your, uh, bambarongs to duck down. They're too tall to get through it otherwise. There are patches of quicksand on the riverbed, but scouts will point them out to you. Questions?"

The little she-mrem merely sneered at him. They too were warriors and blamed him for depriving them of the chance to gain trophies of honor. But obedience to the Prince Warrior in battle was the most sacred of all Yozgat traditions, and they led their bambarongs toward the west river gate, with a pair of wizards clinging gingerly to the back of each, including Mithmid himself.

He had been tempted to suggest means of alleviating pressure on the walls while they were gone, but decided he had been sneered at enough for one day. Glancing back, he expected to see the warrior kings conferring on battle plans, but was curious to see old Severakh in conference with Sruss, while young Branwe stood by with the tearful old she-mrem. Another sortie was supposed to cover the outburst from the west river gate. He wondered what they could be discussing so earnestly. Severakh looked as disgruntled as had the little Yozgat prince a few minutes ago.

"A warrior's first duty in battle is obedience to orders, my lady," he was explaining in a controlled voice. Once more in his proper element, the old soldier, like Changavar, wanted to assert his authority. The interference of she-mrem—though it be the legendary Sruss herself—annoyed him. "Branwe has indeed shown valor and initiative. I won't deny that. But either he's a warrior or he's not. This is no time for individual exploits. He's as fine a young swordsmrem as I've ever drilled—"

"Yes, but what sword does he wield?" asked Sruss. "And what will become of all your sorties and strategy if the Evil One gains control of what you journeyed so far to get? Srana is a mere she-kit, not a wizard. And she's now pitted alone against the most cunning and evil sorcerer in the world."

"Very well, my lady." Severakh yielded at last. "You may be right after all. But he'll be on his own. Little Changavar is already gnashing his teeth with impatience. I can't delay his first sortie much longer." He bowed and started to turn away, then hesitated. "Good luck, lad. Be sure to watch for the red flag. May the All-Mother guide and protect you."

"Amen to that," said Mamre, although she knew nothing about red flags. "I just got my dear boy back, and now I must lose him again."

She wanted maternally to groom him, but Branwe released himself, bowed courteously to Sruss, and hurried toward the big sumpter bambarong he had unloaded for his own use. The Yozgat warriors, all riding triple and eager for battle, had no interest in a lone rider at the tail of their column.

Severakh gave the signal, and a deadly rain of fire-spears and catapult missiles swept the riverbank opposite the Southland Gate. The drawbridge was lowered with a wild clangor of chains, the grinding and creaking gates were heaved open, and hundreds of bambarongs charged out into the dust-hazy sunlight. This was battle. There was no random leaping and gliding now. The huge creatures leapt from the same point, glided over the heads of the swarming hordes of attackers, right through the advancing giant-army towers and siege machines, and landed in a concentrated mass, a hundred yards behind the enemy vanguard.

Swarming down from their mounts, swarming over one foe after the other, charging, retreating, and swarming again with their uncanny battle empathy, the Yozgat males hacked and slashed and thrust with their great swords; the Yozgat females clawed from all sides at once, faded back, then swarmed over the next surprised enemy. No signals were given; none were needed. The ring of slaughtered enemies widened outward from the mass of waiting bambarongs like a pond ripple.

But the odds were overwhelming, and at last flying columns rallied against the Yozgat—only to find themselves converging on an empty space littered with corpses. Every Yozgat seemed to know at once the instant the battle turned against them, and if motivated by a single reflex, they all remounted, ran, leapt, glided, and repeated their swarming attack upon another quarter of the battlefield.

Nothing intimidated the doughty little warriors, not even the terrible contingents of liskash, so hideous in their reptilian sliminess that it was like attacking a nightmare. But attack the Yozgat did, plunging right down into the midst of the most hideous contingent of all. These liskash towered over eight feet high; gangling bipedal reptiles with huge round eyes and sloping foreheads, they wielded their monstrous battle-axes with a power and ferocity incredible to behold. No single opponent could have withstood one; but the Yozgat fought in swarms, and a score of cuts, hacks, stabs, and deadly slashes forestalled every swipe of a battle-axe, a swipe that futilely cut through empty air. Then once more the Yozgat were gone, leaving behind them a disconcerting carnage.

All the hordes besieging the southern wall—despite their massed array of booms, towers, and siege engines—were now disconcerted, their confusion more demoralizing than the relatively few casualties warranted. Leadership also bogged down, and while the attacks on the walls faltered, the catapult barrage raining down on the attackers continued to take a deadly toll. The numbers were too overwhelming for this condition to last, but every minute that it did brought the sortie upriver that much closer to the new dam. Mithmid and his fellow wizards were already out of sight.

Meanwhile Branwe sought an opening for a sortie of his own. Simply gliding off by himself would have left his mount too vulnerable whenever it landed; it was the mass landings of the whole troop of hundreds that threw the enemy into panic.

His chance did not come until, by some empathy or signal he did not catch, the Yozgat suddenly outflanked the enemy hordes and wheeled toward the dry riverbed. Pressure had grown intense upon the northern wall. Something had to be done to relieve it before it was overrun.

Branwe also wheeled around, but in a contrary direction. He had caught only glimpses of Srana across the dust-hazy plain. She had not moved from the hilltop, but the dragon, whether feinting or because its evil rider sensed that he wielded the sovereign magic, had moved closer. Wielding only the Demon Sword, Branwe dared not approach too near himself, and running, leaping, and gliding he circled the stumps of a despoiled orchard, and halted in the ruins of an old farmstead.

A liskash sorcerer, the very embodiment of all that was hideous and evil, and a beautiful young she-mrem, a White Dancer: the duel was epical. And all Branwe could do for the moment was clutch the Demon Sword and watch for an opportunity.

▲

Other eyes were even now watching for other opportunities. Sruss felt that something was wrong the moment she entered her garden with Mamre, who still dabbed at her eyes with a handkerchief. The entire troupe of White Dancers was dressed and ready for the supplication at the Temple of the All-Mother. Even if the Crockercups barred their entrance again, which was almost certain, the people would be less inclined to heed the insinuations of the Silent Ones. But where were the guards assigned by the king? Her own watchmrem were missing.

"Removed by orders of the queen mother, my lady," reported her factotum, the faithful Pepik. "The runner I sent to inform you never did?"

She shook her head.

"Then something stopped him in the streets. There's dirty work afoot, my lady. Mark my words. Naming no names, somebody's up to something."

Sruss had heard a rumor that her daughter-in-law was preparing for flight, probably with all the palace treasure her servants could bear. It was unlikely, however, that Rhenowla would go anywhere without retribution, and there would be no better opportunity than when the entire city was in turmoil. Mercenary priests had already reconsecrated their temples to Narlock. It was important to forestall any public outcry for the sacrifice of the Chosen. But could Rhenowla have the temerity to attempt a more direct retribution, also disguised by the turmoil in the city? Guards were needed, many guards, and at once.

"They won't stop me in the streets, my lady," Mamre shrewdly guessed the problem. "I'd like to see 'em try. Anyways, they'd think I was just going home to the Dragon, which is two streets north, a jog to your left around the fountain, turn left again till you reach Hammersmith Lane, then right. I've gathered some stout lads there for you. Not too nice in their ways, mind you, but all ready to earn themselves a night's free drinking—no matter what my husband says about it." Her eyes narrowed. "He's up to something himself, though he pretended it was just some business about saving our furniture in case we have to flee again. But he didn't fool me, because this isn't the first time lately he's wanted me out of the way, the unnatural wretch! His own wife, too! But that's no worry of yours, my lady. The lads I've gathered for you will guard your Dancers, though they may not be too nice about how they do it, and they'll guard you too if need be. Shall I go fetch them?"

Sruss had no choice but to agree, and sent Mamre off with her blessing. She would only have discredited the White Dancers further by having soldiers withdrawn from the defense of the city to protect them, something Rhenowla no doubt knew very well. If the highest moral authority in the land could be saved only by the lowest ruffians, from the most infamous quarter of the Old City, then so be it.

And Srana? What hope had she against so powerful a sorcerer? Sruss dared not watch the duel out on the plains. Though one White Dancer perish, even the most beloved of all, the order itself must somehow be preserved. Nothing was more important than that: not herself, not Srana, not the very city of Ar. And yet, she could not resist thinking about the message of love and honor her beloved Srana had sent her through young Branwe; as comely a lad as she had ever seen, whose own feelings toward Srana spoke through his every word and expression. The All-Mother guide and protect them . . . .

Hardly an hour had passed when her meditations were interrupted by a commotion at the gate. Pepik was not supposed to open it for anyone but Mamre, and the White Dancers fell back toward their tents in alarm, Sruss herself stared in astonishment.

Mamre was there all right, and behind her a troop of ruffians armed with clubs, chair legs, daggers, whatever weapons had been handy. But in their lead was a great strapping female, dragging, bouncing, and shaking a trio of surly rogues along before her. She held one by the ear with her sharp powerful teeth, and the other two by the scruff of the neck. There were grins and ribald comments from the ruffians following her.

"Her name is Kizzlecosh." Mamre trotted over to Sruss. "A lad as used to drink regular at the Dragon—the old Blue Dragon, that is, back in Kazerclawm days—sent her to me for protection. Against what, I can't imagine. But she says she's kept order in rough houses before, and I believe it. She came with my lad Branwe and the rest, on them big funny-looking critters. Pounced on them three villains there the moment she laid eyes on 'em."

"Bring her to me, please," said Sruss.

Relinquishing her prisoners, after thoroughly intimidating them with threats, glowers, and an admonitory snapping of teeth, Kizzlecosh hurried across the garden. Her bow was clumsy and uncouth, but even she was deferential in the presence of the legendary Sruss.

"One look was all I needed, my lady. Spotted 'em skulking down the street, and knew they were up to no good. And they've all got a parcel too much money on 'em. Mamre here told me you expect trouble today, and I expect that trio is part of it."

"Have they said anything?"

"No, but I'll get everything they know out of 'em, if that's what you want." She bit the air with her sharp powerful teeth.

"We've no time now for interrogation," said Sruss, who recognized at once a staunch ally in Kizzlecosh, despite her uncouth bulk, and quickly summarized the threat posed by the Crockercups to the White Dancers.

"Just point 'em out to me, my lady." Kizzlecosh drew her familiar cosh out of her belt and strapped it to her wrist. "I'll crocker their cups for 'em! And here's some rough lads who'll back me up. Give me the word, my lady, and it's as good as done."

And it was. The ranting of mercenary priests over a revival of Narlock petered out soon after word spread through the city about the magnificent supplication inside the Temple of the All-Mother, and the inspiring dances performed there by the White Dancers. Or perhaps the priests were more impressed with events that occurred beforehand outside the temple.

The general population was certainly impressed, for these events were the true origin of the adage: "As scarce as ears on a Crockercup."

▲

All that impressed Mithmid and the wizards of The Three at that moment was the task before them: to bring down in minutes something that had needed months to erect, by tens of thousands of laborers, working relentlessly day and night. The valley at its narrowest point was miles across; the colossal dam reached from wall to wall, impounding two major rivers into a vast artificial lake many leagues in extent.

"That's what will do our work for us," said Mithmid. The troop looked down from a weathered eminence, some two miles down the valley. "It won't be an easy job, nor as quick as we'd like, but it can be done. Looks like most of the guards have deserted their posts. They've probably slipped away to Ar, in hopes of getting their share of the booty. That should make the job a bit easier for us."

The little Yozgat she-mrem seated in front of him glanced back with her most contemptuous sneer yet—whether because she knew who would do the real fighting, or was merely commenting on the martial prowess of wizards, was not clear. What was clear was the distance they still had to travel to reach the spur that tied down the northern wing of the barrage. Only there could they get near enough to concentrate their mindforce effectively, but it was also the best-guarded approach.

It was early afternoon, and cloud shadows drifted down the valley toward them. A haze of dust and smoke marked the location of Ar, although the city itself now lay hidden behind intervening ridges, silver-gray with vegetation.

"Let's get going," cried Mithmid, trying to sound authoritative.

He was ignored, and started to shout the order again, but then noticed that the Yozgat she-mrem, those guiding the convoy of wizards and those riding triple as escorts, were strapping sets of razor-sharp steel claws onto their wrists. Only when they were good and ready did they at last deign to obey him.

Running, leaping, gliding, down the wooded slope, across a corner of the grassy valley below, then up the steeper slopes beyond. The wizards clung grimly to their saddles; no one would stop for them if they tumbled off, certainly not the fierce little Yozgat females, who rejoiced that they had not been excluded from battle after all, and would let nothing delay them.

There were more defenders than Mithmid had realized, perhaps one of the reasons the Yozgat warrior guiding their bambarong out onto the mountain spur had sneered at him. He prudently decided to leave all military decisions to her, and concentrate on magic. His fellow wizards seemed to feel the same way, although at the moment they concentrated exclusively on clinging to their saddles.

Even this did not avail them when the whole troop of bambarongs came to a flying halt, and a welter of startled wizards went tumbling, bouncing, rolling, and somersaulting to the ground. Shaken and disheveled, they found a path being cleared for them to the brink of the mountain spur, overlooking the dam and its vast impounded lake below, by the Yozgat she-mrem, who had reached the ground still faster.

Swarming, fading out of range, then swarming again with amazing battle empathy, their razor claws flashing electrically

in the sunlight, the Yozgat quickly overwhelmed the defenders. The attack had been spotted from the far side of the
valley, and hundreds of armed mrem could now be seen
descending from the blockhouse that defended the southern
approach to the barrage. But Mithmid had already assembled
his wizards into a unified formation. He pointed his left hand,
remultiplying their concentrated mindforce through the fragments of the Khavala, like some primordial god directing
thunderbolts down upon the enemies of heaven.

Several minutes passed. The reinforcements were already
halfway across the valley. At last a crack opened athwart the
entire summit of the barrage. It was neither very wide nor
very deep, but reached below water level, and the trickle
that pushed through began to eat away at the sides and
bottom. It widened slowly at first; then faster and faster.

Mithmid continued to point, and his invisible lightning
seared deeper and deeper into the blockage. The trickle
forcing its way through was now driven by the hydrostatic
pressure of many cubic miles of impounded water, and shot
into the valley in a silvery jet.

The advancing reinforcements spotted it, and faltered. Then
the jet widened into a veritable fountain, and they cried out
and fled whence they had come. But it was too late for them.
They had over a mile to run, and the waters now poured
through the crumbling barrage like a vast and unstoppable
tidal bore. The roar of the tremendous flood drowned their
screams of terror . . . .

▲

Srana knew she had lost the initiative; she also knew that
Khal, groping his way through the warps of concealment and
illusion she wove around him and his dragon, had recognized
her as the granddaughter of the Sentinel, his most implacable
enemy. His malice assailed her like a physical force, again
and again deflecting back on her the very magic she herself
had created.

All familiar references had dissolved. The sun stood in the
sky, and yet it seemed to be night, as if she was being drawn
against her will into some evil dimension. Hideous liskash
began to materialize all around her.

She sensed from their groping that they could not see her

yet, and she raised her scepter and redoubled the concealment magic deluding them. Not one of them looked in her
direction.

Neither did Khal himself, although he seemed to know
exactly where she was. His three ruby eyes glittered evilly in
the strange darkness. Turning her bambarong, she retreated
down the far side of the hill. She knew he would follow her
anywhere she went. He seemed to have forgotten all about
the battle raging around the walls of Ar, such was his passion
for vengeance.

The longer and farther she lured him away, the better. She
knew not whether Ar could long withstand the siege, only
that with his evil magic guiding and reinforcing the besieging
hordes, the defenders would be doomed.

Why had Khal begun summoning forth reptile-demons to
do his bidding? A sign that he could not defeat her alone? So
potent an exorcism must surely dissipate the magic he
remultiplied through the Third Eye. Nor could his monstrous
dragon, for all its powers of levitation, overtake so fleet and
agile a creature as her bambarong. Perhaps she had not
irretrievably lost the initiative after all.

She had been schooled by the Sentinel himself, the mightiest wizard of his time. She too wielded vast powers of magic,
powerful enough to keep liskash now closing in on all sides
from looking at her. Their movements seemed to be coordi-
nated, and she at last recognized them as groping patterns of
containment, which Khal was somehow directing. Toward
what end? She peered through the unnatural darkness.

The devastation would need a generation of peace to redeem. Should Ar fall, neither redemption nor peace would
ever come, and the land would remain a desert forever. She
had concealed herself in the single grove she found still
undespoiled by the enemy hordes. Its leafy branches circum-
scribed her vision, and it was some moments before she
spotted the canyon, which seemed to narrow toward the
southeast. Once herded inside, her bambarong would no
longer have room for its elusive running, leaping, and gliding.

She had pierced the wild and terrible illusions with which
Khal had first tried to ensnare her, all but the unnatural
darkness, which for all she knew was not an illusion at all, but
some sinister effect of the Third Eye. Now he seemed to be

attacking her indirectly, through her bambarong. Without it, she would be left helplessly on foot.

Nor was there anything she could do but leave the futile concealment of the hilltop orchard, and move in exactly the direction she least wanted to go. Even the mouth of the canyon dangerously constrained the elusiveness of her mount.

Each time she looked around there seemed to be more reptile-demons converging on her. Both Khal and his dragon had slipped from sight. Was this so he could safely divert more of his power to exorcising the evil host against her?

Their duel had been a stalemate until now: vast resources of magic the remultiplication of which was comparitively mean, against a mere novice, who by an odd chance of destiny was able to remultiply such magic as she had by the untold powers of an evil dimension.

Yet even a stalemate served the purpose of withdrawing Khal from the siege. But what if he now tipped the scales against her? Grimmer still, what if he took possession of her scepter? Could anything on the planet then withstand his dark ambitions? Certainly not the city of Ar.

If only she had been able to slip past him when she first arrived here, and give her scepter to Mithmid or some other great wizard of The Three. But Khal had seen her before she had seen him, and she had had no choice but to stand and fight with such powers as she had.

Fire-starting? More intense concealment? Somehow she had to break through the contracting ring of reptile-demons before it utterly enclosed her, and she peered still more intently into the strange darkness, searching for some opening screened from Khal by the steepening canyon walls. Once she broke free their duel could begin afresh, this time on a battlefield of her own choosing, out on the open plains, where the elusiveness of her bambarong would be decisive.

The one point definitely out of Khal's sight appeared at first glance to be the least promising. The reptile-demons were densest there, and more agitated than anywhere else, and she started to turn away. Then she realized that they were not agitated by fury; they were being attacked by a lone rider on a bambarong. A Yozgat warrior? Changavar himself? No, even through the eldritch gloom she could discern that the rider was much too big . . . .

It was Branwe! The Demon Sword flashed as he swung agilely from side to side in the saddle of the bambarong— which was in fact more of a trained warrior than he was— leaping and dodging counterattacks with a battle empathy that did credit to his masters. The reptile-demons fell back in dismay, leaving behind them a foul carnage.

Here was the opening Srana had been looking for, and a flick of the reins was all she needed to exploit it, for her bambarong too was a trained warrior. Sidling through the trees, leaping up the canyon slopes, running wherever there was a clear stretch, gliding over the heads of the enclosing ring; within minutes she had joined Branwe, and together they picked their way through a despoiled orchard and out onto the gravelly farm road beyond.

Their bambarongs, no longer constrained, ran, leaped, and glided over the reptile-demons that loped and slithered into the road before them. Once more they were out onto the open plain, but it was a different plain than Srana had known at the onset of the duel—dark and silent and ominous. Where was Ar? Or the hordes of besiegers?

Then she realized that Branwe was looking oddly at her, and asked him where they were.

"There's Ar before you," he said. "The battle is raging more furiously than ever. Can't you see the Yozgat across the river? Over there," he pointed, "where they've massed their bambarongs, hundreds of them."

She shook her head. "It's so dark, and it seems to be getting darker."

"Here, take this." He leaned across from his saddle. "I know this evil magic, from its very source."

Srana blinked at the sudden onrush of sunlight. She held the Demon Sword in one hand, and her scepter in the other, and the raging battlefield again spread before her in the afternoon light, hazy with dust and smoke.

"But you'll be defenseless," she protested.

"Never mind about me. I'm not the one he's trying to capture. He wants you alive, Srana. Remember that. There! Watch out!"

The monstrous dragon lumbered into view around a low hill and out onto the plain. From every direction emerged reptile-demons, more hideous even than before, and multiplied in numbers. Srana could see them more clearly now, as well as the insane rage contorting the face of the Evil One, who advanced malevolently upon her, heedless of any consequences.

"Over there, behind those ruined buildings," whispered Srana. "I've hidden you in an illusion, but I can't protect both of us. Hurry! He's already trying to penetrate the image."

Branwe had no choice but to obey. He could do nothing at the moment to help Srana; his presence actually endangered her, for she needed all the magic at her command to resist the Evil One. Again he found himself hiding in the ruins of an old farmstead, watching for an opportunity. Only this time he no longer clutched the Demon Sword.

Khal now seemed to be behaving irrationally, as if in his rage for vengeance he could no longer control his impulses. He could not corner Srana out on the open plain, nor could all the reptile-demons he might exorcise from the evil dimension, so long as she rode her elusive bambarong. As she drew him tauntingly this way and that, countering his illusions, confusing him with images of her own, holding him at bay as long as possible, his liskash mind was blinded to all else.

Branwe on the other hand was alert to everything happening around him, both far and near. Having no fragment of the Khavala in his possession, his very presence here was unknown to the Evil One; he was not affected by the unnatural darkness. In the distance he saw the Yozgat once more swarm back onto their bambarongs, then run and leap and glide out of range before a counterattack could be rallied against them. But this time, instead of landing strategically elsewhere on the battlefield, they retreated madly back toward the gates of Ar, just as another sortie burst forth to clear a path for them at the bridge.

It was not this unexpected retreat, but a dull rumble like faraway thunder, that caused Branwe to look up. The red flag! It flew from the highest tower of Ar. The besiegers continued furiously to attack the walls. They did not know what it meant, but neither did Srana, and he spurred his bambarong and raced across the plain toward her.

She had once more halted just out of reach of Khal and his

demon horde. Their stalemate was not passive but dynamic: each had to expend all available powers just to balance those of the other, and was oblivious to all else.

Branwe was never clear afterwards why he acted as he did next. It was a wild impulse, a reflex; had he paused to consider the dangers involved he might never have dared such a feat. He just acted, and his actions were the salvation of Ar.

So intently was Khal's malice focused on Srana that even his danger sense forsook him. The slithering, loping, waddling horde of reptile-demons saw his attacker, and converged with angry snarls and hisses, but they were too laggard to head him off.

Branwe leapt from his bambarong onto the dragon's back, just behind the crouching sorcerer. Boldness and agility were now his only weapons—and the heedless courage of an impulse. Not even the dragon could react quickly enough to thwart him.

Stunning Khal with a blow from the side, Branwe ripped the uraeus mounting the Third Eye from his sloping forehead, and leapt out of reach of the dragon's snapping jaws.

Khal himself nearly followed Branwe to the ground, as the dragon's long flexible neck clumsily knocked him sprawling. But he caught himself in time, and with a hiss of rage, his ruby eyes glittering with malice, he turned to retaliate—only to become aware of a graver peril. For even his dull reptilian senses now perceived the thunderous roar, rising in volume, closer and closer. And he saw a tremendous surge of water, higher than the very walls of Ar, crash through Dragonneck Gorge and rush over the plains beyond in a deadly tidal wave, engulfing everything in its path. He also saw that he had been lured too near the riverbed, too far from the safety of high ground. Not even his passion for vengeance now clouded his survival instincts, and he turned his mount in a blind race for the hills.

The dragon was too huge and ponderous to be very swift; neither could it now levitate itself above the colossal wall of foam and destruction rushing down upon them with appalling speed, since he had lost the power to reinforce its own magic. It was a crude footrace, and Khal's cold reptilian mind calculated only unfavorable odds.

Meanwhile the odds against Branwe seemed even more hopeless. His bambarong had bolted out of reach of the dragon, leaping riderless over the converging hordes of reptile-demons. Branwe too saw the advancing wall of death, but was on foot and weaponless, surrounded by hideous enemies.

"Branwe!"

He looked up, and there was Srana. For an instant none of the reptile-demons around him seemed to know exactly where he was; they looked in every direction but his. The next instant there was a flash in the sunlight, and the Demon Sword stuck blade-first into the ground beside him. Wrenching it free, he fought his way through the reptilian horde with furious agility, once more in possession of a magic that should have made them more visible to him, more vulnerable and real.

Instead he found himself battling mere shadows, as hazy and evanescent as the dust-laden sunlight, shadows that one by one faded into nothingness, as if there was no longer a magic strong enough to hold them in this dimension.

The whole combat lasted but seconds, and he found himself alone on the doomed plain. The mighty flood hurled itself against the walls of Ar, which it no longer overtopped, and was hurled back again with a tremendous explosion; its roar was pierced by the wail of thousands of terrified voices as it swept over the enemy host.

Where was Srana? He could not believe she had deserted him. No, there she was, gliding toward him, with his bambarong beside her own. Then they were running, leaping, and gliding side by side toward the hills, past the ruined farms and orchards, past Khal himself. Their last glide was the longest of all; water swirled beneath them, but they alighted high and dry on a hilltop, beyond its reach.

Only now did they dare look back. The great city of Ar still stood, but the battlefield was a chaos of wrecked towers and machines, drowned food and draft animals, and thousands upon thousands of corpses. The flood waters were already receding toward their natural channel.

And Khal? Neither he nor his dragon were to be seen anywhere. Had they been swept from sight by the mighty flood, or had the liskash sorcerer still enough power to teleport them to safety, perhaps into the evil dimension where they belonged?

Without a word, Branwe handed the Third Eye to Srana.

▲

Chapter 22
The Dragon Book

▲————————————————————————————▲

"I've always done my duty, which is a consolation." Mamre dabbed at her eyes, although there was no evidence of tears. "He thought he was fooling me, saying people were leaving their valuables with him for safekeeping. But I knew he was up to something no good from the start. That's why he wanted me out of the way at certain hours, and why he wanted the little room I'd set aside for you, Branwe. Him and his pals—I warned him against taking up with that set—needed more room to stash their booty. A shame it was, and him a refugee himself, robbing the houses of those poor folk who fled here with all they could carry. Foolish, too, as I could have told him, with so many refugees bearing arms and knowing how to use them. Always was too fond of money, and now he's paid for it. Ah, me." She continued to dab at her dry eyes. "Grujekh had his good points as a husband, I won't deny that, but now he's gone and I'm alone in the world."

Branwe glanced at Srana, and they both smiled. "You always have a home with us, Mamre," he said. "In your kindness you kept a room for me. Well, we've set one aside for you, a whole suite in fact."

"You always were good to me, Branwe." She patted his hand. "And so now you're a great lord, with palaces and estates? Well, I'm not surprised. I knew you were no common lad, even when I first saw you as a kit. Grujekh said: 'Don't get involved; it's none of our business.' He was thinking of the expense, you see. But to me you were a blessing, because I was never blessed with children of my own. House-broke you myself, and a job I had of it too, let me tell you."

303

"Uh, yes." Branwe looked uncomfortable, and Srana had to look away to keep herself from laughing. He changed the subject: "As I told you, the king has graciously restored to me the estates seized wrongfully from my father, the Shadow Warrior. He has also, as compensation for the injustice, awarded me the estates of the noble who perpetrated the seizure. Refugees have informed me that both estates were overrun by the invaders—the noble and his entire family perished trying to flee—and plundered. But from treasure recovered, both from the ruins of the enemy camp here and from Cragsclaw, the king has further compensated us."

"A wedding present," added Srana, "and a generous one."

"And well earned, from all I've heard," said Mamre. "But I shouldn't wonder if the king is feeling generous these days, what with that mother of his banished—and about time, I must say—and him taking a bride of his own. The daughter of a highland king, I'm told?"

"Yes, the eldest daughter of Ortakh of Maragadan," said Branwe.

Mamre leaned closer, and whispered: "A highland gal is just what he needs. She'll teach him what claws are all about, if he tries any of his old tricks with her." She glanced slyly from one to the other, and chuckled.

The Blue Dragon was of only modest size, but thanks to Mamre's diligence it was clean, well-appointed, and success- ful, despite its location in the roughest quarter of Ar. Keep- ing order had been a chronic problem, although not this morning. The tables were already crowded with a motley clientele of rogues, thugs, off-duty soldiers, and constables; two brawny highlanders were cavorting out on the dance floor with a pair of neighborhood slatterns. But more and more eyes watched curiously as one of the new proprietors, an extraordinarily robust female, nailed row after row of ears to the wall behind the bar. Sleek and well-groomed ears, snapped off at the base by sharp powerful teeth.

"We'll see no more of them scoundrelly Crockercups in Ar," observed Mamre. "Good riddance, says I. Imagine their impudence, trying to stop a holy ceremony at the Temple of the All-Mother! Why, I never heard of such a thing. And telling nasty stories about the White Dancers, too. Got just what they deserved, and folks still talk about the lovely ceremony."

"Sruss told me all you've done for us," said Srana. "That's why I wanted so much to come here this morning with Branwe, to thank you."

"You couldn't have made me happier, my lady. All dressed up the way you are. Like you both just stepped out of a painting. Nobody talks about anything but the king's wedding this morning, but there's another wedding I'm looking forward to much more. When's it to be?"

"In three days." Branwe fondly took Srana's hand in his. "Then we journey east to our new estates, to begin the long work of restoring them. I've already made special arrangement to transport your mirror there, and anything else you want to take with you."

"You always were a considerate lad." Mamre looked from one to the other. "So my boy is getting married, and soon— the All-Mother bless them—will have boys of his own, and gals too." She again took out her handkerchief, but this time there were real tears in her eyes. "It seems like only yesterday that you were prattling around the kitchen with your toy dragon, and plaguing the cooks with your childish questions, and helping yourself to cakes when they wasn't looking. How the dancing she-mrem made a pet of you, and when you were older—"

"Oh, uh, here's an old friend of yours." Branwe was glad of the interruption. "I met him in the streets only the day before yesterday, and invited him here this morning."

"And I've invited him here myself as often as he has whiskers." Mamre was as usual half amused, half exasperated by old Hoobel, the schoolmaster. "But he's never once stopped by for the drink on the house I've offered him again and again, never mind what my late husband would have thought about it. And after all the adventures we had together on the road from Kazerclawm too. Hello, Hoobel. Who's this with you?"

"Hello, Mamre," said the old schoolmaster, glancing uncertainly around him at the rascally clientele. "This is my new assistant. My school here has flourished. In fact, I have so many pupils now that I couldn't possibly do all the teach-

ing myself any more. I believe some of you already know
him. His name is Nizzam."

Branwe and Srana certainly knew him; they also knew that
The Three had not only expelled him from their order, but
forbidden his ever dabbling in magic again. But both were
too naturally gracious to chide the poor abject wretch for his
past misconduct, and greeted him courteously. Besides, he
looked so flustered by his classroom duties that there was a
wild stare in his eye, as if he had begun to wonder if even
service to an evil sorcerer were not preferable to trying—
without much success, it appeared —to keep mrem schoolkits
in order. He nodded, but did not raise his eyes from the
floor.

The fate of the Evil One was still unknown, but this was
too joyous an occasion to dampen with further apprehensions of
what had become of him. The talk was open and friendly,
although Nizzam could hardly bring himself to look anybody
in the eye. Mamre was again tickled by Hoobel's naive un-
worldliness, and could not resist teasing him. She also hinted
slyly about the need for a private tutor to the children of a
certain noble family, in the not-too-distant future.

Master Hoobel smiled benignantly at her good-natured
raillery, but could not spare any more time between classes;
nor was he comfortable with his surroundings, either at finding himself among so many grisly rogues or at the gruesome
spectacle unfolding behind the bar.

The wretched Nizzam still kept his eyes on the ground as
he departed behind his new master; but now he had a hunted
look, verging on desperation, at the thought of facing his
afternoon class.

"Moved in, just like home." Kizzlecosh at last laid the
hammer, which she had been wielding all this time, down on
the bar. Cajhet had already installed himself as bartender.
"Always wanted a place of my own," she said. "It's like a
dream come true for me. I see you folks are dressed for the
wedding this morning."

Branwe smiled. "I understand you've just celebrated a
wedding of your own. My congratulations."

"Thanks, and the same to you both. Yes, now that we have
our own tavern, I thought it best to be married. Property
owners should be respectable folk. Without going too far

about it, of course. So me and Cajhet here decided to do the proper thing."

The weak grin on Cajhet's face suggested who had really done the deciding. He nodded in agreement of everything his wife said, a custom he prudently continued throughout the rest of their married life.

"Then there was no trouble about getting an early discharge from the army?" Branwe turned to Cajhet, but it was Kizzlecosh who again spoke.

"Went right to old Severakh myself, and asked him point-blank. No trouble at all. Wrote up the discharge certificate right on the spot, with his own hands, and I thanked him for the favor. 'Madame,' he says, 'any time I can do you a favor like this, please don't hesitate to come to me day or night, no matter what the hour. I'm always looking for ways to improve the quality of the service.' "

"It's all on account of the fluffy pink dressing gown," said Cajhet. "I hear he's going on an inspection tour soon, beginning at Namakhazar. Who knows what he'll end up wearing this time?" He chuckled pawkily to himself, but did not explain.

▲

Whatever costumes he might don later, Severakh was in fact dressed this morning in the splendid regalia of a Grand Marshal of Ar, whose army he had already begun reforming, to ensure that the Eastern Lords never again found so flagrant an opportunity to invade the land.

Captain by captain, soldier by soldier, he inspected for the second time already this morning the honor guard he had posted in and around the Temple of the All-Mother. Candles blazed, flags and banners draped colorfully from every wall, and icons and idols of burnished copper scintillated with light. The resplendent battle dress of the kings of the League of Ar, the raiment of the great nobles of the land, the silken finery of their consorts, and the trappings of the priests vied in magnificence.

The Three, less disheveled than wizards generally were, were just now filing down the center aisle to their assigned pews.

"Everything is in order, my lady," Severakh reported to

Sruss. "My lord, my lady." He also greeted Branwe and
Srana, who had meanwhile joined Sruss in the place of honor,
directly below the glittering altar.

Moments later they were also joined by Mithmid, who
glanced back in exasperation at The Three, now comfortably
ensconced in their own places of honor below the first balcony, where the temple musicians had just begun to tune
their instruments.

"Silly old biddies," he muttered. "Exhaustion from their
recent ordeal I could understand, but some of them act as if
they were senile. Dollavier's the only one who seems to have
kept his wits, and he left Ar the day before yesterday, to
ensure that Rhenowla is both comfortable and carefully watched
in her place of exile. The rest do nothing but whimper and
complain. I truly believe that the savagery of the Yozgat
she-mrem was more of a shock to them than the siege itself.
Not even the flood washed it away. I had to reassure them—
for about the ninth time, I believe—that all the Yozgat have
gone home, that not one of them would be here today, before
I could get them to come."

"With no treaty of alliance, and not even the courtesy to
attend the wedding of the King of Ar," added Severakh,
shaking his head. "All I could get out of Changavar was that
such things were alien to their most sacred traditions. You
saw how, after the flood receded, they camped outside the
city? Well, he said the Yozgat were warriors, and that signing
treaties was as contemptible for them as cringing behind
walls. By the way, now that I think of it, he and some of his
captains were also disgruntled about the behavior of their
females. What happened?" he asked Mithmid.

"You mean why were the Yozgat males disgruntled? I can
only guess it's because of the beastly trophies of honor. That
ride back here, after the flood, was the most harrowing
experience of my life. Not only did we have to watch the
little horrors flay the enemies they had slain, but had to sit on
the very pelts all the way back, while the she-mrem twirled
fur cloaks—sewn from the pelts of other enemies, in case you
didn't know—raked the air with their steel claws, and hallooed
like demons. They took it as a double victory. That is, those
excluded from battle ended up with the only trophies. The
Yozgat males didn't get any because of the flood. Appalling,

really appalling. They danced half the night, before it was finally settled about who got which trophy."

Severakh smiled grimly. "I wouldn't be surprised if the she-mrem rubbed it in a bit?"

"Yes, and more than just a bit," said Mithmid. "Some of the old fools over there wouldn't take my word for it that they were gone. They actually sent messengers up to the ramparts for confirmation. The All-Mother save us if we ever have to rely on them again."

He no longer wore the golden bracelet, nor had Srana possession any longer of either her scepter or the Third Eye. The magic was from an evil dimension, but so far no remains of Khal or his dragon had been recovered from the grisly jetsam strewn across the plains by the receding flood. Neither were the eggs nor the hatchlings Nizzam had reported seeing in the dungeons of Cragsclaw found there when the great fortress was retaken. And so long as their fate remained unknown, no power of magic dared be renounced.

All the fragments of the Khavala, large and small, had been entrusted to Sruss, who had had them sealed within a secret repository somewhere beneath the Temple of the All-Mother. Not unless some new challenge threatened the very survival of the mrem would they ever again see the light of day, and then only under the auspices of the reigning king of Ar. Magic was too important to be left to the magicians.

The magical attractiveness of Rhenowla had been the bane of Ar, and very nearly its undoing. Her lust for power had not blenched even at assassination. The confessions wrung from the three rogues she had employed had proven her own undoing. There was some cynical speculation about whether more people today were celebrating the king's wedding—or his mother's banishment.

Sruss was not sure herself, although she had played the leading role in both events. Her prestige and moral authority were now transcendent in the land; never had the White Dancers been so honored. But if Sruss was still determined not to interfere in the everyday administration of the kingdom, she had been more forthright this time in counseling the young king on the choice of a bride.

The daughter of King Ortakh may have lacked Rhenowla's magical attractiveness, but she was a sensible girl with claws, qualities more needed at this time in a queen of Ar than ravishing beauty. Tristwyn had a good heart, but had been so corrupted and demoralized by the ambitions of his mother that he needed a strong consort to guide him. Ortakh's daughter would make short work of any Crockercup who tried to insinuate himself back into the palace.

She would also tend to bridge the tragic disunity of the mrem, to ally at least spiritually the highland kingdoms and the city-states of the plain.

The White Dancers would continue to foster a common history and justice among all mrem, with more telling effect now than ever. The worship of the All-Mother grew daily in influence, reaching ever deeper into those backward regions which had long been the strongholds of bigotry and dissentient priesthoods. Not that the mrem would ever be anything but fiercely independent, nor should they be; it was the very essence of their nature. But the Eastern Lords would be watching for any new opportunity to avenge their recent humiliation. If the mrem could never agree among themselves, they must at least learn not to allow old feuds and enmities to be exploited against them by a common enemy.

The White Dancers had now taken their places before the icon of the All-Mother; the musicians had at last ceased to tune their instruments; the kings of the League of Ar, each in his traditional battle regalia, including Ortakh himself, formed the escort which would lead the nuptial pair up the grand aisle. The ceremony would begin any moment now.

"You have no doubts or regrets?" Sruss confided to Srana, at her side.

"Doubts perhaps—we all have those—regrets, never," she replied. "Not so long as I live. Our heritage has been despoiled, but we have our whole lives in which to rebuild it, to teach our children a love of justice. Who could regret such a choice?"

Sruss nodded with the wisdom of a long lifetime. Who indeed? As she looked at the beautiful she-mrem beside her, radiant with love and youth and happiness, she recalled nostalgically the choice she herself had made at the same age. The only regret she had over her life with her beloved Talwe was that it had been too brief. But, then, wasn't life itself too brief?

The traditional march music started up. The White Dancers began their graceful ceremonial dance, and the kings of the League of Ar marched solemnly up the grand aisle. All eyes turned toward the bride and groom, charming in their nuptial finery, as they followed beneath the gold-and-scarlet canopy, held for them by the sons and daughters of noble houses.

Despite her age and wisdom, Sruss felt tears welling in her eyes. Were the priests right about lives being reincarnated after all? It seemed to her now that the old stories were retold again and again, that the same wars were lost and won, that the ancient struggle against evil was waged each generation on new battlefields. Once more goodness had prevailed—but for how long?

She glanced from the young bride and groom beneath the canopy to the young bride and groom beside her. The heroic exploits of Srana and Branwe were now being celebrated throughout the land, and a renowned poet had been commissioned to record them in the *Dragon Book*, so they might never be forgotten.

▲

"This is world-building on a major scale...
[*Guardians of the Three*] may rank as one of the most distinctive
creations of modern fantasy."—*Dragon Magazine*

GUARDIANS OF THE THREE

For centuries the feline people of Ar and the powerful Lords of
the East have been at peace. Legends surround the Eastern
Lords and their servants, the liskash—lizard warriors—but
few have ever seen them. This series tells the exciting story of
the sudden rise and devastating assault of the Eastern Lords
against the people of Ar, the catlike Mrem. The Council of the
Three—a group of powerful Mrem wizards—must fight with
their every resource to protect their vulnerable world.

PHILIP JOSÉ FARMER'S

ᴛʜᴇDUNGEON

☐ 27346 **BLACK TOWER:**
Dungeon #1 *Richard Lupoff* $3.95

☐ 27640 **THE DARK ABYSS:**
Dungeon #2 *Bruce Coville* $3.95

☐ 27958 **VALLEY OF THUNDER:**
Dungeon #3 *Charles de Lint* $3.95

☐ 28185 **THE LAKE OF FIRE:**
Dungeon #4 *Robin Bailey* $3.95

☐ 28338 **THE HIDDEN CITY:**
Dungeon #5 *Charles de Lint* $3.95

Look for them at your bookstore or use this page to order:

KATHARINE KERR

THE BRISTLING WOOD

"Kerr fluently and gracefully limns her Celtic-based medieval world, depicting attractive and colorful men, women and elves."

—Publishers Weekly

◆

Deverry: a world of high magic where the actions of men and women extend beyond their deaths, a world in which magic has definite laws—and a very definite price.

◆

"Kerr has a deft touch with characters, supple prose, and a refreshingly natural vision of magic. **The Bristling Wood** is a rewarding entry in a better than average series."

—Locus

◆

Katharine Kerr follows up the successes of **Daggerspell** and **Darkspell** with **The Bristling Wood,** her third novel set in the world of Deverry. In this volume, the ancient wizard Nevyn discovers the actions of the Dark Council interfering in the already tangled politics of war-torn Eldidd. Ruthless and powerful adversaries, their dark arts are dedicated to chaos and greed. Their evil webs are nearly spun before even the powerful Nevyn realizes there's a war of magic destroying his world.

―――――――

And coming in May, 1990
The Dragon Revenant
the fourth novel of Deverry
A Foundation Hardcover and Trade Paperback

―――――――

The Bristling Wood
"A sure winner."—*Booklist*
A Bantam Spectra Book